FINDING TAYNA
Book One

STRANGE PLACES

Jefferson Smith

creativityhacker.ca

Strange Places

Written by Jefferson Smith
Edited by Fleur Macqueen
Cover Art by Merridew Smith
Published by Creativity Hacker Press (creativityhacker.ca)

Printed in the United States of America

First edition: June 2011
Second edition: March 2014 (Rev. 2014-03-12)

ISBN 978-0-9919334-0-2 (print)
ISBN 978-0-9919334-1-9 (EPUB/Kobo/Nook)
ISBN 978-0-9919334-7-1 (MOBI/Kindle)

The greatest poem I ever wrote is just four words long,

yet it contains my entire world:

Brinnameade, Merridew, Rigel, Tayna.

My tribulation. My solace. My muses.

chapter 1

"They're coming!" Eliza ran into the dingy little room with wild excitement in her eyes and very little breath in her lungs. All around her, children's eyes snapped up from their sewing and cleaning activities.

"Who's coming?"

"Wannabes! Real swanky. She's wearing a fur coat–I think it's real– and they came in a limo. They're coming up the stairs right now."

"So what, Lies? Hasn't anybody ever told you? Nobody ever comes to the fifth floor, except Sister Regalia, and she only ever comes up here to give us more work."

"That's what I'm trying to tell you guys," Eliza said. "They didn't stop on four. They're coming *here!*"

The girls stared at her in disbelief, and then, suddenly, the room was electric, punctuated with shrieks of panic. Nobody was dressed for an interview! What would they say? How should they behave? These were the so-called Unlovables–the girls who had done so poorly in the few interviews they'd ever been granted that the Goodies had moved them to the fifth floor, so that they wouldn't mess things up for the other, more likable girls. You know, when the wanna-dads and mommy-bes came by to inspect the latest stock and select their coordinating family accessories?

But they never came here. The fifth floor was where all the scratch- and-dent merchandise was stored, the difficult girls, who were expected to work for their keep until they reached the age of sixteen. That's when the government would stop paying for their care and the Good Sisters could legally turn them out onto the streets, to make room for other, more profitable orphans. Of the twelve girls in the ward, several had been interviewed repeatedly before finally being declared Unlovable. But it was not to any of these grizzled veterans that the now panic-stricken group looked for advice. Instead, all heads turned to a single, raven-haired girl in the corner. She was the queen of rejection, the most unlovable of all the Unlovables, the girl so obviously lacking

1

in adoptable qualities that she had never been given even a single interview and had been moved to the fifth floor on her very first day.

When she was just three years old.

In the ten years since then, Tayna still hadn't received so much as a request for an interview, not one, but she had seen it all. She knew every trick in the book. If there was a trick that Tayna didn't know about getting girls adopted, it was a trick that didn't work. No matter that they never seemed to work for *her*–they had always worked well for other girls. So now, every eye in the room was on her.

The pressure of eleven desperate, pleading faces dragged her out of the book she had been rebinding, and she looked intently from one terrified face to the next. With a sigh, she closed her book and stood up. "All right. Let's do it." She looked a question at Eliza, who was standing vigil by the door.

"They've stopped to tour the junior bunks. You've only got a couple of minutes."

"Right! Let's go!" Tayna clapped her hands enthusiastically, jolting the entire room out of their fear-trances in the process. "Let's partner up. Everybody raise your right hand."

The girls threw their hands immediately into the air. Beside her, four-year-old Rachel was holding up her left. Tayna pushed the errant hand back down, and pulled up on the other, which was determinedly clutching a small, plastic toy camera. "This one's your right, Rake," she said quietly, as she took the camera and hung it by its cord around the girl's neck.

"Okay, now everybody grab somebody else's hand. Whoever you grab, that's your partner. No swapsies."

After a few frantic moments, the girls had all arranged themselves into pairs, with hands clenched in the air between them. "Your job now," Tayna said "Is to look your partner over and find everything major that needs to be done. Neat hair, clean face, tidy clothes. Everything tucked in. Socks up. Sleeves down. Tallest girl in each pair inspects the shorter girl first. Go!"

The girls were accustomed to Tayna's quick, decisive instructions–especially when something important had to be done quickly. She was a quick thinker and fearless about taking action once the decision was made–a quality that her ward-mates had learned to trust. As soon as she said "Go," the shorter girl in each pair began to turn slowly, allowing her partner to scrutinize every inch of her appearance and rhyme off a list of the most serious issues.

Tayna pointed out a few things for little Rachel to fix, then she glanced toward Eliza, who turned away from her own partner to check the hall again. Eliza shrugged uncertainly, so Tayna returned to the task at hand.

"Okay, now everybody switch," she said. "Short girls inspect the tall ones. After you're done, both of you can take a minute to fix up whatever your partner suggested."

Now the other half of the group began to rotate. Rachel tugged at Tayna's sleeve, trying to get her to turn, but the older girl just smiled. "Don't worry about me, Rake. Any mommy-be that I could stand to live with will like me just the way I am. If she gets hung up on little stuff like this, I could never fit into her life anyway."

As the girls attended to their personal grooming, Tayna looked toward the door again. "How much time, Lies?" Eliza opened the door a hair and checked the hallway again.

"Still clear. They're getting the full tour, but they won't be long. Better hurry."

Tayna nodded. "Right. We don't have time for anything fancy. We'll just go with your basic Smile Parade." She stepped forward into the center of the room, facing the door and held her arms out to the sides. "Give me the two smallest girls on my left and right. Uh, Rake and Amanda." She paused for a moment while a couple of girls shuffled away and made room for those two girls to move in. "Now the next tallest beside them, and then the next tallest, and so on." There were only a few minor collisions as the girls got themselves sorted out. While they were doing that, Tayna excused herself from the line and went to the door to look for herself. The shadows spilling out into the hall were now coming from the open door of the senior bunk-room. The tour was almost done.

"Okay, when I say go, everybody goes back to the job they were doing before Lies came in. This always works better when they think they've surprised us. As soon as Sister Regalia opens the door, you all run back to the position you're in now, got it? When you get lined up again, each of you turn to look at your neighbor and pretend to adjust something on her shirt or hair. Then turn and give the hubby your biggest smile, and I mean big. Ham it up. Try to split your face in half. The wanna-dads always think it's great how committed you are and the mommy-bes love anything that gets him to show an interest."

"Tayna?" Little Amanda had her hand in the air.

"What is it 'Anda?"

"I don't know if I can remember all that."

Tayna smiled and hunkered down a little. "It's okay kiddo. Just look at who's beside you now. Rachel and Becky. All you have to do is make sure you get back in line between them when the door opens, okay?" The little girl nodded. "And once you're in line, give 'em your biggest smile. But don't worry if you make a mistake. They'll just think it looks cute."

Suddenly, Eliza went stiff at the door. "Incoming!"

Tayna spun around. "Okay! Everybody back to your jobs until the door opens." Then she crossed back to her work table, sat down and picked up the old book with the broken spine. The other girls raced back to their own tables in record time. A few pretended to work, but in reality, every girl in the room was focused intently on the door knob, like sprinters waiting for the starter's pistol. And behind those eyes, each and every girl was deep into the what-if game. What if this time it's *me* who gets an interview? What if they decide they *like* me? Would they ask me to come live with them, like a real family, with my own room and a cat and a gramma who likes to bake? The only sound was the clicking and clanking of the old radiator in the corner and Becky's shoes rubbing nervously together.

Then the light vanished from beneath the door and it began to swing in. "...and we can store the rest of them in here." Sister Regalia strode into the room, talking briskly to somebody behind her. Tayna realized instantly that something was wrong, but before she could stop them, the girls were already scrambling into position. The parade line formed perfectly in front of the door, with each girl turning to check her neighbor for last-minute lint and stray hairs. Then they hit the high-beams, turning on their maximum, high-voltage smiles, any one of which was bright enough to melt the hearts of a Porscheful of divorce lawyers. But it still wasn't enough to thaw even an eyelash off Sister Regalia's scowl. When the senior Sister turned back to face the room and saw the crisp line-up of beaming faces, she stopped short.

And then she laughed.

She laughed so hard, she nearly doubled over. The eyes of every girl in the room widened in surprise when the old nun actually slapped her thigh in delight and then had to place both hands on her knees to keep from collapsing to the floor. "Who, who, a who taught you to do that?" she asked, struggling for breath. Then she caught Tayna glaring at her from the end of the line. Regalia smiled cruelly and drew herself upright, the laughter draining quickly from her face. "Oh! Tayna, was it? Well that's just priceless!" She turned to the other two people in the hallway–crazy-eyed Sister Anthrax, and a short, ill-kempt and rather hairy looking man. Tayna couldn't recall seeing him before.

"Get a load of this bunch!" Regalia said. "They actually thought you were parents, coming up here to visit them!" The man chuckled non-committally, as though he wasn't sure exactly what the joke was, but Sister Anthrax erupted in a fit of hateful laughter as Regalia turned back to the girls. The faces that had so recently been beaming with excitement, were now beginning to lose their focus, as the girls realized that this Smile Parade might not be proceeding according to plan. Rachel was the only one who didn't seem to understand and she was busily snapping pictures of anybody and everybody with her toy camera while the scene played out around her.

"Hasn't anybody told you?" Regalia asked the group. "You're the Unlovables. Don't you know what that means?" She looked up and down the line. "It means that it isn't possible for any worthwhile person to actually love you. Why on Earth would I waste my time bringing people up here to meet children as hopeless as you? I've got much better things to do with my time, you can be sure." Her keen eyes flicked past the girls to the tables, still laden with unfinished tasks, and then she noticed little Rachel. With a smirk, she took two steps and snatched the camera from the girl's hand. Then she tossed it into the garbage pail next to the door.

"Now stop this ridiculousness and get back to work."

Regalia turned to her companions. "Never mind. We don't need to look in here after all," she said. "Once you've seen one storage room full of rejects and throw-aways, you've seen them all." With that, she turned and marched out of the room, pulling the door closed behind her with a bang.

The Smile Parade was still half formed. None of the girls was sure what to do next. Some turned uncertainly to the left or right, looking at their neighbors as if they might have some kind of plan. One or two of the younger girls sobbed, but nobody said a word. Rachel quietly walked over to the door and retrieved her camera from the garbage. When it became clear that no one was going to jump out and yell "Just kidding!" the girls finally drifted back toward their chores, but they did not all take their disappointment in good stride.

"Nice going, Eliza," Dana said. "Now we know why everybody calls you 'Lies.'"

"Yeah, I think they must have been movie stars," Jenny said.

"No. It was definitely the King and Queen," said a third.

"Yeah, the royal couple from downtown Ugliville."

Eliza ignored the catcalls. After Tayna, she had been there the longest, so it would have been understandable if she, of all the girls, was the most crestfallen to discover that they were not going to be interviewed today. But if there was one thing an Unlovable learned early, it was that life under the Good Sisters of Salvation seldom paid off in smiles. By now, they'd all had plenty of practice bouncing back from disappointments, especially Eliza, who still allowed her imagination to torment her with visions of a sunnier future–an instinct that all the other girls had long since learned to suppress. If this latest kick in the shins had left any mark on her, it was completely invisible as she went quietly back to her job, sewing crests onto the clean, new uniforms they had made for the lower-floors girls.

As Eliza dove back into her needle work, Tayna watched her out of the corner of her eye. This place could get under your skin real fast if you let it, and lesson number one in avoiding Sister Regalia's patented Sucking Vortex of Despair™ was that you had to think about life in her "care" as open warfare–a war in which ridicule was the enemy's chief weapon.

Being the most spirited of the Unlovables, Tayna and Eliza had always been the primary targets of Regalia's campaigns, because nothing attracted barrages of Goody-Goody ridicule like a rebellious imagination or a strong will. It was this constant fire that had made the two girls inseparable–comrades-in-arms against nunnish tyranny.

Unlike physical injuries though, despair wounds could only hurt if you let them, and with the help of a good friend, they could actually be shaken off. Mostly. So Tayna always took pains to watch her friend for early warning signs. Secretly, she was convinced that Eliza always got the worst of the nuns' abusive attention, but as far as she could tell today, Lies was doing fine, and she seemed scarcely even aware of the verbal daggers being thrown her way by the other frustrated girls. After all, compared to the arsenal generally employed by the Goodies, a bit of girl-snark was nothing.

Now, you might think that with a name like "the Good Sisters of Salvation," the women running the Home would be your typical, cheerful, hard-working group of Jesus-freaks in Batman capes, but you'd be wrong. Most people called them the Goody-Goody Sisters, or even just "the Goodies," but it was used only as a short form. They weren't actually implying that the Sisters were good people. In point of fact, the old crones were about as horrible as you could imagine, and it was a galaxy-sized joke that the universe allowed those harpies to even come within a hundred miles of any children, let alone permit them to run an orphanage—even one as flea-bitten and decrepit as Our Lady of Divine Suffering's Home for Orphans and Evictees. In all her years of incarceration there, Tayna had never met a single evictee. In fact, to the best of her knowledge, only two of the words in the place's entire name even came close to being accurate: "orphans" and "suffering." But it was better than living in a burned out car under a highway overpass. Wasn't it?

Tayna sighed and bent back down over her work. There were only two hours to go before she had to make her collection rounds, and she'd still have to be back in time to supervise dinner. Friday was always a very busy day for the senior Unlovable.

———

Late that afternoon, Tayna's collections were almost done. Rain fell in relentless sheets, dragging the bleakness from the sky and spattering it across the sidewalks and low-income apartments, increasing the shabbiness of the city with every drip. An old, yellow taxi pulled up in front of a particularly horrific building. It was a squat gray, concrete structure with iron bars on the windows and a rusting, barbed wire fence running around the yard. Tayna shuddered as she stepped out into the rain. Like all the other buildings run by the Goodies, it looked like it had once been a maximum security prison or maybe a mental hospital, but unless somebody told you, you would never have guessed that it was actually a private school. Holy Terror Collegiate. Tayna couldn't imagine what sort of people would send their children to a place like that, but clearly, somebody did.

The front of the building was almost face-like. The enormous, hulking structure had only two windows, set high on the upper floor, and a tiny, surprised looking mouth of a door, set back from the sidewalk at ground level. Even the building itself couldn't hide its surprise at being allowed to eat children every morning. Tayna went up to that little iron mouth and knocked. Before she could even rub the flecks of rust from her knuckles, the door jerked back, squealing piteously on its ancient iron hinges. Fierce gray eyes peered out from the gloom.

"You're late!"

Tayna knew better than that. There was no schedule for her to keep, other than to be back at the Old Shoe before dinner time. Not for the first time, she wondered if it was possible that the kids at Holy Terror might have even worse lives than she did. Sure, they might have homes and families, but they couldn't have very *loving* families–not if they were forced to spend their days here. But, of course, Tayna said nothing of that to the eyes watching her from the gloomy interior.

"I'm sorry, Sister Inquisita, there was a traffic accident and we had to come by the other bridge." One thing about Tayna was that she never lied. Not quite. But she was very good at making true statements that encouraged other people to leap to untrue conclusions on their own. Take this comment about the traffic accident for example. Sure, there *had* been an accident and they *had* come by the other bridge, but those two things had not happened on the same day, and neither of them had happened today. If the glowering nun wanted to jump to the conclusion that they had happened today, and that such a combination of events somehow constituted an excuse for being late, that was hardly any of Tayna's concern.

"Hmph!" the nearly invisible nun said, but she pulled the door open a fraction wider and thrust a gold-colored urn out through the door. "Tell Regalia that they only filled one this week. The power has been out since Thursday, but the little sprats will have three filled next week to make up the shortfall or I'm going to–"

Tayna cut her off before she could finish. One thing she knew for certain about the Goody-Goodies was that they never made idle threats. This didn't keep them from making up outlandish punishments to motivate the children under their care, though. It just meant that they were particularly persistent when it came to following through on whatever horrible consequences they had invented. Never let it be said that a Goody-Goody had failed to deliver on a promise. So Tayna cut her short, hoping to protect the kids inside, if only just a little.

"I'm sure that will be fine, Sister Inquisita. Two urns per week is still a very good average."

The steely eyes continued to glare from behind the door, but not another word followed. Then, with a snort of satisfaction, they vanished and the door clanged shut.

"Lovely talking to you, too," Tayna said to the cold, rusty door. She turned and went back to the waiting taxi, setting the urn on the seat beside her. It clanked noisily against the urns that she had picked up earlier from Sister Gruesome at the funeral home. No one had ever told her what was in them, or why they needed to be collected every week and taken to the Old Shoe, but the lids were sealed and she knew better than to ask. Any question deemed "nosy" or "impudent" by the Goodies was quick to earn a beating or some harsh chore assignment. Tayna found that she usually learned more, and truer information by simply using her brain and paying attention, but so far, that had not paid off with any of the juicy details about the urns. "Probably dead monkey fetuses," was her usual answer, whenever the topic came up among the girls, in bed after Failing Light. That was the one time of day when the Unlovables had a moment to themselves, to think or to talk quietly. Something about lying in the dark waiting for sleep to come seemed to loosen the tongues of even the most work-weary children.

But what was in them? Eventually, Tayna tore her gaze from the metal jars and looked out through the rain-spattered window at the face of Holy Terror, as a feeling of dread welled up inside her. I hope it's nothing bad. Then she gave herself a shake. Who am I trying to kid? Of course it's something bad. Nothing good ever comes from the Goodies. She sighed heavily and traced a raindrop with her finger as it ran down the glass.

"We can go back now," she said.

The taxi pulled smoothly away from the curb as lightning flashed and a rumble of thunder boomed its disapproval. Even the sky didn't want her going back to that miserable old place.

Tayna never noticed the tall, oddly dressed figure standing motionless in the rain, watching from an empty lot. But he had definitely noticed her. As the taxi reached the end of the block, the mysterious watcher stepped out from behind a pile of broken cinder blocks to follow behind on foot.

It was almost six o'clock by the time Tayna had unloaded the urns and delivered them to Sister Regalia's office, and all the other children were seated at their tables, waiting for dinner. The Old Shoe had five floors, not counting the dining hall and kitchen in the basement, or the roof-top garden. On the ground floor were the nun's offices, and the classrooms in which the girls did their schoolwork. The second floor was the Sisters' residence, where the nuns slept and held their private parties. Most of the girls–the Old Shoe was a girls-only establishment– lived on the third and fourth floors. Each floor was divided into two wards. Infant and toddler wards were on the third floor, where they could be close to the nuns. Then juniors, aged five to ten, shared the fourth level with the older, senior girls. Each ward consisted of a communal dorm room, a bathroom and an activity room. The dining hall was also arranged according to the ward system and there was no mingling permitted between tables.

Fifth floor girls–the so-called Unlovables–ranged in age all the way from toddler to senior and it was their job to help in the kitchens, do the laundry and serve meals to all the other residents. They would eat only after everyone else had finished and after all the dishes had been done. As senior girl of the fifth floor, it was Tayna's job to supervise these tasks. On Fridays, when she was out collecting the urns, she was permitted to put someone else in charge of dinner preparations until she got back, but she was still responsible for anything her deputies did–or didn't do–while she was gone. So after looking around to be sure that everything in the dining hall was okay, Tayna went into the kitchen to find her assistant, Lies.

Eliza Drummel was second in seniority. She was two months younger and had been at the Old Shoe for nine years–almost as long as Tayna herself. She was a thin, slightly mousy girl with an active imagination, and she shared it with her ward-mates with an intensity that was often mistaken for either lying or insanity, depending on who you asked. That's why everybody pretty much called her Lies. You could never tell whether what she was saying was true, or just another part of some fanciful distraction she had invented for herself. As far as Tayna was concerned, with Lies around, who needed TV?

Tayna found her lieutenant busy pulling plates out of the enormous army-surplus dishwasher. Becky was helping. She was one of the shortest girls in the whole place, even though she was nearly twelve, and she was rather sensitive about it, which caused trouble from time to time because she was aggressive and surly, even at the best of times.

It was Becky who first saw Tayna come in. She nudged Lies. "Look who's back." Deputy Eliza looked up and then snapped herself to attention, saluting her returning commander with a sloppy ladle.

Tayna smiled and saluted back. "Generalissimo Tayna, returning to duty. Colonel Drummel, you are relieved. What's on the menu?"

Lies leaned in and made a gruesome face. "It's Sister Disgustia Stew," she said, referring to the cranky old cook. "I snuck up behind her with a hammer and..."

"Eww! That's disgusting!" Becky shouted.

"Not 'disgusting,'" Lies said. "Disgustia."

Tayna laughed at the thought of actually cooking one of the hairy old nuns. "She would probably taste like fried dryer lint," she said.

Becky harumphed and went to load the serving cart, rather than listen to any more crazy talk. Lies grinned at Tayna and then followed after Becky to help with the cart. In no time at all, Tayna and her crew were out in the dining hall, marching up and down the long table rows, ladling out bowls of beef chili with fresh bread and setting them in front of the impatient diners who immediately dug in with noisy abandon.

By the time everyone had been fed, the dishes stacked, and the dining hall tidied up, Tayna and the rest of the Unlovables were sitting wearily at the kitchen prep-table, eating the last of the stew and the few left-over heals of bread. Rachel, who was technically too young for the job but insisted on helping with cleanup anyway, was leaning heavily against Tayna, losing her ongoing struggle to stay awake. The toy camera hung loosely from the cord around her neck and Tayna could feel the warm dampness of the little girl's breath on her skin through the thin material of her own shirt.

"The Rake is gone," she said to the others. "I'm going to take her up to bed." But Rachel must not have been completely asleep because at that point she stirred, mumbling something about still having to put her laundry away.

"It's okay, kiddo," Tayna said. "I'll do it for you tonight. You need to sleep. Okay?"

" 'Kay, Tayna." But before she could say "Thank you," the thin little girl was fast asleep.

Tayna turned out the light and closed the door. Already, she could hear the other girls coming up the stairs from dinner. Soon, the youngest would be climbing into their beds alongside Rachel, and then Tayna and the seniors would retire to the activity room to get some more of their mending and cleaning chores done before their own Failing Light. On the floors below, the more "adoptable" kids would all be sitting in neat little rows in their own activity rooms now, attending to the only evening chore the Goodies ever assigned them: watching television. "Best thing for a young mind," the nuns liked to say. "Healthy, edutainment programming. Two hours each morning and three more after dinner. Can't grow up right without proper knowledge of the world around you, and what better way to get it?"

If anybody needed proof of their sincerity, they only had to look here on the fifth floor, where there wasn't a television in sight–a clear indication that in the collected minds of the Good Sisters of Salvation,

TV truly must be a good thing. They couldn't manage to cut the fifth-floor girls completely off from the modern world, though. Unlovables still got to see plenty of TV while cleaning the other girls' lounges, or the Goody-Goody party room. Then there were the magazines lying around–the Goodies were always reading–celebrity gossip and rumors, mostly. Anything else was just idleness and filth, and not to be tolerated.

Tayna had completed her book-spine repair job that afternoon, so she was busy looking for her next project, but this time her heart wasn't really in it. There were times when what she really wanted to do was grab a marker and scribble all over the damned things, or tear their pages out one by one, imagining each book to be a Goody in disguise. But then she'd take a deep breath and remind herself that such defiance would only end up hurting the other kids. It probably wouldn't affect the nuns at all, and in her view, that would make her just as bad as the Goodies. So Tayna set aside her dreams of petty vengeance and dove back into the pile of injured books. She would just continue waging her private little war, undoing as much Goody-damage as she could until they kicked her out. She was still trying to decide which patient was most salvageable when the other girls began drifting in to resume their own chores. A few of them glanced oddly at her as they took their seats, but she barely noticed.

"I tell you, it's true," Lies said as she came through the door with Becky and Marie. "I could hear them, plain as day. I took Regalia's dinner up to her, but there was somebody in there with her, so I set it on the table in the hall. The door was open a crack and I could see some woman sitting in the visitor's chair." Whatever Lies was talking about, the girls around her were spellbound.

"The woman did all the talking," Lies said. "Something about knowing in her bones that there was 'a girl here who needed her, the one who'd been here the longest, who might have given up hope of ever getting adopted. Not some primping princess, but the most lonely, the most desperate, the most despairing girl in the entire place.'" As Lies repeated those words, every girl in the room was looking at Tayna, their eyes wide with envy. Then Becky broke the spell.

"Yeah, right. Lies-R-Us is just making stuff up again. Like the rich lady in the fur coat, remember? What happened to the limo and all the jewelry, huh? Turned out to be some hairy little monkey-man and Sister Anthrax–not what I'd call choice mommy-daddy material, were they?"

Lies protested. "I'm not making it up," she said. "Sure, this afternoon I made a mistake. I saw a man and a woman in the stairwell and her musty old habit looked like fur in the darkness, but there was a fancy car out front, even if nobody else saw it. And when have I ever made up whole conversations, huh?" One or two of the girls seemed inclined to side with her, but Becky just snorted.

"Oh, gimme a break!"

But even though Becky seemed to turn her attention to her sewing work, Tayna couldn't help but notice that the angry girl kept stealing glances her way. Great. As if she didn't have enough pressure. Tayna knew that things like this, like interviews and adoptions, never happened to girls like her, and now she was going to be the center of everyone else's envy until this latest opportunity proved the rule by blowing up in her face. Still, she sighed, wouldn't it be nice if, just this once, something did go her way? The rest of the evening passed quietly for Tayna as two more damaged books were reclaimed from the heap of shame, but she hardly even noticed them.

Was it possible, after giving up hope for so long, that she might actually be worthy of a loving home?

———————

Outside, the thin man gazed at the Old Shoe from the deep recesses of the alley across the street. It had been a long walk from Holy Terror, yet he showed no outward sign of his exertion. He watched with apparent surprise as an older couple walked out the front door, arm in arm, chatting in animated tones. Then his fascination doubled two hours later, when another man stepped quickly from his car and dashed up the steps to disappear inside. These relatively innocuous events somehow excited him, but there was one last thing he saw—invisible to anyone else who might have been watching—that thrilled him to the very core. In his mind's eye, the Old Shoe roared and twisted, engulfed in brilliant, ravenous, multicolored flame.

He wriggled with delight and settled himself back into the shadows to wait for his chance.

chapter 2

That night, Tayna had a dream. Rising from her bed, she floated silently across the room with her arms stretched out to either side. Her fingertips gently brushed the walls as she drifted out into the hall. Two bare feet hung limply below the hem of her nightgown and her toes bumped idly against the hardwood floors as she rose up and then dipped back down, in time with the slow in and out of each breath.

Her eyes saw nothing. In fact, they were closed, but within the dream, she could still see herself, drifting along the hall and down the stairs, as though she was a little bird, hovering silently near the ceiling above and behind her sleeping self. Down, down she went, past the other floors of girls, past the party on the Goody-Goody level, past Regalia's ground-floor office and down into the basement. She drifted calmly through the dining hall and beyond, into the kitchen. At the back wall, next to the large, walk-in freezer, she came to a small door that she had never noticed before. It swung silently open and she swept past it into a small, brightly lit chamber.

Her body floated around the perimeter of the secret room, facing the walls, where she could see nothing but the rough, orange brick surface that occasionally scraped her nose. Behind her, she could hear things: a man talking in muffled tones, the drone of a television turned down low and something else that sounded like wind chimes, but no matter how hard she strained and twisted, she could not turn to see. It was so frustrating! She was certain that if she didn't somehow discover what was in that room, bad things were going to happen. And the answer was so close. Right there behind her.

Tayna continued to struggle against her invisible restraints, even as her nose continued its tour of the musty brick work. When at last she had completed her circuit of the room, a wave of relaxation washed over her and she drifted back out through the still-open door, which closed again behind her. Back across the empty hall she went, retracing her path up the stairs, level after level and finally returning to her dorm where her body sank back down to the bed.

She tried to keep the dream and all its parts fixed in her mind. It felt so important, as though she was the only person in the world who could figure it out, but even as she tried to study them, the events and details evaporated like mist in the garden. Before long she lost the battle completely and slipped reluctantly into a deep but troubled sleep.

Dear Shammi:

Wasn't that the weirdest dream? I know you must have seen it, since you're supposed to be watching over my thoughts and everything. If only I could see what was in that room. Figuring that out felt like only the most important thing ever. And what room was that, anyway? I've been in the kitchen a million times and there's nothing there—just a brick wall. But there I go, don't I, taking a stupid dream and expecting it to make sense. Maybe it's just a stupid dream. Or I could be cracking up.

Oh, guess what? I think I'm going to have an interview! Lies heard a mommy-be talking about wanting to meet "the girl who's been here just forever." Well everybody knows I'm the queen of that country! She didn't hear anything about a him though, but there's always a him. Wanna-dads and mommy-bes: get your own matched set, available in all this fall's hottest colors Not sold separately. Offer void where prohibited by nuns. The Goodies don't even let solos come into the building, which is too bad, 'cuz I'm sure there are probably some really cool mono-moms out there. We could be all buddy-buddy and have girls-only movie nights every night, with popcorn and soda and candles...

Aww, who am I kidding? I haven't even seen her yet. When was the last time one of the Unlovables even got an interview, huh? It's so... unnatural. The other girls are looking at me like I've got a goat's hoof sticking out of my forehead or something. I still don't really know what's going on, but keep your fingers crossed for me, okay?

Hmm. Do you even have fingers? What does a child-watching god look like, anyway? Interventions are still in your job description, though, right? Do you need fingers for that? What about arms? Legs? For all the help you've been in my life, you might just as well be a multiple amputation victim. What's the matter? My existence isn't pathetic enough for you yet? What does it take to get a little divine meddling around here?

God, I am such a freak! And now, as if I didn't already have enough wrong with me, I think my ears are starting to swell up. They're really sore. Who gets pain of the earlobe, anyway? Maybe I'm getting the plague. That would be intense, wouldn't it? Would you get involved then?

Sometimes I wish you would just give me a sign—show me that you're actually out there, on the job, listening and all. Then I think, no, don't answer that. I'm not sure I could stand to find out if you aren't real. I've been keeping this journal for years now, but still the only writing in here is mine. So I'm just wondering: if you don't write letters and you don't do personal appearances, how am I going to know it's you when you finally show up?

Oh. Right. You'll be the all-powerful being with no arms and no legs. What was I thinking?

Keep your ears on,
T.

Tayna trudged slowly down the stairs, looking curiously at the walls and steps. After that weird dream, it was as though she were now seeing the entire building for the first time. When she finally reached the dining hall for breakfast, she was almost ten minutes late.

"Well, look who's so important that she feels she can keep us all waiting until she graces us with her presence." Sister Regalia glared at her from her place at the head of the fourth-floor table. Everybody knew the senior girls were her favorites.

"Well? Sit down girl! I'll not let these fine young ladies starve another moment to convenience you."

Tayna didn't bother to point out that Sister Regalia and her seniors were all sitting in front of half-empty bowls. Instead, she made her way silently over to the Unlovables table. At the far end, two places were vacant. Those girls were on breakfast duty today. By now, they'd be elbows deep in the porridge pot, sucking down their own hasty breakfast in the kitchen before the avalanche of dishes started washing over them. But at least they were excused from their first lesson period of the day. It wasn't a lot of time, but it was usually enough to get the chore done. The Unlovables rotated breakfast and lunch duties, with two different girls assigned to breakfast and two more to lunch each day.

Sister Regalia finished her breakfast at the same time as the last girl at the senior table, which was not a big surprise. By nature she was as ravenous as a leopard but she usually managed to hold off the last mouthful or two until most of her favorites had finished. Never, however, did she go out of her way to wait for any of the Unlovables, even though they always got their meals last. And today she caught nearly all of them only half-way through their porridge.

"A few items for today, children." Meal time was now officially over. Tayna was sure she saw Sister Regalia smirk in delight when Dana and Jenny groaned in protest. They had made the mistake of chatting instead of eating, but the Sister Superior was not about to back down for a pair of hungry Unlovables.

"First, a word about the televisions..." She looked around the room, waiting to be sure she had everyone's attention. When the muttering had died down, she continued. "I expect you to remember that they are to be left on the channels that I have set them to. They are there for your education, not for your amusement." Sister Regalia's face twisted in distaste at the thought. "Television time is from seven o'clock until bedtime. You are to be seated, in your group lounges, watching the approved programming during those hours unless you have been assigned other duties. Is that perfectly clear?"

By reflex, the entire dining hall chanted in reply. "Yes, Sister." Sister Regalia grunted her satisfaction and moved on.

"Secondly, we have a number of visitors lined up for today. As usual, those of you who are to have interviews will be summoned from your classrooms at the appropriate time. So I expect every girl to keep herself presentable at all times. You never know," she said, looking several girls in the eye at random, "today might be *your* day." Tayna felt her insides turn to butter. Today! How long had she been hearing those words and hoping they might be meant for her? And if Lies was right, today *was* the day. She felt both excited and terrified at the same time.

"That will be all. Off to your classes."

Everybody was talking excitedly and none more so than the Unlovables themselves. By now, they had all heard the rumors and their heads kept turning furtively to peek at Tayna, who tried her best to ignore the attention. She had almost reached the stairs when she felt the grip of a clawed hand on her shoulder.

"A word with you, girl."

Tayna was too startled to speak. This is it! She nodded meekly and followed Sister Regalia through the flow of bodies, up the staircase and into her office. The old nun sat at her desk and Tayna, long-since accustomed to the routine, assumed her position in front of the desk with her hands clasped in front. She didn't have to wait long though. The Sister Superior considered silence golden–except for her own.

"Sister Diaphana is having some trouble with the basil. She's asked me if you might be excused from class to assist her." Tayna blinked. Basil?

"But I thought..."

Sister Regalia cackled. "Oh? Your little friend told you what she overheard last night, did she?" Her expression made it clear that she was enjoying Tayna's confusion. "And you thought the pushy little doll woman meant she wanted to see *you*, is that it?" Tayna couldn't help herself. She nodded. "O ho! I thought so. And you have so much experience with visitors that you trust your own thoughts in the matter, do you?" Tayna felt crushed. Lies had got it wrong after all.

"Well," said Sister Regalia. "I'll have you know that *nobody* comes into this establishment and tells me who they want to see. I make all the decisions around here, and don't you forget it. Nothing could possibly convince me to risk our sterling reputation by having any of our visitors meet the likes of you. Nothing." Regalia watched Tayna carefully as though she was waiting to be certain that all spark of hope had been smothered before she continued.

"Now, as I was saying, Sister Diaphana has been having trouble with the basil. She wondered if you might be excused from classes to help her, although I'm sure I have no idea what possible use you might be. Still..." Regalia paused as though she was studying a complicated calendar in her head before continuing. "I suppose even a complete klutz like you can help with digging and shoveling or whatever daft nonsense that woman has in mind. So, go find her and do whatever you can to help tidy up her little mess. I trust you can find her?"

Tayna's heart was in tatters. She hadn't realized just how much she had come to believe in Lies's latest tale, nor how desperately she had wanted the chance, just the slimmest chance, to find a mother who would take her away from this hideous place. She thought she had successfully buried those fantasies years ago, but rather than give Regalia the satisfaction of seeing her misery, Tayna grabbed at her invisible wrist-bracelet instead and twisted her frustrations down into it. There was no real bracelet there of course–invisible or otherwise. It was just some silly habit she'd picked up as a child–a way of calming herself down when she was feeling stressed–but she'd been doing it for so long now that she no longer even noticed herself doing it. Still, it wouldn't be good for Regalia to see how easily she had been brought back to the edge of hope.

"Diaphana isn't all that difficult to find," she said.

When Regalia dismissed her with a wave of her hand, Tayna stormed out of the office. She was so tired of being pressed under the thumb of that self-important harpy. Even after a few more twists of her bracelet, she still wanted to scream, throw things, maybe even hurt a basketful of puppies. She stopped. Then she giggled. Puppies? She had never been any good at nurturing a good rage. Whenever she tried, she eventually came up with absurd images like that, which ruined the whole effect. She just didn't have a knack for brooding. Tayna grinned a goofy grin at herself and cocked an ear to listen for Sister Diaphana. Imagine. Puppies.

"Whoops! Oh, my."

Of all the Goody-Goodies Tayna knew, Sister Diaphana was the only one she could honestly call harmless. She was a large woman. Her habit billowed out around her like a tarpaulin caught on a boulder in a hurricane, and her voice was as big as her frame, which made her extremely easy to find. Classroom 1.

"Oh, hello Tayna, dear. I was just clearing up the board in here and I think I've made a frightful mess."

Indeed, Sister Diaphana was covered from head to ankle in yellow chalk dust. As she strained to reach the writing at the top of the board with the eraser, her ample frame saw to it that all the chalk below the level of her shoulder was transferred directly to her robes.

In a nicer world, Sister Diaphana might have been that one, warm soul who made living in the Old Shoe bearable for girls like Tayna. But, sadly, Sister Diaphana never seemed to be completely in the world– not the real one, anyway. She was one of those people who laughed for no reason at all and carried on conversations with the empty air. Sometimes, when she really seemed to be with you, she was very sweet and motherly, but then there were other times when she seemed to be lost in a world that only she could see, one that didn't even have you in it. Either way, she was too out of touch with what was going on around her to guide or protect any of the older children, though she was quite good with the infants.

So instead of having the mentor she so genuinely needed, Tayna could only take pity on the poor woman–just another victim of the savage pranks and humiliations that were the stock in trade of the other Sisters. For example, Sister Anthrax's favorite joke was to use a long pointer to write meaningless sentences across the top of the board after teaching a class. Then she would pretend to have some urgent errand and ask Sister Diaphana to clean the board for her. It was a sport she never tired of, but poor Diaphana never seemed to catch on.

"Come on, Sister. Let's get you tidied up and then go see about your basil."

Sister Diaphana sparkled at the suggestion. "That would be wonderful, dear. It's been giving me such trouble this week."

———

At the very top of the stairwell, above even the fifth floor, a heavy iron door let them out onto the roof, at the rear of the building. Tayna led the way around the little hut that capped the stairwell and went directly to the edge of the old pool that now served as the orphanage's sunken, rooftop garden. She was already partway down the ladder before she noticed that Diaphana was no longer with her. A noise from the flag pole caught her attention and she whipped her head around. Horror grew in her eyes and she swarmed back up the ladder. The portly Sister was at the front of the building, leaning out over the edge of the roof, with one arm clutching the rickety old pole, and the other waving wildly in the air.

"Yoo hoo! Yoo hoo! Hello Duck Man! Thank you for your help but I have Tayna now! She's very good with the plants you know! She'll fix everything! Bye bye!" And then she swung back around, coming very near to toppling herself off the edge in the process, but Tayna was there just in time to grab her by her flailing arm.

"Oh my God, Sister! What was that all about?" Diaphana gazed serenely back at her, clearly unsure what Tayna was referring to.

"With the flag pole!" Tayna said. "The whole 'Yoo hoo! Duck Man!' thing." She gave a fair impersonation of Sister Diaphana swinging precariously from a rusty pole while waving the other arm over her head.

"Oh, do you know the Duck Man too, dear?" Tayna sighed. Conversations with the big Sister often went this way.

"No, Sister. I don't know him. Is he nice?"

"Oh. I don't know that I'd call him 'nice,' dear." Then she leaned in close and lowered her voice. "Between you and me, he's a bit odd." Tayna suppressed a grin. Coming from Sister Diaphana, she didn't even want to guess what that might mean. She tried again.

"Where do you know him from? Does he live near here?" Tayna's full attention had been on the flailing nun. She hadn't seen who the waving was directed at, if indeed there had been anyone there at all.

"Oh, yes, dear," Sister Diaphana replied, "He lives right there across the street. In the alley. At least, he's living there for now."

Tayna did not like the sound of that. "You mean, there's a strange man living in the alley next to the orphanage? Sister, are you sure he's real? How did you meet him? You haven't been outside in a month."

"Of course he's real, child. I spoke to him last night in this very garden. He can't talk, poor dear, but he offered to help me with the basil today, only I don't need his help anymore, do I? Now you're here." Tayna was getting seriously creeped out. Some weirdo had actually been climbing around on the roof?

"Why do you call him 'Duck Man?' Does he have feathers?"

Sister Diaphana smiled. "Oh, no, dear. Don't be silly. He was quite tall and very distinguished looking with his nice beard, and he wore a long pink coat.. Come to think of it, maybe he thought it was going to rain. He was wearing long rubber pants, too. They came all the way up to his chest, and he had his coat tucked inside to keep it dry. Oh. And he had the most darling hat on his head. It had a bright yellow bill, and big googly eyes on the front–just like a duck "

By the time Sister Diaphana had finished her description, Tayna's fears had subsided. Nobody dressed like that could have survived for long on these streets without getting picked up. This Duck Man sounded like just another one of the fantastical people who inhabited Diaphana's invisible world. Tayna put the matter behind her and led the nun back to the garden.

Most people would not expect basil to be a viable crop in a city-bound, rooftop garden not in November–but such people were not making allowances for whose garden this was. Sister Diaphana was the gardener of record. She was a sympathetic soul, in her way, and in a more stable person that would have given her a greener thumb than the average nun enjoyed, but even that would not have been enough to bring herbs and flowers to full bloom at the bottom of an abandoned swimming pool on a windy roof, with the chill of winter beginning to set in. While Sister Diaphana got all the official credit, everybody knew that this was really Tayna's garden.

It had been several days since Tayna had last found the time to visit her refuge, and in that time it appeared that Sister Diaphana had been busy, although, what she thought she had been doing was anybody's guess. Tayna's garden was not generally the orderly and regimented grid-work of plants that most people associated with modern, efficient horticulture. Instead, hers was a riot of chaotic associations, seemingly clumped in random patches. Roses climbed the stalks of tomato plants, herbs sprouted from the crotches of tree branches. There was even a vertical row of carrots growing from a crack in the wall between the old tiles. But somehow, under Tayna's careful guidance, it all just worked.

Or, at least, it usually did. Today, mayhem was strewn about her carefully managed chaos. Yellow bits of rope were tied to various shrubs and stakes and then trailed out randomly across the beds. A water cistern had been turned on its side and rolled through the cabbages. And there, in the corner, where the basil normally flourished, was a large, square patio stone, smack on top of the herb patch.

Tayna sighed. "What have you been up to, Sister?" It was a rhetorical question. She didn't expect an answer, but she got one anyway.

"Regalia wanted to have a patio, dear. I did my best. Do you like it?"

Tayna felt a brief flare of anger. Sister Regalia. She might have known. But the hopeful expression on Sister Diaphana's face dowsed her anger. As usual, there was a pile of work to be done and a shortage of volunteers, so Tayna pulled up her shirt sleeves and set to it.

"Come on then, Sister. We've got our job cut out for us today, haven't we? And I think," she added with a friendly grin, "that I know what's been troubling the basil."

The hours of the day slipped away while Tayna set about, restoring order to her sanctuary. The stakes and ropes were the first to go. Then she righted the cistern and with Diaphana's help, shoved it back into its corner where it could collect rainwater that sometimes poured in off the roof. They even got the patio slab levered up and off the herbs.

And that's when her real work began.

Most gardeners would have given up on all the crushed and tattered plants, but not Tayna. Starting from scratch would take weeks. Besides, you don't shoot people just because somebody beat them with a rock, do you? Why should it be any different with vegetables?

For hours Tayna worked her way through the beds, propping up stems here, stroking leaves there. She was really quite good at it and before the day was out, all the members of her little chorus were singing again. True, a few of them were still shaky and off-key, but they'd be fine with another day or two of attention. She squinted up at the sun, sinking now toward the western wall. "Well, we'd best get back inside, Sister. It will soon be time for supper."

After ensuring that Sister Diaphana found her way back down to the ground floor, Tayna hurried to her dorm to get cleaned up. She came through the door just in time to see Lies, standing in the middle of a crowd of girls, wearing her best outfit and talking at a hundred miles an hour.

"Lies?" Tayna said. "What are you guys doing here? Who's downstairs on dinner prep?" The girls didn't even hear her. As soon as Lies saw Tayna, she came running forward, waving her arms excitedly in the air.

"Oh, Tayna, they're fabulous! Just exactly like we've always imagined. They're so polite, and friendly. They actually wanted to know about my life! Can you believe it? Nothing at all like the Goody-Goodies. I told them all about you and the stuff we've done and they asked questions and everything. Oh this has just been the best day ever!"

Tayna had no idea what was going on, but obviously something exciting had happened. Or at least, Lies thought so. She laughed.

"Slow down, Lies. What's going on? Who's not like the Goodies?"

Lies just giggled in delight. "Why, Mr. and Mrs. Nackenfausch, of course. I had my interview today and they're everything we've always dreamed about in parents. They are just so cool! They run a hospital for dolls and she's awesome and I think they're going to adopt me!"

———·———

Out in the alley, Duck Man pulled his hat lower on his head. He was crouched inside a dumpster. A bitter wind whistled along the streets, forcing him to hunker deeper down into the garbage for warmth. He had seen her again, on the roof. And now *she* was burning too. His time was coming, his time to be with her. He felt it in his bones, he knew it. It was a good feeling, one that made him feel bubbly inside. He took an apple from his pocket and began to eat. He could wait. He was really good at that. Waiting. And watching.

All around him, the wind continued to howl.

chapter 3

Tayna turned away from Lies and her gaggle of admirers without saying a word and bolted from the room. Behind her, she could hear the
excitement drain from Eliza's voice. "Tayna? What's wrong? Aren't
you happy for me?" But she didn't go back. Her fury drove her on,
blinding her to everything else. And when she reached the end of the
hall, not even Eliza's last plaintive call could stop her.

"T? Come back. I'm sorry."

Tayna thundered down the stairs, unable to think. Barely even able
to breathe. The only thought she could hold was that she needed to get
out. To flee. No punishment was deterent enough to keep her there for
even a moment longer. So when she reached the ground floor, Tayna
didn't even stop. She ran down the entry hall, pulled open the heavy
wooden door, and proceeded to commit one of the greatest offenses
in the Goody-Goody Book of Shalt Not, as she bolted down the front
steps of the Old Shoe and out onto the darkened street. Unescorted.
She didn't care where she went. It didn't matter, just as long as it was
some place nunless. And Lies-less. Then she jammed her hands deep
into the pouch of her hoody and stalked off to find it.

Tayna walked for a long time, oblivious to the turns she took or
which abandoned buildings she passed. She avoided the more brightly
lit areas, favoring the shadows in case the Goodies decided to come
after her. The Old Shoe was not in one of the nicer neighborhoods,
and the Goodies had always used that as an excuse to ban the children
from going out into the streets. The few times she *had* been out, Tayna
had always been under the glare of a Sister or in the back of a taxi–
always guided by some adult who knew where they were going. The
only thing Tayna ever knew was the name of their destination, which
was usually one of the other Goody-run institutions–Holy Terror or the
Gruesome Harvest Mortuary–but those places might just as well have
been floating on crackers in a vast sea of onion soup for all she knew
about how to find them. As her blind fury began to fade, she looked

around, and for the first time in her life, Tayna realized just how little practical understanding she had of the world she lived in. Nothing was familiar.

Even if she had been here before, that would have been by daylight. She'd never be able to recognize it now. Your attention always gets drawn to the bright things. By day, that means things like shop signs, billboards and cars, but darkness has a way of changing what you notice. At night, the bright things are fewer and farther between and of an entirely different character: a section of sidewalk glowing beneath a rare, working street light; the glow of a television from a ground-floor apartment window; a flickering neon light over the doorway of a seedy bar. The more Tayna looked around, the more alien things became and the more uncertain she felt.

This unfamiliar world, filled with its sputters of harsh, unnatural light and backed by the smell of damp concrete and grime, suddenly felt... wrong. That instinct, which was her only guide now, gnawed at her for several blocks. Little by little, shadow by shadow, tinkle by tinkle of broken glass, it whispered in the back of her mind. Wrongness. Strangeness. Danger. Finally, when she reached the next corner, she'd had enough, and instead of continuing along her current course, Tayna turned and marched away from the electrified night of the avenue, drawn into the darker side-street by what? A smell?

The smell of leaves. Ahead of her, hanging above the sidewalk, she could almost make them out, winking and shimmering in the moonlight. A park. The nagging in her skull relaxed. This was something she understood. It reminded her of her rooftop garden, and somehow, of childhood. When she finally reached the trees, it seemed the most natural thing in the world. She stepped off the sidewalk and into the blackness of the silent urban thicket.

At first, she felt soothed by the dense foliage, by the sounds and smells of greenery and life all around her, but the further she wandered into the trees, the more she realized that, even here, things were less than they seemed. The trees were all of the same kind, all the same size. There were very few animals and nothing at all larger than a squirrel. The grass showed no variety, no flowers, no weeds. There was no marsh or any hills. It was as though the entire wood had been planned by someone who had never actually seen a real forest. The vibrancy of life that had attracted her initially, turned out to be little more than illusion, just as bleak and uninspired as the electric lights and concrete had been.

"But this is crazy." She spoke the words aloud, trying to make the trees around her feel less creepily silent. "This isn't my first time in a park. It isn't even my first time in the woods. And you trees are no different from any of the others I've seen. So why do you feel so strange all of a sudden?"

"It is your flower." The voice was muffled by intervening leaves, but not many.

Tayna went still. There was someone else in the forest with her. And that someone was way too close.

"Who's there?" she called out with more confidence than she felt.

"I have many names."

This was shaping up into a trailer for a bad horror movie. Teenaged girl, walking alone at night in an abandoned city park hears creepy voices from out of the shrubbery. Definitely not a scene from a light comedy. This had slasher film written all over it.

"Where are you?" Something about the conversation felt odd, the way subtitled movies are odd, as you try to watch the actor's lips and read the text at the same time, and she fidgeted nervously with her invisible bracelet. But despite her rising stress, she tried to keep her voice positive and naively curious, like she was honestly trying to find this psycho-dude. Meanwhile, she was backing up, retracing her steps as quickly and as quietly as she could manage, and glancing from side to side for a weapon. Anything.

"I am here," said the voice, but this time it was not muffled by trees. The speaker had come out into open air and was now directly behind her.

Tayna whirled around to face him. And then she gasped. There, standing in front of her, was the tall bearded man in rubber pants that Sister Diaphana had described. Duck Man. And he was reaching out to grab her.

No child can reach the age of thirteen in the modern world and not realize that this was a life or death situation. Nor can that child–especially a girl–have escaped hearing at least some of the details concerning how one should react. First, she screamed. Then she kicked as hard as she could. And then she ran. She was pretty sure her foot had made solid contact. There may even have been the reward of a satisfyingly surprised grunt from her assailant, but she didn't hang around to conduct any post-kick victim surveys. She just ran.

And she continued to run. After a while, she was surprised to discover that she had seemingly boundless reserves for running. In the end, she ran for what seemed like an hour and it was only when she realized that she recognized her surroundings that she stopped. She was right back where she'd started, standing on the street in front of the Old Shoe. Even though she didn't know the layout of the city, her subconscious must have been keeping better track of her route than she'd realized. When she had pressed her internal panic button, her brain had simply rewound the tape to the beginning. That was probably pretty cool, but right now she was too frazzled to care. A strange and entirely unexpected emotion flooded through her and it took a moment to realize what it was. She was glad to see the old dungeon.

Shuddering at the thought, Tayna trudged up the steps and went back in where she belonged.

———

"You selfish, arrogant little sprat!"

It was late, after Failing Light, and Sister Regalia was in a high rage. She seemed to almost fly across the lobby when she saw Tayna walking past her office door. Never pretty, the senior nun was now terrifying to behold, all angular elbows and bony legs, gliding across the floor as though she was on rollers, with a heavy wooden rod raised above her head in a clenched fist. Regalia wasn't a particularly large woman, but she was densely built. And hairy. Her ears could easily do with a good brushing and the only thing keeping her eyebrows from merging was sheer dogged persistence with her tweezers. If the wind had ever had the courage to blow the woman's habit up over her head, Tayna doubted anybody would notice. In all likelihood, the hair went all the way down. Still, with her recent experiences still fresh in her mind, Tayna wasn't much in the mood to fight. Instead, she hung her head in quiet submission, ready for the blow that she herself felt she deserved. But it never landed.

"Sister."

The sound of that calm, patient voice coming from Regalia's office did more than a team of draft horses could have done in that moment. They stopped the Sister Superior cold in her tracks.

"Am I to assume that this is the spirited young lady we have been so concerned about all evening?" Again the voice spoke, in fluid, appealing tones that seemed both compassionate and powerful, accustomed to being obeyed.

"Yes, sir," Sister Regalia replied.

Sir?

A small man stepped out of the Sister's office. Tayna recognized him as the man who had been touring the fifth floor the other day with Regalia and Anthrax, although he seemed to be much more expensively dressed now than he had been then. He wore a dark gray business suit that did a decent job of disguising his somewhat knobby shape. In his hand, he carried a white and equally knobby wooden staff, capped at both ends with little hand-carved skulls. Blood-red gemstones winked at her from the eye-sockets as he walked toward the immobile nun. He smiled warmly at Tayna and pushed Regalia's arm down gently with his staff.

"Come, Sister, surely you won't insist on beating her before I've had the pleasure of a chat."

He turned away from the Sister Superior with a decided air of dismissal. "Tayna, isn't it?" he said, inclining his head toward her. "Sister Regalia was just telling me all about your mysterious arrival and subsequent, shall we say 'energetic' history here. Since the Sister seems to have taken temporary leave of her manners, allow me to introduce myself. I am Angiron. Well, Lord Angiron, actually."

Tayna nearly choked. "She told you about my arrival?" In all the years Tayna had been living with the Goodies, nobody had ever told her even the skimpiest of details concerning how she had come to be there. The closest any had ever come was when Sister Inquisita had threatened to roast her 'just as crisp and black as that other one.'" But when Tayna had pressed for details, the viperous old hag had said, "Well, you're not the only orphan in the world, are you? They're not all lucky enough to have a good home and protection. I'm sure many have died, probably in gruesome accidents. *Very* gruesome, you can be sure."

Tayna had been just seven at the time.

Sister Inquisita disappeared later that same week and in all the years since, Tayna had wondered what had ever happened to the crusty old woman, but she hadn't been able to learn a thing, until the day she'd become Senior Unlovable and made her first trip to collect the urns. And there she'd been. Crotchety as ever, and apparently now in charge of Holy Terror.

Yet that one comment, made so many years ago, had been the only thing Tayna had ever heard that even hinted at her own secret, untold origin story. And you really had to stretch to even read that much into it. But now, here was some smooth-talking, twisted up little man casually talking about how much Sister Regalia had already told *him*. Tayna glared jets of fury at the Sister Superior. Lord Angiron's gleaming eyes flicked perceptively from the orphan to the nun and back again.

"Am I to understand, Sister, that the young lady has been told nothing of her past?" Tayna's expression was all the answer he needed. "Well then, let's you and I have a little chat, shall we? One that no doubt is long overdue." Then he turned away, beckoning for Tayna to follow him, while simultaneously shooing Sister Regalia out of her own office and striding past her.

Tayna followed him warily into the room, and closed the door behind them.

Even with it closed, they could still hear Regalia sputtering in the hallway, but Angiron just smiled and seated Tayna in a very gentlemanly manner, before seating himself in the large office chair. He gestured toward the door. "She does seem to be every inch the grounded harpy tonight, doesn't she?" Tayna returned his ingratiating smile, with a cautious half-smile of her own.

"Well, my dear. I expect you have a great number of questions. I'm scarcely the most knowledgeable person to answer them, of course, but since the good Sister hasn't seen fit to do so herself..." He let the words dangle there between them, like a life-preserver thrown just short of a drowning swimmer. All she had to do was reach out and take it, but that inner voice was still whispering words of warning to her. Danger. She held her tongue and watched him mistrustfully.

Lord Angiron waited, leaving a silence that begged to be filled. The oak desk loomed between them, and the coat rack in the corner, hanging darkly with one of Regalia's old habits, seemed to glare at the young girl's impudence, as though the nun herself was actually inside it. The silence stretched out and Angiron reached casually into a drawer, from which he withdrew a thin-bladed knife and began to trim his fingernails. Tayna watched his eyes peering at her from over top of the blade. They were dark, calculating eyes, hidden beneath a thick and almost furry brow. As much as she wanted to learn what he could tell her, she just didn't trust those eyes. Instead of taking up the conversation, as he so clearly intended, Tayna raised her own eyebrows a trifle, challenging him—as if to say, "It's your meeting. If you've got something to tell me, then get on with it."

Angiron's eyes widened in surprise, but he chuckled good-naturedly. "Well, you're feisty enough. That's for sure." When she still said nothing, he shrugged and spread his arms genially. "This tale—at least, as much as I've heard of it—has precious little meat, I'm afraid.

It's likely to disappoint you, but as I understand, it was a foreigner who found you. He approached the city, late one night, having just arrived from some distance away." He paused again, now picking at something in his teeth with the tip of the blade, then he pointed it at her in an off-hand way. "Now, what you must realize is that this was ten years ago, in the middle of winter. The poor man knew nothing of the local geography, nor the laws of the land. He claimed he saw something out of the corner of his eye while traveling on a dark and lonely stretch of road. Upon investigating, what should he find but a small, nearly helpless child, alone in this world, save for himself and the howling coyotes."

"Where did this happen?" Her tone could not disguise her curiosity.

Lord Angiron smiled more broadly, apparently pleased to have dragged her out of her silence. "On the north highway," he said. "Somewhere near the old Indian museum, I believe."

"Wasketawin," Tayna said. "And then?"

"There isn't much more to tell, my dear. A good deal of time was spent combing the area, but no evidence was ever uncovered that might suggest who you were, how you came to be there, or where your people might be found. With no family to be notified, your case was turned over to the skilled hands of the Good Sisters of Salvation here. Quite a remarkable case, actually. It is common enough for them to *dis*-appear, but very unusual for a young girl of that age to *appear* without a trace. Had you spoken the language even slightly, perhaps the investigators might have learned enough about you to do more." Tayna sat bolt upright in her chair.

"I didn't speak English?" This news shocked her no less than if he had told her that she'd been found in the remains of a crashed rocket ship. "What language did I speak?"

"Well," he said thoughtfully, "that was the puzzle, wasn't it?"

Tayna looked at him warily. "What do you mean, 'puzzle?'"

Lord Angiron waved a hand at the nameless, faceless perpetrators of bureaucracy. "None who were assigned to your case were ever able to fathom the language in the slightest. It was eventually assumed that you were merely imitating the idea of speech and had not yet learned to talk at all."

Tayna sat back to think about that for a moment and then a thought occurred to her. "Is that why I was placed immediately with the Unlov–um, on the fifth floor?"

Angiron seemed surprised by the question. "Well, I suppose you'd have to ask Sister Regalia for a full accounting on that point," he said. "Although, that certainly sounds plausible to me." Then he turned in his chair and opened a cabinet behind him, placing the knife inside before turning to face her once again.

"So I was speaking gibberish?"

He smiled sympathetically. "It hardly sounds surprising for a child as bright as you to have invented her own style of speech, does it?"

Tayna shrugged. "I suppose not." She lifted her gaze from the floor up to the strange man behind the desk. "The language I made up. Did it even sound close to any real languages?"

Angiron sputtered and coughed for a moment. "Ah, er, ahem. I'm afraid I, uh... Languages are not really my area of expertise." Suddenly, his face brightened. "Although, I do remember reading about the case at the time. There was one fellow who thought it bore a passing resemblance to the local aboriginal tongues, though I gather nothing helpful ever arose from the theory."

Tayna perked up a bit at that. "Really? Which language?"

"All of them, my dear. The poor fellow was quite exercised about it, though I never did understand why." He smiled benevolently.

"And no specific words were ever worked out?"

Angiron was beginning to look uncomfortable. "Just the one, if I remember correctly. Just the one."

"And what was that?"

The tiny Lord now took his feet. "Your name, my dear. Your name. Sister Regalia had taken to calling you Mowgli, but every time she said it within your hearing, you pointed to your chest and declared with inescapable certainty, 'Tayna.' A most impressive display of character from one so young."

Tayna was pleased with the sound of that. The image it formed in her mind was so... Tayna. But before she could frame another question, he had rounded the desk and was ushering her toward the door.

"It really has been charming to get this chance to know one another, but I must say good night now."

Tayna looked bewildered. "But I thought you had questions for me," she said.

"Another time, my dear. A rain check, perhaps?"

Tayna looked at him uncertainly. "I think I'd like that," she said. "You've been very helpful."

Angiron face clenched slightly into a scowl. "I'm sure I have, girl. I'm quite sure I have."

When he opened the door to let her out, Sister Regalia huffed her way past with her nose in the air to reclaim her lair. Lord Angiron ignored her and took Tayna's hand in his own, his demeanor suddenly smoothed again from whatever had upset him. "If you'll excuse us dear, the Sister and I have a few matters to discuss." Then he reached up and stroked Tayna's cheek with oily fingertips, which caused a shudder of revulsion to run screaming up her spine, but she fought down the urge to flinch. "I'm sure we'll see each other again very soon," he said, "I'll be staying for a while. The Good Sister has kindly offered me the use of the guest quarters. I look forward to our next meeting." Tayna could swear he actually blew a silent kiss at her, and then he turned to follow Sister Regalia back into the office.

Ew, ew, ew, ew, ew! Tayna's mind screamed in disgust, as soon as the door closed. His touch had been like oiled sandpaper and what the hell was that kissy face thing all about? She shuddered convulsively and reached up quickly to try to scrub away the memory of his caress. When that boiling pot had finally simmered down, it dawned on her that she had just had one of the most baffling nights of her entire life. Not only had she learned more about her past from some creepy dwarf in ten minutes than she'd been able to pry out of anybody else in ten years, but then there had been all of that "Yes sir, Lord Angiron, sir" business earlier with Regalia. And how do you even begin to talk about the whole "Duck Man meets Mr. Kicky Foot" thing before that? Yup. Altogether a very confusing night. She needed to let it all soak in for a while. More importantly, she was exhausted and needed sleep. Maybe by morning she'd be ready to try to tell Shammi all about it.

———

Lies crept quietly out of the ground floor washroom and trotted down the hall toward the Sister Superior's office, looking over her shoulder as she went. Nobody else was around. Like most of the girls who had spent any time in the Old Shoe, Lies had developed her own way of surviving. It was all well and good for Tayna to have that whole "quiet competence" thing going on, but there was only room for one Tayna in the house. Lies had a different strategy, one that she liked to call her 'policy of superior knowledge.' The only problem was that acquiring useful information required taking risks. Like being caught out of bed after Failing Light. She raised her hand as though she were about to knock at the office door and held it there–just in case. Then she leaned in to listen.

"–can't risk giving them to Tayna." An unfamiliar voice carried through the heavy wooden door.

Lies's eyes popped. "Superior Knowledge" usually just meant bits of dirt–what Regalia thought of one of the girls, or one of the Sisters, maybe. But lately, she'd been batting high numbers, scoring all kinds of useful tidbits, and this definitely sounded useful. She still didn't know what she'd done to upset Tayna, but maybe if she got something good now, she could use it to make peace. That would be nice. Lies looked around the hall and quickly checked the stairwell over her shoulder. Everything looked quiet, so she took a chance and moved in a little closer.

"How have you managed to keep the little f'znat in the dark for so long? She almost pinked me twice in less than ten minutes." It was a man's voice, but Lies didn't recognize it.

"I told you it was risky." That was Regalia. "She's trickier than she looks. The best way to keep a secret is to forget you even know it, but in her case, she has a knack of digging them out of you anyway. I find the best policy is to go on the offensive every time she speaks."

The man grunted.

"Did you get anything useful out of her while she was standing you on your head?"

Immediately, there was a bestial snarl, followed by the sound of something heavy smacking into something soft. Lies jerked her head back instinctively.

"Speak to me in that manner again and the next time, I'll use the pointy end."

"Yes, Lord Angiron. I forgot myself. Please forgive me."

Lies was more startled by the Sister's groveling than she had been by the sounds of violence, and it suddenly dawned on her that she might be in danger herself. Something intense was going on, and if she got caught out here, chances were good that she'd learn about the pointy end too. But to her credit, Lies didn't even consider bailing. This had something to do with Tayna, and it sounded nuclear big–so big that something as trivial as Lies's own fear wasn't even going to be given a vote. Throwing caution down an elevator shaft, she stood her ground and pressed her ear more firmly against the door.

Shortly after falling asleep, Tayna had the dream again. Rising from the bed, she floated silently across the room with her arms stretched out to either side. Her fingertips gently brushed the walls as she drifted out into the hall. Two bare feet hung limply below the hem of her nightgown and her toes bumped idly against the hardwood floor, in time with her breathing.

As before, her eyes were closed, but she could still see herself from the hovering little bird position, above and behind her body. Down she went, past the other floors of girls, past the Goody-Goody level and past the ground-floor offices. Lies smiled and waved from the doorway where her interview was happening. She looked so happy, but Tayna continued drifting, down the steps and into the basement. She floated calmly through the dining hall and beyond, into the kitchen. At the back wall, next to the large, walk-in freezer, she came to a small door that she only ever saw in the dream. It swung silently open before her and she swept past it into the brightly lit chamber. Her body floated around the perimeter of the room, facing the walls, and even her dis-embodied, floating viewpoint could see nothing but the rough, brick surface that almost scraped her nose. Behind her, in the middle of the secret room, she could hear things: Lord Angiron talking in muffled tones, the drone of a television turned down low and something else that sounded like wind chimes.

As she strained to listen, she became aware of a tickle in her toes, which quickly intensified into an almost painful burning sensation. Still floating, Tayna arched her back and kicked, trying to shake the feeling from her toes, but that only made it move, first into her feet, and then flowing up through her calves and thighs, and then on, up through her torso, chest and neck, where it divided and ran down both her arms to her fingertips, only to rebound back up her arms, where it recombined and shot straight upward into her head. When at last it faded, all that was left was a mild buzzing feeling that settled into the flesh of her ears. But still the sounds droned on.

The words made no sense and even as she strained to hear them, her body continued its tour of the musty brickwork. Tonight, however, when she tried to turn to look at the middle of the room, her body cooperated, turning easily and allowing her to see what had previously been hidden. A thick wire hung from the ceiling and at its end was a shimmering watery sphere. Distorted images of television programs rippled in the water and the sounds of laugh-tracks and insipid banter whispered from its depths. On the floor, below the sphere, there was a round, three-legged table. Each leg was a made of a whitish, knobbly wood, capped at either end with intricate skull carvings, and on the table, sat one of the Goodies' urns. Each time the voice of Lord Angiron spoke, a single drop of liquid fell from the sphere and struck the urn, causing it to reverberate with the sound of wind chimes.

As her gaze swept across it, the urn seemed to shudder in startlement, apparently surprised to see her, but Tayna only smiled. Her dreams were so weird lately.

By that point, her body had completed its circuit of the room, and a wave of relaxation washed over her once more, as she drifted back toward the still-open door. She was just about to float through it when a dull throb of light pulsed from several of the bricks to one side. Tayna paused and reached out curiously with an upraised finger, probing gently at one of the bricks. As she touched it, a new voice echoed within her thoughts. "Urgent fear." The voice was warm and inviting, but it conveyed great sorrow and distress. Tayna ran her finger across the bricks, each one reverberating with gong-like word pairs in her mind. "Family yours. Peril great. Flee now. Home come." Tayna hated this kind of dream. Every orphan had them and she was disgusted with herself. Hadn't she given them up a long time ago?

In any case, her dream body turned away from the bricks and she resumed her stately progress out the door, which closed silently behind her. Back across the kitchen floor she went, arms outstretched and toes bumping along the floor until Lies stepped out in front of her with arms of rope, that looped and coiled about Tayna's shoulders, bringing her to a bobbing halt.

"What have you done?" Lies screamed. Her fury took the form of ruby-red sparks, spraying from her eye sockets like venom. "Get out! Get out!" Lies's ropey arms shook Tayna in violent jerks of rage.

That was enough to wake Tayna from her dream and she tried to sit up. Lies was leaning over her. "You have to get out!" she hissed. Tayna blinked uncertainly at her friend, who looked like she had been crying. Or was about to. Lies shook Tayna's shoulders again, vigorously, unaware that it was no longer necessary.

"I'm awake," Tayna mumbled, as she looked around, trying to make sense of her bed. Then she gasped. She wasn't in her bed at all. She wasn't even in the dorm.

She was standing with her arms stretched wide beside her, in the center of the kitchen floor.

chapter 4

Tayna shuddered. "Wha? This can't be..." She swiveled her head around slowly, as though she were still caught in the dream. The brick wall in the kitchen behind her was blank. No little doors of any kind.

"Come on, Captain Space-for-Rent. Mission Control needs you back in your body. We've got to get you out of here! Pronto!"

Tayna turned toward the voice. "Lies? What happened to your rope-arms?"

Eliza looked back at her with as much confusion on her face as Tayna felt herself. But there was something else there too. Panic? That wasn't good, but what did it have to do with her? "So... not in bed...?"

Eliza stamped a foot in frustration and grabbed Tayna by the arm, dragging her across the room. Tayna felt her hand being pressed downward, against the floor.

"Feel that? Stairs, right? Not dorm room. Stairs. We're in the basement, T. Got it?"

Tayna nodded slowly. "I guess..." The solid feel of wood under her hand gave her something to focus on. She ran her thumb along the worn edge of the step. Then she looked at her bare feet and a smile gradually bloomed. "You're right," she said. "It can't be a dream." She looked at Lies and began marching in place, lifting and lowering each foot with large, exaggerated steps. "Dream feet never touch the floor."

Lies blew out a sigh of relief. "Thank God. I thought you'd never wake up." Tayna started to say something but Lies interrupted. "Ear practice, T, not mouth practice." The expression was one they'd both heard Sister Anthrax use a million times in class. Tayna made face, but she didn't interrupt.

"Sister Regalia just went upstairs looking for you. Any minute she's going to find you out of bed and they're going to start searching. We cannot let her find you."

Tayna frowned. "So? I'm out of bed after Failing Light. It's hardly the worst..." Lies shook her head.

"The problem's not her, it's him."

"Who?"

"Lord Angry One, or something like that. I heard them talking in her office. You have got to stay away from him."

"Lord Angiron?" The memory came back slowly. "I... I met him earlier. There's something seriously bent about him, but..." She shuddered at the sudden memory of his touch.

Lies waved her hands in a that-doesn't-matter motion. "Forget what you thought about him then. That was before bed, right?" Tayna nodded. "Well, everything changed a few minutes ago. When he made his decision."

"What decision?"

Lies stamped a foot in frustration again. "This is taking too long, T! They're upstairs right now and time is running out!" Then she drew a deep breath and turned to look Tayna straight in the eye.

"Look T, I heard a bunch of stuff when I was up there, and there's a lot we need to talk about, but there were two things that really scared me, okay?" Tayna had never heard her friend actually frightened like this before. She nodded but didn't interrupt.

"The first thing I heard was Lord What's-his-name beating Sister Regalia. A real punch-her-in-the-eye-and-bounce-her-off-the-furniture kind of beating. And that was just for smart-mouthing him." Tayna's eyes went wide. She remembered how Lord Angiron had ordered the Sister around earlier, and how quick the woman had been to obey. That behavior suddenly made sense.

"And the other thing?"

Eliza'a face darkened and she lowered her voice. "He said he was going to kill you. Tonight. 'Take you out of this world with one quick swing of his staff.'"

The blood drained from Tayna's face. For the briefest moment, she wondered if maybe this was just another of Lies's secret fantasy games, but one look at her friend's eyes laid that idea to rest. Eliza Drummel wasn't that good an actress. If she was saying that the sky was falling, then judging by her face, she must have already been hit by a couple of chunks.

"Okay. What's the plan?" The two girls had pulled hundreds of pranks and schemes in their years together. Missions. They were used to sketching things out for each other quickly and quietly.

Lies shrugged. "We've got three gargoyles: Lord Angry Guy and

Regalia on five, with Diaphana last seen checking the babies on three. I'm thinking Operation Lookyhere. Should give you plenty of time to make the front door."

Tayna considered for a moment and then nodded. "Sounds good, but after you set the shrill, take off for bed, okay? No point in both of us getting caught. I'll take it from there."

"You sure?"

Tayna nodded. "Yup. Positive." Well, maybe not *positive*. The two girls looked at one another. They both had the sense that this was goodbye.

"Listen, T. About earlier..."

Tayna shook her head. "Bridge-water, amiga. Into storage until we have time to giggle over it. Deal?"

Lies nodded, her eyes brimming, then she lunged forward and trapped her best friend in the world with an enormous bear hug. "Watch your back, T."

"You too."

After a moment, Tayna pulled herself out of the embrace and saluted Lies with a goofy flip of her hand, then she darted up the stairs without looking back. Behind her, she heard Lies sniff once and then turn to bolt for the kitchen.

Apparently, now would be a great time for some tea.

Tayna stopped on the second-last step, just below the first-floor landing. It was decision time. She peered cautiously around the wall into the hallway. Everything looked clear. The light was on in Regalia's office and its door was partly open, but she couldn't see if anyone was in there. Her gaze slid longingly toward the front door, just a few steps further down the hall. Lies had made it sound so easy, but Tayna knew better. There were many things Sister Diaphana might be talked into doing, but letting Tayna out the front door into the dark of night was not one of them. The front door was not an option until they *knew* where Diaphana was. If she was on night-duty, she'd be sitting at Regalia's desk, right now, and that made the chances of getting caught while she was unlocking the front door pretty high. Even if she did manage to get through it, she still had no way to lock the door behind her. Somebody was sure to notice and come after her, and her experiences getting lost earlier that afternoon had proven that she was going to need as big a head start as she could get.

No, the front door was a no-go. What she really wanted was in the office. Regalia's window was the only ground-floor window that wasn't either barred on the outside or painted shut on the inside. Hopefully, all three gargoyles would be drawn to the basement in response to Lies's distraction, and that would leave Tayna's way clear to get out the window and close it behind her. *Then* she might have a reasonable chance at a head start.

Besides, she thought, as she turned and looked up the next flight of stairs. This is my turf. Nobody chases me out of here until I'm good and ready to go. And that isn't going to happen until I've got my journal.

Tayna stalked quietly across the landing and began to climb once more. A new plan had already formed. She still had time to get up to the roof door, above the fifth floor, before Eliza's distraction summoned Regalia downstairs. Once the old bat had left, Tayna would be able to drop down and get her stuff. Then she'd make her way back down and out through the office window while everyone was running around trying to find her. She trotted down the second-floor hallway toward the base of the next flight of stairs, smiling at her own craftiness, when she heard the unmistakable sound of feet on the stairs. Adult feet. They were coming down too soon!

"She's not in her dorm," said a muffled voice from above. Tayna slowed down to listen. It was Regalia.

"She's not on the fourth floor either." Lord Angiron's tone was no longer as ingratiating as she remembered it.

"Skip two and three for now," Regalia said as their voices got louder. "We can check those later. First we have to keep her from reaching the ground floor and the exits."

Dammit! Tayna looked quickly back in the direction she'd come from, wondering if she should double back, but until she knew where Diaphana was, that was too risky. The large Sister would never intentionally hurt her, but she had a way of trapping everyone around her in the slow, sticky tar of her own confusion, and tonight that amounted to the same thing.

"You do that," came Angiron's reply. "I want to check the basement. Then we can take our time working up from there more thoroughly. She'll have nowhere else to go."

Oh no. If he goes down into the basement now, he's going to catch Lies! Tayna took a step, reversing herself, back toward Lies, but then she stopped. Lies would just have to watch out for herself. Angiron and

Regalia were about to come down those very stairs and she needed to worry about herself! She looked around quickly. Second floor. Nun territory. Great. Goodies behind every door, and nowhere to hide. Then her eyes fell upon the door at the end of the hall. Well, sure. That room was empty, but that would just be stupid. Wouldn't it?

The heavy footfalls booming from the stairwell were getting impossibly loud. There was no time! Tayna sucked in her breath. I am *so* going to regret this. Then she turned, and with the imagined shadow of Regalia looming over her every step, she ran down the hall for all she was worth. It was impossible to tell which sound was loudest: the thumping of her bare feet on the worn hardwood floor, the thunder of her heart that seemed on the verge of blowing her ribs out through the sides of her chest, or the cannonade of Regalia and Angiron's feet hurtling down the stairs behind her in their louder-than-life, Tayna-killing frenzy.

Fortunately, the cannonade must have been the loudest, because neither Angiron nor Regalia appeared to have heard either of the other sounds, and she could hear them turning the corner at the bottom of the stairwell just as she bolted through the bedroom door and pulled it shut behind her. Safe!

If you could call Regalia's bedroom safe.

———⟋——⟍———

With her task in the basement complete, Lies was now paused at the main floor landing. She quickly saw the problem posed by Regalia's half-open office door, and the front door was still locked, so Tayna hadn't gone out that way. She must still be somewhere in the building then. Eliza was just beginning to wonder what she could do to help when she too heard the din of adult feet on the stairs above. Oh crap! Were they chasing T? She listened carefully. No, worse! Something about searching the ground floor! Suddenly, Lies could feel the walls closing in. In a few seconds, she was going to be locked in a game of cat and mouse with an enraged Goody and her best friend, Mr. Impulse Control Issues.

Without another thought, Lies crossed the hall and started checking the handles of the closed doors. The magic of her afternoon with the Nackenfausches must still have been with her though, because when she tried the interview room door, it swung open silently in her hand. Nobody had locked it! Thank you! She slipped inside the room where only hours ago, she had had the most exciting conversation of her life, and closed the door gently behind her. Then she took a deep breath. This was about to get very interesting. The inner door that connected this room to Regalia's office was open slightly. Eliza trotted quietly across the carpeted floor and closed it, then she held onto the knob with both hands and waited.

It seemed like only moments later that the pounding feet on the stairs reached its crescendo. One set of feet seemed to continue down into the basement, but whose? Her attention was quickly drawn back to the other set of feet, as they crossed the hallway and entered Regalia's office.

"Where are you, girl?" Lies breathed a small sigh of relief. It was Regalia. "Come out, come out, wherever you are!" She listened as the old crone pushed her desk chair out of the way, presumably to look under the desk itself. She was standing right on the other side of this door! Lies tightened her grip on the handle and hung on for dear life. A moment later, she had to stifle a shriek as the handle jerked in her hands, but she didn't let go.

"God damn all sticky doors and troublesome girls!" Lies could hear the swirl of fabric as Regalia whirled around and stormed out of her office, punctuated by the sharp *clack!* of the office door lock. Eliza swallowed once, terrified of what she was doing, and then she pulled the inter-office door open, stepped through it, and pulled it shut again behind her, just as Regalia entered the interview room through the outer door. Again Eliza held tight to the doorknob. From within the room she had just vacated, she could hear raspy breathing as the Sister Superior searched. And once again, her heart leapt all the way up to bounce off her tonsils when the doorknob shook in her hands.

"Why doesn't anything work properly around here?" Regalia raged, but the nun didn't take the time to investigate, and a moment later, she was gone again. Eliza let out a long, slow breath of air when she heard the outer door of the interview room being locked. Only then did she finally relax her grip. It would take at least fifteen minutes for Regalia to check all the rooms on this floor and to lock them all–especially if she wanted to be thorough.

Just then, a shrill whistle pierced the night, and nearly startled her out of her skin. But then she smiled. In all the excitement, she'd almost forgotten. One made-to-measure distraction, coming up! Any second now, Regalia would go tearing off toward the basement and-

But as suddenly as it had started, the whistle died and Eliza rolled her eyes. Damned gremlins. She should have known better. They were always getting into things and ruining her plans. Like the time she had left the water bomb above Sister Anthrax's bedroom door but it had burst when nobody was around? Gremlins. And the time she'd set her alarm to get up at five o'clock in the morning to catch Sister Disgustia putting dead cats in the stew pot, only it had gone off at five in the afternoon instead? Gremlins. And now they'd pulled her distraction kettle off the stove before it had finished doing its job, too. Not fair! This time it was important! She stamped a foot in frustration, and then immediately recoiled in horror. Had anybody heard that? Was Regalia about to come running back in to investigate?

Eliza strained to listen, stretching her ears as far out into the silence as they would go. There was the ticking of a clock... and the clank of the radiator... Then she heard a cupboard door close in a nearby room, followed by low muttering, but there were no sounds of a raging nun, no whisper of habit cloth as the Sister Superior stormed down the hallway. The gremlins had succeeded, and now Tayna was out there somewhere, hiding from a killer and waiting for a diversion that would never come.

Eliza's shoulders sagged. Why did anybody trust her to do anything important? She went to the window and leaned against the coat rack, burying her face in the folds of Regalia's old habit. She should have followed her usual Pylon Law: *When you get confused, just stand still. When you're in danger or you don't know what's going on, pretend to be a deaf mute and wait. Sooner or later, the situation will reveal itself and tell you everything you need to know, so long as everyone thinks you're an idiot.* But she couldn't do that tonight, could she. It's fine to play dumb when you're the only one in danger, but not when your best friend was about to be murdered. That was the time for some serious non-pylonry. Eliza wiped her eyes on the habit sleeve and then peered through its folds to the street beyond. There was Anger-man's limo, parked at the curb. And to the right, the dull gray concrete of the front steps beckoned in the moonlight. Freedom was so close! But she was now further than ever from getting Tayna out that door–out onto the street and safely away from all this insanity. She let the nun's habit settle back into place and turned away from the window, disgusted. With herself, mostly. She'd botched the relatively simple job of creating a diversion. How on Earth was she supposed to create one now, from here? She might just as well pick up the phone and dial 1-800-MIRACLE for all the good that would–

Eliza paused, and the forlorn expression that had been melting her features relaxed. She looked back at the window and the coat rack, and then a mischievous grin germinated at the corners of her mouth. A glimmer of hope. Maybe there was a way after all. Before she could risk killing the plan by over-thinking it, Lies turned around and grabbed the telephone from the desk.

It was definitely worth a shot.

———◦———

If there was any room in the entire building that was sacred, it wouldn't be the tiny chapel on the ground floor. That oversized closet had been stuffed with boxes of paper and old office equipment for years now. No, for sacred–as in, the room treated with the greatest of awe and respect–you'd have to look somewhere else. Regalia's bedroom. In her ten years of residence, Tayna had been in absolutely every single room of the building, save this one. The urge to somehow mark the moment was powerful, but Tayna was not Eliza. She knew better than to let her fanciful imagination take control. Tonight, this room was nothing more than temporary shelter. Her eyes darted around the room, flicking from one odd bit of nun decor to another, when a loud rapping froze her blood in her veins.

A knock at the door. Regalia had found her!

But then Tayna paused and cocked her head. Regalia? Knocking at her own door? Unlikely. But who else could it be? Panic grabbed Tayna by the shoulders. Now what? What should she do? Throwing caution to the wind, Tayna steeled her nerves and grunted an answer.

"Unh?" She made her voice as gravelly and raspy as she could and hoped for the best.

"It's just me, Sister. I heard you come in and I just wanted to thank you, dear. For letting me stay for another night, and for the joy of working with these wonderful children for another day." Diaphana.

Tayna tried to imagine how Regalia would react to such undiluted sweetness. "Hngh!" Then she reached out with a trembling hand and locked the door. Loudly.

There was a silent pause, and then Diaphana replied quietly. "Yes. Of course, dear. You're tired. I understand. Well, good night then. And thank you." Again there was a pause, and through it all, Tayna's heart was breaking, but what else could she do? She couldn't let the warm-hearted Sister find her–certainly not here, of all places. And she was pretty sure that, had it really been Regalia in here, the old bat's patience would have worn out by now, so Tayna remained completely silent. After another moment, she heard the large Sister sigh and then shuffle away down the hall, until at last she heard a bedroom door open and then close.

Whew. That was close. Well, at least now she knew where Diaphana was. The Sister must have come up to bed shortly after Lies had seen her. Then Tayna kicked herself in the shin, because that meant that Regalia's office had been empty all along. She could have just sauntered in there and climbed out through the window any time she'd wanted! Damn! Oh well. It might have been empty earlier, but it certainly wouldn't be now. This great plan of hers was going off the rails in a go-dawful hurry. The situation just kept changing, and now, her mission to the fifth floor was going to have to wait, too. What she needed most right now was somewhere to catch her breath and to think. Somewhere safer than here in the heart of Goody Country.

She couldn't go down, that much was clear. With two gargoyles below her, any front-door strategy was now hopeless. Where was Lies's distraction? Operation Lookyhere was pretty reliable, but it actually needed the "looky here" part to make it work. Something must have gone wrong. The best thing to do now would be to find somewhere to sit and wait–give Lies time to work out a Plan B. And the only place that was unlikely to be searched any time soon was up even higher–the roof. It wasn't perfect and it wouldn't last forever, but it would be safe enough for a while. Maybe an hour if she was lucky. Hopefully Lies would have something by then.

Tayna unlocked the door as quietly as she could and slipped out into the darkness. Fortunately, her lifetime of sneaking around the building after Failing Light had taught her about all the trick steps and unexpected squeaks in the floor, and she made it to the roof in relative silence. The stairwell door let out at the back of the roof, where the rusty iron ladder of the fire escape arched up over the chest-high parapet before disappearing down into the gloom on the other side. But seeing it now, Tayna could only shudder. Nope. Not in a million years.

She had been on the fire escape a few times before, just the top couple of rungs, to prove she wasn't scared of it. But in truth, she was. Its dull orange rungs were thick with flaking rust. Some steps were so corroded that she could actually see through them in places when the light was bright, and two of them were actually missing. Nobody knew when anyone had last actually tested the thing, and the general belief was that, if there ever was a fire, attempting to use it would only ensure that your charred remains would fit into an even smaller box, because there wouldn't be any long bones left unbroken after you had plummeted to the alley below.

And then there was the noise to consider. Even the best fire escapes were designed to get people to the ground during a crazy emergency–not to be silent highways for burglars and runaways–and this one was far from the best. Every bolt and bar shook and rattled whenever you touched the stupid thing, making it bang and clang like a blacksmith's shop in a drainage culvert. Even if it did somehow manage to hold her weight, Tayna's chances of reaching the street that way, without being heard, would probably be better if she just jumped. She shivered at the thought. Hopefully, she wouldn't ever have to make that decision. Lies would come through. The girl might be wacky, but she was a reliable kind of wacky.

No, her best hope now was information, so she turned her back on the metal death trap and headed forward, toward the flag pole at the front of the building, skirting past the ominous dark rectangle of the swimming pool garden on her left. A moment later she looked down onto the streetscape below. There was Angiron's car, sitting nonchalantly at the curb, waiting to drag her away to some unimaginably creepy fate. And across the street from that was the alley–to the best of her knowledge, the home and castle of a completely different homicidal maniac–one who wore rubber pants and who had apparently chosen Tayna as his next chew toy. So many choices lay before her. Death by creepy short guy, or death by creepy tall guy. The world was nothing if not generous. If Lies didn't come through soon, Tayna might be left with no choice but to risk the Clattering Cage of Flaming Death.

Tayna hunkered down out of the wind, with her back to the parapet wall and was just beginning to settle when she heard a car horn. Terror flooded through her. Had somebody seen her up here on the roof? Was Angiron honking his horn to alert Regalia to what he'd just seen? Well, if that was the case, it couldn't hurt to look again. Slowly, she turned around and leaned her head out over the wall and peeked down.

What she saw baffled her completely. A taxi. There was a yellow taxi sitting at the curb, idling, in front of Angiron's car. He appeared to be waiting for a passenger, but who would–?

Again the horn blared, a little more stridently this time. And then, as Tayna watched in mystified disbelief, Sister Regalia scuttled out the front door and over to the waiting taxi. For some reason, the bizarre old hag was abandoning the hunt and leaving. Had Angiron beaten her with his stick again? As soon as the passenger door closed, the taxi pulled smartly away from the curb and headed off into the night. Tayna slumped to the ground, completely befuddled. It was getting so that you needed some kind of computery wiring-type diagram just to keep track of who was trying to kill who around here. Then, before she could even get a handle on these latest developments, more commotion sounded from the street below.

Tayna raised herself up and looked over the wall again. There was Sister Regalia, miraculously back on the sidewalk, and pointing down the street at the disappearing taxi she had only just moments ago fled in. She turned and yelled something up the stairs toward the open front doors. In a flash, Angiron was out onto the sidewalk, pulling her toward the street. Regalia made a move to jerk away, but Angiron cuffed her brutally with the back of his hand and flung her into the car. Then he ran around to the driver's side, jumped in and gunned the engine, giving chase to the taxi that had now vanished from sight.

Up on the roof, Tayna slumped back down again, trying to figure out what had just happened. How could her luck get this good, so quickly? She simply couldn't believe it. Again she stuck her head out over the edge, to confirm what her brain was having trouble accepting. And again she saw that Angiron's car was gone, the front door was open and both Regalias had left the building, along with the vicious Lord Angiron.

Tayna allowed herself five full seconds of additional incredulity and then she pulled herself to her feet. "Not much of an escape if I stay here," she said, and then she ran back to the stairwell door and plunged inside.

It took her exactly forty seven seconds to detour from the stairwell to her room and collect the few things she owned that were worth taking with her. Her journal and the few bits of clothing that didn't absolutely shout "homeless orphan." She dumped it all into her ratty old knapsack and paused briefly to salute her sleeping ward-mates before racing back out into the hall.

When she reached the ground floor, she slowed down. Sure enough, the front door was still open, but she just couldn't shake the feeling that this was some elaborate trap. Tayna edged her way cautiously down the hall to the point where she could look out without being seen from the street. Yup. The car was still gone. She was almost ready to run out the door and escape to her freedom when lights appeared on the pavement. A car was coming.

O crap, o crap, o crap, o crap! I waited too long! Now Angiron's back and he's going to find me and I'm going to be dragged off to some swamp and murdered. Tayna crouched down at the edge of the door, too terrified to look out and equally terrified not to. But finally she did, only what she saw still didn't make any sense. Now the taxi was back and Regalia was getting out. Before Tayna could tear her eyes from the scene to run, something about Regalia caught her attention. She wasn't as ugly as she ought to be. And then, in another moment, realization flooded through her.

Eliza closed the taxi door behind her, being careful to pull the hem of the habit out of the way first. The damn fabric was everywhere! Then she looked up and saw the wide-open door of the Old Shoe. This was it. The moment of truth. It was obvious that the limo was gone–Angiron had taken the bait–but had Regalia gone with him? Eliza took a deep breath and did the bravest thing she had ever done. She walked up the steps and in the front door. And then something grabbed her hard around the shoulders.

"Oh my God, Lies! Thank you! That was the coolest, smartest most bad-assedest thing I've ever seen!"

Relief flooded through Eliza's still-terrified body and she sagged against Tayna's enthusiastic hug. "Thank God, T. You still haven't been hacked to bits. Did Regalia go with him?"

Tayna pulled away and looked at her. "You think I'd be standing here like this if she hadn't?" Then she smiled. "How on Earth did you come up with that stunt?"

Eliza blushed. "Well, it just sort of came to me while I was hiding in Regalia's office," she said.

"You hid in her office?" Tayna looked shocked. "And she didn't find you?"

Lies smiled slyly. "I kinda faked her out with the 'sticky door-knob' trick." Tayna's jaw dropped.

"Girl, you must have enormous brass chaninkas where your brain used to be. That is so freaking awesome!"

For a moment, Tayna just grinned stupidly at her friend. Eliza had come through spectacularly. But time was against them, and it was Eliza who broke the spell. "Look, T," she said, "I would love to take time to catch up–you know we've got a lot to talk about now–but you have *got* to go. I told the driver to wait for me–I told him I'd forgotten something and that I'd be right back out." As she talked, she pulled the bulky habit over her head and handed it to Tayna.

"Just pull this on and he'll never notice the swap. I think all nuns look the same to most people."

Tayna grabbed the robes and pulled her head and arms through the appropriate holes. "How am I supposed to pay him, Lies? I don't have any money."

Eliza smirked at her. "Would I go and set you up with a great exit like this, and then forget something as basic as that? I called the taxi service using the Goody's account. You know, the one they use to send you out collecting and when Sister Disgustia goes to the supermarket?"

Tayna just shook her head in disbelief. "Eliza Drummel, you really are my hero."

Eliza bowed deeply. "And you've always been mine, T, so we're even. Now scoot! Before somebody comes back and ruins this little love-fest."

Tayna picked up her knapsack, then she turned and gave Eliza a kiss on the cheek. "Thank you so much, Lies. I owe you. Big time." Then she turned and darted out to the car.

Eliza watched until the taxi pulled away, then she closed and locked the big front door and went up to bed. It occurred to her that through-out this entire escapade, not a single grown-up had laid eyes on her, so she was feeling very good about herself as she climbed the stairs and headed toward a well deserved night's sleep.

chapter 5

Sitting in the back of the taxi, Tayna realized that she had no idea what to do next. She'd spent all her time worrying about getting out of the building, and none of it planning what would happen next. Now that she was out, the tension that had been building between her shoulders and in the pit of her stomach was beginning to melt away, leaving nothing to hold her together but the shakes. She had just fled the only home she had ever known, in fear for her life. Worse, the only adults she had ever met who weren't Goodies themselves, either worked for them, or were little more than cardboard cutout strangers. There wasn't a soul in the world she could actually run to. She looked up and the driver's eyes meet hers in the rear view mirror.

"Where to now, Sister?"

Good. He hadn't noticed the switch, but she still had no idea where to go. She lowered her eyes and said the first thing that came to mind. "The Wasketawin Center, please." Then she pulled her veil down a little lower. Wasketawin? It took her a moment to recall why that destination came so readily to mind. Oh. Right. That's where Angiron said they found me. Obviously there wouldn't be any clues still lying around–not after ten years–but it gave her somewhere to go. And at the very least, the trip would give her some time to think.

Tayna's biggest worry now was the driver. What if he wanted to talk? What if he was the kind of guy who did this job because he liked people. She couldn't afford to get dragged into a conversation. If that happened, he would soon figure out how young she was and might even try to take her back to the Old Shoe. Rather than wait to see what he would do, she decided to head him off. As soon as they were under way, Tayna raised her hands up, clasped them together in front of her face, and started murmuring under her breath. There were two things that gave most people the willies: public displays of religious fervor, and a habit of talking to imaginary friends. (Or were those maybe the same thing?) At any rate, she didn't much care whether he thought she was praying strenuously or having a serious argument with the man who lived inside her fingers–so long as he left her alone, and he did. She felt a little guilty about being so rude, but then again, he was probably used to it–especially if he'd ever had Goodies as fares before.

The next problem on the horizon was how to handle getting rid of him when they reached the park, but that turned out to be the easiest thing in the world. Fortunately, thanks to Eliza's quick thinking, there was no need to pay the man. When the car slowed down at the entrance to the park, Tayna told him to pull over. And when he did, she just got out and said goodnight. If he wondered what a young Sister of Good Salvation was planning to do on the side of a desolate highway in the middle of the night, he never mentioned it. He just turned the car around and drove away. Tayna waited until his tail-lights were a dim glow in the distance before she felt safe enough to look around. Angiron had said something about her having been found out this way, not in the park, but near it, on the highway. And that meant somewhere around here. Maybe something would look familiar.

This far from the city, the sky was a brilliant wash of stars. Reflections off the thin skiff of snow gave her enough light to see by, but there wasn't much to see. She was standing at the edge of a two-lane highway. In front of her, a few shrubs and low trees flanked the large, stone sign that marked the entrance to the park. From there, the entrance lane ran back toward the interpretive center, hugging close to the lip of the coulee all the way. And that was it. There was nothing else. Just flat, wind-scoured prairie spilling to the horizon in every direction. Seeing it now, on a cold and windy winter night, Tayna found it easy to understand why native clans had sought shelter here for so many thousands of years. Not in the interpretive center, of course–that was new–but down in the fold of land beside it. Some dim, distant taste of memory teased at her. There *was* something familiar feeling here, but as soon as she tried to examine it, it melted away like a hoar frost in the sun. And all the while, that feeling was serenaded by four disjoint phrases, teasing at her from the depths of her unconscious.

Family yours. Peril great. Flee now. Home come.

Could that have been something more than just a stupid orphan's dream? Tayna shrugged. If there was something familiar here, she'd better get in gear and find it. Ignoring the lane, Tayna turned to her left, hefted her knapsack higher up onto her shoulder and set off, following her instincts across the crunchy, snow-packed grass down into the ancient, wooded ravine.

A coulee is a narrow, steep-sided valley that forms on the prairies. Elsewhere, people have other names for similar things, such as "ravine" or even "canyon," but around here, they were coulees. They occurred when run-off from heavy rains dug deep scars into the earth as the water collected and then rushed away to some nearby lake or river. This particular coulee was a deep one and rather long, with a good-sized brook flowing down the middle throughout most of the year. That's part of what had made it so attractive to the plains people. Most coulees make good short-term shelter, but this one was excellent and could be used all winter long. It was deep enough to protect larger trees and game, and large enough to offer all the amenities a nomadic family could want from first snow to last. Some local scientists even believed that this location provided the oldest known evidence of humans in North America, but that belief didn't fit with the popular theories of the day, so the claims were dismissed as just being silly, or worse, as bad science.

At first, Tayna had trouble seeing the steeply sloped ravine walls as anything but a pain. Picking her way down through all the shrubs and bushes on the sloping terrain was slow going, especially because the nun-wear kept getting snagged on the bare twigs and branches. Before long, she was sweating quite heavily under the voluminous robes, despite the cold, November night air. Eventually, though, she managed to get herself down to the flatter ground at the bottom, where she found a well worn trail. In older days, it might have been a game trail, worn by timid woodland creatures seeking refuge from the howling winter above, but these days, it was almost certainly a groomed trail, beaten flat by park staff and the few tourists who still wandered around the site during the snowier parts of the year. Regardless of which particular species of timid creature had broken the trail for her, Tayna was glad of it and followed it off to her right, deeper into the coulee and the park.

She walked for what felt like a half hour, keeping to the trail, even when it wound left and right, crossing the brook several times over low, wooden bridges, until she arrived at a crossroad. Straight ahead, the trail continued along as it had been doing, following the brook in a meandering sort of way, and to her right, a paved path branched away to run up between the shrubs until it vanished over the coulee's lip, which seemed to be much higher above her here than it had been where she'd started. This was probably the path up to the interpretive center. She was still contemplating her options when she heard voices ahead of her on the trail. Oops. Not a good time to be caught snooping around the grounds. Looking around quickly, Tayna took a few steps back up the trail and then ducked off into the brush. She hunkered herself down beneath the upturned root ball of a recently toppled tree–probably brought down under the mountain-load of snow that always drifted into places like this–and there she waited. The voices were getting closer.

"Do you really think she's coming here?" The voice was all too familiar.

"Of course she's coming here, you dim-eyed cow! I've just told her the only thing she's ever heard about the night she was found–that it is somehow connected to this place–and you think she might have decided to go shopping? Don't be an idiot. She'll come. And she's a bright girl, too. When she does come, she just might find it. And if she figures out how to use it, this whole thing will have been in vain." That voice, ringing with disdain and self-confidence, was unmistakable. Angiron. Tayna's heart raced and she gave her non-bracelet a violent twist for good measure. How many different gods have to be angry at you to pull down this kind of bad luck? She looked around to check her hiding place. Obviously, the tree had collapsed very recently. The root ball was still dark with freshly upturned dirt, although it was thoroughly frozen. The dark cloth of the habit would be almost invisible against it. Still, she couldn't escape the sudden feeling that she was completely exposed.

"Do you suppose she might have doubled back, my Lord?" Regalia's voice was almost simpering. "I mean, if she noticed us following..."

"Corpses!" Angiron cursed as the two of them came into view around a bend in the main path. He swung his walking stick angrily at a young sapling, which snapped cleanly in two, as though it had been felled with an axe. "Yes, she might have done just that. Might be too frightened to think it through yet. Yes. It's more than possible that she went back, or that she soon will."

Angiron turned and grabbed Regalia by the throat. "I'm going to take you back to your precious Home now. If she does come back, you'd better be able to handle her this time." Then he looked back the way they had come. "But in case she does find her way here while I'm gone, I want to be sure she waits for me." Angiron snarled and flung the frightened nun away from him, toward the uphill path. "You drag your miserable carcass back up to the car and wait for me there. I'll be along in a minute." As he stalked off down the trail, Tayna could hear him making a strange, gurgling noise. It sounded like laughter.

Tayna could almost feel sorry for Regalia, as the usually domineering woman, now under the impression that she was completely alone, made no effort to hide her weakness, and limped slowly up to the top of the slope and out of sight. No more than ten minutes had gone by when Angiron appeared again on the path, and turned uphill at the fork, following Regalia to the parking lot. Tayna held her breath as he strode right past her hiding spot. He had his hands jammed deeply into his pockets for warmth, but he didn't even glance her way as he passed. Tayna shuddered. He had passed closely enough that she could even smell his cologne lingering in the air. It smelled like blood and wet fur. Charming.

She waited several minutes to be sure he wasn't coming back, then she stepped cautiously out onto the path. There was something down there that Angiron didn't want her to see, and that alone would have been sufficient reason to go find it, but there was more to it than just that. This was somehow connected to her own past! Without so much as a second thought, Tayna tugged the habit's veil down firmly around her face for warmth, and set off down the snowy game trail.

The further she pushed into the coulee, the deeper and more protected it became, and the deeper the snow got. She also saw more signs of life and diversity. Dozens of different kinds of trees and shrubs huddled together, both cooperating and competing with their neighbors for survival. Beneath their roots and branches, everything from chipmunks and prairie dogs all the way up to foxes and coyotes fought for territory, food and shelter. Even a herd of mule deer browsed the bare pickings down in this natural menagerie. Tayna didn't see all these creatures, of course, but she knew they were there just the same. Here and there, tracks criss-crossed the blanket of snow, darting back and forth across the path and through the underbrush. And even if she hadn't seen the signs, Tayna felt as though she could actually sense their presence. She could almost feel the hum of their tiny heartbeats vibrating in the air.

What interested her most, however, were the big, clumsy gouges left by the most recent animal to pass. Angiron's tracks were a chaotic contrast to the almost polite perforations of the other wildlife tracks in the smooth blanket of snow. His trail ducked beneath a low-hanging branch. Following it, Tayna ducked down low and was about to scoot beneath it, when a pair of rough hands seized her from behind and a dark sack settled down over her head.

"This trail ends *here* for you!" The voice was deep and familiar.

Tayna stamped a foot in furious frustration. "Gimme a freaking break! Is there, like, an uber-villain bush-party going on down here and everyone just forgot to invite the victim?"

For the second time in twenty-four hours, she had been surprised in the woods by Duck Man, only this time, she was completely helpless to do anything about it.

———————

His hands spun her about quickly as they bound her arms to her sides with cord. Once she was securely pinned, he fumbled at the folds of her habit that he had pulled up over her head. It wasn't a sack after all. There was a moment of awkward tugging and then cool fresh air washed over her face.

"Are you harmed?"

The ropes were tight and she turned her head to glare at him, but when her eyes finally found his, she was surprised to see genuine concern on his face. She shook off the feeling. *He's not worried about me—probably just worried that my meat is bruised or whatever it is psycho killers worry about after trussing up their victims.* She forced her gaze away from his eyes, and allowed it to settle on his beard and mouth instead.

Duck Man repeated his question. "Have I harmed you?"

Wait a tick. Something looked wrong. What did he just say?

"Has your hearing been damaged? I was as gentle as I could be, but you had to be stopped. Have I hurt you?"

Now that she was watching his mouth as he spoke, she was certain of it. He wasn't speaking English at all. She could see his lips moving as he spoke, but they seemed. . . wrong—like she was watching an Asian film dubbed into English by deaf Swedish mimes. Nothing fit, nothing sounded familiar, but she understood him just the same. It was the creepiest thing she'd ever felt.

"Please answer me. Are you hurt?" Duck Man was beginning to sound a bit panicked, but how could she answer? It was one thing to *understand* the sounds he was making, but could she actually speak it? Had she said anything to him in the parkette the other day? She didn't remember. So, there was only one way to find out. Tayna cleared her throat.

"Do us think tomorrow or lifetime?" she said, hesitantly.

Duck Man's face visibly relaxed now that she'd finally broken her silence, but then what she'd said registered and a look of puzzlement clouded his eyes. A moment later, his face lit up with understanding, and before Tayna could react, he raised a hand and set it on her head as he hummed a strange melody.

The humming stopped. "I have helped your tongue to see its error," he said. "Try again. Have I harmed you?"

Tayna looked at him suspiciously, but she repeated her answer. "Do you mean now, or ever?" After saying them, Tayna repeated the words to herself, concentrating on the movement of her tongue within her mouth. She had been doing it *incorrectly*–pushing it too far forward. She couldn't imagine what his little song might have done about it, but for whatever reason, the words were now coming out clearly.

"I had meant 'on this night,'" he said. "But if I have done you harm in any other time or manner, speak of that as well."

Tayna glared at him with all the contempt she could muster. "You mean physical harm?" she said. "Sorry to disappoint you, but no, nothing's broken Although if you want to talk about emotional scarring, then yes–miles of damage. All these attacks in the bushes will probably keep me from ever having a good relationship with my gardener and I doubt I'll ever be able to enjoy quiet walks in the moonlight again. Does that count?"

Duck Man chuckled dryly. "I fear I have made a dreadful mistake," he said. "By correcting your speech, it seems I have handed you a powerful weapon. It is a decision that I may long regret." Then he leaned in closer. "Tell me, what is a 'gardener?'"

Tayna tried to keep her mad on, but this guy was just too whacked. Instead of leaping about and screaming, or brandishing chainsaws and toenail pullers, he just stared at her, as though he was seriously expecting her to explain what a gardener was. This was not the kind of crazy they tell you to expect when they're doing their little song and dance about 'don't accept candy from strangers.' This was just too weird for words. "What?"

"This 'gardener' you speak of. Is your relationship with it truly in danger?"

Tayna closed her eyes. "Look, forget about the gardener, alright? We're fine. Copacetic. I think we're going for tea and crumpets on Tuesday. I've just got one question."

Again, he stared at her expectantly.

"What the hell do you want from me?"

The suddenness of her outburst startled him back a step, but he smiled. "Child, you are delightfully strong. If I judge your tone rightly, the 'gardener' was a jest. But you are correct–the manner of my approaching you has been rather... harsh. Forgive me. It was necessary. One cannot be too cautious in such an unfamiliar place. Seemingly, you live with the minions of Lord Angiron, yet you flee from them, only to seek them out again here, under cover of night. You burn, and yet you use it not. Truly you are an enigma. What is your name?"

Tayna's defenses were suddenly on high alert and she ignored the question. "You know Angiron." It was not a question.

Duck Man seemed stumped by that one. "Of course. Am I not the Watcher?"

What? The ropes allowed her just enough freedom to reach her hands together and she gave her invisible bracelet a quick turn to settle her nerves. "Listen, Duck Man, or whatever your name is, it's creeping the hell out of me that we're standing here and talking some secret language I didn't even know I could speak, but let's forget about that for now, because even speaking the same language, it's like we're from completely different planets or something. Just because I know the words doesn't mean I have any idea what you're talking about. Could you maybe tell me something useful? Like why you jump me every time I walk past a tree?"

Duck Man nodded sagely. "Even when you jest, you cut deeply into the veil." He too glanced nervously up the hill, as though expecting trouble at any moment. "You have many questions," he said. "Yet, time washes over us and if we do not make haste, we shall still be here for the trapper's sport when he returns."

Tayna's eyes instinctively flicked up the hill to where he had been looking. "You're just as worried about running into him as I am, aren't you?"

"Indeed," he said. "Though I do not fear him, as perhaps you do."

"Look," Tayna said. "Maybe we can help each other out a bit. You sound like a nice guy. Why don't you untie me and we can get out of here. Then I'll teach you how to play twenty questions."

Duck Man stared deeply into Tayna's face for several moments, then he shook his head. "You are cunning, child, but you do not yet see all the paths in your own forest, nor understand who walks upon which."

Tayna sighed.

Duck Man smiled at her frustration. "Know this, child. I am the Watcher and you are in my gaze. Soon, our trail will deliver us to an appropriate clearing, whereupon I shall reveal to you another path. Once you have seen its fullness, there you shall have your freedom. I will invite you then to make a journey with me, and upon the end of *that* trail, what answers there are to give can be freely shared between us." Then he took hold of the length of rope dangling from the knot at her elbow. "But until then, we must hasten away from this spot. Come." He set off at an angle, up the hill and to the right of the main path. Tayna had no choice but to follow.

She didn't like the look of this. Creepy-boy here was dragging her off the path into the bushes. She had a vague memory of some advice she'd heard or read somewhere. Try to get the killer to see you as a person instead of a victim. It may weaken his will to hurt you. "Uh, since we're going to be all buddy-buddy, you might as well call me Tayna. What should I call you? Duck Man?"

He looked back at her over his shoulder. "A charming name to add to my collection, no doubt, but you may call me Veest."

"Okay. Veest. That's a nice name. I had an uncle named Veest once. Do you know him?"

The old man didn't slow down, but he did glance back over his shoulder at her. Despite their obviously different upbringings, some body language is universal. The look clearly said, "Yeah, right. What kind of moron-flakes do you think I eat?"

Tayna grinned sheepishly. "Okay, sorry. It was worth a shot. But, uh, why did we leave the trail?"

He seemed to ignore her as he continued to stride ahead with his long legs pushing through the snow, drawing Tayna behind him in his wake. He remained silent until they had broken past a tall pine. "There," he said, pointing back down toward the main trail. "That is why I have diverted you from your path."

Tayna turned to look. "Oh my God." What she saw almost made her heave. Angiron's tracks emerged on this side of the pine tree, from beneath those low-hanging branches she had been about to duck under. In an open space between there and the next tree, three small animals—a fox and two squirrels—floated helplessly in the air. Their bodies writhed and twisted, but they made no sound. Below them, a large hare lay dead in a patch of blood-stained snow, skewered to the ground by a familiar length of stick. A carved skull on the end gleamed at her with blood-red, ruby eyes.

"Can you do something for them?" she said, weakly. The floating creatures looked like they were in agony.

Veest shook his head. "I have life-magic. It can do nothing against this."

Right. He has magic. Of course he does. Still, no better explanation offered itself to her. "We have to do *something!*"

Veest turned and looked at her. "To enter the clearing is to take the trapper's bait. Their fate would become your own."

Tayna looked at him in horror. "You mean, they're suffering there... because of me?"

The older man nodded. "It is well that you would ease their suffering, but to enter the circle unprepared would be folly."

"And there's really nothing we can do for them?"

He shook his head. "Lord Angiron's power flows from the dead. Like mine, yours flows from life. The magics of life and of death do not walk the same path."

"So that's a 'no?' "

Veest thought for a moment and then he offered her a grim smile. "Indeed. That was a 'no.' " Then he reached out and, to Tayna's surprise, released the knot at her elbow and unwound the cord.

She looked up at him in surprise. "You're letting me go?"

Veest looked amused. "Did I not so promise?"

Tayna wasn't sure of half of the things he'd said. It was possible that he'd promised something like this. It was also possible he'd promised her a death by slow torture; the Swedish mimes were still making a mess of his dialogue. But the fact that he'd untied her was a point in his favor. "So now what?" she asked.

"Your previous path wandered into the snare unprepared. Now you are set upon a new path and you must choose. It may pass that I hold answers to the riddles that beset you. If you would seek the wonder in that, you must travel the way with me, to a quiet place for the seeking. If you would not, then it were best that you decide now and make your haste before the trapper returns." He pointed at the floating animals to underscore his point.

"Answers to what riddles?" she asked.

"The greatest riddles," he said. "Who you are, where you come from, the purpose of your life..."

The words went through Tayna like an electric current as they triggered a memory–something from her dream. "You know my parents? They're really alive? And they're in trouble? Have you come to take me to them?" The words came out even before she could plan what to say, and they startled her almost as much as they seemed to startle the old man.

He looked at her uncertainly for a moment and then raised his shoulders in a shrug. "Am I not the Watcher? I know many things, and suspect a great many more, but how can we know where our feet will wander if we do not first take a step?"

Tayna didn't know what to think. Angiron's trap made it fairly plain that Lies had been right all along–he really was trying to kill her. Then there was the wacko dream message to consider, about her having a family and them being in some kind of danger. Next thing she'd known, ol' Ducky here had shown up and said he might know what's going on, but he'd also admitted to knowing Angiron. And how exactly did he know so much about her, anyway? He knew that she lived in the orphanage, so it wouldn't have taken a PhD in Villainy for him to guess what an orphan would want to hear. On the other hand, he couldn't be in cahoots with Angiron–he'd actually kept her from walking into the trap, hadn't he? Tayna twisted again at her bracelet. Things just weren't adding up! Maybe this Veest guy was playing his own angle. The fact that he had saved her from one trap didn't necessarily mean that he didn't have one of his own lined up. Psychopaths were probably very territorial about their victims. She looked back at the struggling animals again and then at the old man. In reality, her options were pretty limited. And strange as he might be, he might also be the safest choice. Besides, it wasn't as if she had a long list of other places to go.

"If I did come with you," she said, carefully. "There'd be no funny stuff, right?" Veest looked at her with a befuddled expression. Tayna sighed. "You wouldn't, like, hurt me or anything, right? No more ropes? No electrical probes or inappropriate touching? No more sneaking up on me when it gets dark?"

Veest shook his head in bewilderment. "If my suspicions are borne true, than I will prove incapable of harming you–in any way–just as you are incapable of harming me."

Tayna snickered. "Oh, I think I could find some way to leave a mark."

Veest frowned and rubbed his shin. "Yes. When you believe yourself to be in grave danger, the Dragon's Peace is lifted, and clearly you do not lack talent for the task. But you have no such belief of danger now. You cannot strike me."

Without warning, Tayna lashed out at him with Mr. Kicky Foot again, but to her complete and utter astonishment, the air thickened around her like hot taffy and her leg came to a dead stop several inches short of his. As soon as she stopped straining to complete the kick, the air resistance dissolved and her foot dropped back into the snow.

"What the hell was that?"

Again Veest glanced up the hill. "A million questions, but only a handful of moments. There is no time for answers now. You must decide. With me or with none, you must leave this place quickly, as must I. Choose."

Despite her reluctance, Tayna had already made her choice. There were just too many signals pointing the same way. "Okay," she said. "Let's go."

If Veest was surprised by her decision he didn't let on. He turned immediately and struck off up the hill. "Hurry. This way." Tayna moved to follow, but then she paused and looked back toward the trap–the one that had been meant for her, and that had instead only succeeded in trapping several small, helpless creatures. It was like they were being punished for something she had done, and as soon as she put it that way, Tayna couldn't live with it, no matter what Ducky said. Instinct took over. Before she lost her nerve, she turned around and darted back toward the blood-drenched snow. She could hear Duck Man yelling for her to stop, but she ignored him. When she reached the skewered hare, she snatched both it and Angiron's staff from the snow, and, whispering a silent apology to the dead rabbit, hurled them into the black night, toward the river.

The moment the staff pulled free of the ground, the hovering animals dropped into the snow and lay there panting. Behind her, Veest burst from the bushes with one arm raised above his head, whirling something at the end of a string. He was singing a deep, forceful melody, but as the offensive trap arced across the snow and into the water, his song died on his lips. He looked around in confusion. All of this, however, was too much excitement for the exhausted creatures and they dragged themselves off into the underbrush. Veest let his arm drop and the object that he had been whirling over his head stopped in its arc and the shrill note it had been emitting died away.

"You are not ensnared," he said, looking mystified.

Tayna looked around, more than a little surprised herself. "Apparently not."

Veest hurried forward and clasped her by the shoulders. He turned her left and right, looking at her carefully. When he was satisfied that she was unharmed, he released her, but he still looked agitated, peering one way and then another into the darkened trees that surrounded them. "Now is not the time to seek the wonder in it. For now, be thankful for the fact of it. We must hurry away. However you came to break the trap he has set for you, Lord Angiron will now be aware that you have done so and his return will be swift." The old man took Tayna by the shoulder and urged her back the way they had come. Sensing the new urgency in his voice, she followed without complaint.

The two of them pushed on through the snow in silence for another ten minutes, with Veest stopping every now and then to listen for sounds of pursuit. After several minutes, he finally turned sharply aside and clambered straight up the steep bank of the coulee. Tayna was surprised at how well he moved through the snow, even with the hip-waders slowing him down.

"Where do you get your fashion advice?" Tayna asked. "Clown school?"

Veest paused and looked down at his wardrobe—the pink coat tucked into green rubber pants. "Surely they are appropriate for your world," he said, looking somewhat confused by the question. "I found them here."

"Never mind," she said. "It's a long story. But next time, try the mall. The dumpster look is definitely not working for you."

The old man looked at her curiously for a moment, and then shrugged and turned to resume his march up the coulee slope. Tayna followed along, trying hard to suppress the amused grin that kept sneaking onto her face, but she was only marginally successful.

They reached the top of the rise at a place just beyond the interpretive center. The weather had turned while they were down in the protected fold of the valley, and now it was getting mean. Tiny pellets of ice and snow sleeted into their faces, driven by a swirling wind that came at them from across the open plain. They were less than thirty yards from the entrance to the center's coffee shop, but Tayna could barely see it through the snow, and the wind nipped at them in shrieks and whistles, making it hard to hear or be heard. With one arm thrown across his eyes for protection, Veest bent down to thrust his other hand into the snow, and then withdrew it, clutching a small fistful of dry, hard soil. He then moved forward, probing anxiously into a snow drift with an extended toe. After several attempts, he nodded in satisfaction and crouched down, beckoning Tayna forward to come see. Taking his free hand from his face, Veest brushed at the snow, exposing a white rock about the size of a child's head.

"Life and death brought together with non-life," he shouted, apparently for her benefit.

She nodded to tell him that she'd heard. The old man slapped the handful of dirt down onto the stone and opened his mouth in... song? His lips were moving, anyway, and she thought she heard a note or two, before the wind caught the melody and flung it away.

When he was done, Veest threw a quick smile at her and stood up. At first there was nothing. Then, through a brief pause in the wind, she heard a faint sizzling, like eggs on a hot pan or the sound of television static. Veest waved an arm out toward the snowy field in front of him. "The way opens!" he shouted. A circle of snow collapsed around Veest's rock. And then, beside it, another. And then another. Soon there were fifty or sixty similar holes in the snow, arranged in a large circle. From the bottom of each, a white stone glistened up at the howling sky. Veest turned to her and cupped his hands to yell over the howling night.

"It seems to take longer on the winter side. It often–"

Suddenly, his eyes went wide as he looked over Tayna's shoulder, but before he could say another word, a scarlet rose appeared on the old man's shoulder, spinning him halfway around before he pitched head-long into the snow. Tayna whipped around and peered into the night. A shape was stalking toward them from around the corner of the inter-pretive center, purposefully, striding directly into the wind. Angiron.

And he was reloading his rifle.

Before Tayna could scream, Veest regained his feet and grabbed her by the arm. He staggered forward across the ring of stones, pulling her along behind him. She tried to yell at him, but the wind shredded her words as they left her lips. She wanted to ask, "Where is there to go? What's the point in running?" They'd lost. Angiron had won. But then, as she stumbled along behind him, across the far edge of the circle, everything changed. Winter vanished. The storm vanished. The snow and the building vanished. Angiron vanished. Tayna was left standing in stunned amazement, surrounded by brilliantly colored trees, standing on the bank of a rapidly flowing stream, under a warm and sunny azure sky of summer.

"Cool," she said. And then she passed out.

chapter 6

Quiet. That's the first thing you noticed. Not an "oh-my-god-have-I-suddenly-gone-deaf" kind of quiet–there were still birds and crickets chirping and all those mysterious-but-completely-natural sorts of sounds that one might expect to hear in a typical forest clearing–but that's *all* there was. No honking horns in the distance, no car alarms, no ambulances or jackhammers, no air conditioners, dump trucks, school bells or portable stereos. Just a soft, whispering blanket of tiny, polite sounds to let you know that there were a thousand different creatures nearby, each going about their busy lives, and that all was right with their world. It was *that* kind of quiet.

Tayna slept within that quiet for a long time. For most of the last week, every single night had been interrupted by strange dreams, malicious Goodies or death threats, and her day-time activities hadn't been much of a picnic either. So quite simply, management had finally been forced to take action and Tayna was now closed for repairs. Watch for the grand re-opening, coming soon. For all she'd been aware, it could just as easily have been a troop of circus monkeys that had picked her up and carried her after she fainted instead of the old hobo. But none of that mattered. With her brain on forced vacation and taking no notice of the passing time or distance, it had refused to stir even when she'd been lowered onto a rough bed of leaves and grass. During the whole experience, only one thing had mattered. Sleep. Long, deep, delicious and entirely dream-free sleep.

After a day, or maybe three, of this self-imposed oblivion, management decided that it had done what it could do, and at last threw the switch to turn the lights back on. Tayna stirred. She yawned and spread her arms slowly in a cat-like stretch, keeping her eyes closed and savoring the feeling. Her earlobes tingled faintly, but she couldn't quite remember what that was all about. Sleep still hung lazily over her thoughts and it took a few moments to put it all together. Wow. Had all that stuff really happened? Or had it been a dream? Waking up now was almost like a game show. "Okay, this is it folks. Last night while L'il Orphan Tayna was sleeping, we moved her to a secret location. When she opens her eyes, where do you think she'll be? Is she face down in a snow-swept coulee? Lying on her back along the technicolor banks of a freshwater stream? Or is she all the way back in her own bed, on the fifth floor of the orphanage? What's it gonna be? So many choices, but only one of them can be right. Let's watch now and find out, as we take you back to Tayna's brain, just moments before the big reveal." Tayna smirked to herself. I'll take door number three, Monty. It's all a dream and I'm back in the Old Shoe. Cautiously, she took a deep breath and opened her eyes.

Nope. Not a dream–not unless the Goodies had gone hippie over night. The bed she was on was low, not much more than a soft pile of bedding on the floor near the wall. She pushed the blankets off and started to sit up, but then she stopped. Not blankets at all. They felt wrong. More like moss.

She looked around carefully, struggling to understand what she was seeing. The whole room was... weird. It was roughly circular, but that was all she was sure of. As with the blankets, everything appeared normal at first, but then she'd look closer and the whole scene would suddenly twist, like an optical illusion. Take the walls for example. They looked like ordinary walls, lit from below and decorated with a warm, leafy patterned paper. Then the scene twitched in her mind's eye and she realized that they weren't even walls at all. They were tree trunks! Not concrete or plywood or even flat, these walls were woven together from the branches of a ring of actual trees. They came together in a point above the center of the room, and were widely spaced at the bottom. That was where the dim, silvery moonlight reflected off their bark from outside, creating the illusion that she had mistaken for low-mounted wall lights. The gaps between the trunks that let the light in let air in as well, and it flowed freely through the room, carrying the scents of grass and pollen. But higher up, as the trunks came together, the branches intertwined to form a sturdy, solid mat. And over top of that, a thick layer of leaves completed the structure, shutting out wind, light and rain. Not wallpaper at all, as she had first assumed.

Where the hell was she?

Judging by the dimness of the light it must still be night time, but how late? Predawn? Dusk? She had no idea where she was, and her time sense was all out of whack too–she had no clue how long she'd been asleep, nor even what day it was. For now, though, she didn't care.

She knew exactly what time it was, in the only sense that mattered: time to figure out what the hell was going on. She started to get up off the bed again.

"You are not ill."

Tayna froze. The voice had come out of the dark recesses at the far side of the room and she stared at it now, intently. It was him. She could just make out the slightly paler darkness of his features peering out at her from the gloomy shadows. How long had he been watching her? She was suddenly intensely aware that she was no longer wearing Regalia's habit, and the implications of that thought made her shudder. At least she still had the T-shirt and jeans on.

"Okay," she said. "Are you actually trying for creepy pedophile, or is that vibe just a happy accident with you?"

"No," he said, ignoring her. "Clearly you are not ill."

"I thought I warned you about sneaking up on me in the dark."

That seemed to get his attention. "The sun was still within the sky when I entered," he said. "It is the darkness that has stolen upon us both."

"So, what, you've been standing there in the shadows all day, just watching me sleep?"

"Am I not the Watcher?"

Tayna rolled her eyes. "I've had just about enough of that crap," she said. "You promised me some answers. Why don't we start with what the hell that whole 'am I not the Watcher' thing is supposed to mean."

"Born to see, my task is to watch. It is my function."

Tayna sighed. "Great, so you're like, what, the local Peeping Tom?"

"I am the Watcher. My purpose is to observe."

"And you've got nothing better to do than watch me sleep? Wow. Talk about a million channels and nothing on."

"May I approach?"

That was odd. Did weirdos usually ask for permission? "Yeah. I guess," she said, hesitantly. "But not too close." She listened as his footsteps shuffled softly across the grassy floor, but she still couldn't see very well. "Can we turn on some lights?"

Veest paused for a moment to consider before answering. "Let us step out into the world, instead," he said wearily. "That may be best." Tayna heard more movement, and then a rectangular panel of lighter darkness appeared in the wall to her left.

"This way."

The night sky provided enough light for her to see him standing there, holding the door open, waiting. She kept her face turned toward him as she sidled past, still not ready to trust him in such close quarters, but as she passed, she could see his skin in the pale moonlight. Her eyes widened in surprise. His face was drawn and sunken, as though he'd lost twenty pounds since she'd last seen him. He looked horrible– and sleep-deprived, too, judging by the vaguely tortured look around his eyes and the big, dark blotches below them. As reluctant as she was to admit it, his face had been rather kindly before. Thinking back, that's what had unnerved her the most. He had looked too much like a friendly uncle to be for real. But now that the trustworthy look was gone, now that he looked just haunted and crazy, it also made him seem less threatening. How weird was that?

"Are you, um, okay?" she asked. "You look like you've been sick or something."

His free hand came up slowly to rub at the shoulder of his door-holding arm. "I have been taxed," he said. And then Tayna remembered the crack of Angiron's rifle and the rose that had bloomed on the old man's shoulder.

"You were shot!" she exclaimed, and the old man winced at the loudness of her voice, but Tayna ignored him, thrusting her hand forward to push the collar of his shirt aside. The skin beneath it was warm to the touch and damp with sweat, despite the cool night air, but otherwise it was unremarkable and completely wound-free.

"How? I mean, I saw..."

Veest meant his smile to be reassuring, but the pale moonlight lit only his exhaustion, which pushed the effect firmly into "ghoulish" territory. "There is much to tell," he said, waving a hand toward a comfortable looking hump of ground just beyond the door. "Let us sit."

Outside, Tayna could see moonlight glimmering over grasses and wildflowers that flowed across an open field, surrounded by trees. It was like something from one of her dreams. Nighttime voices–those of crickets, frogs, bats, and the like–murmured in the darkness, adding texture to the living quiet of this forest glen, without seeming to add any actual noise. This was not some cheap, token imitation of the natural world like the one in that gross little parkette–this was the platinum card, members-only version. This was real.

"Wow," she said as she looked around. "It's like magic." Within her chest, Tayna could feel a tension she had never known was there, relax.

Beside her, Veest raised an eyebrow. "Indeed," he said, groaning slightly as he settled himself down on the hillock. He patted the grass in invitation. "I am tired. Let us take our fullest ease within this 'magic.'"

Tayna sat beside him. To her surprise, the ground was softer and more comfortable than she had expected it to be. The thick grasses bent stiffly under her, providing a springy cushion–much nicer than the cold, hard touch of packed soil or stone that she had expected. It brought to mind how harsh things had become lately–especially yesterday–with the sudden appearance of this Lord Angiron guy and his apparent obsession with all things Tayna. And let's not forget the certifiable creep show of that rabbit-trap in the coulee. Her eyes flicked automatically to Veest's non-existent shoulder wound. If we're counting weirdness, that's gotta count for something, too, right? And speaking of which, what had the old guy done with winter? And what had happened to Angiron? In less time than it took for Veest to arrange his robes about him, she had blasted the old man with the firehose of her questions–each one seemingly more important and more perplexing than the one before. Veest sat quietly, listening intently until the surge of her eagerness had abated.

"Yours is not the calmly flowing path of a river, is it?"

Tayna smiled a little self-consciously, but then she shrugged. "Nope. I guess I'm all boulders being thrown in from a cliff today. And I'm feeling like, if I don't get some answers soon, I might go nuclear."

Veest smiled weakly. "No doubt that would be unpleasant, so we shall strive to avoid it," he said. "But I have only one mouth to speak with, and little energy. We must settle on one question to lead us. Which is the most connected?" He looked at Tayna expectantly, but she just looked back at him, perplexed.

Veest nodded. "Questions are like the end links in a dangling forest of chains," he said. "Behind each of these question-ends, an answer follows, which then pulls the link of another question, revealing the link to another answer and so they extend, beyond sight, pulling us forward along their length. Such is the nature of conversation. But once started, the lure of the chain in hand is strong. It becomes difficult to let go, that we might pick up another. The wise seeker chooses the first question with great care–in the hope that many other, profitable links will come to hand in its sequence."

Tayna was used to dealing with Goodies–an entire order of women who seemed to have all taken vows of defiance, sworn to obstruct everything Tayna did or wanted. It was in their very nature to contradict whatever she said and to deny every request, but over the years she had learned how to handle them. Veest, however, was a different cauldron of spiders. Instead of obstructing her, he gave every appearance of being on her side. But she couldn't help noticing that, despite all the promises he'd made in the coulee, he still hadn't actually told her anything useful.

"So, you want me to think about all my questions, and then pick the one that will lead us to all the others?"

"Precisely," he said. He smiled happily at this apparent meeting of the minds.

"But wouldn't I have to already know what the answers were before I'd know if the questions were connected?"

Veest nodded. "Indeed, that is sometimes true, but questions about cats seldom connect to those regarding boot repair."

"In your world, I'll bet that seemed like a helpful comment."

Again he nodded. Sarcasm did not appear to be something he'd had much experience with. Tayna sighed. Every time she met somebody who seemed to have answers, he started getting weird on her. Then a thought occurred to her. In this case, with Veest, the weirdness had come first. Maybe that was a good sign. "Alright," she said. "You want a good question? I've got a great one. Who am I?"

Veest's eyes widened and then a smile broke through his weary features. For the first time, Tayna caught a glimpse of an entirely different person, one who was home at last, on familiar ground, with all his demons safely barred outside the gate. "Now *that*," he said, "is a worthy chain to unravel, indeed. Some have even said that it is the only chain there is, and that all others are but illusion." He paused and looked out over the sea of grass, rippling in the moonlight before continuing.

"Lamentably, while my knowledge of the people and histories of this world is great, my knowledge of you and your world are limited. I fear the answer you seek lies far beyond us on the joined path we now tread."

"If you don't know who I am, then why waste so much of your time trying to kidnap me or watching me sleep? Or do you follow all the teenaged runaways who go into the bushes without an escort?"

"All of them," he said, "Who have flowered so spectacularly in a desert."

"Come again?"

A look of confusion tickled at the old man's brow. "It is what drew me to you," he said. "The fire of your flower burns brightly upon you, yet I know not the how of it–to have walked your path in such a barren world and still have found taste enough of wonder, the so-called 'dragon's vim,' to fuel the change... Such a thing is a marvel in itself–a flame in the sky, dancing about you. It called to me, as it must, for am I not the Watcher? Yet still, that I should have been there, then, at such a curious time. It cannot have been mere idle chance... Tell me, it came upon you only recently, did it not?"

Tayna put her hands in the air. "What the whaty what?" After ten years of rubbing up against Goody tactics, Tayna had developed callouses in the part of her brain where trust was supposed to form. In her experience, adults could be trusted only for as long as they spoke plainly. As soon as they started with the gobbledegook, her internal alarms started ringing. And even though she'd understood every single word he'd said, she still didn't have a clue what they meant. She was trying, she really was. She *wanted* to trust the old guy. He seemed so sincere. He looked like crap–and somehow that counted in his favor. Tayna knew instinctively that he was more than just some crazy lunatic who had dragged her away to his magic forest. But no matter what she wanted to believe, he had this annoying habit of triggering that pesky scam-radar of hers, and the constant adrenaline shots were really frazzling her happy place.

She took a deep breath. It was simple, really. Either he was a nut job who would eventually snap and do something pervoid, or he was on the level and deserved her trust. But which was it? In the end, it was a sound that made her decision for her, or rather, the memory of one–the sound of a shrill whistle emanating from the end of a whirling cord, and of an old man crashing through the bushes to come to her aid when he had believed her to be in danger.

Tayna lowered her hands. "I'm sorry," she said. "I'm just getting tired of being stuck in the middle of conversations I don't understand. I have no idea what you're talking about. You expect me to know all about wonder fuel, and what that has to do with fire and flowers, but I'm completely lost."

Veest looked at her carefully. He seemed to sense that some decision had been made–that she was no longer fighting him. He nodded then, acknowledging this new understanding. Then he closed his eyes in thought. Tayna watched him, as his expression grew increasingly perplexed, and then, suddenly, he opened his eyes again, and his face shone with a new-found realization. "I, too, must apologize," he said. "For I have only just glimpsed the truth of something I should have seen before. There are things that I believed you knew, which evidently you do not. Things which change all."

Tayna breathed a sigh of relief. Finally someone was had realized that she might not be up to speed on what was going on. "What things?"

"That you have reached your flower–your coming of age into the flame of magic that permeates all things–and that you yourself were born within the embers of that flame. Here in *this* world."

Even the crickets were stunned into silence.

Tayna's jaw sort of hung there, twitching. Her instinct, honed to razor-sharpness on the Goody-Goody whetstone, was to scoff, and her reflexes already had her primed and ready to go–ready to launch into a patented tirade of mocking indignation. *Bad move, Buddy! You've just subscribed to sixty-four channels of round-the-clock, in-your-face Tayna, and in tonight's exciting episode, get ready as we bring you some of the heart-poundingest, show-stoppingest, most exciting chop-socky action you've ever seen!* But she held the scoff at bay. Instead, she took a deep breath and let that instinct go. She'd made her decision. Veest was one of the good guys. Therefore, this was not the flaming crack-pottery that it appeared to be. She just had to figure out what it was.

"I was born here," she said at last. There was only a slight trace left of her sarcastic disbelief. It would probably take some time to completely cool her jets on that. "And I have magic." She looked at Veest with a level gaze. "You know, I've got to tell you. If you had hit me with just one of those announcements, I'd have probably decided you really were crazy. But somehow, telling me two impossible things before lunch makes both of them more believable. Knocks 'em down to just overwhelming."

Veest sat quietly, watching her, and allowing her to work through her thoughts in her own way.

"Let's start with the slightly-possible-but-really-whacked one first. I was born here?" He nodded. "How do you figure that?"

"You have flowered," he said. "In a world where none have capacity for the vim, no ability to hold it, or to channel it."

"And you can actually see this... magic stuff? On me?"

Tayna watched his answering nod closely. He seemed so matter-of-fact about it–as though it was the most natural thing in the world, like finding lint in your pocket or wearing socks inside your shoes. Magic.

And worse, it came a damned sight closer to explaining her last three days than any other theory she'd come up with on her own. But did it have to be *magic*? Come on! Abracadabra and hocus-pocus? A la peanut butter sandwiches? That was totally ridiculous, right? And there it was, right there: ridiculous. As in "ridicule." The one thing above all others that Tayna simply could not tolerate. Every fiber in her brain was screaming, "Incoming! Intelligence Wedgie at twelve o'clock!" Trust was all well and good, in theory, but it was also another word for inviting someone inside your guard and giving them the chance to pull your credibility up over your head, exposing your tattered emotional underwear to the entire world. And no matter what decision she might have made to trust him, her pride just would not let her go there.

"Magic is just tricks for kids," she said. "Stuff done by carnies with two rabbits and the jack of spades. It isn't real."

Veest nodded. "And the creatures floating in the trap–those were 'tricks' done by 'carnies?'"

Tayna looked away. "Magnets," she said, half-heartedly.

The Watcher fixed her with a disbelieving stare. "Magnets. They explain everything you saw?"

Tayna spun around and glared at him. "What do you want from me, huh? You want me to take something I've always been told was a fairy tale and now, suddenly, just change my mind–decide that, hey, it's real after all? Forget everything I've been told, forget everything I *know*"–she thumped herself firmly on the chest–"deep in here. And I'm supposed to take your word on this because why? Because you're an old man who says he's going to give me some answers? You don't offer any proof. Not one shred of it. It's just your word against what I know is true. I don't suppose you'd care to give me a demonstration? Something real, something I can touch, and prove that there are no wires or mirrors or hidden springs? You do that, and then we'll talk. But until then, you're just a crazy old man telling me that the sky is green and the moon is made of cheese."

But the look on her face didn't say, "You're a liar and I don't trust you." It said, "I want to believe you, but I'm scared." The old man seemed to understand that though, and he nodded.

"So be it."

Then he coughed a little to clear his throat, followed immediately by a long, slow... croak–a sound that was impossibly low-pitched, like a bullfrog at the bottom of a well. It went on for almost ten seconds. At first, she thought it was only a belch, but it was too long and precise sounding for that. Then he did it again, and that's when she realized that he was actually enunciating the sound. No way it was just a bit of gas–there were words of some kind, rattling around in that well with the frog, although she couldn't quite make them out. After the long, low rumble had faded away, he did it a third time. This time was by far the loudest and Tayna had to clap her hands over her ears to keep them from rattling off the sides of her head, as if the low-grade burning sensation hadn't been enough. Even the stones at her feet trembled and quaked in response, but when the sound at last abated, not all the stones returned to their former stillness. Three of them, each about as big as her fist, continued to bounce and shake, as though they were still hearing the Watcher's throaty call. Right there in front of her stupefied gaze, the trio of rocks hopped across the grass toward her. They didn't stop when they reached the toe of her sneaker, either. They just hopped aboard and kept coming, bouncing one over the next in leapfrog fashion, along the top of her foot and up her leg. When they reached her waist, Tayna reached down, mesmerized, fully expecting her hands to become entangled in the invisible wires that must surely be controlling this rock and roll sock hop.

But she found no wires.

Curiosity gripped her and she wrapped her hand around the smallest of the three stones. It was smooth and cool to the touch–just what you'd expect from a rock. The only thing out of the ordinary was the way it twitched faintly in her hand, as though it eagerly wanted to return to its place in the dance, which had now paused while the other dancers waited for their little brother to catch up. Tayna opened her hand and released it, feeling just like she had once before, on the roof of the Old Shoe, when she had released a butterfly that had gotten itself tangled in her hair. With their ranks now restored, the conga line resumed its dance, continuing up Tayna's torso and then onto her shoulder. From that perch, each stone did a little pirouette and then leapt up into the air, to settle at last into a delicately balanced pillar on the top of her head. Tayna's eyes were now wide with wonder and she glanced up at him, just in time to meet a widening twinkle in Veest's own.

He seemed to be almost as surprised as she was. "I've never done more than one before," he said, looking down at the grass and stones around him, as though he might find some kind of explanation there. As soon as his attention wandered away, the pillar of stones collapsed from Tayna's head and rained down around her feet. The sudden clatter broke her trance and she shook her head violently.

"No way! Magnets," she said. "Gotta be. Or air jets maybe..." But her voice trembled with uncertainty and her eyes darted around looking for the secret. Unconsciously, she brought her right hand up, closing it over her left wrist. She twisted fitfully at her imaginary stress bracelet for a moment, but Veest just stared at her, openly, waiting for her to work things out for herself. Then Tayna grabbed at his hands, turning them over carefully, looking for secret control rings or something. The old man didn't even object when she pushed the sleeves of his robe up to his elbows, but there were no wires, no computery gadgets, not even so much as a suspicious length of fishing line.

"Is it really so difficult to accept?" Veest caught her gaze with his own, curious and still slightly bemused. "There are wonders far greater in your world," he said. "Yet those you do not question."

Tayna shook her head. "That's not magic. That's science. It's got rules and limits and stuff."

The Watcher nodded. "As does magic," he said. "These rules and limits—you know them? You have studied them? You are able to employ them readily?"

Tayna eyed him suspiciously. "Well, I can use things, like light switches and telephones, but I don't really know how they work."

Again the Watcher nodded. "And yet you accept them. Or is it your custom to search the forearms of all users of your science as well?" His gaze dipped briefly toward his still bare arms and Tayna blushed.

"Well, when you put it that way..."

Veest smiled. "Perhaps they are not so different," he said. "Perhaps what you call science simply works differently in this place and employs a different name. Can either of us know otherwise?" He looked at her, expectantly. After a moment, Tayna sighed in resignation and relaxed the nervous fidgeting of her hands.

"Magic, huh?"

Veest nodded. "Magic." Tayna looked down at the three stones now lying completely inert in the grass.

"And you say I've got it?" Judging by her tone, they might have been talking about a rare, tropical disease.

"Of that, I am certain," the Watcher replied. "Indeed, never before have I seen it burn so ferociously."

Tayna shrugged. She'd asked for proof and he'd provided it. What more did she want? A government investigation? At the very least, he was right about one thing–she didn't know enough about any of it to make an intelligent decision. So rather than waste more time in denial, as some might, offering more challenges and more debate, she simply moved on, doing her best to accept the idea. And having done so, she had to admit she was a little intrigued.

"So, what does that mean, exactly? Can I change rabbits into chain-saws or shoot lightning from my fingertips?" She held her hands up experimentally in front of her, gesturing into the cool, early morning air, half-expecting something freakish to happen.

Veest's forehead wrinkled into a frown, confused as much by her sudden acceptance as by the question itself. "What? No! Lightning is as hot as the sun! Even if one could convince it to leap from the fingers, it would almost certainly burn them off in the passing."

Tayna's face wrinkled in puzzlement. "So what good is magic if all you can do is make rocks dance?"

Veest rolled his eyes. "What use is singing if all you can do is make pretty noises? What use is gravity if it can only make things move down? Magic is what it is. It does not know that it is supposed to be 'useful' to the likes of you or me." Then he winked. "Still, even as useless a thing as magic can sometimes be tricked into being helpful."

"Like blowing stuff up or raining fire on your enemies?"

Veest just stared for a moment, dumbfounded, and then he shook his head sadly. "Your notion of what magic should be is most disturb-ing. No. One cannot do such grandiose, destructive things with it. Even in the days of our fathers, when we were capable of greater feats than today–even then–such cataclysms were not possible. And since those days, the vim has faded from the garden of us, though we know not why. Perhaps it is simply the way of such things, but great or small, understood or not, magic is a part of the world, based on wonder and joy. It does not destroy."

"You said something about the 'vim' fading. Is that like the wonder-fuel you talked about earlier?"

Veest nodded and reached down to pick up a flattish stone, smaller than the ones lying at Tayna's feet. He laid it in the palm of his open hand. Quietly, almost under his breath, he muttered a short phrase of song, but again she couldn't make out the words. The stone rose gently into the air between them, quivering where his breath washed over it.

"Magic," he said, "is wonder. Wonder is magic. To use it, one must maintain an aspect of delight in all the nuances of a thing's ex-istence. Note the pebble and marvel at the rushing waters that must have tumbled it through streams and rivers for how long to smooth it so. See how even the caress of my breath makes it shudder like a frightened moth. Why should it move thus while floating here, yet not do so when it was lying flat upon the ground? It is this wonder, this vim, from the world around us, that nourishes the tree of magic within. That is why the words we sing are called 'charms.' We truly allow ourselves to be charmed by the world and then give expression to that feeling." He reached out with his thumb and forefinger and plucked the pebble from the air and with a flick of his wrist, spun it out over the glade.

Tayna lost it in the darkness, but heard it as it hit the grass. "Only children believe in magic in my world."

"They are wise," Veest said. "For are children not the natural harbors of wonder? Its magic helps them to survive the world and to grow. Yet greatest among us are those who can retain that sense of wonder into adulthood, long enough for it to brush up against the wisdom of experience. This is a very difficult feat, one that takes considerable skill and concentration: to experience life, and, at the same time, to remain delighted in each and every aspect of it, as though one were constantly encountering the universe for the very first time. In all of my experience, these two qualities are the rarest to find in equal abundance: wisdom and wonder."

The Watcher reached over and picked up a dry twig that he then held out to Tayna. "Now you try," he said. There was a hint of quiet expectation in the off-hand way he said it.

"Could you repeat the words of your spell? I didn't hear what you were saying."

"A charm is not a 'spell,'" he said. "Not a memorized set of words or incantations. It is a feeling, one that you try to put into words–any words, in any language–as long as you understand them, and can feel them strongly enough."

"And I can use any tune I want?"

Veest nodded. "Or none at all. It is the thought that matters–the idea. You must strive to tell the stick how much you appreciate the complexity of its existence. Describe also your delight in its ability to float upon the air. Be specific, describe it fully, as though it were simply another of the stick's features that you are admiring. Sticks are not especially bright. If you can be convincing, then it will believe that it can float, and hence it shall."

Tayna took the piece of wood from his hand and looked at it, then she began a sing-song sort of melody. "Hello Mr. Stick, uh, you're so dry and pointy and all alone..." Her voice petered out and her cheeks flushed with embarrassment. She rubbed irritatedly at the itching sensation that still lingered in the fleshy part of her ears. "This feels so stupid."

Veest grinned. "Indeed, it might," he said. "Especially if one believes that magic consists principally of explosions and violence."

Tayna smiled. He'd actually made a joke! She turned her attention back to her twig and hunched her shoulders around a bit, protecting it from any stray breezes that might come along to interfere.

"Hello Mr. Stick, you're so dry and pointy and all alone. You must miss being in the tree with all your friends. Maybe when the wind blows across the grass and mixes you up with other sticks, you get a little of that feeling back. So that's why you're rising now, rising up into the sky in search of your friends." She knew her song was horrible, but so what? If this actually worked, though, she was definitely going to have to learn a whole bunch of better melodies and rhyming phrases. There was no way she was going to go prancing through the forest doing magic to the tune of TV jingles or the Happy Birthday song. But for now, she shut out all thought of sounding ridiculous, she just focused. And she sang. But no matter how much wonder she poured into it, her twig just sat there on her hand, refusing to do anything even remotely unsticklike.

Veest watched curiously and after a while he reached out and folded her hand closed with his own. "Perhaps later," he said, but Tayna got the feeling that he was more disappointed than he let on.

"Still think I'm all uber-magic?" she asked. "Maybe I really was born over there, magicless, and your sensor is just out of whack. I'm probably so non-magical that I'm right off the charts and you're just misreading it as extra-big mojo with special sauce."

"For everything that may happen in the world," he said, "there must be a first time. Perhaps it is as you say, but I think not. Being raised in such a place may well have altered the path of your flowering, but there is no question as to which world nurtured your actual birth. You still know nothing of our history. When you do, there is a tale within it that you may find explains much."

"A story about me?"

"It is a tale for your eyes, not your ears."

Tayna gave him a look. "You're the one who started this, you know. You brought me here, you started babbling about flowers and fires, you told me to sing love songs to dead sticks. Did I give you any trouble?"

He arched an eyebrow and she smiled. "Well, okay, I guess I did, but I'm not giving you any now. Even though I feel completely ridiculous, I'm doing my part. Why do I get the feeling you're still holding out on me?"

Veest looked at her in silence, but Tayna only watched him back, waiting for an answer. He seemed torn between a number of conflicting thoughts, as though he had better things to be doing and wasn't sure how much of his time she was worth. After a moment, though, he nodded.

"You are correct," he said, getting slowly to his feet. "Come. I will show you." Tayna watched the old man shuffle away toward the forest.

"Now?" she said. "Where are we going?" But if he heard her, he didn't answer, and Tayna was forced to hurry off after him, or risk being left behind in a strange forest. Alone. At night.

chapter 7

A little ways into the second hour, Tayna realized that, wherever it was the Watcher was leading her, it was not nearby, although she wasn't going to complain about it. If this old man could make the trip in the middle of the night without any preparation, on top of having a gunshot wound, then Tayna the Healthy Teenaged Orphan wasn't going to be the one to complain. The only gripe she might legitimately have had–the darkness–had been handled right at the beginning. The old man, noticing that Tayna had not yet developed a grace for waltzing effortlessly between trees and shrubs in the dead of night, had simply held his neck talisman briefly in one hand and muttered a charm. From then on, it had glowed brightly enough for them both to see clearly where they were going.

What she did worry about, however, was whether she had made the right decision. *Family yours. Home come. Peril great.* The further she fell into this rabbit hole, the more those words seemed to resonate, and if they were more than just the dream-time yearnings of a desperate orphan, then she was pinning an awful lot on this strange old man and his promise of answers. What he'd told her so far was pretty wild, but it didn't add much to her picture of the larger Tayniverse. And if that didn't change soon, what was she going to do as a next step?

More than once along the way, her impatience welled up inside her, producing an almost painful need to yell "Where the hell are we going?" But each time, that bit about it being "a tale for her eyes, not her ears" echoed in her head, and she decided to hold her tongue just a little longer. When she found herself doing so for the third time–suppressing her own driving need for immediate answers, simply because the adult-who-knew-more wanted it that way–she actually came to a complete stop on the trail and dropped her jaw in amazement. What the hell was going on? Had he put some kind of mojo on her to shut her up? But then a simpler explanation occurred to her, and she realized that, in a way, he had put a spell on her. A one word spell. Trust. He had simply trusted her to respect his request, and for some reason, she was doing so. After that revelation, the question never occurred to her again. That doesn't mean they walked the forest in silence, though. No. But she was able to relax her anxiety a bit, and she found a million questions to fill her thoughts instead–and his. Questions about this world, this "Methilien Forest." And he in turn had just as many questions for her about her world–which he insisted on calling "Grimorl." There were more than enough "question chains" in those two arenas to keep the two of them occupied for the rest of the trip.

For example, he found the Old Shoe endlessly fascinating and he returned to the topic often, whenever some other chain had fizzled into a tangled mess. He seemed most interested in hearing about Lord Angiron and the other orphan girls, what they were like, how they dressed, where they went, how they acted–stuff like that. And her questions to him were all about the world of Methilien itself, how it worked, who lived there, and so on. You might think that she should have asked about why he believed she'd been born here, and about why she'd been raised in Grimorl and what had happened to her family and all that, but she knew instinctively that those questions were for later, for when they finally reached their destination. In the meantime, the Forest of Methilien was turning out to be a fascinating place in itself.

According to the Watcher, Methilien was a vast territory, populated by three different races–the Wasketchin, the Gnomileshi, and the Djin– and each race practiced a similar form of magic, although they drew their vim from different sources. Djin strength came from non-living things: rocks, stones, metals and the like. The Wasketchin–her own people! –drew their vim from living things, such as trees, birds and animals. This left the realm of death and decay to serve as the power source of Gnomileshi magic. It was a dizzying conversation. Here she was, having a serious discussion, treating the world of magic as real, with actual rules and procedures. The sheer number of details and facts behind it all, helped to make it seem more real to her, and less like a bad movie plot, but it was still hard to get over the idea of flash-boom, flying rocks and dancing twigs, magic. So every now and then, Veest would illustrate his lectures with practical examples.

At one point, Tayna asked how many creatures lived in the forest around them. Instead of laughing at her ignorance though, Veest simply sang a short snatch of song and showed her. Suddenly, the light of his talisman shattered into a thousand fragments and shot out into the landscape around them in every direction. The entire forest, for as far as her eyes could see, was now filled with drifting shards of pale blue light—each moving in its own little path, along the ground, through the air, hugging the twigs and bark... There were even little blue glows dancing in the air between her and the Watcher. His charm had transferred a tiny pulse of light to all the living creatures within the range of his voice. Tayna was startled by the sheer number of them pulsating and shimmering all around her. The charm only lasted for a minute or so, but that was enough. She'd had absolutely no idea how rich and alive a real forest could be. And after the moment had faded and all the little shards of light had returned to Veest's chest to light their way, Tayna found that she was listening more attentively when he spoke.

A little while later, after almost four hours of walking in the dark, they arrived at the perimeter of a large clearing, just as the sun peeked through the trees in the east. This, Veest assured her, was their intended destination, and it was made all the more magical by the glimmer of brilliant colors that the rising sun was beginning to pick out on the leaves and flowers in the surrounding forest. If she had needed any convincing that she was in a different world, there it was. No way could anybody fake a rainbow-colored forest.

But for all that color, the clearing that now lay before them was all the more unusual for its total grayness. Clearly, it was an unusual place. Tayna sensed that even before Veest led her through the dense ring of trees standing vigil around it. Within the ring was not a forest glade like the one surrounding Veest's hut had been. This was no riot of wildflowers, grasses, colors and insects. This was a lifeless, blasted, barren hole in the landscape—a rocky scar, three feet lower than the surrounding forest, about fifty yards wide and denuded of every blade and twig; every insect, bird or mammal; every scrap of soil and every drop of water, save for at its very center. There, a circular disc of soil stood upon the bare rock. It was no more than twenty feet across and was capped by a layer of thick, green grass with a crooked, dwarf oak no taller than a man standing alone in the center. Its gnarled branches clutched and twisted upward toward the brightening sky, and from where Tayna was standing, they appeared to be holding a shimmering metal plate up into the air. It was as silent as a church.

Veest climbed down from the outer rim of soil and motioned Tayna to follow as he made his way across the blasted rock to the central dais. A series of whitish stones formed a stairway leading up onto the grass-topped platform and Veest ushered Tayna ahead of him with a sweep of his arm.

"Behold the Weeping Glass."

The object at the center of the tree's branches was not metal, as Tayna had thought, nor was it glass, as the name suggested. In fact, it was an oblong panel of polished stone, about as wide as her shoulders and half again as tall. It rippled wetly in the early morning light, which is what had given her the impression of metal from a distance. Tayna looked among the branches and around the stone itself, but she couldn't find a source for the water anywhere. Beads of moisture just seeped out along the top edge of the stone, apparently arising from nowhere, and then ran down the face of the "glass." A quick check determined that the droplets only formed on one face–which she automatically called the "front"–the side facing toward the steps. Veest came up quietly behind her and laid a hand on her shoulder.

"What do you see?"

Tayna peered into the wavering reflection for several seconds and, to her surprise, an image formed. "It's a woman," she said. Behind her, Veest grunted in satisfaction, as though this was the answer he had expected.

"Can you describe her?"

"Yes. She's young. And thin. Her hair is long and kind of dark. She looks sad." Veest nodded again, eagerly, and urged her to continue.

"Oh. Wait. There's another woman now." The hand on her shoulder tensed.

"Do you mean that she has changed her appearance? Cut her hair or some such thing?"

Tayna shook her head. "No, it's definitely a different woman. This one has darker skin and a larger mouth. Oops. Now there's a third. Wait, four." In a matter of seconds, the Weeping Glass filled with dozens of faces, old and young, thin and fat, adult and child, but all of them sad and all of them female.

Veest seemed disappointed by what she reported seeing and he wandered away from her to sit on the steps, lost in thought. Tayna watched the faces a moment longer and then went to stand beside him.

"Who are they?" she asked.

The old man shrugged. "There are many possibilities."

"You thought you knew though, at first. Who was I supposed to see?"

Veest looked up at her with the expression of an uncle about to tell his niece that her goldfish wasn't just "resting." "During a dark period in our history," he said, "dozens of young girls vanished over the course of nearly four years." He waved a hand toward the tree behind him. "The mothers of these 'Lost Ones' built this memorial in their honor. People come here to remember them. When they look into the glass, they see the faces of the lost. It was hoped that while paying respects, someone might recognize a face, that of a missing child now living somewhere else, perhaps with no knowledge of her past. All of them had fewer than five summers when they disappeared."

"But you seemed pleased when I saw that first face. It was a woman, not a child."

Veest nodded. "There was a second charm placed upon the Glass," he said. "If one of the missing girls herself should look into it, she would not see the children."

Tayna's breath caught short. "Who would she see?"

"The face of her own mother," Veest said.

Tayna's heart skipped a beat, and she was forced to sit down as well, on a step below the Watcher.

"After years go by," he said, "it was thought that a Lost One might not even remember the look of her own mother's face. The Weeping Glass is not just a memorial. It is also seeks to restore the families, if someone should ever become 'unlost.' "

Family yours.

Tayna made a quiet sobbing noise in her chest. "You think *I'm* one of the Lost Ones, don't you? And you think my parents are here in Methilien somewhere?" she said slowly. "Alive? As in 'not dead?' "

"Here, yes. Perhaps," he said. "More I cannot say."

Home come.

The world turned itself inside out and Tayna could feel herself being flung up into the air and being buried under a mountain, all at the same time. There was a fantastic roaring sound in her ears and her tongue suddenly tasted of iron and bile. She reached out and grabbed the Watcher's knee with both hands to keep from sliding off her step and spinning away into deep, dark space. A very long time later, the feeling subsided.

"So if they are alive, then I could go find them, right? Like, today?"

Veest nodded. "That too may be possible," he said. "Though, without the Glass, the finding of them may not be easy. Yet, if you did, what would you tell them?"

"Oh, I don't know. Maybe, 'Hi, Mom. Sorry to worry you. I was just stuck in Grimorl for a few years, but I'm back now. Everything's okay. What time is supper?' "

Veest smiled, but it seemed more sad than enthusiastic. "It is more complicated than that, I fear."

Tayna glared at him, defying him to burst this amazing bubble of hope that was forming between her lungs, but she didn't interrupt.

"The world you have come from, Grimorl, is a place well known to all the forest as a myth. Most believe it to be the place where the Dragon Methilien sends those who have died. To claim that you come from there would be to confirm their worst fears–that you are not Lost and are, indeed, simply dead. Moreover, it is said that only those who were evil in life might be willful enough to escape that place. They will believe that, somehow, you have managed to do so, fleeing your just punishment and returning to wreak havoc upon the lives of those who have long since given you up. Your family's honor would thus be in jeopardy and no doubt they are respectable folk who would have no course but to shun you. They might even take it as their duty to see that you are returned to your oblivion."

The mountain suddenly doubled in weight. "But that's crazy!"

Veest nodded. "No doubt it is, but belief is a powerful guide. I have no doubt that you would be welcomed openly if you could but give your kin some explanation that would not immediately terrify them."

Peril great.

Tayna looked at the old man, her enormous eyes, brimming with liquid frustration. "But it's the truth! I *was* in Grimorl! And now you tell me that everyone here thinks it's Hell and that I'm some kind of zombie. Well, you know what? They're right! It *is* Hell! It is the biggest, suckiest place in the known Universe, where orphans are worked like slaves, and suck-up toady girls are treated like princesses! The harder you work and the smarter you are, the more the grown-ups try to crush you under their big stompy boots! Nobody wants to know who you really are, or what you can really do–they're only interested in making you as miserable and as boring as everybody else! And they hack at you, and they hack at you, and they just keep hacking and slashing and chopping until everything good about you and everything that makes you *you* is gone forever!" And then Tayna did something that she had not done since she was a little girl. She cried.

Veest watched her patiently. He didn't sweep her up in his arms and cuddle her, or even rest a hand on her shoulder in sympathy. But he didn't make her stop, either. And when it had run its course, she looked up at him, wiping the tears from her face with her sleeve as she did.

"You said 'most.' Most of the people would think I was back from Hell. Grimorl."

"Yes," he said. "Most. There are some who do not believe that Grimorl is a real place at all. To them, you would appear to be deranged, claiming to have returned from your adventures in a place that they believe to be only a fanciful tale."

Tayna couldn't help herself. She burst into laughter. What else was there left to do? "This is just so amazingly screwed up, isn't it?" she asked, when she could finally catch her breath. "I'm either a death-eating zombie from beyond the grave, or a complete whack-a-doodle. What's not to love about that?"

"Indeed," said the Watcher. "Clearly you must tread carefully in this matter, if you would avoid tarnish upon your happy reunion."

"Let's just find them first," Tayna replied. "After that, we can worry about the paint job all you want." Then a thought occurred to her. "Are you sure all the mothers were here?" She waved a hand at the Weeping Glass behind them. "Would it work for me even if my mother was sick the day they built this? Or if she was a freak and didn't get invited by all the cool moms?"

Veest seemed to brighten in response to this idea, and he sat up a bit more perkily. "Now that is a fine question indeed," he said. "No. From what I understand of the charm used, it will only lay claim to a direct blood offspring of its weavers, and now that you give air to the question, there was one such absent, as you suggest."

Tayna's heart stuttered. "Well? Who was it?"

"E'thiel, a young forest auntie," he said. "At the rising of the White Moon, when the mothers were gathering in this place, E'thiel was elsewhere, bound by duty. Though it grieved her heart in the choosing, she was attendant to a difficult birthing and would not put both doe and fawn at risk."

"A deer? Since when do wild animals need midwives?"

Veest scowled in irritation. "Since when does caring have limits?" But then he shook his head ruefully and seemed to recall how much of this was all new to Tayna. "It is the role of the forest auntie," he explained, more patiently. "They tend to the creatures of the wild as need be. For a people to hunt the game and to harvest the fruits of Methilien without otherwise giving back would be unjust–power without responsibility, taking without giving. Balance is the way of all things."

"And this E'thiel has that, huh? Some kind of mothering streak for plants and animals?"

"And also for children," he said, gazing at Tayna thoughtfully. "Such things often follow blood. Perhaps there is more to your speculation than idle fancy."

But Tayna knew better than to sink her teeth too deeply into that line of thought. Not yet, at least. And certainly not out loud. So she shifted the topic. "That's pretty tragic, though, huh? Giving up any hope of finding her own lost child in order to help a frightened animal. What happened to her? E'thiel, I mean. Where is she now?"

Veest spread his hands uncertainly. "Who can say? She and her husband Alon spent much of their time apart from others, and it is a large world. I have not had word of them in some time."

"Alon? Is he a forest auntie too?"

"Of sorts. He is a waterbringer, but where most who take up that calling bring water from the river to the villages, Alon elects instead to assist E'thiel in her labors, herding his mists to the drier places of the Verge, helping flora and fauna to thrive where they otherwise might not."

"They sound like good people," Tayna said, unable to resist the temptation of a maybe-real family. "Almost like hippies. That would be kinda cool. 'My mom, the forest auntie.' She probably eats granola. I suppose that would make me some kind of forest cousin, right? Once removed, maybe?" Then she recognized the warning signs–signs she usually noticed in Eliza–and backed away a little from her daydream with a sigh. "Well, at least now I have a name to ask around about. Two names. That ought to make things easier."

Veest must have caught the same warning, and he cocked his head. "You understand that it is only speculation, do you not? There is no cause to believe that she is your mother, nor even that she still lives."

Tayna nodded. "Sure," she said. "And tomorrow I'll let that sink in. But for today? Today maybe I've got a real mom. And her name is E'thiel. I just want to feel that for a while, okay?"

The Watcher nodded his understanding.

———

But dwelling on fancies was not really a part of Tayna's thing. Lies would have run with the E'thiel story, and in four or five minutes, she'd have had it worked up into a complicated plot involving royal families, international intrigue and at least three dashing suitors, all competing for her love and affection–not to mention the sizable inheritance of money and power that were awaiting her once she could finally prove her identity. Such things did not interest Tayna, however. And after fifteen minutes or so, once the shininess had dulled from her excitement, her mind drifted back to more practical things.

"Is there anyone I *can* talk to freely? Someone who knows the truth about Grimorl?"

"That," Veest said, rising wearily, "is what I have been attempting to discover of late. Other than myself, I had believed there to be only one other—one who, unlike you, was actually born there. He discovered the way of crossing many years ago, by accident, and now chooses to live here among us. But for the same reasons, he keeps his origin a secret. Plainly though, Lord Angiron has now discovered the portal. I do not know what he hopes to gain from your world, but I begin to suspect that it is of no good intent."

"You mean that *you've* only just discovered it," Tayna said.

Veest looked sharply at her, unaccustomed to being contradicted. "No. It was I who discovered Nafosh when first he came. And it was I who taught him our ways and our language so that he might disguise himself among us. He is a well-hearted spirit and he does the Forest a great honor by choosing to remain. No, I have known about him and about the secret of the portal for more than twenty summers."

Tayna shook her head. "That's not what I meant. You said that Lord Angiron has now discovered the portal. What you should have said was that *you* have now discovered that he knows about it. You haven't got a clue when he found out."

Veest began a retort, but it died on his lips and the old man's eyes clouded over in thought. But Tayna pressed on.

"So let me get this straight," she said. "I can stay and I can try looking for people who knew E'thiel, but if I tell anyone the truth about where I've been, they'll either try to kill me or they'll lock me up in a rubber room. So how do I go about looking if I can't tell anyone why? What do I say? That I've been asleep under a tree for ten years and that I just woke up?"

Veest's attention was still focused in the distance, and his reply had all the warmth of an answering machine. "That might work," he said.

"Oh brother! Now you're not listening to me, either." Tayna rolled her eyes. Could this world possibly get any weirder? Just then, the itchy sensation in her ear lobes, which had been tingling dimly ever since she woke up, flared again, and she rubbed at them roughly. "I don't suppose you could magic me up a good skin cream?," she asked. "Or would that be another one of those things that are too useful to be possible with magic?"

She got no answer.

"Hello? Earth to Watchery dude! Itchy ears? Skin cream?"

Veest waved absently toward the forest. "Merlhora leaves will relieve irritations of the skin." Then he seemed to come out of his thought-coma and his eyes registered her presence again. "Yes, merlhora will do the trick nicely. You'll find them in the forest there," he said, pointing. "It is a small hedge with yellow flowers and orange leaves. Crush two or three of the leaves in your fist and then brush those fingers gently over the irritated skin. And if that should not prove sufficient, there is always the Wayitam's home, a mere two hours in the direction of the rising sun." He pointed to the obviously rising sun, as if she might have trouble finding it, but the tingling had become an almost burning sensation, so Tayna was in no mood to discuss the whereabouts of the local hospital. Instead, she almost bowled the old man over in her haste to race off into the forest to find some relief. It didn't take her long, and just as he had promised, the juice of the crushed leaves brought nearly instant numbness. Tayna almost danced with delight as she returned.

"Hey, Veest! This stuff is amazing! How often should I use it?"

There was no answer.

"Veest? Hey! Grumpa! How long does this stuff last?"

But again there was only silence. And when she returned through the ring of sentinel trees, the sight that met her eyes stopped her short.

The clearing was completely empty. The Watcher was gone.

chapter 8

"Sign here, girl. And for goodness sake, write neatly."

"Yes, Sister." Eliza stared in amazement at the sheet of paper in front of her. All the other documents arranged on the desk were covered in dense, black adult-speak, in the smallest font she'd ever seen. But her page was almost bare–written in child-friendly language and everything. Or at least, what the Goodies thought child-friendly language must look like. In truth, it was easy enough to read, but it was a long, long way from friendly.

My name is Eliza Drummel and I understand that when I sign my name, I become the property of Sue and Ned Nackenfausch. I also understand that after signing this page, there are no do-overs and I am stuck with my decision until I am eighteen years old. I promise to work hard, to do all my chores, to not talk back, and to respect my new parents just as I would respect any Sister of Good Salvation. And most of all, I understand that I can never come back to Our Lady of Divine Suffering's Home for Orphans and Evictees. Ever.

But Eliza couldn't care less what the actual words were. To her, they didn't matter at all, because she knew exactly what they *meant*.

My name is Eliza Drummel and I understand that when I sign my name, I am free free free free free free free free free free free free free free free! And did I mention? I'll be free! I also get to live with Ned and Sue, my new mom and dad, for the rest of my life, and I promise I'll do anything for them–not just because they aren't Goodies–but also because they're totally amazing and they're taking me away to live in a castle full of dolls and I get to be the Doll Queen and this is all just so cool because I'm so totally in love and so are they and each of us would do absolutely anything for the other, I just know it, because we're a family now and that's what families do!

It took her exactly three tenths of a second to sign her name.

"Fine," said Sister Regalia, as she snatched the paper away and pushed it aside. "Now get back to class while the grown-ups do the real signing." Sue caught Eliza's eye and managed to give her a smile that said, "Pay no attention to her, dear. You just signed the only paper in the world that matters." So Eliza left the room, glowing from head-to-toe and ear-to-ear, and closed the door gently behind her.

———

"Now we can get this over with," the nun said. And for the next forty minutes, she pushed document after document across the desk, first to Ned and then to Sue, waiting impatiently and tapping her pen on the desk in irritation as each of them insisted on reading every document from beginning to end before signing it.

When the last signature had been signed and all the papers were stacked neatly in the corner of the desk, the Sue woman asked the question she had no doubt been burning to ask all morning. "So, when do we get to take her home?"

This was the part Regalia loved, and she raised an eyebrow in mock confusion. "How should I know? Whenever they get around to approving the paperwork downtown, I suppose. A week. Maybe two. We'll be in touch." She pulled the pile of documents toward her and riffled through them again, dismissing the Nackenfausches as obviously as she could and hoping they would leave.

"A week?" Sue said. "Maybe two?"

Regalia watched the woman exchanged glances with her husband. They had come ready to take Eliza home with them today. Now. They always did.

"That can't be right," Sue said. "Surely there's a way to speed things up?"

Regalia sighed and raised her eyes from the paperwork wearily, doing her best to look like a harried public servant, buried in important work and patiently dealing with inane distractions from ignorant yokels.

"We are dreadfully understaffed," she said. "This is Tuesday. Normally, papers are taken to City Hall on Fridays, by the senior girl, but our senior girl has gone missing." The Sister Superior was certain that Eliza herself had been involved in that, but she could prove nothing.

Although that didn't stop her from letting every nuance of that suspicion ring in her voice. "So it will probably be Monday or Tuesday of next week before we can even think of getting to it. Then another week or so before we can get back again to retrieve our copies. So you see, it really will be at least two weeks, now that I think about it, before we'll have everything squared away. And we can't possibly release her to you until everything has been done properly."

"You're joking," Sue said. Regalia delighted in the pair of long, horrified faces across the desk from her. "Two weeks, because you can't spare anybody to deliver the papers? How long does it take City Hall to sign them once they've been delivered?"

Regalia waved a hand in the air dismissively. "A day, usually. Don't worry, that won't add any more delays if that's what you're thinking. Just look at this as a chance to enjoy the anticipation. She really is going to turn your lives upside-down, you know. And considering your age, you had best make sure you get all the rest you can get before that happens."

"Enjoy the anticipation? Why, I'll have you know–" So, the woman had some spunk, did she? Regalia liked it when they struggled. Unfortunately, the husband chose that moment to join the conversation, and he put a hand gently on his wife's arm to restrain her.

"What Sue means to say is that we'd be happy to deliver the papers for you, to help relieve the burden of what is no doubt a very hectic time for you now, given the absence of such a crucial child from your workforce."

Regalia looked up sharply. There had been a taste of iron in the way he'd said that last bit. Could he actually be threatening her? Maybe he wasn't the dead fish she'd taken him for. Her eyes narrowed. The last thing she needed around here now was trouble with the authorities, and if she read him right, that was exactly what he was suggesting. There was nothing this little man could stir up that Regalia couldn't handle, but the timing would be... awkward. And there was no sense in letting a little fun get in the way of the big picture. If Angiron was going to make a move, he was just going to have to do it quickly. She'd done everything she could to buy him more time, but now that indulgance was looking to be more costly than its worth.

"Well, if it's not too much trouble," she said, doing her best impression of sweet and grateful.

"No, none at all," Sue replied with relief. She gripped the husband's hand in a show of solidarity.

Regalia shrugged. "Then I suppose we'll have Eliza ready on Friday morning. You can pick her up at noon, after morning classes."

The husband smiled. "Oh, I think we'll take the papers with us when we leave now. With any luck, we'll have them back later this afternoon. Tomorrow afternoon at the very latest. We'll pick Eliza up then."

The man was playing with a fire he did not even realize surrounded him. But Regalia resisted the urge to snarl, and simply put more teeth into her smile. "I really must insist that she spend one last night, after you've returned with her papers. We have a tradition here, a sort of going away celebration when one of our darlings gets adopted. I'm sure you wouldn't want to deny Eliza this special time with all her friends, and we couldn't possibly do it any earlier, just in case there's a problem at City Hall. It would be devastating for a girl to go through the farewell party only to have things blow up and fall apart afterward. Quite humiliating."

Ned locked glares with her for several long seconds, then he looked away and nodded. "Fine," he said. "We'll pick her up at lunch on Thursday, then."

Regalia cackled with delight inside. "Of course," she said. "Assuming that there are no problems, and that you get all the papers signed and back here before dinner tomorrow."

"Yes," Ned said. "Assuming all that."

"Right, then." Regalia stood up and handed Sue the stack of papers. "The address for the registration office is on the top form. I look forward to seeing you tomorrow."

Sue smiled as she hefted the stack of forms, but Ned leaned past her and plucked at the corner of a piece of paper that had somehow gotten shoved under the telephone book. "I'm pretty sure they'll want this one too," he said. It was the one that Eliza had signed.

Curse the man! Regalia didn't even try to look embarrassed though. "Why, yes," she said. "They will definitely want to see that one, too. I shudder to think how much that careless slip might have delayed things."

Ned's eye gleamed. "I'm sure you do," he said. Then he put an arm around his wife and they went out the door.

Regalia watched out her window until the couple had climbed into their old car and driven away. As soon as it had passed from view, she was out the door and flying down the hallway toward the little chapel that had been hastily converted into a guest suite. She knocked impatiently at the door. A pained groan acknowledged her from within, and the Sister Superior couldn't resist a chuckle of satisfaction as she opened the door and stuck her head in.

"M'lord? It's Regalia. Another of your precious chickens is about to slip through your fingers. I've done all that I can. You have until sun-high on Thursday to mend it." Then, without waiting for any more unintelligible grunting, she closed the door and almost skipped with delight all the way back to her office.

"Two hours, my grumpy butt!" Tayna's voice rose in frustration as she struggled up another steep hill. All around her, the chattering of the birds and squirrels went silent, allowing her frustration to echo in dignity. After a moment of respect, the chattering resumed. "And where the hell did he take off for in such an all-of-a-sudden hurry, anyway? Doesn't he know I'm just a kid?"

For the fifth time in as many minutes, Tayna swept her hair back out of her eyes and pushed it behind her ears. One strap of her knapsack hung loosely at her side, torn and useless, and the bag kept swinging around in front of her, driving her crazy with every thump and bang. Her jeans were now thoroughly drenched with sweat, and they clung to her legs like drowning sailors. The further she walked, the more she perspired, and the damper her clothes got, the harder it was to move. With one hand gripping tight to a purplish tree branch and the other waving wildly at the swarm of insects feasting on her sweat, she pulled hard to hoist herself up over the last rocky outcropping. She had almost clambered all the way up...

And then the branch let go.

Tayna fought valiantly to catch herself, teetering on the lip of rock, with her arms pinwheeling wildly. She was just inches from stability. And she might have made it too, but then the strangest thing in an already strange day happened. The tree she had pulled herself up with started yelling.

"Oh, leaf rot!" it shouted. "Tell me you did *not* just snap my branches off!"

Tayna was so distracted by the sudden shout that her arms stopped pumping. And without their wild circular arcs to hold it at bay, gravity rose up to claim her. She tumbled backward down the rocky rise, yelping and screeching all the way. The tree was not pleased by her sudden departure either, and before Tayna could complete even her first backward somersault, the bark-skinned fury was already pelting after her, throwing the rest of its branches aside as it coiled itself on the rocky lip and sprang into the air.

Tayna watched helplessly as the world of leaves, dirt and sky orbited blurrily around her, interspersed with nightmare flashes of some crazed purple tree-creature plummeting from the sky above, hungry for the kill. Her end-over-end tumble stretched itself out into a slow, leaf-lubricated slide that seemed to go on forever, until her knapsack fetched up against a half-buried log and jarred her to an abrupt halt. Momentum carried her feet up over her head, and threatened to start the whole tumbling thing all over again, but she managed to haul them back from the brink.

And in a flash, the tree-fiend was on her.

Tayna tried to offer some resistance, but a half-hearted cringe was all she had left. Little more than a twitch of her eyes, really. Her tanks were completely drained. The cry of defiance she had planned came out as little more than a weak sigh of resignation. Her legs flopped back down into the muddy furrow that her back had carved through the rotting ground-cover as she fell. She knew she was beaten and she tried to offer her arms to her captor in a sort of hand-cuffy gesture of surrender, but she couldn't make her vision hold still, let alone her arms, so they just sort of waved in the air like smiling daisies in a gentle breeze, oblivious to her peril or any role they might play in averting it. It wasn't enough that no walk in the woods was complete these days without a stalker or two hiding behind every tree, but now, even the trees themselves had joined in on all the stalkery action. Tayna realized that she was just too tired—she couldn't hold up her end of that game for even a moment longer. Or even her arms. The daisies dropped uselessly to the ground, somewhere near her sides.

"Take me," she moaned. "I won't even struggle. But whatever you're planning to do, better make it quick. You don't want me to die on you before you get around to killing me." Then she closed her eyes to wait for the end.

The tree knelt down beside her. "Are you okay?"

Tayna opened one eye to peer up at her strange tormentor. In her confusion, she could almost swear she saw a face. Stupid eye. She closed it again in disgust.

"Hello? You're not dead, are you?" She could feel rough tree-hands shaking her shoulders and prodding at her cheek.

The hands withdraw. And then she heard an unexpected sound—

ragged, stuttering breaths, like a toddler who's trying hard not to cry. After a moment, she opened her eye again, but it was still on the blink, because now it was telling her that this tree-thing was sitting on its butt, with its head in its branches, sobbing.

"Oh this is just great!" it wailed. "Three days of waiting all ruined, and to put sunlight on top of it, now I've gone and killed someone!"

Tayna could scarcely believe her ears. How could she? They were actually agreeing with her stupid eye! This tree-thing, that moments ago had seemed ready to tear her into bite-sized Tayna strips, was now crying into its own bark because it thought it had killed her.

"Not dead," she said weakly. The tree, however, was not convinced.

"You're just saying that!"

Tayna smiled weakly. "Right," she said. "I'm stone dead. The talking will probably pass once the rigor mortis sets in."

There was a long pause while her assailant thought about it, and then she caught what sounded like the ghost of a chuckle.

As Tayna watched, she realized that he wasn't even a tree at all–just a young man dressed as one. "So you're not going to kill me?"

Tree-boy looked at her quickly. "Oh. Sorry if I scared you," he said. "I wasn't mad at you or anything. Just my rotten luck." He sighed heavily. "I've been out here for days, and I think I was getting close. If only you'd just kept going! I couldn't break disguise to wave you off– that would have ruined everything. But did you go peacefully about your business? No, you had to actually walk right up to me and grab hold of my branch!" He shrugged his bark-encrusted shoulders and smiled weakly at her. "I held on as long as I could, you know, but then you just yanked it out of my hand and, well. . . "

"Sorry. I didn't know you were there."

"Of course you didn't. That was the whole point! As far as you knew, I was just another tree, right? At least I got that part right."

"But I don't get it," she said. "Why were you standing all alone out here, dressed like that?"

"Putting our question to the trees," he said, as if that answered everything. "But clearly, if the trees know anything, they aren't talking. Or, not to me anyway." Then he dropped his head back into his hands. "And she hasn't said so, but I've got a feeling this was my last test, which I've now failed. When she finds out, she'll probably send me home, and I just don't even want to think about what that'll do to my folks. Our family has served Methilien with distinction for as far back as anyone can remember, but this golden prize of a son can't even cut it as a second-rate story uncle."

Tayna wasn't sure what to say to that. Clearly, she'd managed to stomp into a delicate situation with her big, clumsy feet, and, whether intentionally or not, she was beginning to feel just a bit guilty about it. But with the rush of excitement now draining out of her, she was finding it difficult to concentrate on what he was saying. While she was trying to puzzle things out, tree-boy seemed to realize for the first time that she was lying on her back in the dirt, and he stuck out his hand. "Can I at least help you up?"

Focusing on his hand turned out to be a tricky thing, and her gaze kept drifting beyond him, to the carved up slope and its outcropping of rock, which looked more and more like a mountain that had to be climbed. "Only if you have some kind of plan for keeping me up, once I get there," she said.

The young man squatted down beside her, glancing around the hilltop as he did. "Well, for good or ill, I'm obviously done for the day. Might as well head back for some food." Then he asked a very perceptive question. "Say, when was the last time you ate?"

The words echoed in Tayna's head for several seconds. What? Good question. When had she last eaten? In her hurry to find answers, she'd sort of let a few of the basics slip. Let's see. Her memory was mostly a blur now, but Veest definitely hadn't given her anything yesterday, and Angiron had not been shooting bagels at them the night before that. She'd spent the preceding dinner hour stomping through that stupid parkette, and lunch before that had passed while she was in the garden with Sister Diaphana. "Uh, two days ago," she said uncertainly. "Might have been three."

The young man's eyes widened. "Well, maybe we should do something about that, huh? Think you could stay on your feet for ten minutes if there was a hot meal at the end of it?"

Tayna groaned. "I think so." The thought of food made her stomach rumble. "But only if you're sure it's ten. If it's eleven, you'll have to carry me. Any more than twelve, you might as well just cook and eat me. I'll be dead by then."

"Fair enough," he said. He clasped her by the wrist and stood up, hauling her to her feet in the process. "You can start counting now." He put a guiding arm around her shoulder and directed her gently across the slope of the hill, taking an easier route toward the other side.

Now that the crisis was over, Tayna's systems were standing down from full alert, and weariness seemed to leap through her from point to point like a chain reaction. She fought to stay awake by counting her steps, but lost count somewhere between six and parking meter. Eventually, at what might have been about three hundred if she'd been able to keep counting, she caught the sound of voices and bustle coming from beyond the trees ahead. "Oh. Forgot to ask," she said, in a foggy manner. "But where am I?"

Beside her, her guide smiled. "You've crashed into the Heart of the Verge," he said. "Home of the Wayitam. We're almost there."

"Oh, good," Tayna muttered. "Not lost after all." Her new friend had to pretty much carry her the last hundred yards.

"Wasy'r num?" Tayna said. Her mouth was crammed with bread and she was trying to shovel soup in along side it. The welcome addition of fuel to the cavern of her stomach was like adrenaline to a race horse. Her exhaustion, which had been more from lack of food than actual fatigue, receded with every swallow and the sparkle slowly returned to her eyes.

"Sorry?" Her rescuer sat on the log beside her, politely holding her half-eaten loaf of bread so that she could more easily splash soup at her teeth.

Tayna held up one hand—hold that thought—and chewed vigorously. Twice she tried to swallow and realized that she still couldn't get it down. Eventually, after one last precision delivery of wet soup to act as a lubricant, she got the mass of bread down where it belonged, which did wonders to clear up her speech.

"I said, 'What's your name? '"

"Oh," he said, apparently relieved. "For a moment, I thought you'd said 'Wah tzior nham.' In old Djin, I think that means, 'Monkeys can paint my cactus.' I was afraid the lack of food had damaged your brain."

Tayna smiled and tapped the side of her head with a finger. "Nope. Any damage in here is purely hereditary."

The thin young man smiled back at her. "Good. Then to answer your question, my name is Elicand. And to answer the questions that will no doubt follow along in your chain, I am a story uncle—or rather, I was training to be one. So naturally, I've been living here with the Wayitam."

"Naturally," Tayna replied. Then she remembered what he'd told her on the hill, about how she'd interrupted some kind of test he was taking, and how his life was now ruined.

"Uh, sorry about barging into your... whatever you called it. With the trees."

Elicand sighed. "It's okay," he said. "Really. It's not like one test was going to change anything. Even if I'd succeeded, she'd have just found some other reason to get rid of me. I don't think she likes me very much." Then he sat back. "But enough about my problems. You're here to see her yourself, huh? The Wayitam? What's it about? She's pretty busy right now."

Tayna waved her arms in the air in dramatic uncertainty. "I have no idea! None at all! Stupid Veest! He just said, 'Hey, there's a place over that way called the Wayitam's Home.' Then he vanished. He didn't exactly say what I should do when I got here."

Elicand's eyes drew narrower. "You saw the Watcher? You actually spoke to him?"

Tayna looked at him curiously. "Yeah? So? Is that a big deal? It's not like gophers have ripped out his tongue or anything. All he ever *does* is talk." She scratched roughly at her ears. In all the excitement of finding civilization and food, she'd forgotten to gather any more of the soothing leaves, and the itching was back worse than ever. "I don't suppose you could tell me where to find some merlhora bushes around here? I think I've got army ants building spider webs in my ears or something."

Elicand stood up and suddenly didn't seem to know where to put his hands. "Sure, er, um, no," he said clumsily. "I mean, yes I do, but maybe the Wayitam has some on hand. Wait here. I'll go find her."

Tayna only half heard him. The damned frostbite in her ears was somehow still getting worse, and it was consuming all of her attention. Would they have to amputate? That's what they did for bad cases, wasn't it? She thought she could remember reading something like that in stories of northern adventure the kind where one character or another invariably loses a toe as a result of some heroic, selfless act, out on the frozen wastes. What would she look like with no earlobes? She gave up on scratching and tried slapping sharply at both ears with the flats of her fingertips, hoping to swap all the burning and itching for the more manageable sting of slapped skin. She was still doing that a few moments later when an old woman approached her.

"You must be the girl the Watcher sent. Do you bring word about the Quest?" But Tayna was so preoccupied with her ear-slapping that she scarcely heard a thing. The old woman stood beside her, watching

Tayna's bizarre behavior with apparent impatience.

"Wonder to you, stranger," she tried, as though she was reading from a script that she didn't have time for. "Be welcome in my home." But Tayna was still oblivious. At last the woman sighed and dropped herself onto the log bench at Tayna's side, jostling her quite bluntly with an elbow in the process. "Hello there. It's a lovely day, don't you think?"

That, finally, got Tayna's full attention, jolting her out of her itch-trance, and she looked up briefly. "I guess," she said. "If you enjoy having trappers hack your frozen ears off with a blunt hatchet."

The woman, who looked to be in her sixties or so, looked confused for a moment, then her tiny, triangular face softened, filling with compassion. "Oh, my! That's just awful! When did this happen?"

Tayna blinked, now startled completely out of her slapping experiment. "What?" Then she realized how she must look, pawing spastically at the sides of her head and talking about bloody-minded trappers. She blushed. "Oh, uh, it didn't," she said, lowering her hands. "I was just thinking about how things could possibly get worse. I wasn't actually serious or anything." Seeing that the woman still looked a bit skeptical, Tayna turned her head to show off her entirely intact audio equipment. "See? All still there. No bloody stumps. Although, I'm beginning to wish they had been hacked off." With that, she couldn't hold back any longer and her hands flung themselves up in a renewed frenzy of scratching and rubbing.

"Hmph," said the old woman, casting a glare back over Tayna's shoulder. "You mean to say you've never seen this before? The a'dinesh?" Tayna's gaze flicked up at the sound of the stern, chiding tone, but the comment was obviously directed at somebody else, so she went back to rubbing.

"Uh, no. Sorry," Elicand said, stepping forward bashfully into Tayna's peripheral.

"Well, come on then, don't just stand there. Come and learn something useful." The old woman raised her hands toward Tayna's ears. Then she stopped and inclined her head, pausing to look Tayna in the eye. "May I?"

"Uh, sure," Tayna said. "If you think you can do something about it, knock yourself out. Or else knock me out."

The fingers were firm, but gentle, as they explored the tender flesh. "As I thought," the woman said. Tayna tried to keep from fidgeting as both earlobes were taken gently between thumbs and forefingers and massaged. Meanwhile, the old woman continued a running commentary, apparently for Elicand's benefit. "When they show at the ears, they can be troublesome. Be still a moment, dear." The probing fingers felt nice enough, but they did exactly nothing for the burning and itching. Tayna was about to say so when, suddenly, the old woman yanked harshly and twisted. Stereophonic pain shot through Tayna's head and she jerked back to get as much distance as she could between her ears and those vicious fingers.

"Hey! What the hell are you doing? That hurt!"

The old woman grinned impishly. "Forgive the deception," she said as she stood up. Then her voice changed back to lecture mode. "It is an old mother's trick. Without it, the discomfort might endure for days. Best to get it over with quickly, before the sufferer thinks to offer resistance." She paused and peered down, with a hand on Tayna's chin, turning her first left and then right, appraising the ears. "A cobalt trefoil," she said. "Quite fetching, if I'm any judge. She will no doubt be the envy of all her friends. See how spectacularly they match her eyes? They don't always get so lucky." The old woman laid a hand on Tayna's head. "Many happy days upon you and your young man," she said. Just then, a voice called out urgently for the Wayitam, and without another word, the woman melted away into the bustle of villagers, and was gone.

Tayna gaped after her and shook her head. "Who was that?"

Elicand grinned. "Kind of intense, huh? That was Lan'ia Sha. The Wayitam."

Tayna probed gently at her ears. Surprisingly, there was scarcely any trace of the burning itch any more, but stranger still, now they felt almost... puffy to the touch. "Wait a minute," Tayna said, as the old woman's benediction finally wormed its way to the surface of her attention. "My young man? What was she talking about? I don't have any young men."

"Sure you do," Elicand said. "You must." He pointed to Tayna's ears. "Those are your a'dinesh–the lovers' links. They were–" Whatever Elicand had been about to say died on his lips, as Tayna felt a tugging at her side. She turned and looked down to find a young girl, who couldn't have been any older than three or four, standing there with one finger hooked into Tayna's belt loop. She was dressed in a pale green, knee-length version of the robe that all the locals seemed to be wearing, save for Elicand, who was still dressed in the remains of his grape-colored tree disguise.

"You're very pretty," the little girl said. Tayna smiled and squatted down to the girl's level.

"Thank you," she said. "You're very pretty, too." The girl shook her head vigorously.

"No I'm not. I'm jus' cute. I won't be pretty 'til I'm all growed up, like you. Then I'm gonna be *ravishing*." The girl's complete sincerity made Tayna laugh and her little friend giggled along with her.

"I'm sure you will. My name's Tayna. What's yours?"

"Whin An're Tesh, but that's too hard for Jaiden to say. He calls me Winry. You can too if you want."

"Well, it's very nice to meet you, Winry. Who's Jaiden? Your little brother?"

"No, silly! He's my hobban."

Tayna's face pinched in confusion. "Hobban?" Elicand crouched down beside them.

"You mean 'husband,' don't you, little one? Did the Wayitam ask you to come over here?"

Winry nodded. "She said I should come to see the new lady's ears and tell her what I think. So that's what I doned."

Tayna looked at Elicand. "Husband? She's married? She's only a little kid!"

Elicand blinked in quiet confusion. "Um, yeah?" Each of them seemed confused by the other, but Winry paid no attention.

"Wow," she said, craning her neck and peering at the side of Tayna's head. "Yer lucky. You gots really beautiful 'nesh. So pretty an' blue." Winry reached out her small hand and touched Tayna's ear delicately. "Are mine gonna be like that?"

Elicand shook his head. "No," he said. "When you and Jaiden have both flowered, your vim will mingle and create something special, just for the two of you."

Winry nodded at him and then turned back to Tayna. "Wanna see 'em?"

"See what? Your ears? They're nice too."

Winry giggled uproariously. "No, they not! They just ears an' I don't even have any 'nesh yet! I haven't fowered yet. Don't you know anything?" Tayna shrugged. "I *meaned*, do you wanna see *your* 'nesh?"

Tayna made a silly face, crossing her eyes and trying to look at the sides of her head, which made Winry giggle harder–a sound that bubbled and echoed among the trees like a brook in springtime. Winry reached inside her robe and pulled out something that dangled from a cord around her neck. "If you wanna, you can use my behind-looker," she said. "Nafosh gave it to me, but you can try it too. It's easy." Winry pulled the cord off over her head and stuck out her fist, offering the contents to Tayna, but what fell from her hand was totally unexpected: a small, plastic hand mirror–obviously designed for some stylish fashion doll. There was a large, swirly B on one side, and a tiny, perfectly smooth reflection on the other.

"You just look inna shiny side an' it shows stuff behind you," Winry said, then her voice dropped into a reverent whisper. "It's doll magic."

Tayna looked back and forth between the little girl and this impossible toy from her own world. Then she turned to Elicand, but he didn't appear bothered by anything.

"Well," he said, nodding toward the "behind-looker." "Does it work?"

Tayna's first thought was, d'uh, of course it works! It's a mirror! How could it not work? She held it up and tried to position it, although it wasn't easy to get everything lined up. It had been designed for a doll less than one foot high, so it was minuscule. To see anything useful, she had to hold it really close to one eye, but then it was so close to her face that her cheekbones got in the way of seeing anything useful over in ear-country. Eventually, though, she found an angle that worked, and got her next shock. Tayna jerked her hand up to prove with her fingers that her eyes were lying–only they weren't. Her ears weren't just puffy–the entire earlobe had almost doubled in length and turned a bright, sapphire blue. Worse, there was no longer just one, but now *three* earlobes seemed to hang there, jiggling and bobbling as she twisted about, trying to get a better view. It was as though she had suddenly acquired built-in earrings made of blue meat. The only thing that could have been any more alarming would be if they were pierced. Tayna had always hated pierced ears.

"They're so blue," was all she could think to say.

"Yer lucky," Winry said. "So's Granna–she gots green eye-blinks, but she told me about a man she knowed once who got a 'nesh like a big black bunny nose on his lip. It maked him look just like a rabbit. All twitchy and stuff. You got real pretty ones."

Tayna handed the plastic mirror back to Winry. This was just too weird. She hadn't really believed in this whole a'dinesh story until she'd actually seen them, big as life, hanging there from the sides of her very own head. It was kind of hard to dismiss the whole thing as a quaint religious belief now.

"And this means I'm married?" If people around here got married as young as little Winry, could it really have happened to her, too? Assuming she actually had been born here, of course. That was by no means a settled question in her mind, but there were so many overwhelming things to swallow that it was easier to just sort of go along for now, pretending that it was all true. Any actual analysis and decision-making would have to wait until later.

"Wow." Then she looked at Elicand. "Married to who?"

He shrugged. "Well, to your husband, I guess."

Tayna shook like a dog shedding water. "But I don't have one!" she shouted. "Seeing as how the only eligible guy I know who is even close to the right age is you, and we only just met, I'd say it's pretty much completely impossible. Not to mention that it's just stupid. I'm thirteen! I don't even think it would be legal." She twisted fitfully at her imaginary bracelet again. The skin of her wrist was getting tender from all the attention she'd been giving it lately, but she ignored the discomfort and glared her obstinance at the story uncle, daring him to defy her logic.

"Have you talked to your parents?" he asked helpfully. "Maybe there was a commitment ceremony when you were little. It happens that way sometimes. People get busy and then they forget to tell the kids, although, you'd think they'd have said something by now..."

Tayna shook her head. Where could she even start with the whole "parents" thing? Elicand's eyes narrowed.

"Maybe you'd better tell me what's going on," he said.

Tayna twisted roughly at her left wrist in frustration. How do you answer a direct question like that when you're not supposed to talk about it? She tried giving him her innocent puppy look, but he didn't buy it even for a minute.

"I'm not a complete idiot, you know. Your story is completely barkside in. You come here starving, dressed in weird clothes. You speak the language strangely, using odd words in a bizarre accent, you know next to nothing about anything, you flinch when I mention your family, and the only person you'll admit to knowing is the one person who is famous for being invisible and unknowable to anybody."

Tayna shook her head. "I'm sorry," she said. "But could we just rewind a bit? I'm still stuck at the part about exploding ears equals some kind of secret husband."

"This is exactly what I'm talking about," he said, waving a hand at Tayna's entire... situation. "I've never heard of a girl who doesn't know about the a'dinesh. Little girls dream about it all the time, making up stories about their commitment ceremonies and how handsome he's going to be, from the time they learn to talk. And big girls never shut up, showing off their 'nesh when they get them, and bragging about how theirs and their husbands are more identical than any other couple that ever lived. Are you sure you didn't bang your head?"

Tayna threw up her hands. "Why do you keep asking me that? Would brain damage really help? Should I just go bash my skull in with a rock? Then maybe would you cut me some slack?"

Elicand raised his hands in front of him in a gesture of surrender. "Hey! I'm not the bad guy here. I'm just as confused as you are about what's going on, but you've got to admit that your story is pretty unusual. We both know you're not exactly telling me everything, right? And you couldn't have picked a worse time to drop extra puzzles on the Wayitam, you know, what, with the King and Queen miss–"

Winry had been quiet for a while, letting the older people talk, but she had reached her boredom threshold. "I'm hungry. I'm gonna go see Granna." Then she turned to Tayna. "Do you wanna come?"

Tayna scowled at herself. "I'm sorry, Winry. It wasn't very nice of us not to include you, was it?"

The girl grinned. "S'okay," she said. "Growed-ups do that alla time. Do you wanna come see Granna with me? She's still sad, but she really likes compl'ny." Elicand shrugged a sheepish apology and then raised his eyebrows at Tayna. It was clearly her call.

"Sure," Tayna said. "That sounds nice." Winry let out a squeal of delight and ran off ahead of them to tell Granna, forgetting totally that Tayna was a visitor and didn't know where she was going, but Elicand chuckled and indicated with a wave of his hand that they should just follow in the same direction.

"So? I think you were about to share some more misdirection with me," he said, resuming his polite inquisition as they trailed between the sparse trees, following approximately along in Winry's wake.

Tayna sighed. She was getting tired of all this cloak and dagger stuff. What she really wanted to do was drop all the mystery and just tell him. But that was the one thing Veest had warned her against doing, wasn't it? And he knew this place far better than she did.

"Would you be satisfied if I told you that the Watcher knows the whole story, and that he told me to keep quiet?"

Elicand's eyes widened in surprise. "He did, huh? Silence is like a religion with that guy–his first answer to every situation–still, he knows a lot more about things than some failed story uncle does." He looked at Tayna glumly. "I suppose if the Watcher told you to shut up, there's probably a reason, but did he tell you how to explain yourself? I'll bet it didn't even occur to him that everyone you meet is going to want to know what's going on." To illustrate his point, he gestured back toward three or four villagers who had been trailing along idly behind them, hungry for news. Having been noticed, though, the small group suddenly waved shyly and then hurried off to other, suddenly more pressing tasks.

"People are going to be curious," Elicand said. "That's just a fact. Between any two Wasketchin there is always some cousin or friend who connects them. So if a stranger like you comes along and can't tell people where she fits in, that'll just be downright weird." Then he paused and caught at her elbow. "Or does he *want* you to be some kind of sore tooth, getting poked and prodded by every tongue you meet?"

Tayna wasn't sure what to say to that, and she twisted more fiercely at her wrist. Maybe Elicand was right. Maybe Veest had told her to keep quiet, knowing that it would only make people even more curious, and that they'd end up paying closer attention to her story. Would that make them more likely to remember something helpful? Could he be that devious? Or was he just some batty old codger who didn't know half of what he was saying? She still couldn't say for certain what she felt about him, but a deal was a deal, and she'd made one—even if it was only with herself. So until she had a damned good reason to change her mind, trusting Veest was still the plan. Perhaps doubly so, now that she saw how much sway he seemed to have with people like Elicand. They might not understand him, but they did seem to respect him. Maybe there was something useful in that.

"Well, they might not know me, but everybody seems to know him," Tayna said. "If they ask, can't I just say that Veest sent me?"

Elicand laughed. "Oh yeah. That clears everything up. It's not like he's twice as mysterious himself or anything."

Tayna shrugged. "But it just happens to be the truth," she said. "I have no memory of my family. The Watcher found me, as an orphaned child, and has been rearing me and guiding me since the very day I came into this world. Until today, he is the only person I have any memory of ever having met in all the Forest."

That brought Elicand to a halt again, one foot poised above the log he'd been about to step over. "You didn't say that as a question," he said. "You actually stated it as fact. And the Dragon's Peace let you."

Tayna wasn't sure what that meant, so she just shrugged. "Then it's settled. That'll be my story."

Elicand shook his head in wonder. "You're the strangest person I've met all day," he said. "Raised by the Watcher... That's quite a story all by itself. It doesn't really answer much, but at least it'll get people off your back. Nobody expects stories involving him to be straightforward."

Tayna was glad to have that issue settled, but in her mind, it had been a minor one at best. There was still so much going on. Everyone around her was tense, like they were waiting for the sky to fall somehow–something about a quest and the King. And then there were all of her own questions, too. Ears. Weddings. The whole thing was getting galactic big, way too fast. And to make things worse, people kept getting spooked when they saw how little she knew. How was she supposed to ask questions and get to the bottom of anything without making it sound like she was an even bigger idiot? All she could do was keep her ears open and hope for the best. Who knew? Maybe Shammi would write her another one of her weird letters tonight, explaining everything. Yeah, right. As if *that* mysterious character had ever done anything as helpful as actually write a letter. Tayna adjusted the knapsack on her shoulder, suddenly conscious of the journal tucked inside with her extra clothes. The questions were piling up deeper and deeper, with no answer-shovels in sight. But this was no time to get buried, so she pushed them aside with a final twist of her invisible bracelet and hurried to keep up with her guide.

Compared to the little clearing around Veest's hut, the Heart of the Verge was almost crowded–both with people and the strange, multicolored trees and plants. The village was scattered across a low, flat area where the forest thinned out a little, nestled within a ring of low surrounding hills. She had never heard of a village set up *between* the trees before. Usually those would have been the first things to go, to make more room and provide some firewood too. According to Elicand, though, all Wasketchin villages were like this. What made the Heart different, however, was its location. Centrally located in the region, the Heart served as a meeting place, convenient to most of the Wasketchin in these parts. Convenient because it lay precisely on the intersection of four major trails, at least, insofar as the forest had any actual trails. Tayna hadn't seen any bare, beaten tracks anywhere–not even during her walk with Veest. He'd told her that to allow such things to form would have been highly disrespectful to the forest's balance and diversity. In Methilien, a trail was more like a general set of directions–say, from the base of this rock, up over that hill, and down to the field on the other side–not a precise line for where to actually put your feet. People used these "trails" frequently, but they took great care to walk a slightly different path each time, to spread any disruption of their passing over a wider area.

The Heart itself was made up of a little more than twenty of the conical houses–"dehns," Veest had called them–scattered around the site wherever they seemed to fit best. And at the western-most side of it all, tucked in at the base of a sheltering hill, was the communal area they had just left, with a cooking fire at its center, surrounded by a ring of seating logs. It served as a combination town hall, school house and community kitchen–for any activity in which people needed to gather in groups larger than four or five. But Elicand was leading her away from all of that, making for the opposite corner of the village, toward what Tayna could now see was a solitary dehn of reddish-orange trees, set back a fair ways from its neighbors. Winry had long since vanished among the trees ahead of them.

"So, what is a 'story uncle,' anyway?"

Elicand frowned. "Uh, how much do I need to tell you? I assume you know what a Wayitam is?"

Tayna shook her head. "Until I got here, I thought the 'Wayitam's Home' was some kind of hospital."

The young man sighed and shook his head. "Wayitam is the name for what she does," he said. "Her job is to talk to people, find out what they're doing, what they're worried about, what they need, and stuff like that."

"Sounds like another word for 'Watcher,'" Tayna said.

Elicand grinned. "You're right, but she does more than that. The Watcher watches. That's his whole thing–to 'bear witness to the progression of events that form our history.' Some people think he's also a kind of deterrent–it's surprising what some people will do, or won't do, if they think somebody might be watching them–but nobody, other than the Watcher himself knows the whole story. The Wayitam, on the other hand? Her job is simple: find needs and then do something about them."

"That sounds like a big job," Tayna said. "How many are there?"

"Wayitam skills aren't very common. At the moment, we only have

Lan'ia Sha, but at other times, there have been as many as maybe four or five. My grandmother was the previous one. She trained Lan'ia and then we had two Wayitams for years and years, but ever since grandmother died, it's just been the one."

"One Wayitam? To handle the problems of an entire world?"

Elicand shook his head. "Not the entire world–just us, the Was-ketchin of the Verge. And they don't do it entirely alone, either. There are all kinds of people who sort of fill in the smaller stuff–forest aunties, story uncles. There's a lot to do and..." Elicand's voice trailed off for a moment. When he continued, there was a bubble of regret in his voice that hadn't been there before. "Anyway, the forest aunties work more or less on their own and they can train each other, but the uncles work really closely with the Wayitam, so they come here for their training. It has to be done by an actual Wayitam, but because there are so few of them, they pretty much have to stay put, or people who really need them won't know where to find them. That's where the story uncles come in–they're kind of like the Wayitam's traveling ambassadors–free to wander around, gathering information and speaking in her name. Sometimes they carry messages or advice to specific people, and diffi-cult problems are usually brought back to mama, but otherwise they just make stuff up based on common sense. Men are good at that part–men from my family especially. In the last few generations, our clan has produced eleven story uncles. Dad was so proud–I was supposed to be the twelfth–only that doesn't look likely now. I think Lan'ia only agreed to take me in because she felt obligated to my grandmother, but I'm hopeless. Any day now she's going to realize that it just isn't work-ing, and when she does, she'll send me back and I'll have to face my whole family."

Tayna couldn't help but notice how proud he was whenever he spoke about his family, or how deflated he became when the topic turned to his own abilities. She tried to change the subject.

"So that's it for career choices around here?" She ticked the list off on her fingers as she recited it. "Watcher or story uncle for the men, and Wayitam or forest auntie for the women?"

Elicand grinned. "No, not at all. I guess it must have sounded that way, but my family is actually pretty weird to have so many in service to the Dragon. Most people, men or women, do normal work–baking bread, making cloth, that kind of thing. After all, it takes a whole village to make up a village. But you're right. Story uncles are always men and Wayitams are always women. Most Watchers are men too, although I did have a girl cousin who was supposed to become the Watcher's apprentice once, but she was one of the first to be Lost. A girl Watcher is pretty unusual, though. Normally, when girls are called to serve, it's as forest aunties. There've been a bunch of those in my family too–both my sister and my dad's sister are aunties." Then his face brightened. "Hey! Do you think being the first failure in such an unusual family makes *me* special. I wonder if dad would buy that argument?" But it sounded flat and hollow.

Tayna had a hundred more questions to ask. Elicand sounded really well connected and she was dying to ask him if he knew anything about E'thiel and Alon, but by that time, they were approaching a solitary dehn. In front of it, a stooped old woman sat on a rock, mending a broken pot. And behind her, Tayna could see Winry sitting silently in the doorway, watching them approach.

"Wonder to you, Arin Far'eh," Elicand said. The woman looked up, and Tayna was startled to see that she had brilliant, green eye-lids. Eye-blinks.

"Wonder to you, Uncle Elicand," the old woman said, managing to sound both formal and a bit cruel at the same time. Elicand winced at her use of the title he was convinced he would never earn, but he said nothing about it, and the old woman just sat there, glaring up at him, challenging him to state his business.

Elicand waved a hand toward Tayna. "My friend here has come to us without much chance to prepare for her journey and her clothes are not well suited to this region. The Wayitam wondered if you might have a kirfa in her size. And possibly some boots?" Tayna looked at him quickly. The Wayitam wondered? The woman hadn't said a single word about clothes. Elicand caught her stare and winked at her, then turned back to Winry's granna.

Arin Far'eh glanced suspiciously at Tayna and then turned her glare back to Elicand. "You know that I do. My Siani P'leth took nothing with her on the Wagon, did she? I suppose now it will all have to pass to this stranger, will it? It's not like my feelings matter any more. Wait here."

The bitterness in the woman's voice took Tayna by surprise, and she was about to give up and apologize for being a bother, but Elicand set a hand on her arm and squeezed gently. "That would be very kind of you, Arin. We'll wait."

Winry scuttled out of the doorway to let her granna pass, and once the old woman was inside, she bolted forward. "Don't let Granna fool you," she said. "She's real happy to see you. I can tell. She's just awful sad since mummy died."

Somewhere in Tayna's chest, a hollow space opened up and she knelt down to give Winry a quick hug. "I'm an orphan too," she said quietly. The little girl hugged her back, but then she broke away as Arin emerged again from the dehn. She was carrying a neatly folded bundle of cloth, with a pair of soft-looking leather boots piled on top. Arin pushed the garments toward Tayna, who accepted them with a smile.

"Thank you."

"Don't spill on 'em," the old woman said. "They ain't been charmed or nothing. Just simple clothes. They'll take a stain like grassweave."

Tayna looked uncomfortably from Arin toward Elicand, uncertain what to say. He just smiled and gestured for her to say something. Anything.

"Um, I'll be careful," Tayna said, still puzzled. Then it all clicked, and she understood what was going on. Emboldened, she took a step toward the old woman. "I was wondering. May I come back later and visit you and Winry? I really am new around here—you have no idea—and it would be so nice to have some girls to talk to." She thought she saw Arin's face thaw just a little.

"If you must." Then the old woman looked at Elicand. "Has she been accommodated yet?" When he shook his head, Arin turned back to Tayna and yanked the clothes back out of her hands. "I suppose you'll be staying here, then, eating all my food. And I'll just have to go put these things back inside too then, won't I? I'm sure I don't have anything better to do than fetch things back and forth like some kind of traveling Djin." She eyed Tayna up and down, taking in the spattered grime, the wear and tear, the knapsack hanging in tatters from her shoulder, then she clucked her tongue like a disapproving hen. "And I suppose you'll be coming inside, wanting help out of those muddy clothes, too, won't ye? I'll just go sit there and wait on ye 'til yer done and ready. Take yer time. I'm only gonna rot so quick." Without waiting for a reply, Arin turned away and disappeared back into her dehn.

Tayna just stared after her, a little startled, but as soon as the old woman disappeared, Winry ran and jumped up into Tayna's arm, kissing her on the cheek. "Tayna! She *likes* you! I'm so happy yer gonna stay with us!" Then the little girl hopped back down and ran after her granna, slowing down to a somber pace only when she reached the door.

Tayna smiled as the little girl vanished inside, then she turned to Elicand. "That was an example of you and the Wayitam at work, wasn't it?"

Elicand looked at her with surprise, but there was still a trace of the wink in his voice. "Oh? What makes you say that?"

"Well, I was thinking about what you said earlier," Tayna said. "About how she pays attention to what people need, and about how you're supposed to help her do something about it." She glanced down at her own damp and muddy clothes, indicating with a disgusted wave of her hand how constraining and inappropriate they were, especially in comparison to the tough but loose, knee-length "kirfa" everyone else was wearing. "Lan'ia Sha probably noticed how exceptionally functional these are," she said. "And then I think she remembered Arin here, and how she might have something that would make me look slightly less homeless, that wasn't already being used, so she did something about it. But she was sneaky. She didn't just say, 'Hey Elicand. Take this hobo over to Arin and get some of the good clothes from her dead daughter.' Instead, she sent little Winry over, and just figured the rest would happen by itself. Especially if you were with me."

"You think so?" Elicand said. "Why didn't she just get me to take you to Arkenol? He's a great weaver and loves to prove it. Why send you to Arin at all? Especially in such a complicated way?"

Tayna paused to think. "Well, I don't know about him," Tayna said. "But Arin's obviously really depressed. And I think maybe Winry is, too. Maybe the Wayitam thought they needed to feel helpful more than Arke-buddy needed his ego stroked."

Elicand dropped the naive act and let out a low whistle. "Wow!" he said. "You're good! Yeah. Siani P'leth died a few months back. The three of them were really close and Arin's been in a real dark way ever since, feeling useless and old, I guess–and probably feeling overwhelmed trying to keep up to a kid as busy as Winry. The Wayitam saw a way to help all of you at the same time. That's the way she likes to work–taking a bunch of problems and sticking them together so they solve each other."

Tayna looked at him. "It seems to me that you actually did more of the 'sticking them together' than she did. Maybe you're not as hopeless as you think."

The story uncle blushed a little and looked away. "You're new around here," he said. "Wait til you see her in real action. Then you'll know how pathetic I really am."

110

"That's too bad," she replied."I was hoping that maybe I'd finally met someone around here who was connected enough to help with whatever secret agenda I have that I'm not telling you about."

Elicand laughed. "You've only got one?"

That shocked Tayna and she glared at him for a moment, but she couldn't hold it and it dissolved into a grin. "I guess I am pretty much the drama queen around here, huh?"

He shrugged. "Something tells me that whatever is going on, you're doing well just to keep your nose above the sand right now. Don't worry about it. You're probably right. If I know the Wayitam, before you leave here, she'll end up giving you just what you need, but don't bother hunting for it. You probably won't recognize it when it happens."

Tayna looked at him, and shook her head. This guy had a serious case of self-defeat. She'd been talking about *him*, but he had instinctively assumed that anyone who was actually helpful had to be the Wayitam.

"I don't know about that," she said, glancing past him toward her two new friends in the dehn. "I think maybe the helping's already started." And then she pushed past him and went inside.

chapter 9

Tayna had never flown anywhere before. She knew about airplanes, of course, but she'd never actually been in one. Where would she have been going? It's not like the Goodies were in the habit of selecting lucky orphans to send to Hawaii every winter. So she didn't even have that experience to draw on, when, the next morning, she found herself sailing through the air over top of the trees, facing backward, with the wind whipping her hair into her eyes. And she owed it all to a little girl with a case of early-morning giggles.

Sunrise comes early to those whose bedroom walls are little more than a street-gang of saplings standing in a leafy huddle, and nobody is as sensitive to morning light as a four-year-old girl on her first sleep-over. Tayna awoke to a gentle nudging at her shoulder.

"Tayna, you 'wake? Huh? You 'wake yet? Come onnnnn!" Winry had extricated herself from Arin's side at the very first twinkle of light, unable to contain her excitement once she remembered why she wasn't in her own bed. And Tayna knew from years of experience that there was no way she'd be allowed to go back to sleep now, so she rolled over and shushed Winry, casting a warning glance toward Arin.

"Let your Granna sleep, kiddo. I'm up. You can help me get dressed."

The twenty minutes that followed were both baffling and hilarious, as Winry explained the proper way to put on a kirfa, while giggling at every awkward mistake Tayna made. As if the garment wasn't strange enough to begin with, the entire lesson was further complicated by the fact that, though Winry used the terms "right" and "left" liberally in her explanations, it soon became clear that she had absolutely no idea what they meant. She thought they were like spices on food, to be thrown in at random to make everything more interesting. And it appeared to work, too, judging by the amount of laughter it provoked. By the time Tayna finally got the important bits of skin covered, she and her crazed little fashion-guide were fighting hard to suppress their giggles.

But then came the boots. The first one went on well enough, but as Tayna picked up the the second, she was interrupted. A frightened little chipmunk popped out of the boot between her thumbs and then screamed a high-pitched, squeaky "chit-chit-chit!" at the two home invaders, before dashing up her arm and making a break for the forest through the dehn wall behind her. This was more than any person should be expected to keep bottled up, and the two girls exploded into helpless convulsions of laughter on the floor.

Loud laughter.

"By the love of the hairless, hopping Dragon!" Arin bellowed, waving an arm angrily at them from the day-defying darkness under her blankets. "Go take a flying jump and leave an old woman in peace!" Later, Tayna realized that Arin must have been half dreaming in that moment, and had visualized her instructions a little too vividly, because without warning, Tayna was suddenly flung up and out of the dehn, crashing through the thinnest branches near the top, in what could only be described as a "flying jump." And now, here she was, several minutes later, still holding the left boot in both hands and gaping in surprise at the blues and grays of the treetops flowing quickly by beneath her, with absolutely no idea where she was going or how to abort the trip. Somehow though, despite the million other impossibilities she had been forced to swallow lately, this one bordered on actually being easy. It wasn't that big a stretch from seeing Veest's floating rocks to imagine magically flying people, and besides, it was almost fun. She wasn't moving dangerously fast—like, so fast that she had to worry about the air getting sucked out of her lungs and suffocating or anything. But it was definitely car-fast, and by the time the shock had worn off, she was already too far from the village to bother calling for help. A gust of wind tugged hungrily at the boot still gripped in her fingers. Tayna quickly tugged it onto her bare foot before anything else could go wrong, and then turned her attention to the next problem: figuring out what to do about her predicament. But that kind of depended... What was a flying jump anyway? Was it flying? Or jumping? The distinction made all the difference in the world as far as she could tell, because with a jump at least, there was an implied coming back down, and maybe she wouldn't need to actually *do* anything. But flying? That could go on forever. One thing seemed immediately sure though: staring back the way she'd come wasn't shedding much light on anything. So, with an effort of contortion, she got herself twisted around into what seemed like the only proper position for the situation–the Superman pose. Although it only took a minute or two of that before her arms gave out and the wind blew her hands back into her face. The third time it happened, she gave up in disgust–what does superman know about real flying, anyway? Instead, she clamped her arms firmly at her sides. More of a Bulletman pose, really, if there was such a guy, but it seemed way more practical.

Now that she could see better, it was pretty obvious that what she was doing was definitely more fly than jump. The coming back down part was nowhere to be seen. Movies, however, were clueless about a lot more than just arm position. According to the laws of Hollywood flight, all a heroine has to do is lean a little, one way or the other, to gracefully bank and twirl her body through the sky like a ballerina. In practice, however, leaning did about as much good as wishing. She tried sticking out a leg, on the theory that maybe jump-flying used the same principles as toboggans–drag steering. But that didn't work either. Just to be thorough though, she tried again with one arm, and then two, and in various combinations with her legs. Still bupkiss. Finally, in a fit of frustration, Tayna tried to just slow herself down by standing upright and facing front, with her arms clawing at the wind, like some murder victim's chalk outline hurtling through the sky, but even that had absolutely no effect on her flight plan. All she managed to do was invite cold jets of air to blast her in unladylike places through the flapping gaps of her kirfa. Depressed, Tayna flopped back down on her belly. Wherever she was going, her destination seemed to be completely beyond her control.

In the end, it happened rather suddenly. One moment, she was peering down at the mighty river that now curved through the lemon-colored treescape below her, and then, in the next moment, she raised her head just in time to see a rugged cliff rushing toward her face. She threw up her arms and scrunched her eyes closed tight to wait for the impact, but it never came. When she finally risked peeking out from between her fingers, she could see that she had risen and come to a complete stop, hovering in mid-air, not six inches above the rocky top of the cliff. Tayna reached down tentatively and poked a finger at the rough slab of rock below her.

Which promptly broke the spell and returned her to the attention of Mr. Gravity.

———⌣———

Tayna just lay there for a moment, unsure whether she could trust that the ride was over yet. She was also a bit dazed still from all the flying, and then the sudden not flying.

So it wasn't until a few moments had passed without any further dramatic changes in motion that she finally allowed herself to relax. Not that she was complaining, exactly. The whole thing was actually pretty cool, and if she ever did figure out where *family yours* was hiding, maybe she could convince Arin to fly her there next. How would that be for *home come*, huh? Mix in a little of this fast floaty *flee now* and– "Bang!–"she'd be the flying ninja of daughterly vengeance, coming out of sky. Take that all you *peril great*, whatever you are! But first she'd have to find her way down off this hill and back to the Heart of the Verge.

When she got to her feet and dusted the pebbles from her knees and looked up, the scene spread out in front of her was enough to make her breath catch in her throat. The river carved its way through the thick, yellow-green blanket of treescape that seemed to stretch all the way from one horizon to the other, changing color every hundred yards or so, perhaps responding to changes in the soil or something. Glittering like a wet snake, it raced in toward the cliff-face below her at a glancing angle, only to thunder past its rocky base and turn away again, scraping a little more of the cliff away with every rock-chomping splash. Eventually, the entire hill would be gone, eaten over the eons by that voracious ribbon of fast-flowing water. As rivers go, it wasn't especially wide–Tayna was pretty sure she could throw a stone across it if she tried–but it was fast and deep–more than enough to pose a near-impenetrable barrier to a city girl who had never been taught to swim. And assuming her flying days were indeed truly over, that was going to be a problem, because the Heart of the Verge was back that way–on the other side.

The morning sun hung brightly above and sparkled off the forest below, as ripples of breeze stirred its canopy like the surface of an ocean. For the first time, Tayna could see how beautiful this landscape really was. Words like "unspoiled" and "breath-taking" suddenly didn't sound as trivial as they once had, and it became easy for her to set her problems aside for a bit. Tayna had never really understood the fuss about the "great outdoors," but maybe that was because she had never seen it like this. Up close. Natural. And wild. Or maybe this forest was out of the ordinary, given the extra colors and all. "Gotta stop and smell the merlhora sometime," she said, then she moved carefully to the rocky outcropping that jutted out over all that splendor. Her new boots were comfortable, but a little weird feeling–cushy–as if they were always floating just a fraction of an inch above the uneven stone of the cliff top. She didn't trust them. Not yet. So instead of walking, she crawled to the cliff edge on hands and knees. When she got there, she sat down quickly and dangled her legs over the edge. With nothing but shimmering water below, and spectacular forest as far as the eye could see, it was a perfect moment.

But such things were not meant to last. Tayna was scarcely ten minutes into her psychic recharge when the sound of talking floated past her ears. No. Not talking–singing. From somewhere up river–beyond the bend, still out of sight. Forgetting about the weird cushiness, Tayna stood up to get a better look, and she was craning her neck out over the water, peering into the distance, when her boot slid just a fraction. But that was enough. The heel caught in a crag of stone and Tayna stumbled. Off the cliff. And plunged toward the raging current, forty feet below.

Then the water closed over her head.

———————

Vaguely, from the depths of memory, Tayna thought she remembered hearing that a human body would naturally float. All you had to do was hold your breath and not panic. Her body however, did not stop at the water's surface. It plunged downward into the suffocating darkness. Tayna felt oddly detached. What about Wasketchin? Do we float too?

Time ticked by in bubble-slow fashion. Shining little spheres of air trailed up from the folds of her kirfa, jiggling past her eyes in a taunting dance as they accelerated up toward the light–and the air. How fair is that? The only thing down here that doesn't need oxygen are those stupid bubbles, yet there they go, leaving, and taking it all with them. Oh, and where were they taking it? Why, up to where the rest of all the oxygen was of course. Stupid bubbles. Come back!

Tayna watched them go–so many of them that they merged together in her mind's eye, forming a hollow silver tube of precious air that stretched all the way up from her arm-pits to the sky above–a clean, slender snorkel of vanishing hope. She felt her boots strike bottom, dimly aware that the current had her, dragging her feet swiftly across the riverbed stones. Instinctively, she coiled her legs beneath her and kicked out, hard. The trip back to the surface seemed to take another eternity, giving her plenty of opportunity to stick out her tongue at the now painfully slow pockets of air as she rocketed up past them. Her lungs burned, and Tayna wondered if she had somehow taken a wrong turn somewhere. Wasn't "up" supposed to include refreshing things, like breathing? But then the wondering was over. Her head broke out of the water and she sucked in a great lungful of precious air.

And a teaspoon or three of river water.

Whatever composure she might have had left was swallowed with that water, and Tayna began to thrash. She raised her arms to claw at the surface, trying to pull her head forcibly up above the frothing waves, but every time she got there, her body did its best to knife back downward, back into the very depths from which she had only just escaped.

By the third time she had scrambled her way back to the surface, Tayna's lungs were on fire. Her arms, too, were exhausted, and they now drifted down to hang uselessly at her sides. Bulletman at sea. Tayna shook her head. She had nothing left. Her legs kicked feebly. Once. Twice. She knew she should be fighting harder, not giving up, but without even consulting her, various parts of her body were now going on strike, one by one, demanding drier working conditions and more air. Finally, even her legs gave out and drifted slowly down, following the example of her arms, to hang uselessly in the water. When she slipped again beneath the waves, for the fourth and surely final time, Tayna felt herself relax, resigned now to her fate, even though it was such a sucky way to die. At least the whole husband problem was being resolved. *She* was about to give *him* a divorce. And what about all the other goodbyes? Dear Shammi...

Just then, a powerful, dark-skinned hand appeared in the water beside her. It bobbed about in languid slow motion—up, down, up, down—before seizing her suddenly by the hair and yanking. Ow! What's the point of pulling my hair? Isn't drowning painful enough? She looked up, consciousness fading, barely alert enough to notice that she was rising toward the light. A distant, murky thought swam into her mind through all the glue. Light, new and improved, now with a special offer. Just include six box tops and for a limited time only, your light will include a free supply of air. Be the first on your block to not die! Now, where had she put all those box tops? They were around here somewhere.

"By the bands of gold on my father's arm!" a far-off voice exclaimed. "It seems Abeni has caught a fish!"

With a few strong strokes of his paddle, the enormous, dark-skinned warrior guided his little canoe out of the current. There was scarcely room in the craft for all of him, let alone her flailing body, so he simply dragged her along in the water behind him, using her as a crude rudder, while he paddled with his other hand. As soon as they reached the shore, he tossed her in a heap onto the bank beside the boat and started to climb out after her.

Tayna may have been too tired to fight him off in the water, but one look at the mountain-sized man looming over her now gave her a renewed sense of desperation. With every ounce of strength left in her, she tried to drag herself up the muddy bank with her fingers–the only part of her body not exhausted by the struggle to swim. She didn't know if she'd been caught for dinner or for something more sinister, but she didn't intend to find out the hard way. The big man though, did not give chase. He merely threw back his head and laughed. It was a deep and booming sound. Almost musical. Like a kettle drum fall down a flight of stairs.

"Where do you think you are going, little fish? You are young and Abeni has spared you from an early death. Among his people it is custom for the rescuer and the rescued to share the recovered life– half for you and half for Abeni. Abeni will take his half now." Then he leaned down low over the exhausted girl, whose fingers were no longer cooperating in her quest for freedom and had joined Body Parts Local 103 to stand idly by as management slipped back down to the water's edge at her captor's feet.

"Of course," the big man added in a conspiratorial whisper, "you may wrestle Abeni to win back your freedom, but it is no use. Abeni will win."

Tayna groaned and let her head sink into the mud. She didn't even have the strength to spin her imaginary bracelet in frustration. He was right. "Sorry *family yours*," she mumbled as the light began to fade. "I tried." And then the world went black.

—————

Tayna regained consciousness some time later. Every part of her body ached, and the aches were made worse by all the bouncing. She was slung over a massive black shoulder, with her head hanging down. All she could see was a great back and the colorful spray of bent grasses springing back into place below, as his powerful legs pushed through, carrying the both of them across an open field. She could also hear singing. It sounded like the same melody she had heard above the river.

"Hey! Put me down!" Tayna said, more weakly than she had intended. She thumped a fist against her captor's back, but it was barely even strong enough to get his attention. At the sound of her voice, the legs stopped plowing through the grass. before she knew what was happening, Tayna felt herself being swung through the air, and then she was standing woozily on her feet. Although, now that her legs had to support her weight, she wasn't so sure that this was an improvement.

"Ho now, Little Fish," said the big man standing in front of her. He was easily the biggest man she'd ever laid eyes on. "Perhaps Abeni should throw you back into the river," he said. "You are too small to make a good meal. In another year, perhaps you will be large enough for a snack." He stood with his fists planted on his hips, waiting for her to say something.

"A year? I'd have been dead in another thirty seconds."

The big man grinned. "Oho! So the Little Fish agrees that Abeni has saved her life. That is good. Now we will not have to wrestle to see who holds the truth of it. According to custom, you must now be Abeni's servant for one half of your remaining life. He shall call you 'Little Fish' in honor of this day. Here, Little Fish, you may carry Abeni's pack." He quickly set an enormous leather sack on the grass beside her.

"You think I'm going to carry that?" she said. The bag was almost as big as she was. Abeni looked down at it and then at her.

"Perhaps the Little Fish has a point," he said, nodding his enormous head. "She is still tired from her swim. The Djin are not cruel masters. Abeni will carry the pack for today. Little Fish will carry another item for him."

He was a Djin? No wonder he was so big. Tayna looked around. She couldn't see anything else that needed to be carried. "What's left for me to carry?" she asked, looking pointedly around at all the nothing else he had with him.

"Why, Abeni's most valuable possession," he said.

"What's that?"

"It is his servant, the Little Fish!" he said, bellowing his deep, musical laughter once more. Then he jerked the sack back up to his shoulder, and resumed his march across the field, singing his song in time with his great, striding legs.

Tayna thought frantically. She didn't have any intention of following this big galoot around the forest for the rest of her useful life–she had other plans–but she couldn't exactly fight him. He was a one-man mountain. Then a thought occurred to her. It was worth a try. "Um, Abeni?" The giant halted his song and turned around.

"Does the Little Fish wish something from Abeni?"

Tayna nodded. "I was wondering if this custom of yours includes protecting me from danger."

Abeni looked around. "Abeni sees no danger."

"But you would protect me, if there was any?"

"Yes, Little Fish. A servant is a valuable possession. Abeni would protect all his possessions from harm." He turned to resume his walk, but Tayna wasn't finished.

"Wait!" she called out. Once more the man turned to face her. "If somebody tried to kill me, what would you do?"

Abeni looked confused. "The peoples of the Forest cannot do such things to each other," he said.

"But if someone tried?"

Abeni shrugged. "Then he could not be of the People and would not be protected by the Dragon," he said, thoughtfully. "As well, he would be a danger to others, who did not know of his treachery. Abeni would have to kill him." The big man frowned, as if this line of thought disturbed him.

Tayna, however, smiled. Bingo. "Then I have saved your life, Big Whale, and now *you* must become *my* servant for half of *your* remaining life. You can start now."

Abeni laughed. "That is very slippery, Little Fish, but from whom have you saved Abeni? There are none here to challenge him." Again he looked around and shrugged to emphasize his point.

"I have saved him from a great and powerful Djin," Tayna said. "One who was sworn by duty to slay him."

"Who is this Djin and why has he sworn such a thing?"

Tayna grinned. "His name is Abeni, and he has sworn to protect me, his servant, from all who attempt to do me harm. Back there on the river, you almost killed me–you startled me with that song of yours and made me fall into the river far below. Abeni is my sworn protector and is duty-bound to kill you–to protect me and all others who might be snared by your sneaky song attack. Unless..." She allowed her voice to trail off. Abeni looked wary, as though he didn't like the turn this conversation had taken.

"Unless what?" he asked suspiciously.

"Unless I tell him that your song was not intended to harm me, and that it was only a simple accident that nearly caused my death."

"Hmm," Abeni said. His eyes narrowed as he considered this new perspective on the situation. "Abeni wondered why the Little Fish was in the river if she could not swim." He considered for another moment, and then he smiled. "So be it! Abeni releases his servant, but only if the Little Fish will release him as well." Tayna nodded. "Then it is done." Abeni bowed to Tayna and she bowed back. "That is well," he said when the bowing was over. "Abeni already has too many stomachs to feed. Where would he find the gold to feed still another?" He smiled widely then, showing Tayna a vast expanse of teeth, including plenty that were gold. Then he winked, and roared again with laughter.

After a moment, Abeni clapped his hands in a sound like nearby thunder. "If the Little Fish is not to be Abeni's servant, then she must become his friend. Perhaps his new friend would come with Abeni and share a meal with him, after he has delivered his most important message."

"Uh, I'd like to Abeni, but I can't. I have to get back to the Wayitam's place. I was visiting her and I kind of ran out unexpectedly." Then she lowered her eyes and added sheepishly, "Can you point me in the right direction? I'm sort of lost."

Abeni looked at her in frank surprise and then threw back his head and laughed again. "She is lost!" he cried with great merriment. "The Little Fish journeys to the same end as Abeni, who travels from a distant land, but she is lost in her own back yard and asks *him* for help!" As he laughed, he turned her around by the shoulders and pointed. There, coming through the trees to see what all the commotion was about, was a small crowd of villagers. Arin and Winry were in the lead.

———

Since flinging Tayna bodily into the sky with a flick of her arm, Arin had become completely hysterical. She had run like a demon all the way from her dehn to the center of the village—with Winry at her heels—screaming "Help! Help! I've killed her with my powers! She's gone! Her brains have been dashed upon the Anvil by now! Help!"

Elicand had been the first to reach her, and had managed to calm her down only a little before the Wayitam arrived to take over. With the poor woman sobbing and wailing, and Winry chiming in about "turning her left to the right and zoom went the chipmunk from Tayna's flying boot til she esploded all over the sky," it took Lan'ia Sha almost two hours to get a half-ways coherent story, and then to organize a search party. That group had just been setting off, led by the still-flustered grandmother, along Tayna's last-known flight path when the loud laughter of the Djin had drawn them aside to investigate.

Finding Tayna unexpectedly whole and well, Arin had done nothing since but fawn and fuss over her. By Tayna's count, she had received eighteen separate apologies from the woman before the group had even made its way back to the village proper. And every time she mentioned her adventure, Arin's eyes would grow wide, and her head would shake with disbelief.

"It has been ages since I last saw a skimmer," she said at one point. "Nobody's been able to fly anything bigger than a cooking pot since I was a much younger woman. And even then, it took more vim than I've ever held. I am so, so sorry." The old woman reached down and laid a hand gently on Winry's head. "And I tremble to think what might have happened if I'd yelled at the little one here, instead of someone big enough to look out for herself."

Tayna was exhausted from her ordeal, but she did her best to smile reassuringly. "Nobody hurt, nobody dead. I'm okay. Just gotta stop shaking first. And sleep. Don't know why, but terror makes me sleepy." Once back in the Heart, Tayna was trundled quickly off for a long nap, safely tucked back into the dehn from which she had so unceremoniously been ejected only a few hours earlier. But it still felt cozy.

———————

"Guest Tayna! The Wayitam requests a consultation! Will you come?" The voice sounded oddly muffled.

"Not if I have any word in it, she won't. Not until she's rested up proper!"

Tayna rolled over on the bed to see what was going on. Arin stood at the door, holding it shut with both hands to keep the young man out, though he showed no signs of trying to force his way in. Tayna smiled. Something told her she was going to be smothered with motherly concern for at least another day or two. And in her heart, she was actually tickled to death by the idea.

"It's okay, Arin. I'm all napped out. You can let him in."

The old woman looked uncertain, as though not even sure she should let Tayna herself decide what was good for her, but then she sighed. "If you're sure," she grumbled, and let go of the door. But even with Arin no longer offering open resistance, Elicand wasn't prepared to subject himself to her glare, so he repeated his message from outside and waited there until Tayna emerged.

"A consultation? About what?"

But he had no idea. Tayna wasn't exactly feeling a hundred percent, but the nap, which had lasted most of the afternoon, had restored most of her senses, if not her energy. "No arm wrestling, or mountain climbing involved?" Elicand shook his head. "Okay," she said. "Talking won't be too hard. Let's go."

They walked through the trees toward the Wayitam's dehn in relative silence. When they got there, Elicand pulled back the springy doorway and waved Tayna to precede him inside. The dehn was about the same Arin's and it smelled of freshness, like after a rain. Lan'ia Sha, was sitting comfortably against the wall, on a pile of blankets. The Djin sat beside her. Both of them looked up expectantly.

"Come in. Both of you." The Wayitam waved them each to a blanket pile in front of her. "Sit."

"You wanted to see me?" Tayna said as she settled herself into a comfortable position.

Lan'ia Sha gazed at her intently, but said nothing. Tayna couldn't remember ever feeling so completely... studied before in her life. It made her wonder if this was how microscope slides felt. After several awkward moments of scrutiny, the Wayitam sat back.

"You're something of a mystery, I don't mind telling you," she said. "And I don't much care for mystery, but these are mysterious times, so what's a woman to do?" The Wayitam pressed her palms together and tapped the united fingertips slowly against her frowning lips as she weighed her decision.

"I find myself with a growing collection of these mysteries," she said at last. "A king overdue from his ritual quest; a lost girl with no history, who consorts with Watchers, and can fly; and a brother Djin arriving from the Anvil, bound to a mission of honor, and bearing a message from the Djin King." She shook her head at the sheer wonder of it all. "When two trails cross," she said, "that may be accident. But for three to meet? Or six? That speaks of cause." Then she narrowed her eyes and looked straight into Tayna's soul. "And something tells me that, in this case, you are the cause, although I haven't the slightest inkling how or why."

Tayna met the Wayitam's stare levelly. Was she in some kind of trouble again? This was starting to feel like a trial or something. "So what are you going to do with me?"

The old woman shrugged. "Who can say? With all that is going on, I have not had the time to grow an opinion of you for myself, but others have. Your friend here," she said, nodding toward Abeni, "Seems to think that you are honorable, and you've also earned the support of an apprentice story uncle. Weighty endorsements, both of them." Elicand shifted uncomfortably in his seat. "I am not accustomed to being rushed in my decisions, but events have left me little choice, haven't they? The world unfolds faster than I would dictate, so I must rely on what I have. Abeni has come with news of the Quest, and I am most anxious to hear it–we all are–but it was decided that you should hear it with us. Your arrival in the midst of these mysteries can scarcely be coincidence, and by placing you together I expect I will learn as much from you this night as I will from our King."

Tayna gulped silently. "Um, I'm sorry I kept you waiting," she said politely, but she was confused. How did Lan'ia Sha expect to learn anything from him? Wasn't he still missing? Maybe she meant the Djin King.

Then the Wayitam lifted a small package from the folds of her kirfa. "That he should arrive in this manner troubles me greatly, but the time has come for answers." With that she broke the seal and unwrapped the bundle, withdrawing a pathetic little collection of sticks and string. It looked like something Tayna would expect a little boy to have shoved in his pockets, along with a dead frog and some jelly beans. It certainly did not look at all kingly in origin.

Lan'ia Sha brought her hand to her face and whispered over the twigs. Almost instantly, they twisted and shuffled in her hand, tumbling around one another briefly before solidifying into the shape of a small person, who rolled over and sat up. One short length of twig served as the head. Its bark had been stripped and the facial features were little more than slits cut into the revealed wood. The stick-man looked around. And then the eyes fixed upon the Wayitam.

"Oh. Hello, Lan'ia," he said.

The woman lowered her gaze deferentially. "Your Majesty."

Tayna's eyes went wide. Your Majesty? Their king was a stick-man who lived in a river hobo's knapsack?

The stick-figure king barked a high, raspy laugh. "Why so formal? Are the Gnomes visiting again?" Then he seemed to become aware of something important and twisted his little head this way and that before slumping back down on the Wayitam's hand. "Oh, leaf rot!" he exclaimed. "A v'ou du?"

"Yes, my Lord Malkior. If I may be so bold, I ask you to think back upon recent events. We wish to know more about something that befell you only days past."

"Oh, all right. Give me a moment," Malkior said. He squatted down and rubbed at his little twig chin with his little twig hand, lost in thought for a moment. Then he looked up suddenly. "Oh." he said. "I see what you mean about important. Yes. Tell me, how long has it been?"

Abeni leaned forward. "Three days you have ridden in Abeni's pack, placed there by your own Lady's hand, Great King."

Tayna knew what the Wayitam meant by events proceeding faster than she would have liked, and she twisted absently at her wrist now as she tried to follow the conversation. She felt like she had been living this way for a month and events still showed no signs of slowing down. It was like she was running down hill ahead of an idea avalanche and getting buried in it before she'd even had a chance to decide which way it was going. Did this magical twig-king have something to do with their being in a forest? Perhaps he was descended from some Great Tree or something, but she resisted the urge to make guesses just now. It was more important to stay ahead of the avalanche. Now was not the time to inspect each boulder as it went by.

Lan'ia Sha was now asking Malkior to recount what he could recall of recent events. If the king thought it odd that he was being asked to report like some servant, he gave no sign. "Nothing would please me more," he said. "The three of us—Grinyak, Mabundi and myself—climbed the Anvil, along with one companion each of our own kin, as is the custom. But of the six who went up, only five came down."

"Was the ritual completed?" the Wayitam asked anxiously, but the stick man only shook his head, and Tayna saw the woman's shoulders deflate as though she had been punctured. "Who was lost?" she asked, with a sigh. "And how?"

Malkior pounded a fist against her thumb in frustration. "Grinyak, dammit! Fallen into the Anvil's teeth. We do not know how he came to be out there, alone in the night, nor what caused him to fall, but Prince Angiron has decided where to lay his crown of blame."

Tayna stiffened. "Prince? Angiron's a freaking prince?" She was surprised to learn that she'd asked the question out loud.

"What?" Malkior said, a little unaccustomed to being interrupted. "Yes, the First Prince—eldest son of Grinyak—but he'll be a Contender for the Crown now. He left immediately, believing the bones of his father to be irretrievably lost, never to reach the cherished harvest tables of their death wardens." Elicand and the Wayitam both groaned. Apparently that was important.

"That'll put them in a good mood," Elicand said.

The stick king nodded sadly. "It gets worse, young friend. For as I was saying, the Gnome Prince believes that it was no accident—and that it was I who lifted the hand in his father's undoing."

"You?" the Wayitam said. "Why you?"

"Because I was the last who would admit to having seen Grinyak before his demise. And because, when I saw him, we argued."

"Argued? About what?"

Malkior shook his head dejectedly. "What other topic is there?" he asked, then he shrugged. "Grinyak petitioned me yet again to remove the Mourning Dove. It is the only path that has ever led us to quarrel. And now that quarrel can never be resolved. Despite many other sorrows, I grieve now for that lost resolution between us."

Tayna felt the avalanche nipping at her heels. The whole "my enemy just might become the king of all the magical Gnomes" boulder was bouncing along right beside her, and it was hard not to stop and stare at it. The grip of her right hand twisted more feverishly into the skin of her bracelet wrist and she managed to force her attention back to the conversation.

"But what about the Dragon's Peace?" Elicand asked. "How can anyone think you did something to him *before* it failed."

Tayna nodded. She still wasn't too clear on what this Dragon's Peace was all about, but even if Malkior had been able to commit violence, what could a stick man do to a full-grown person? Unless... Were *all* the races ruled by twig royalty? And what would that mean for Angiron? He isn't a stick man. Would he have to become one if he took the throne? Oh, right. Ignore the boulders. Keep running!

"Ah," said Malkior. "That is indeed the question, but Lord Angiron is ambitious, and I suspect having answers to such questions would not suit his cause. He departed for the Throat that very morning, vowing not to return until he could do so as the rightful head of the Gnomileshi Horde. He has vowed to exact payment from me and from any who would follow me." He sighed. "No doubt he seeks to use this to his advantage, to stir his people and aid him in his quest for power."

"Perhaps it is good then that he does not know of the Wagon," Abeni said.

Malkior nodded in agreement. "Perhaps that is to our advantage.

Angiron does not know that the sons of Kijamon were able to recover Grinyak's remains, and that even now, my lamented friend rides the Wagon toward his cherished harvest tables. Perhaps that will be enough. The return of their fallen King may quell any froth of anger that the Contender might otherwise incite among the Horde."

"Such is the hope of King Mabundi," Abeni agreed. "It is why the sons of Kijamon have been bonded to this task, to guide the journey of not one, but two fallen kings." He tapped the iron ring that clanked dully among its gold and silver brethren on his arm. "Abeni is sworn to join his brothers in this great duty when they arrive."

"And if they fail, war may fall upon the Verge shortly thereafter," Malkior said. "So Lady M'Ateliana and I make haste for home, to prepare for the unthinkable. We spread caution to as many as we can along the way, but we must hurry. It has been scarcely a week since Grinyak's fall, but I fear that soon, the Verge may be awash in angry Gnomes, without a Peace to restrain them."

"Then it truly has fallen?" Elicand asked.

In answer, the Wayitam reached out and smacked him firmly on the cheek. The blow echoed in the stunned silence that followed–a blow that would not have been possible had the Peace of the Dragon still been intact. "We learned of this only moments before you arrived," Lan'ia said. "Today is the thirtieth day since the passing of King Jallafa and the quest to reaffirm the Oath has failed. The Peace no longer stands. Violence is once again possible, as it has not been since days long past, and a powerful enemy rises, who is ambitious enough to exploit the situation–to his advantage and our peril."

"For all we know," Elicand added quietly, "the entire forest could already be at war."

There was a brief silence as the implications sank in. After a moment, the little king turned to look up at the Wayitam. "M'Ateliana and I are gathering a council at Bethil Glen. We beg the guidance of your wisdom."

"Of course, my Lord. You shall have it. If war comes, the Heart will be harbor no longer. My people and I will depart before highest light tomorrow to join you."

"Thank you," he said. Then, suddenly the little stick man shuddered. It was a wracking, earthquake of a shudder that seemed to set parts of him rattling from one end to the other. His face snapped around in horror. "Hair? They used hair?"

Abeni hung his face in remorse. "There was no kincraft to oversee a proper cutting, Great King. Only the Lady."

Malkior shrugged. "I suppose it was for the best. At least it–" There was a tiny snapping sound, and then his entire body exploded, raining bits of twig all over the three onlookers.

"Oh my God!" Tayna shouted as she leapt to her feet. "Your king just exploded!" She darted around, trying to collect all the tiny fragments of king-stick from the blankets and the folds of Lan'ia Sha's kirfa. Maybe somebody could put him back together.

Elicand looked helplessly at the Wayitam, who was staring back at him. Then, despite the grimness of the news, they both broke into laughter. Lan'ia Sha reached out and placed a restraining hand on Tayna's arm. "There is no cause for alarm, girl. Do you truly know so little? All is as it should be."

Tayna gaped at her. "Your king is *supposed* to explode? What kind of government system is that?"

The Wayitam smiled and patted Tayna's arm. "No. Of course the king is not supposed to explode. You did not think that this was the actual king, did you? It was a v'ou du–a small copy–made with a tiny piece of our real king and animated by the magic of a kincraft. Exploding happens rarely, but the Lady M'Ateliana is not strong with such magic. A true kincraft would have woven much sturdier craft. Nevertheless, I assure you that the real Lord Malkior is no less Wasketchin than you or I."

Tayna took a deep breath. "Okay," she said. "I get it now, but next time, you might want to hang a couple of signs around the doll's neck."

"Signs?" Elicand asked.

"Yeah. Like, 'Your real king is bigger than this' and 'Warning: Monarch may suddenly explode.'"

Everyone laughed, but it was not for shared joy. The Peace was dead, and soon, the jackals would come to feast on its remains. For the moment, there was only their weak laughter to hold the inevitable at bay.

———————

Dear Shammi:

I don't know what it's like for you, sitting up there in the God-jacuzzi, kicking it righteous and contemplating the brilliant oneness of all your faces, but have you ever had one of those days where you open your sock drawer and a flock of screaming howler monkeys fly out? Where did all that come from, you ask yourself, and what am I going to do about it? But you never get any answers–or socks–just more howler monkeys.

Things are just so crazy! It makes me miss Lies. She always knew how to break off the craziest piece of gibberish at just the right time to crack me up. Without her, I don't think I'd have stayed sane in that madhouse. And I'm not sure how I'm going to do it out here without her. She was always the strong one. I hope she's doing okay. Sure, she's still trapped in that entirely crapadelic hole, but at least she understands the rules and knows what to expect. Ha! I never thought there would be anything about that place to miss, but there it is: knowing the score. One of the great benefits of the boring life, I guess. But somehow they forgot to mention it in the adventure advertising. "Family yours. Peril great. Flee now. Home come. Confusion always." See? Kind of ruins the whole vibe.

Speaking of confusion, sooner or later, somebody around here is going to want some real answers. I only met Elicand this morning and he's already tired of the tap-dancing. Dodging the question isn't going to work for much longer. And then what am I supposed to say? Is Lan'ia Sha going to be happy she invited me to that exploding king party when she finds out I'm some kind of escaped lunatic who thinks she's an a day pass from Hell? And what about Arin? Is she still going to be all gung-ho for me to hang around little Winry when she finds out that I come from a land of make-believe where we lock children in big boxes and yell at them all day? It's like howler monkeys aren't enough all by themselves. Every one of them has to hang an extra job or two around my neck as they're flying by.

Groan. Well, I guess I just can't let them tag me, right? Peril great, and all that... Jeez. Listen to me, taking it all serious and everything. I could really use a clue from you about now. That message was real, right? Not just another crazy orphan's dream? I mean, all that burning, tingly stuff–Veest says that's what flowering feels like. And then the next minute–Bam! –incoming message from space. Like I got a new cell phone and as soon as I turn it on, there's a message waiting. "Tayna? It's your mother. Come home right now. You're in big trouble, Missy." It sounds too real to be just a stupid dream. And if it is real... Oh boy!

Ever since that night in the kitchen, I've been kind of going with what-

ever comes along. Mostly because I didn't have time to think, but now I do. Tomorrow, everyone here is going off to see the wizard. Follow the yellow grass road. Do I go with? Visit the King? That would be the easy thing—just keep bobbing along. But that's not likely to help with peril great, home come, is it? I kinda think I have to make that job number one right now—being all peril-defying and home-comey. So ix-nay on the ing-kay. And just say no to needy little orphans, too. (Sorry Winry!) I've got a job to do. The flee now part is done, but I've got to see it through until the final home come. Then maybe someone else can take the important jobs for a while, and I'll see about starting a doll collection, or whatever it is normal girls my age are supposed to be doing.

Sigh. Did I mention that being the hero sucks?

Keep a dolly warm for me,
T.

All night, Tayna dreamed of howler monkeys.

chapter 10

"Philip. You're mourning la vie," said the howler monkey.

What? Tayna shifted in slumbery confusion as the strange voice repeated itself. "Fill up your morning, lovey." She pulled the blanket down to her chin and opened her eyes cautiously.

Arin was standing beside the bed, with a steaming mug in her hand and an embarrassed smile on her face. Nothing more needed to be said. Today was not going to be like yesterday.

"A good day starts with a full morning," she said. "I made you some boh-choh. Siani P'leth used to tell me that a morning without a cup of my boh-choh was not a morning at all–just night time with added glare."

Tayna smiled sleepily and took the rough clay cup into her hands. It was warmer and heavier than she had expected and its thickness released the mug's heat slowly, which helped to soothe the morning chill from her fingers. Tayna nodded her thanks to the old woman and took a sip. Wow. Flavors unfurled across her tongue like a silk flag, pushing back the murk of sleep. Boh-choh was definitely something to wake up to! It had a sultry sweetness, a bit like chocolate, but tangy too, accompanied by spicy notes, which were even more subtle on her tongue than they had been in her nose. She sighed contentedly.

"So, lovey," Arin said, as she sat on the edge of the bed. "Today's the day. Will you be going to Bethil Glen with the Wayitam?"

Tayna groaned inside. Nothing like getting right down to business, huh? She took another sip.

"Well, if it's any influence to you, that's what Winry and I are doing. That child has really perked up with you around. It's been hard on her since... well, since moving in with a sour old grump like me. She would love for you to come with us." Then the old woman lowered her eyes shyly. "And so would I. You shake things up, dear. You really do. And a good shaking up is something I've needed for a long while now, I think."

Tayna raised her sleepy eyes from the mug, and suddenly the entire room was filled with screaming howler monkeys. The largest of them was leaping up and down, exactly where Arin had been standing only a second earlier. She looked around wildly for a moment, and then the leaping monkey smiled.

"So? Do you think you'll be coming?"

Was she still asleep? Tayna looked down at her right index finger. It was still wrapped around her mug, but now it pulsed with quiet, purple power. The Arin-monkey just sat there patiently. Expectantly. Tayna sighed with relief. The purpleness and the monkeys were only in her head. It was her dream, still talking to her. Yelling at her, actually. It was saying that Arin and Bethil Glen were just more howler monkeys–distractions–and for now, not part of the path she had committed herself to. Going with the flow again would be easy, but she knew it for what it was now. Last night, she had made a promise, to Shammi and to herself–a promise that had to start here.

Tayna reached out gently with her purple finger and touched Arin-monkey on the forehead. The words just came without thinking. "I like her too, Arin. A lot. But I can't be Siani. Not for her and not for you. You know that, right?" Flash. The monkey was gone, leaving only Arin. The purple glow faded from Tayna's finger and the rest of the monkeys just melted away into the morning air, as if they had never been there at all.

The old woman saw none of the light show, of course, and she lowered her eyes, but she was nodding. "You're right, of course," she said softly. "I suppose it just seemed so easy. I mean, there you were– young, and strong, and she likes you so much. . ."

"But my life is full of holes," Tayna said. "And I have to start filling them in now."

"Yes," Arin said, pointing at Tayna's ears. "That mysterious young man of yours." Tayna didn't bother to correct her. "Where will you go, lovey?"

"Tayna? You goin' away?" The blanket on Arin's bed undulated and a little head popped out, still blinking and sleepy.

"I thought you was gonna come with granna an' me to see the King."

Tayna looked down at her little friend and drew in a deep breath. Winry looked up at her with those big saucer eyes, trusting and confused, and looking to her older friend for a comforting answer. Tayna sighed. She felt helpless, but she knew now that there was no such thing as helplessness. It's a delusion–just another word for giving up. For every problem, there is *always* a magical monkey-melting finger waiting to be found. You just had to have the courage to wield it.

"Sorry, pipsqueak, but there's something I've got to do first. Maybe I'll see you there later, okay?" And as hard as it was for her to tear her gaze away from the little girl's slowly trembling lip and crumbling happiness, Tayna forced herself to do just that. Then she turned back to Arin.

"You're right, Arin. I need to find some answers first. I don't suppose there's a Town Records office around here?"

Quietly, beside her, Winry began to sob.

———

Tayna was still feeling a bit glum when she found Lan'ia Sha in her dehn, packing a rather small bag. Breaking Winry's heart was one of the hardest things she'd ever had to do, and the experience had left her in a snarky mood. "That's all you're taking?" she asked, seeing no other luggage around.

Lan'ia Sha looked up and smiled. "What would you have me carry? Some trees? A rock? They have those in plentiful supply at Bethil Glen, just as we do here."

"Well, you must have some stuff. What about your party dress, or a soup pot, or maybe a favorite stick shaped like Veest's knee?" The older woman stood up and slung her pack over her shoulder, testing it for weight.

"Who would need more than a pair of kirfas?" she asked, cocking her head in a bemused fashion. "And I'll have you know that I possess nothing as whimsical as a Veest-like stick." Then she winked. "Mine looks more like a Gnomileshi harvester's blade, don't you think?" She withdrew a small piece of driftwood from a fold of her kirfa and held it out for Tayna to inspect. It did look like a wicked, ritualistic dagger of some kind. Tayna hefted it and then handed it back.

"So that's really it, huh? You're dragging your entire village off too see the king, you don't know how long you'll be gone, or when you're coming back, and you're just going to take a pair of undies and your favorite stick? I thought somebody as important as you would have a whole wagon devoted to her personal trophies and magical brick-a-brac."

The woman gave Tayna an odd look, and then marched to the open door, motioning for Tayna to join her. "I am, of course, taking far more than 'undies and a stick,' " she said. "I'm taking no less than twenty-seven of the things that matter most in the entire Forest." She nodded toward the east where a train of villagers were already making their way through the trees. Arin and Winry were in the group and the grandmother waved briefly, but Winry wouldn't even look in Tayna's direction.

The little girl's disappointment made Tayna's heart sink almost to her stomach. She knew full well that she had made the right decision, and that Winry was going to have to learn that little girls weren't always the center of the world, but that didn't make her feel any less the cowardly villain.

Seeming to sense Tayna's resolve, Lan'ia Sha caused the driftwood knick-knack to disappear back into her kirfa and then turned to address her young visitor. This time, it was the Wayitam, Counselor to the King, who spoke. "I do not know even a tenth as much about you as I should like, but I believe that you are honorable, and I suspect that you know more about living outside the Dragon's Peace than you should. How that can be, I honestly cannot guess, but I've learned to put a little trust in my hunches, and my hunch is that your counsel may prove valuable in this new world of ours, where so many distasteful things now seem possible." Tayna blushed at the unexpected, though uncertain compliment, but it did not shake her decision.

"I'm not going with you," she said. "I've decided on the path I've got to follow, only I'm not sure where it is."

The Wayitam looked at her for a moment, and then she laughed. "Spoken like someone who has spent far too much time with the Watcher," she said. "Tell me about this path of yours then."

"Well, I'm assuming Elicand has filled you in on my story." The Wayitam grunted in a way that suggested that he had, but that she didn't find it a particularly satisfying tale. Tayna pressed on. "Well, I think I have to find my family." She fingered her earlobes and thought about the word. Family. *Family yours.* It occurred to her that it could include husbands too. Ick. She lowered her hand and turned her attention back to the Wayitam.

"Anyway, Arin told me about a place she called the 'Stinkhole,' and that it's somehow full of books about people and their ancestors? I was hoping you could clue me in."

"Aah," Lan'ia Sha said. "Truly, a strange people. Yes, I've heard the tales myself, but few Wasketchin have ever had need of the place. We have family and kincrafts and the story uncles to hold our memories for us. What I have heard–and stories have a way of growing in the retelling, mind you–is that it is one of the most sacred of the Gnomileshi shrines. They, of course, do not call it by such a repulsive name. It is rightly called Igli's Book, or something like that. There they preserve records of all the dead who pass their harvest tables. I suppose you might well find some small answers there, but tell me, what good will that do you? What do Gnomes know of Wasketchin lore? You could always come with us and consult with Nafosh, the royal kincraft. I expect he will be at Bethil Glen, along with all the others."

Tayna dismissed the suggestion with a wave. "Arin told me about the kincraft. Something about family stories with magical finger puppets–like the twig king. But she didn't think he'd be much help if I didn't already know who my family was."

Lan'ia Sha nodded reluctantly. "Perhaps not," she conceded. "But I just don't think it wise for someone so... vulnerable, to go deep into Gnomileshi lands without more of a plan. Especially at such a perilous time."

For the first time since meeting the woman, Tayna got a sense of just how much she seemed to care about people. That, more than anything else, gave her a sense of just how much stress the Wayitam had been under while waiting for news of the royal quest. She found herself wanting to set the woman's mind at ease.

"Actually, I won't be alone," she said. "I'm going with Abeni."

The old woman raised an eyebrow at that. "How curious," she said. "He mentioned nothing of it when I asked him to take the boy along." Tayna grimaced. Elicand was going, too? She wasn't sure how she felt about that. Would Abeni have room for another freeloader when he'd already been saddled with one? Well, she wasn't about to take no for an answer. He'd just have to make room.

Then the Wayitam paused and turned to face her. "This is where we must part then, it would seem." She indicated the straggling end of the train of Wasketchin, most of which had already disappeared into the trees. "Your Djin friend will guide you well, and he knows far more of Igli's Book than I do. He's actually been there, you know." Tayna's pulse raced a little. He had? The Wayitam smiled at that, then she leaned in to whisper in Tayna's ear. "Don't worry child. I'm sure he will agree to take you."

The older woman turned away to join her people, and Tayna flushed a little at how easily the Wayitam had seen through her pathetic attempt to sound all in control and on top of things, but she was pretty happy just the same. She stood there and watched until Lan'ia Sha and the rest of the villagers had disappeared completely into the forest, then she turned to survey the silent village.

Now all she had to do was convince Abeni to take her. And that would be a heck of a lot easier if she could actually find him. After criss-crossing the villagy patch of forest three times, all she'd managed to turn up was his great leather travel sack. He had tucked it neatly up against a log bench in the communal cooking area, but so far, that's all she'd found. The entire village population was now on the road to Bethil Glen with the Wayitam, leaving nothing here to find but their silence, which might have been almost creepy if it hadn't been so darned peaceful. So, having exhausted all the places she could think to look, Tayna dropped herself down onto one of the log benches to wait. Sooner or later, Whale-Who-Walks would have to come back for his bag. She smiled to herself. Whale-Who-Walks. That wasn't bad. She was deep in thought trying to come up with a few more poke-names like that, when a series of high-pitched grunts interrupted her scheming.

"Unk! Ert! Ip!"

Tayna looked around. The village was completely still, but the sound persisted, apparently unaware that there was nobody around to be making it.

"Rak! Ayt! Nif!"

On the grass beside her, Abeni's bag twitched. It happened so quickly that Tayna wasn't even sure it had actually moved, and she stared hard at the heap of worn leather. Had it really moved? Or had that flicker just been a bubble of what Lies called "imagination gas?"

The bag twitched again.

This time, it was accompanied by a loud, "Yak!" and Tayna could only watch with bemused fascination as a small, furry butt wriggled its way out of the bag's open neck. The legs attached to the butt were still mostly inside the bag, planted firmly against the side of the log to give purchase, as their owner strained to pull something out. The tufty brown rump wiggled in the air as the legs heaved again.

"Wrrrr-r-r-r! Gnarrr-r-r-r!" Suddenly, the entire furry body shot out of the bag–"Kyap!"–and rolled across the grass, accompanied by glimpses of yellow metal and a clanking sound. The tangle of fur and gold came to rest several yards away, and lay there on the ground, panting and clinking. One furry little arm drooped exhaustedly to the grass, to reveal a gleaming gold chain, clutched beneath the other, held tightly to the matted brown fur of the sneak-thief's chest.

Tayna laughed as she leaned down over the little miscreant. "Don't you think that's a bit big for somebody your size?" she asked. "The guy who owns that could eat you and your entire family as a snack." Tayna reached a hand out for the chain. "Maybe we'd better–"

Just then, two brilliant green eyes snapped open and blinked at her. She was immediately struck by a sense of warm, friendliness–and more than just a little mischief. His eyes were each ringed by a cone of stiff brown fur–making the little guy look for all the world like a koala doing an impression of a barn owl. Lower down, a thick band of darker fur framed his mouth in a great handlebar mustache. But before Tayna could process the full comedy of his appearance, the excitable little felon clutched his hard-won treasure tightly to his chest and leapt to his feet.

"Fun play! Fun play!" he shouted, and then he turned tail and ran off between the log benches, trailing two feet of golden chain behind him that bounced and jingled as he ran.

"Hey! Come back here!" Tayna jumped to her feet and ran to cut off his escape route.

"Pikabu!" shouted the thief, and Tayna's ears were filled with the sound of soda-pop fizz as she leapt over the benches .

"Peek-a-boo yourself, you little munchkin!" she snarled, but even as her feet hit the grass on the other side of the bench, there was already a hole growing in the pit of her stomach, draining all her happy away. There was no sign of the thief or his booty. Either booty. Somehow, he'd gotten away clean.

———————

"Um, Abeni? About your mother's wedding chain... No, that's not it. Too blunt. *Oh, by the way big guy... You remember that choice piece of bling you had stashed in your giant man-purse? Funny story about that..."*

It was an hour or so later and Tayna still hadn't figured out how she was going to explain the bizarre theft, nor her complete failure to stop it. She was still searching for the right angle when Abeni suddenly barged out of the trees.

"The Little Fish is here!" he cried, and threw his arms open wide in greeting. "Abeni is happy to see her!" Then he stopped short and looked around, taking in the utter silence with a broad glance. "Why did she not go with her people to visit the King?"

Tayna glanced down at the leather bag, still lying open on the ground beside her, and then back up at the big, trusting Djin face. She sucked in a deep breath and stood up. Like band-aids, right? She gave her bracelet wrist a quick jerk. Better to just get it over with.

"Look, Abeni, I came here to ask if you would take me with you on this wagon ride deal or whatever, because Lan'ia Sha told me you were heading to Gnomelandia or whatever they call it and I need to get to Igli's Book to look up my parents, who are kind of missing, but I don't know how to get there, so I was going to ask you to drop me off on your way by, only you weren't here, so I sat down to wait for you and then–Bam! –this little ninja squirrel appears out of, like, freaking nowhere, and before I know it, he's got your family fortune in his furry little mitts and he's running for the hills going grunt, squeak, wheeze, and I am so totally going after him, you know, 'cuz what's a friend supposed to do, right, but he starts yelling these squeaky little nursery rhymes at me and before I can figure out what *his* damage smells like– Poof!–there he was, gone, so now here's me, worried you'll think I took it, but I didn't, only how could that matter, because I had the chance to stop him and I blew it, so it really is all my fault anyway and, like, now you're gonna refuse to even talk to me, let alone take me to the Book placey place, and that's okay, I mean, I totally understand, but I don't know what I'm gonna do, either, because I pretty much don't know anybody else around here, except for that creepy Veest guy and we all know how reliable he turned out to be, so I'll probably just wander the forest blindly and do babysitting for table scraps until someone finally feels sorry enough to put me out of my misery, but if Grimorl really is Hell, then we all know that that's going to wind up all nuns, all the time, multiplied by, like, a bajillion, but that's my problem not yours. So will you?"

Abeni just stood there for a moment, blinking slowly as he looked at her, sifting through her blurt-spree, trying to make sense of it. But to her surprise, he did not laugh, and he did not seem to be angry.

"Yes," he said.

Tayna's eyes widened in surprise. Yes? Had he actually heard everything she'd said? After all, it really had been kind of a firehose. But the Djin nodded at her reassuringly. "What the Little Fish does is most important," he said. "To restore her family–nothing could be greater than this. If she must go to the bone house of the Gnomes to do it, then the sons of Kijamon will light her path." And then he touched his wrists together in front of his face, and bowed over them in some form of salute.

"And you heard everything I said, right? About your gold, and about the fuzzy guy and all that?"

Now Abeni threw back his head and bellowed with laughter. "This thief was as tall as her knee, was he not? Covered in fur and filled with great energy?"

Tayna nodded. "You know him?"

Abeni grinned. "He is Shondu, the chalat. Very hard to catch. The Little Fish must not worry. Not even Abeni can catch him when he jumps, but he will return. And then the Little Fish will see how Abeni deals with such things."

The way his eyes twinkled with anticipation when he said it made Tayna wince. Nobody deserved to have to face an angry Djin. She found herself hoping that the little guy was miles away by now, with no intention of ever coming back.

⁓

Tayna fell in behind Abeni's broad back, hypnotized by the leather travel bag that bounced gently left and right in time with his great strides.

"So why are you going to see the Gnomes, exactly?" she asked, as they made their way up one of the steep hills that ringed the Heart of the Verge.

In answer, the Djin raised his left arm to display a collection of gold and silver bracelets. They clinked together musically, but one darker ring clanked cheaply against its neighbors "Abeni is bonded to the Wagon," he said. "As are all the sons of Kijamon. There can be no other task for any of them until that duty is complete and the Wagon has been delivered to the harvest tables of the Gnomes."

"Bonded? As in 'tied to?' "

Abeni shook his head. "A bonded task is a great honor for Abeni. To fail is to bring shame to all Djin everywhere—especially to Abeni's family. Besides," he said, dropping his voice into a loud stage whisper, "Abeni much prefers the sound of gold and silver." He raised his arm again and shook it to emphasize the point. "Black iron sings an ugly song."

"Cool," Tayna said as she clambered over a fallen tree that the Djin had simply stepped over. "So, what, you get to take it off when you're done, and put on a gold one?"

Abeni whirled around and gaped at her, horrified. "No Djin would do such a thing! To remove a bond ring is a great crime. The Little Fish dishonors Abeni with such a suggestion."

Tayna back-pedaled quickly. "I'm sorry," she said. "I didn't mean to jerk your chain, but how do you switch them if you can't take them off?"

"Abeni has been properly bonded," he said with pride. "The Dragon will know when the task is done." And that seemed to be all the explanation necessary. The Djin turned back to to the task of leading her up the hill.

"So what makes this trip so important?" Tayna asked. The steep climb was beginning to take its toll on her calves and to tire her out.

"It is the Trail of Two Fallen Kings," Abeni called back, enthusiastically. "In all of history, such a Trail has never been warded."

"And these dead kings... They're actually inside this Wagon? And delivering it is supposed to stop a war?"

"That, too. Yes," Abeni agreed, laughing.

Tayna was trying to picture a cart loaded with the bodies of dead kings, and how that was going to stop a war, when suddenly, a loud shriek sounded from the branches above them, and a blurry rocket of brown hurtled out of concealment, headed straight for Abeni's head.

"Look out!" Tayna cried, and ran forward to push the Djin out of the way, but he was higher up the hill than she was and she ended up falling against the backs of his knees, which did just enough to his stability that when the brown fur-rocket made contact, all three of them went tumbling down into a heap. Tayna wound up trapped firmly beneath one of Abeni's enormous legs. She pounded and heaved against the dark mountain of meat that held her down, terrified that Abeni was unconscious with that little Shindig character eating his head or something. The leg on top of her jerked spasmodically and Tayna went nuts. He was! He was eating Abeni! Or he had jabbed a stick in through the big guy's ear or something. Only direct, physical brain scrambling could cause those kinds of convulsions!

Then she heard the deep, boom of thunder, and a moment later, the darkness rolled aside, off her face, and she recognized the thunder for what it was: a scream of battle rage.

"So! The great brown fur-eagle thinks to attack Abeni again, does he?"

Tayna looked around quickly to see Abeni with both powerful arms wrapped tightly around the little thief, who struggled and strained to get free. There was no way such a tiny body could stand up to those arms, not for a minute, and without even thinking, Tayna flung herself across the Djin, grabbing his arm by one of the gold bands and heaving for all she was worth.

"No, Abeni! No! You can't kill him! It was just a chain! What would Kijamon say? It isn't a fair fight!"

Slowly, the big Djin's arms came down, and two sets of eyes peered at her–one brown, the other green. Then they looked at each other and laughed–Abeni, with his deep, musical drum laugh, while the furry munchkin had a rapid, high-pitched giggle that sounded like a five-year-old on helium.

It occurred to Tayna that this might not be a death match after all. In fact... She pushed the Djin's massive forearm out of the way to be sure. Yup. It was a tickle fight.

"I take it he is not your sworn enemy then?"

Abeni brought the rough-housing to an end by ruffling Shondu's belly one last time, and then he placed the little guy up onto his own, broad shoulder. His new passenger seemed familiar with the proce-dure, and happily grabbed onto the ring that dangled from Abeni's ear, for stability.

"Does the Little Fish not remember?" Abeni asked. "Shondu is the chalat. A Brownie."

Tayna nodded. "I remember the words," she said. "But they don't mean anything to me. What's a 'chalat?'"

"It is a Djin word," he replied. "It has many meanings–'partner,' 'helper,' 'pet'–all at one time."

Tayna and Abeni got back to their feet and dusted themselves off while Shondu simply hung on to the earring and enjoyed the ride.

"He's your partner?" Tayna said, incredulously, as they got them-selves pointed back up the hill and resumed their climb. "How does that work, exactly? You carry him from town to town, and he con-tributes what? Mischief lessons for the local children?"

"Oho! Many would take lessons from such a Great Master!" the Djin said. "But Shondu does not teach. He is Abeni's protector."

That brought Tayna to a dumbfounded halt. "*He* protects *you*?"

Abeni seemed amused by Tayna's confusion. "Certainly!" he said. "Brownies are revered throughout the forest for their great skill in the face of danger."

"And that skill is...?"

Abeni smiled. "Why, running away of course!"

Tayna smiled. That part made sense, anyway. Shondu was pretty small, and with his attitude, probably got lots of practice at making quick escapes. "But how does that help you?" she asked. "He can't exactly carry you on his back."

"Not in the way the Little Fish means," Abeni agreed. "But the chalat indeed takes Abeni far away, if Abeni is quick with the pikabu when danger comes." Tayna actually pulled Abeni around so he could see her, and then she pointed at her face, loaded with as much disbelief as she could muster. Abeni smiled. "Like this," he said, then he opened the travel sack and pulled it down over his head.

Tayna rolled her eyes. "Oh yeah, right," she said. "I can see it now. The pits of hell spit out a hundred warriors to attack and little ol' me turns to face them while big strong you pulls a bag over his head and throws his puppy at them. We're saved! You're my hero."

Abeni pulled the sack down off his head, still grinning affably. "The Little Fish mocks what she does not understand," he said. "It is the pikabu. Does she not remember? The jewelry thief who vanishes in the blink of an eye? Shondu can jump to the pocket at any time, but he must use the pikabu to bring Abeni with him." He gestured toward the empty sack in his hand. "The doorway to the pocket." Her sustained don't-try-that-crap-with-me look encouraged him to elaborate. "Shondu's pocket is very dark and very far from here," he said. "Where it is, no one can say, but it is far enough that no danger can easily follow."

Tayna looked at Shondu, who blinked happily back at her from his seat next to Abeni's head.

"Now that is something I'd like to see," she said. "I suppose it would make you one heck of a spectacular get-out-of-jail-free card, wouldn't it little guy?"

A muffled sound from the chalat, somewhere between a cat's purr and the cooing of a dove, was more than answer enough.

When they reached the top of the hill, Abeni turned and flashed her a toothy smile. "Behold! The sons of Kijamon!"

Tayna's eyes sparkled. She couldn't wait to meet Abeni's brothers. "Any sons of Kijamon have gotta be friends of mine," she said. Beyond Abeni, at the bottom of the hill, she could see three more Djin busily rearranging boxes and bundles on the grass beside an absolutely enormous wagon. No two of the men below seemed to speak the same dialect of body language, but even from the top of the hill, the family resemblance was unmistakable.

Abeni led her down the hill to stand at the head of the Wagon, where he made introductions. "The largest and ugliest is Abeni's eldest brother, Zimu," he said, indicating an enormous hulk of a Djin, even bigger than himself, who nodded a silent greeting as he worked. His chest was banded with heavy knots of muscle upon muscle. On impulse, Tayna stepped forward and tried to hug him, but she couldn't even come close to getting her arms around Zimu's steely musculature. It was like trying to hug a mountain, but this mountain smiled widely in acknowledgment of the attempt. Tayna realized then how lucky the Wasketchin were to be on peaceful terms with these people.

"Next to him," Abeni continued, "In rank, in birth order, and especially in lack of beauty, is Sarqi." This brother, while still tall, was almost skinny by Djinnish standards, which just made him look even taller. As Tayna attempted to repeat her greeting hug, Sarqi recoiled, but after a glare from Abeni, he squared his shoulders and accepted her unorthodox welcome, although he remained rigid throughout the experience, and broke away as quickly as he felt politeness–or Abeni–would permit.

Then Abeni turned to the last brother. "The littlest one who, fortunately for him, is almost as handsome as Abeni, likes to be called Hambu," Abeni said.

Tayna smiled at the small Djin, but his arms were too loaded with packages to attempt a hug. "Likes to be called?" she said. "What's that all about?"

Judging by his grimace in response to the question, his name was a topic that arose too frequently for the youngest Djin's tastes. He shrugged sheepishly. "Because, friend-of-my-brother, the longer path of my name is 'Hamunijabu,'" he said, "Which means 'Keeper of Pimples' in the old tongue. And some people," he paused to rake his brothers with an accusing gaze, "take far too much delight in reminding me of it." The other Djin laughed uproariously, Then Zimu threw a damp cloth that smacked Hambu on the side of the head and then clung there for a moment before dropping to the grass at his feet.

Tayna laughed. There was an honest fun in the banter of these brothers, regardless of how oddly matched they appeared to be, and it was a kind of fun she could only envy. She didn't even want to think about how much trouble the four of them must have gotten into as kids. But wait a tick. Tayna paused and then snapped her gaze around the group quickly, from bulging bicep to bulging bicep. Then she turned to Abeni with a sly smile growing at the corners of her mouth.

"Hold on, Whale-Who-Laughs. Something's a little out of whack here. How come Little Hambu doesn't have a bond-ring?"

Abeni stared at her in surprise. Then he roared with laughter and turned to his brothers. "You see?" he cried out happily. "Did Abeni not say that she would penetrate this glamor?" Then he turned and nodded to Hambu, who fumbled at his collar. With a sudden jerk of his hands, the Djin physique vanished, leaving only Elicand standing in its place, by comparison, looking almost as skinny and fragile as stick-Malkior. He was grinning sheepishly and clutching a pendant made of yellow metal.

"I forgot all about the bond ring," he said. "I'll have to figure out how to add one." If he was disappointed at being so easily discovered, he didn't let on.

Tayna was still gawking at the sudden transformation. "How did you–?"

Elicand grinned and hefted the gold chain, from which a circular pendant hung, bumping gently against his forearm. "It's called a pre-tendant," he said. "They used to be really common, back before the magic started to fade. Parents used to give them to little kids, long before they flowered. It was a way for them to experience magic on their own and to learn about wonder in the world. Not many of them left, these days. Not in the hands of kids, anyway."

"It was given to Abeni," the big Djin said. "when he was small."

"Stolen, you mean. It was actually mine," Sarqi complained. "And you were never small."

"Complain not, little brother," Zimu added. "It was mine even before it passed to you, but perhaps losing it is why you are still small. Would you like it back?"

Tayna ignored the banter and returned her attention to Elicand. "But why a disguise?"

Elicand shrugged. "I want to get the true experience of being a Wagon Warder," he said. "And Warders are always Djin."

"So wearing a disguise is going to make you feel different?"

"No," he said, shaking his head. "But it will change how other people feel. Wearing the pretendant, I am just another Djin Warder, but without it, I become a spectacle: the disgraced story uncle, and breaker of the Djin tradition. What I would experience then would not be the traditional experience of a Warder–only that of a freakish curiosity. It would ruin everything."

"Disgraced?" Tayna asked, before she could rein in her tongue.

Elicand winced, but he nodded. "You haven't heard? That's why I'm not going with the Wayitam to see the king. I've been sent away."

The Djin brothers were suddenly busy with their tasks, not wanting to embarrass their new "assistant" by hearing his confession of defeat. Tayna put a hand on his shoulder. "Oh. Sorry. That doesn't seem fair. It wasn't your fault you messed up the tree thing. That was all me."

But Elicand shook his head. "It was more than that, I think. That was just kind of like the last leaf on the pile."

There didn't seem to be much point in arguing about it, so Tayna changed the topic. She reached out and touched the yellow metal pendant wrapped around his fist.

"What if you get caught though? Won't you be in trouble?"

"Why would I?" Elicand replied, with a shrug. "If the real Warders don't mind, who else is there to complain? Although, even if there were complaints, I would still be going. Being a story uncle is in my blood. I don't know what kind of work I'll end up doing, but I'm always going to collect and tell stories. And the one thing a story teller craves more than anything else in the Forest is a new experience to add to his list. I've never heard of anyone who's ever done anything like this before. The Trail of Two Fallen Kings? It should be a great tale."

Then his face brightened. "Hey, have you ever seen the Wagon up close?" Tayna shook her head. "I thought not. Come take a look. It's pretty amazing."

Elicand moved to the Wagon's side and ran a hand almost reverently along the polished stone siderail. "They say, 'Touch not the Wagon, save with the hands of grief,' but that only applies when it's in motion."

Tayna had to take a step back to see the whole thing. It was enormous, and horrendously over-built. Its size and shape gave it a distinctive profile–one that was apparently famous and immediately recognizable all throughout the forest. The frame was carved from solid granite, topped with rows of cylinders that Elicand called "sky chambers." And those were the most unusual part.

Arranged in three courses on each side, the cylinders projected above the top of the frame and provided a majestic cap to its silhouette. Each chamber was over two feet wide and six feet deep, standing almost upright, but tilted out slightly from true vertical, with its upper end open to the air. At each village that needed it, Elicand explained, the Wagon would stop, while the body of the recently departed was placed into an empty chamber. This was apparently how every resident of Methilien expected to take their final journey–on the Wagon with their faces raised to the sky, in a salute to the wonders of life.

And when that path at last reached its conclusion, deep in the Throat of the Forest, they would receive their final release at the hands of the Gnomileshi death wardens, transformed from a simple, fleshly shell into the very stuff of magic itself. It all sounded weirdly complex, but sort of natural, too, Tayna thought. Like magical recycling. Very neat and tidy.

Elicand recounted all this as he walked slowly around the structure, running his hands over its famous features and speaking in hushed, respectful tones. It seemed to Tayna as though he was garbing himself in the kirfa of the Wagon's history, borrowing the nuances of its mystique to bind himself more completely to it, align himself with the sons of Kijamon, who, unlike him, had been steeped in that history since birth.

She followed along behind him, listening to his stories in fascination until she suddenly noticed the Wagon's base. "Hey, there are no wheels," she said, pointing to the ground where the Wagon rested on long, silver runners. Abeni's brothers looked up sharply in curiosity. To them, it was as though she had announced with great surprise that the sky was blue and the forest a rainbow. How could she not know such things?

Zimu's eyes widened, but Sarqi actually snorted in disgust. "It needs no wheels!" he spat, his tone dripping with scorn. "Any fool knows that the Wagon of Tears floats upon the Way Chanter's song. Wheels would be an abomination! Would you want your body's last experience of the world to include having its organs churned into butter by the constant shaking of a wheeled journey across desolate, dragon-blasted lands?"

Tayna cringed a little and shook her head, but Abeni came to her rescue, stepping in quickly to tell his brothers what he knew of her story–of her recent return from a distant land, where she had been isolated from the culture and traditions of her people, and that, sadly, this had included ignorance of the Wagon and its rich history.

"And what is more," Abeni added, sensing that this was the right time to broach the subject, "The Little Fish has decided that she will now correct this tragedy. She joins the sons of Kijamon upon the Trail of Tears."

"Bah!" Sarqi barked derisively. "The girl is totally unsuitable–she has no lore!"

Zimu, on the other hand, dismissed Sarqi with a wave of his hand.

"There is no law save that of the Wagon itself," he said. "It will accept her or it will not. And should it do so, who are we to say else?" He looked pointedly at Sarqi, who turned away quickly, muttering to himself. Not exactly a fun-at-parties kind of guy, Tayna noted. But if there was to be some kind of test, nobody told her what it was.

In fairly short order, the loading was finished, and Zimu announced that the Wagon was ready to resume its journey. The quartet of warders moved quietly to take up their positions near the Wagon–Abeni in front, Zimu and Elicand, who was once again draped in the guise of "Hambu," on either side. Sarqi brought up the rear. Tayna just kept herself out of the way and watched the proceedings. She had no idea how this "approval" was supposed to happen, but she held her breath and waited. Hopefully, it didn't involve trial by flaming pants or anything. She'd had enough weirdness lately.

From the rear position, Sarqi began to sing. It was a low, sorrowful lament and the Wagon shuddered in response, lifting smoothly into the air, and then gliding forward in total silence. Had there been a test? Was she approved? She couldn't tell. The procession had almost disappeared into the trees when "Hambu" finally turned around and waved an arm.

"Come on!" he shouted. "What are you waiting for? If it was going to reject you, it wouldn't have lifted off the ground!"

Tayna grinned and ran to catch up.

chapter 11

Now that she had decided to take charge of this little adventure her life had become, Tayna was more determined than ever to get a handle on anything and everything that happened around her. Dumb-assed ignorance was getting to be a real pain–there was no telling how many useful clues she might be walking past *right now*, simply because she didn't know enough to recognize them for what they were. So, as the entourage made its way through the Forest, she seized the opportunity, and filled the air with a steady hum of questions. Her only exposure to death in Grimorl had been her weekly trips to Gruesome Harvest, the crematorium run by the Goodies, and that had consisted of shuttling back and forth between the rear service door and the taxi, carrying urns as they were thrust out to her by some nameless hairy-armed nun. To be honest, most of what little she knew of death came from movies and TV–scarcely what you might call "intimate experience with the hereafter." This Wagon deal, on the other hand, was about as intimate as you could get. There were actually real, live, dead bodies in this thing.

Maybe her fascination was gruesome, but if they thought so, the Warders said nothing. They just answered her as best they could, though it soon became obvious that Sarqi wasn't taking part. Not because he was a cranky and ill-tempered person–though he was that–but because he was far too busy. Sarqi was the Way Chanter, responsible for the continuous singing of the flotation charm that held the Wagon aloft and kept it skimming over the ground in all its smooth, quiet dignity. The job was apparently so engaging that even the simple task of talking had to be left to his brothers, who were busy enough with their own tasks, but could at least spare the occasional comment.

"When a Djin king dies," Abeni explained. "There is much feasting and merrymaking. The newly dead linger between the stars for a time, to observe and remember the living, before crossing over to Grimorl."

Zimu, who was listening intently between the incessant *Swik! Swik!*

of his Way Maker's whip, chimed in. "It is an important time," he said. "It is said that what they witness then sets the mood for the eternity of their Grimorl-life. *Swik!*" His whip darted out and snapped a large stone from the path in front of Sarqi's feet. Tayna held her tongue. All this Grimorl talk—what would they say if they knew that she was *from* there? With Zimu's attention now caught up in clearing Sarqi's path, Abeni continued.

"So the living must celebrate with great joy," he said. "To a Djin, weeping over the loss of a friend is most disrespectful. That is why one full month must pass before the Djin elders will summon the Wagon for a fallen king. We must wait until the spirit of the king has tired of the festivities and moved on."

However busy he might be, Sarqi just couldn't resist adding his own unique perspective at that particular point. "Otherwise," he said. "Some stupid clod might run up to the Wagon and doom him to an eternity of torment by singing one of those depressing Wasketchin funeral songs." But even that was too much of a distraction and he had to return quickly to his charm song as the Wagon suddenly sank toward the ground.

The other brothers carried on, sharing the explanation between them, about how escorting the king on his last journey was one of the highest honors a Djin could expect. For such a task, anyone would accept the iron bond ring with great pride and much boasting to his friends. Then, Zimu admitted, he would no doubt proceed to worry himself sick, contemplating the floods, the landslides and any of the million or so other things that might conceivably go wrong on the Wagon Trail. Honor aside, it was hard to imagine a more nerve-wracking way to earn a gold band. Or a more shameful way to earn rust-stained wrists if you failed. King-warding was about as stressful a job as any they could think of. And this particular time, it was even moreso, because this time, the sons of Kijamon didn't just have the honor of their dead king to protect.

They had *two* dead kings to worry about.

When newly crowned King Mabundi had returned from the failed Oath ceremony at the top of the Anvil, the three brothers had been preparing to set out as warders on King Jallafa's Wagon Trail, but Mabundi was apparently not satisfied that this was sufficient honor for House Kijamon. So he assigned them all an even greater task with which to begin their journey: recovering the so-called "irretrievable" body of King Grinyak. Mabundi had hoped that if the Gnomileshi

King could be returned to his people and given his proper rites and ceremonies, their First Prince might be mollified into letting go of his thirst for vengeance. With so much at stake, Kijamon himself had insisted on accompanying his sons on this first task, and had proved instrumental in devising the method by which they finally did manage to recover Grinyak's body. Then, in accordance with the instructions Mabundi had given them, they placed Grinyak into the Wagon alongside King Jallafa. It was a gesture of utmost respect that the two great leaders should set out thus upon their final journey, in precisely the same way that they had ruled their respective portions of the world–as peaceful, dignified neighbors

Time, however, was pressing, and if there was to be any chance of averting a war, the Wagon had needed to set out at once. But who now would guide it? Somebody still had to see Kijamon safely home, which was a journey in the opposite direction. If left to get himself back down off the mountain top alone, Kijamon, who was old and much more frail than he liked to admit, would almost certainly have died in the attempt. So in the end, the four Djin settled on a bold plan. The older brothers would begin the Trail at once, without benefit of a Way Finder. This would leave Abeni free to accompany their father safely home, and from there, he would then join the Wagon by the faster wild-water route, arriving at the Heart of the Verge ahead of them, where he could then prepare the way for a swift journey beyond. It was a risky plan– the Wagon had never journeyed with only two Warders before. Such prideful risk-taking might even offend the Dragon himself, and subvert the ancient covenant that had always protected warders upon the Trail from harm. But these were desperate times and there seemed no other, safer course to follow.

So Zimu and Sarqi were sent out on the next leg of their journey alone, without a guide. Still, despite this handicap, the two of them had managed to reach the rendezvous only a single day behind Abeni, despite having to share the jobs of three men between them, through the ruggedest, most mountainous terrain in all of Methilien. By the time they arrived, Abeni was ready with their additional supplies. The whole thing had been handled so efficiently that the entire stopover had taken less than a half hour, which was exactly the kind of competence that had earned the sons of Kijamon their exemplary reputations among the Djin.

As the day wore on, Tayna became aware that the story uncle wasn't saying much. He was listening, obviously, but his attention was focused more on what the brothers were doing than on what they were saying. Maybe he was hoping to pick up a new career. Tayna caught his eye and gave him a big grin, nodding at the lightning-fast whip that had so completely mesmerized him. Elicand grinned back sheepishly. Clearly, they were both fascinated by the strange brothers, who made everything look so easy. According to Zimu, the job *was* easy. At least in theory. Guide the Wagon from village to village, collect the waiting Seekers, make sure that the proper respect was shown to the Wagon and its passengers, and try not to run into any trees or fall off any cliffs while doing it.

"Of course, no task is ever as easy as the describing of it sounds," he said. "Nobody ever says what 'proper respect' might mean. It *sounds* like it means, 'Do not let children put dead frogs in the chambers,' or, 'Keep Gnomes from tying claim strings to the choice body parts.'"

Sarqi grunted his annoyance. "Oh, fracture! That's all we need— claim stringers!"

Abeni nodded his agreement, and when Tayna raised an eyebrow at him, he went on to explain. "On every Trail," he said, "There is at least one such Gnome, too eager to wait for the Seekers to reach the harvest tables."

Zimu frowned. "They try to beat their brothers in laying claim to a prize tooth or finger while it still lies within the very Wagon. It is very undignified." The tongue of his whip snaked out and jolted a dead branch from the path with a "Snap!" that seemed to underscore his feelings about such over-eager body harvesters.

Throughout the entire afternoon, Sarqi kept up his raspy tune without break, save for the occasional cutting remark that he was unable to keep bottled up. Tayna was sure that there were many times when the sour-faced Djin must have been struggling to keep his thoughts to himself and his mind on his responsibilities. His song was the only thing that kept the Wagon off the ground and moving forward, although in Sarqi's case it was hard to even call it a song. It sounded more like a rope being pulled through a pile of leaves and branches, full of hissing and snapping. It might have been better described as an aria from an opera sung by injured snakes. But when it came to charms, quality was not what mattered, it was heart, and because he was a son of Kijamon, Sarqi had more than enough of that. His job did indeed come first, so his pleasure at adding caustic side-comments to the conversation was held to a minimum and the Wagon stayed on course and out of trouble.

If the Way Chanter served as the legs of the Wagon, then the Way

Maker might be called its hands. Sarqi's task was so completely absorbing, and his attention so thoroughly riveted on the Wagon itself, that he had little time to even watch his own feet or the ground in front of them. If it wasn't for Zimu, he'd have tripped, stumbled or outright fallen at least a dozen times in every hour. And to hear the brothers talk, even one such distraction would surely have caused the Wagon to spin wildly out of control, strike an upturned tree root and burst into spectacular pillars of flame. But each time disaster seemed imminent, there was trusty Zimu–*Swik! Swik!*–clearing the obstruction and making way for his younger brother. Sometimes he even stepped in to guide Sarqi by the elbow, around a shallow depression or protruding rock that couldn't be cleared. The Way Maker's task may have been a bit less absorbing than the Way Chanter's, but it was far more physically demanding. At least three times, Tayna and Elicand stood aside to watch in fascination as the enormous Djin raced ahead, bent an entire tree to one side and then stood there, straining against its relentless pull for several long moments while first the Wagon and then Sarqi himself made their way by, completely oblivious to his efforts. It was no wonder Zimu was so big. Some of those trees were as big around as Tayna herself.

Of the three brothers, the most talkative by nature was also the one whose job afforded him the most mental leisure for conversation. Abeni's task was that of the Way Finder–the eyes of the Wagon. While his brothers had their attention focused on what was immediately in front of them, Abeni's eyes were turned outward, scanning the horizon and the landscape, looking for the least taxing path to their next goal. On some few occasions, Zimu would make a quiet churking noise in his throat and Abeni would appear almost miraculously at his side, ready to lend a hand. Each time, he seemed to know instinctively what needed to be done, and he did it, with scarcely a word exchanged on the matter.

That was really the most intriguing thing about the whole business, Tayna decided–the effortlessness–the grace and almost eerie silence with which the brothers negotiated obstacle after obstacle, rarely having to resort to more than a nod or a hand gesture to coordinate their efforts. If it hadn't been for her non-stop questions, the entire day might have passed with little more than a grunt and smile passing between them. It was a natural bond of elegance and efficiency, and not for the first time in her life, Tayna found herself wishing she had siblings.

By early afternoon, the rhythm of the Djins had become almost hypnotic. The conversation had tapered off, and Tayna had joined Elicand in just observing their quiet grace. But even the most fascinating rhythm eventually begins to repeat, and while the graceful ballet of interactions between the three Djin brothers was truly a marvel, watching them execute endless variations on the theme became less and less fascinating. Confident that he had now absorbed about as much as he could concerning the day-to-day handling of the Wagon through forest, Elicand allowed himself to fall behind a bit, joining Tayna, who had slowed to examine the wondrous assortment of colors taken by the trees and plants through which their path wound. She looked up and smiled a greeting at "Hambu" as he approached.

"It's so nice to see them like this," she said.

He couldn't hide his bias. "What, the stately majesty of Djin warders upon the Wagon's Trail?"

Tayna shook her head and turned back to run a hand down the trunk of the oak tree beside them. "No, not them–the trees," she said. "I mean like this, real. The colors are beautiful of course, but they're made of wood, too."

Elicand gawked at her. "Uh, what else would trees be made of?"

Tayna blushed. In her fascination, she'd forgotten that she wasn't supposed to talk about what she was beginning to think of as her "previous" life. Fortunately, keeping silent on that topic was made easier by the complete lack of a common vocabulary. How do you explain plastic to a medieval forest bard?

"Never mind," she said. Then she straightened up and looked into the distance, where the somber Wagon was vanishing into the trees. Elicand saw it as well, and indicated with a nod of his head that they should probably catch up, so the two of them set off in its wake, at a slightly faster pace.

Something had been bothering Tayna for a while now, but she'd been afraid to ask the Djin because it might sound insensitive. So she took the opportunity now to ask Elicand. "I thought we were supposed to be making stops to pick up, uh, passengers."

"Seekers," he said, correcting her. "Yes, we will, but there aren't many villages here in the water-shadow of the Spine. Abeni says our first stop is on the other side."

Tayna sighed. "People keep doing that–talking about places like

I'm supposed to know what they are. Or where. I'm not a walking Tour Guide to the Methilien Forest you know."

"Places? What do you mean?"

Tayna threw her up hands in exasperation. "Like just now–the Spine. And the mountain whatchamacallit, the Anvil? And the Throat. Is there a Kidney, too? Maybe a Great Spleen?"

Elicand's Hambu face laughed. "You're kidding, right? I mean, how can you not know about them? You can see them from just about everywhere." When Tayna refused to meet his gaze, Elicand's eyes narrowed in suspicion. "Say, where is it, exactly, that you've been living, anyway? Somewhere where you can't see the Anvil? I don't think that's even possible."

"Trust me," Tayna said. "It's possible. But you wouldn't believe me if I told you." Elicand looked at her sideways as they clambered over a fallen tree. The Wagon had been forced to deviate around it, and by going over it, they had managed to close much of the gap. Tayna could now hear the familiar *Swik! Swak!* of the Way Maker's whip just beyond the cluster of trees ahead.

"I find that... fascinating," Elicand said. "So you really haven't ever seen the Anvil?" Tayna just shook her head. If it had been visible during her Bulletman adventure, she'd been to busy panicking to notice. Elicand looked at her for a moment, and then clapped his hands together decisively. "Okay, then. Come on. We're going to fix that right now." He grabbed her eagerly by her sore wrist and set off at a trot. In no time at all they had caught up to the Wagon and Abeni's real brothers, but Elicand ignored them and kept going. A minute or so later, they found Abeni himself, scouting further ahead. In response to a breathless question, the Way Finder assured "Brother Hambu" that he did indeed plan to cross at a place called "the Cleft."

"We'll meet you there, then!" Elicand shouted over his shoulder. "There's something your Little Fish needs to see!" And he was off again, with Tayna still close at his heels. It didn't take much for them to pull ahead of the Wagon. With its greater bulk, the brothers were forced to weave back and forth, staying clear of the denser clusters of trees, and that slowed them down. Once Elicand felt they had stretched a sizable lead, he relaxed back to a quick walk. "We need to get to higher ground," he said. "And fortunately, the Spine itself should be just ahead. We'll be able to see everything from there."

Even at their brisker pace, it still took them almost a half hour to reach the point where the trees thinned out, and as they emerged from the dimness of the shaded forest, Tayna realized that it wasn't just the trees that were responsible for all the shade.

Elicand swept a hand majestically out toward the giant shadow looming in front of them. "Welcome to the Spine."

"Whoa. Anybody need a wall of rock?" Tayna looked to the left and right. As far as she could tell, the massive barrier ran to the horizon in both directions. Had it been perfectly straight, it would have been difficult to judge its size, but fortunately, it undulated slightly along its length, giving her eyes something to grab onto. It was enormous. Tayna turned to her friend in disbelief. "We're supposed to climb that thing?"

Her guide laughed. "A little, I guess, but it's not as hard as it looks from here."

Tayna wasn't so sure. From where she was standing, it might just as well be covered in festive, holiday razor-wire. The Spine was a solid, rocky ridge, several hundred feet high, that rose sharply from the ground in front of them. Not quite vertical, but close enough that it didn't make much difference. The base was green with a slick-looking moss, which, higher up, gave way to glossy black granite. It looked impossible to climb.

Elicand pointed off to the left. "See that dip in the upper ridge over there?"

Tayna looked to where he was pointing. About a half a mile away, she could see what he was talking about: a small, V-shaped notch in the otherwise continuous silhouette of the Spine's upper edge.

"Well, that's the Cleft. When we get there, you'll see that it's really a big crack that reaches most of the way to the ground, and there's a path leading up to the base of it. That's where we'll be crossing over."

Without trees to get in the way, or the bulk of the Wagon to slow them, they covered the remaining distance quickly. Long ago, some calamity had apparently split the Spine, forming the giant Cleft and dumping masses of rock out to the side. That debris hadn't gone very far though, and that mass now formed an apron, upon which a gentler approach of switchbacks had been tracked by untold years of travelers. When Tayna at last strode up the last slope and reached the base of the massive cloven gap, she stepped out into the direct sunlight shining through it. "So that way is west," she said, pointing through the gap toward a point on the distant horizon, below the lowering sun. It felt good to finally have some kind of bearing. "And so this spine thing must run north and south."

Elicand came to stand beside her, nodding. "And this," he said, taking her by the shoulders and turning her to face back toward the forest, "Is why we came here."

Tayna's breath caught in her throat. "Oh, man! That is freaking wild! What a view!"

The entire forest lay spread out before them in an unbroken flow of colors that stretched off into the distance. All the bulk of the Spine stood at their backs, hanging like a frozen wave of rock about to crush the treetop shoreline below, and its shadow was already pounding the threatened landscape with darkness. To her left, it slowly meandered its way to the horizon, but to her right, things were decidedly more interesting, and it was this view that held her attention.

"The Throat of the Forest," Elicand said. "Notice how all the rivers around here flow into it, like a giant mouth?" It was a vast circular depression in the expanse of leafy canopy, miles across, as though the entire forest had been formed from an ocean-sized blanket of wool, and somebody had left an invisible weight on the bed, pressing everything below it down into a bowl shape. Well, the half she could see was bowl-shaped, anyway. She assumed the other half was as well, but it was obstructed from view by the massive wall of the Spine itself, which ran straight out into the bowl–well beyond the rim–before finally slumping sharply down out of sight, somewhere near the middle.

"Can we see the Stinkhole from here?"

Elicand looked at her in surprise. "The Stink–?" A sudden look of understanding warmed his face. "Oh, so *that's* why you suddenly decided to come along, huh?"

Tayna laughed. "Yup, pretty much. So, can we see it or not?"

Elicand looked past her shoulder toward the funnel of the Throat. "Not really," he said. "It's supposed to be right down in the Narrows, near the center, too low down to see from here. The air's too hot and sticky that far down, and the humidity turns everything into a slime–all overgrown and dark. But I hear it's lovely if you're a Gnome."

Then he turned and pointed down to the shadowed forest below them, to where the Wagon could now be seen emerging from the trees, with its three, fly-speck-sized Warders. "Looks like we'll have company soon. It's amazing how quickly they can move with that thing, huh?"

Tayna smiled quietly to herself. There was a smattering of hero-worship in his tone.

"So, can we see the Anvil from here, too?" She had to tap him on the shoulder to get his attention, and her hand sank further into the illusion of his big, muscular Djin shoulder than she expected, but it quickly found firm tappables not too far below.

"What? Oh, right. The Anvil." He turned and looked off into the distance to the left, pointing to where the Spine met the horizon. "Hmm, it's a bit hazy today, but if you far-look to the end of the Spine, you can't miss it."

"Wutta-huh? Far-look?"

Elicand winced. "Oh, I'm sorry. I forgot you don't have your magic yet. That's weird, huh? It usually comes when you flower. Oh well. Let's do it the way my grandmother used to do it when I was a kid, then. Make a circle like this with your fingers." He held up one hand, making a ring with his thumb and scratching finger. Tayna copied him, and he reached out, settled his hand over hers and sang a low melody. "Now, lift the ring up to your eye," he said.

Tayna looked down and saw that the air within the circle of her fingers shimmered, like heat waves rising from a hot stove. As she raised it in front of her, the view through the shimmer flickered and bubbled. When she brought it somewhat hesitantly to her eye, she was startled to see that it was acting like a little telescope. She could see quite a ways further. Elicand reached up and took her hand gently by the wrist, twisting it clockwise and then counterclockwise, showing her how she could control the degree of magnification.

Tayna turned to him and gave him a quick, almost giddy smile. "Magic is awesome!" she said, then she turned back to scan the horizon. And there it was. Just above the last curve of the Spine, a sort of triangular lump rose above the grayed out colors of the distant tree line. She zoomed in and the triangle grew, revealing a high plateau atop of which sat a large, jagged looking form, looking for all the world like the kind of mountain you expect to find in children's drawings.

"The Anvil," Elicand said. "It's supposed to be the sleeping form of Methilien himself. See how the very peak is a sort of reddish color? That's called the Bloodcap. It's where the Oath to renew the Dragon's Peace should have happened. Some people think it's red because it's the one place where Methilien didn't actually turn to stone, and that his blood still flows beneath the surface, but it's just reddish rock if you ask me. The tales don't mention one, but I'm pretty sure the original Oath-takers had a story uncle along with them. He probably suggested that spot–the imagery is just too good to be an accident. See how the Spine comes out from the base of the Anvil, like a tail? Pretty long to be a tail, but look at how it fits. It gives each race a sense that part of the Dragon is theirs, because it runs through all three domains, starting in the Throat with the Gnomes, across the Verge through Wasketchin territory, and then up, finally, to the Djin.

Tayna nodded. It was easy to see how a story like that would catch on. "Does anybody live on the actual Spine itself?"

Elicand shook his head. "No, not really. The stone is pretty hard and there isn't much in the way of soil, so there's really no water or food on it to speak of."

"So if nobody lives on it, who does that part belong to?"

"Depends on who you ask," he said, turning to the right. "See that last bit sticking out into the Throat? That's called the Outreach. According to the terms of the Dragon's Peace, all land higher than the lip of the Throat and lower than the Anvil's Plateau is Wasketchin territory, and clearly, the Spine is higher than the Lip along its entire length–even the Outreach. But if you look at it on a map, the whole Throat looks like a giant circle, except for that one, long, finger-shaped notch that is technically part of the Verge. Every now and then, somebody tries to create trouble with that mappish view, claiming that the Outreach ought to be considered Gnomileshi land, since it's inside the circle of their territory. And the trouble's gotten worse in the last few years."

"How?"

Elicand pointed out toward the end of the Outreach, which curved slightly to the left at its tip, allowing them to see it from where they stood. "Look closer there. Tell me what you see."

Tayna brought her zoom-fingers back up to her eye and the image swirled and danced as she adjusted it. When it cleared, she could see a tall woman standing on the rocks. Then her brain adjusted for the distance and she realized it was actually an enormous statue of a woman, rising up from the end of the Spine. She seemed proud and defiant, pointing with one outstretched finger, glaring the full power of her silent, stony judgment down onto the Gnomileshi homes below her.

"Wow. She's beautiful," Tayna said. "And so angry. Who is she?"

"That," he said. "Is the Mourning Dove. When I was just a little kid, the royal princess, Alia't Ae N'Amiera, died in a horrible fire. It was such a stupid, tragic accident, but her parents, Lord Malkior and Lady M'Ateliana, weren't convinced. They seemed to think that a visiting group of Gnomes had somehow been involved, but nothing could be proved. Of course, the Gnomes denied everything. And since you can't tell a lie under the Peace, what could anyone do? We had to believe them. Everyone except Malkior anyway." Elicand sighed. "That's what's really put the strain on his kingship. We all love him to pieces, but it would be so much easier if he could just let Alia't go. M'Ateliana has. Why can't he?

"Anyway, the Mourning Dove is Malkior's tribute to the great queen that he believed would have blossomed out of his young daughter, if she had lived. He had it constructed as a symbol of the Wasketchin peoples' grief over their loss, and then he had it placed there, right on the border, as a reminder to the Gnomes. They've been angry about it ever since. Malkior says it will stand there until somebody proves them innocent, but privately, I've heard him say it'll probably be there forever. You can just imagine how furious the Gnomes are. Remember? Malkior's v'ou du said that it was the only topic he and Grinyak ever argued about."

Tayna nodded as she continued staring in wonder at the majestic statue through the lens of her fingers. Then she noticed something on the Mourning Dove's knee, and zoomed in a little closer.

"There's somebody climbing her," she said, over her shoulder. "Is that normal?"

"Must be a charm-trimmer."

Tayna looked back at him. "A what?"

Elicand nodded. "A charm-trimmer. Not everybody can use magic. Well, it's not that they can't do it–it's just that they don't have any power. You know that charms need fuel, right? Like logs to fuel a fire?"

"Yeah. Veest mentioned something about it. That's the vim part, right?"

Again he nodded. "Right. Normally, we just sort of absorb it from the world around us. Through our skin and such. But some people can't. And some others can, but not very efficiently. That's where charm-trimmers come in. When a charm is cast, most people are pretty sloppy and not all the vim put into it gets used up. Some of it just sort of hangs around, but it's been changed. Leftover vim like that can be collected and given to people who can't absorb the normal kind. And some people are really good at sniffing it out and gathering it up. Those people sometimes choose that as their calling. That's probably what your Dove-climber is."

Tayna brought her hand back up to her eye and hunted around trying to find the charm-trimmer again. She wanted to watch him in action. But suddenly, she jerked backward, "Oh!" Tayna lowered her hand and looked at her guide uncertainly. "I think he took too much."

"What do you mean?"

"The Dove," Tayna said, pointing with her free hand. "It just, like, collapsed. This is another one of those exploding king things, right? Just keep calm, it happens all the time?"

Elicand grabbed her zoom hand and jerked it up to his own eye. "Let me see!" But it was too late, all he would be able to see now were some billowing clouds of dust rising from the point of rock where the statue had been standing, and a few Gnomes milling around, climbing over the rubble.

"They've pulled it down!" he cried, once he got Tayna's fingers zoomed in. She looked at him sadly. Even through the disguise, his face was drained and pale. "That's about the worst thing that could possibly happen now," he said. "When it comes to Alia't and her statue, Lord Malkior isn't exactly reasonable. There is no way he's going to see this as anything other than an act of war!"

"What do you think he'll do?" Tayna asked.

Hambu shook his head. "I don't know," he said. "Whatever kings usually do when someone starts blowing up their stuff, I suppose. Wait here!" Then he turned and pelted back down the slope to bring the grim news to the Warders.

———

The sun sets late in the summer months, and the sons of Kijamon were able to traverse the Cleft in good time, escaping from the shadow of the Spine and buying a few more hours of daylight to continue their journey. The demise of the Mourning Dove had only increased their resolve to complete this Trail as quickly as possible. From their point of view, the sooner Grinyak reached the Gnomileshi harvest tables, the sooner things might calm down. But they couldn't just make a beeline for the harvest tables now, either. That would be disrespectful to just about everybody involved. The people of Methilien had a right to pay their respects to the dead–any dead–and there were also the waiting Seekers to consider. Their families would not be anxious for any delays in the Wagon's progress. So the brothers had decided to just stick to the plan. The group had barely reached the flat terrain of the Verge on the far side of the Spine, when Abeni announced that they were coming to their first stop. Tayna caught the smell of a cook-fire on the shifting breeze. "What village is it?" she asked. She had to raise her voice to be heard above the sound of rushing water.

Zimu just shrugged. "Who can say?"

She turned to Abeni. "Well? What village has the Way Finder led us to?" But he too could only shrug.

"Abeni is the Way *Finder*," he said. "For what the Little Fish is seeking, she must ask the Way *Knower*." The others chuckled at that.

"Alright," she said with a sigh. "Who's the Way Knower?" Zimu and Abeni both pointed silently at the Wagon.

Tayna gave them her best smirk. "The Wagon knows where we're going? And you don't?"

"That is the magic of the Wagon of Tears," Abeni said. "Always, it knows where the next Seeker awaits."

Zimu coiled his whip and hung it around his neck in order to assist Sarqi more directly. "Ever it points toward the next Seeker, like an arrow," he added. "But it does not know how best to go from here to there."

"Not an arrow, more like a spring," Sarqi interjected. "Whenever I have to force it to turn around a tree, it fights me the whole time, trying to swing back to its target." Right on cue, the Wagon trembled. Sarqi gasped and dove frantically back into his song.

Abeni watched his brother to be sure he had everything under control, before picking up the explanation. "Guiding the Wagon from here to the next place *is* the job of the Way Finder," he said. "But Abeni does not know where the Wagon wishes to be–only its direction. He does not know the name of the village or what people might live there, you see?"

Tayna nodded slowly. "So you guide the Wagon and it guides you?"

Abeni broke into a wide smile. "Yes!" he said. "The Little Fish does understand."

Tayna wasn't sure that saying the words was the same as understanding them, but it didn't matter. They were emerging from the trees now, and they found themselves on the bank of a fair-sized river, churning with the run-off that had been collected and channeled by the great flanks of the Spine. The village was nestled alongside a turbulent course of rapids, and its roar quickly grew too loud for even shouted conversation as they approached. Four or five dehns lay scattered along the nearer bank, and several more were visible through the mist, on the far side.

Sarqi guided the Wagon up to the door of one tiny home and then stopped, as a middle-aged villager emerged. Abeni bowed low and gestured solemnly toward the floating Wagon. The man blinked and gazed vacantly past the party of Djin, seeing only the great Wagon.

After a moment, he nodded and raised his hand, asking the warders to wait, then he turned and went back inside. When he re-emerged, he was carrying a large bundle in his arms. Tayna watched intently, and then a sob caught in her throat when she realized that the bundle was the body of a young boy. She was suddenly glad for the privacy afforded by the noise of the water, leaving each of them alone with their thoughts.

The man stepped over to the Wagon and with the aid of a change in the Way Chanter's song, raised his son's body up and guided him into an empty chamber. The tiny head tipped back, gazing sightlessly at the leaves and sky above. Tayna caught only a glimpse of the face, enough to see that it had a pale, bluish tint, suggesting that the child had met his end under water, which seemed only fitting. Clearly, the river dominated all aspects of life in this tiny place.

When the body had been loaded, the fisherman reached inside his kirfa and withdrew a small wooden carving–a turtle of some kind–which he placed on his son's chest, closing the chubby little fingers around it for him, so he wouldn't lose it. With this last task done, the force that had been animating the man somehow fled him and he sagged against the side of the Wagon. Truly the hands of grief. He lingered there for a moment, with his head lowered and one hand absently stroking the yellowish tousle of the boy's hair with his fingers. Then he slowly straightened himself, nodded to the warders and stepped aside. All around them, other villagers had emerged from their own dehns, in twos and threes, standing in silent family clusters to observe the Wagon ritual and pay their respects. All in utter silence, save for the relentless crashing of water over rock.

It occurred to Tayna that she could look around, distract herself from the unbearable sadness of the scene. Maybe she could scan the villager's faces, looking for some sign of the cobalt trefoil ears. But her own discomfort seemed trivial at the moment, and indulging it would have been disrespectful. So she stood there and watched a man say his last goodbyes to his only little boy. And she was glad that when at last it was time to go and it was her turn to make respectful eye contact with the grieving father, she did so with the full honor of tears upon her face.

The moment was over and the man withdrew his hand from the boy's head. Immediately, the Wagon began a slow rotation, coming to a rest with its nose pointing downstream. Once it had stopped turning, Abeni nodded in satisfaction, and then set off at a brisk pace, paralleling the river's course and leaving the rest to follow along behind.

"Death is different here," Tayna said, as soon as they were far enough from the rapids to make talking feasible. "Sadder."

Zimu's whip flicked out and coiled around a length of driftwood lying across their path, which he jerked aside with a casual motion. "No. Death is always the same," the big Djin said. "It is grief that changes."

Tayna nodded thoughtfully at this, but said nothing. It was not a time for chatter.

The hardest thing about being adopted–Oh my god! It's really happening! Lies rolled over, buried her face in her pillow, and screamed. "Yaaaahhhhh!" When you've been Unlovable for eight whole years, and living with Goodies for nine, it becomes impossible to explain the feeling you get when somebody suddenly comes dancing out of the darkness and picks you to be their very own daughter. It was like she'd been captured by cannibals and taken to some depressing, disease-infested, tropical island and trussed up, ready for the boiling pot, only to have Prince Friedrich, the Crown Prince of Lower Bavaristan come steaming up the lagoon in his private assault yacht, duel his way past a dozen ferocious warriors to the Big Chief's kitchen hut and rescue her one-handed, while he fought off the next dozen tribesmen with his free hand, and then ask her to marry him on the boat-ride home.

No. That wasn't it. Not exciting enough. For the first time she could remember, Eliza's imagination failed her. She just couldn't think of anything that was more exciting, more scream-of-joy-causing–more beautiful–than the fact that somebody out there loved her. It was a feeling that filled her up so often, and so fully, that she just had to spill it out. And the only way she'd found to do that, so far, was to scream into this stupid, fluffy, beautiful pillow. Lies patted her scream-catcher affectionately and set it back down on the bed. Actually, being this happy was kind of fun.

The hard part, though, to get back to the point, was the part about how her happiness was making her friends feel. She was trying not to gloat, and really, she wasn't gloating, but when you're spraying happiness and giggles all over the place on a sixty-times-per-hour basis, it's hard for that to not look like gloating. Especially to the ones who weren't being adopted, because everyone on this floor knew how unlikely that was to ever happen for any of them.

Lies looked around the new "ward room." For some reason that still hadn't been properly explained, the entire fifth floor had been relocated to the basement. Hastily assembled bunk beds now lined the walls of the dining hall and every girl had been required to pack what few possessions she had into a cardboard box that would fit underneath, two boxes to a bed. Sister Regalia said they were being moved so that they wouldn't make so much noise going up and down the stairs to their kitchen duties while everybody else was still asleep, but Lies wasn't buying any of it. Something was going on, only now, without Tayna around, she was finding it hard to come up with a plan for getting to the bottom of it. And to be honest, she was having trouble focusing on Goody issues just now.

The clock on the wall said 09:22. Just one hour and thirty eight minutes to go. Pick-up was always at eleven o'clock. That was one of the Goody's rules. They told the mommy-bes that it was to help get the girl integrated into her new family. They'd get home and immediately have lunch to focus on—no awkward silences. But Lies knew the real reason—she'd heard Sister Anthrax and Sister Disgustia talking about it once, when precious Bethany had been chosen as the trophy child to decorate the Litchfield-Chesterton merger. According to Anthrax, it was simple. "Later than nine so we don't disturb our breakfast, earlier than noon so she doesn't need to be fed another meal, and as late in between as possible, to make the little snot-blower squirm!"

If there was one woman Eliza was going to not-miss more than all the others, it was definitely Anthrax.

"Alright girl, don't just sit there! Get moving! Time to go!"

Lies shook her head. What? Sister Anthrax herself was standing on the bottom stair, tapping her foot impatiently and glaring at her with that creepy, slightly larger right eye of hers. Nobody could glare contempt like Sister Anthrax.

"Go where, Sister?"

"Don't play stupid with me, child! I haven't got the time. The car is waiting, and no doubt, so are those pathetic fools who picked you. So move!"

Eliza looked around in confusion. Her gym-bag was packed and sitting on the floor by her feet. It was all part of the plan. Ned would come down the stairs at precisely eleven o'clock, give her a big hug and ruffle her hair, and then say, "Let's go, Eliza. We're so happy to have you in our lives. Here, let me carry that for you." Then they'd go traipsing up the stairs, hand-in-hand, to meet Sue in Regalia's office, and then they'd all go out to the car together, singing something happy. She'd been planning it for days.

Now Anthrax wanted to change all that?

"But I thought they were coming here to pick me up. That's how it always works. Eleven o'clock. Ruffling hair. The sing–" But Anthrax cut her off with a poisonous cackle.

"That's how it works for the regular girls, not for you lot. Now move it! Or do you want me to tell them you've changed your mind?"

The very thought sent an electric current through Eliza's body and she leapt to her feet. "Alright, Sister. I'm coming!" Then she grabbed her bag, slung it over her shoulder, and raced toward the stairs and the already-vanishing feet of the vilest Goody, leading her up into the darkness.

———————

The river had petered out into a low, wide fen when the Way Finder called a short pause at its edge so he could go ahead to seek a solid path across. As was the custom, Sarqi maintained his lofting song while they waited. Raising and lowering the Wagon unnecessarily throughout the day was the mark of an amateur–one who had not fully absorbed the duty of dignity that was to be accorded the Seekers, although, with the Wagon stationary, he was at least able to change the tempo of his charm to a less taxing mode. Zimu took the opportunity to circle the hovering Wagon, searching for signs of wear or damage that might have occurred during the day. He was on his knees, inspecting the bottom of the runners when the scout returned.

"Abeni has found a path," the Way Finder said, as he strode from between the bull rushes that flanked a narrow strip of higher ground as it ran off into the wetland. "But it is narrow and uneven, and darkness comes swiftly in the forest. The Wagon settles here for tonight."

The words were scarcely out of his mouth before Sarqi let out a deep sigh of relief and gave up humming his tune. The Wagon settled to the spongy ground beside Zimu, accompanied by the scent of freshly crushed wildflowers.

"Hurry up with the tent. I need my beauty sleep," Sarqi said as he sank to the ground beside the Wagon and rubbed at his tired feet.

"You sleep each day, little brother," came Zimu's reply. "But it seems you do it poorly, for each morning you have only become uglier. Perhaps you should try wisdom sleep instead. That hole may be the easier for you to fill, and it is almost as deep." Sarqi groaned and threw a feeble clump of dirt at his mountainous brother, but it fell short. Taking a seat at Tayna's side, "Hambu" gave a contented little sigh of his own, reached up to grab himself by the throat, and vanished, to be replaced by Elicand. After draping the golden chain of the pretendant over a knob of tree root next to him, the story uncle raised his hands to stare at them in wonder. Then he turned to Tayna and grinned. "See? They're back to their proper size." He rolled them one way and then the other so she could see both sides. "They've been bumping and banging into stuff all day–dropping things too. It turns out that hands work a lot better if they actually stop where your eyes think they do."

Abeni laughed at all the playful banter around the camp and went to the back of the Wagon. Now that it had settled to the ground, touching it was permitted and he and Zimu pulled an assortment of packs and bundles from the tailbox. In no time at all, they had erected an enormous red tent that filled what little space there had been between the trees. But even before Tayna was certain that the job was done, the leaves and branches of every tree within earshot reverberated with the cacophony of Sarqi's snoring.

"The sons of Kijamon don't waste any time," she said. Abeni finished cinching the last tent rope and came to join her as Zimu began preparing dinner. Elicand had wandered over and was now hovering next to him–either to help or just to make sure he got early access to whatever food emerged.

"Indeed not," Abeni agreed, as he sat down beside her on the grass. "To waste time upon the Wagon's Trail would be an insult to the Seeker. The Way Chanter travels as far as he is able each day, retaining only enough strength to slow his collapse onto his blankets. At night, the Way Chanter and Seeker seem brothers in eternal sleep."

"Except for the snoring," Zimu called out.

Tayna smiled. "So, we're up with the sparrows and back on the Trail at sunrise?"

"That depends upon Sarqi," Abeni replied. "The Wagon departs when *that* son rises." Tayna rolled her eyes at the pun.

"And then how long until we reach the Throat?" she asked, trying to sound casual, but they both knew she was in a hurry to reach her destination. That episode with the little boy and his father earlier had been a painful reminder of things like *family yours* and *peril great*, and the closer she got to her answers, the more anxious she became.

"Who can say? Only the Way Knower, but Abeni too hopes that the Trail is short. It would be best if the Gnomes did not learn of the most-honored of our Seekers," he said, hooking a thumb toward the Wagon, "until after their journey has ended."

"Why?"

Abeni made a sad face. "Because it is the Gnomileshi way to squabble and fight over bones. Upon every Trail, some will seek to find the Wagon ahead of their brothers, that they might lay their harvest claims in advance–even should the Seekers be but a shoemaker and a cook. Think how many will come if they learn of this twice-crowned temptation."

"So shouldn't we be getting back on the Wagon's Trail as early as we can?" Elicand asked, as he came back to join them, having been chased away from the cooking fire by Zimu. "Why waste time letting Sarqi sleep late?"

Abeni burst out in a new peal of laughter and clapped his younger "brother" vigorously on the shoulder. "Young Hambu has much to learn about his new people," he said. "To the Djin, sleep is never a waste of time!"

Eventually, Zimu joined them as well, carrying four large pewter mugs and handing one to each of them. Inside, Tayna could see that the mug was divided in half by an inner wall. One side held a hot, meaty stew that tantalized her with notes of basil and tarragon. On the other side, she thought she recognized her new favorite aroma. "You made boh-choh? Do Djin Wagon warders always drink Wasketchin beverages or do you only have it because Elicand and I are with you?"

Zimu frowned. "Does 'boh-choh' sound like a Wasketchin word to you? The "traveler's brew" is a Djin invention–one that our softer cousins have stolen from us, but we do not mind. Wisdom cannot be stolen–it can only be shared."

But the day of travel had taken its toll on each of them, especially the two Wasketchin, and soon, exhaustion dulled their tongues. The only sounds to be heard were the contented slurps and grunts as each of them attacked their food with whatever enthusiasm they had left. Elicand was the first to set his mug down and he patted his tummy appreciatively, with a nod to Chef Zimu.

"Sorry," he said as he stretched into a full-body yawn. "I know I didn't do any work today. You guys did it all. I don't have any excuse, but I'm as tired as a stump juggler."

Abeni moved away to the edge of the marsh to rinse the mugs and pots, leaving Zimu to correct their young friend.

"You have been watching all day, and learning about our ways, have you not?" Elicand nodded sleepily. "Then that is the tale of it," Zimu said. "The brain is a muscle, like any other. To do work with it taxes the body no less than work of the legs or arms. What is more, muscle-work can only make one weary. It takes brain-work to create true exhaustion. Perhaps your brain is now telling you that it is full and that it is time to go to bed."

"Sleep time?" A furry head emerged from Abeni's travel bag, which was otherwise empty now that the Djin's things had been moved to the Wagon. The Brownie looked around, blinking sleepily in the fading light.

"Ha! Shondu makes a joke," Abeni said from the end of the Wagon, where he was pushing the dishes back into the tailbox. "He wakes from his all-day nap to see if perhaps it is time for bed." The merry Djin crossed the camp and resumed his seat, reaching out to scratch his little friend between the ears as he did so. Shondu climbed up onto Abeni's lap to bring more scratchable surfaces into play.

"Why do you keep him hidden in the bag?" Elicand asked. "Is he sick?"

"Brownies do not sicken," Abeni said. "But, sadly, they are not common." Then he leaned over and, in an exaggerated stage whisper, added, "Abeni's elder brothers do not yet have chalats of their own. It would be an insult to allow Shondu to remind them of their younger brother's greater skill. They must learn to work harder if they wish to gain such good fortune of their own, but Abeni must not say so." Zimu, who had heard everything of course, glowered at his cocky younger brother.

Elicand laughed, which was an easy thing to do around the large, friendly Djins. "So, 'brother,' will Hambu be permitted to do any work tomorrow?"

Abeni gave him an approving look. "It is well that young Hambu wishes to work. We shall see. Abeni thinks his little brother has learned something of the Warder's Way today, has he not?"

Elicand grinned sheepishly. "If realizing that it is a lot more work than it appears to be counts as 'learning something,' then yes. I've learned plenty."

"Excellent," Abeni replied. "No job should begin until the size of the task has been fully measured."

This sounded encouraging to the young Wasketchin. "So perhaps my brother could find a small task for me to 'measure' tomorrow? To be sure I've got the measuring part figured out?"

Abeni chuckled at the young man's persistence. "Perhaps he will," he said. Then he turned to look at Shondu. "What does the chalat say? Is Hambu ready for his next lesson?"

"Pikabu! Pikabu!" The excited Brownie hopped off of Abeni's lap and ran frantic circles around the startled youth, leaping and clapping his hands as he went. "Fun play! Fun play!"

"Do you know the pikabu?" Abeni asked, turning to make a playful grab at Shondu. At the same time, Tayna reached down to grab the travel sack.

"Here. I think you need this," she said, as she pulled the bag down over Elicand's head, the way Abeni had shown her earlier.

"Hey! What the–" Elicand started to say.

Abeni looked up from Shondu's excited scampering to see his young friend with the sack already in place. "Oh, good. You know it. Shondu, Pikabu Hambu!"

Shondu shouted his reply, "Pikabu!" and the campsite was suddenly filled with a sound like the buzzing of bees. When it died away, Shondu and Elicand were nowhere to be seen.

"Way to go, Shondu!" Tayna cried.

Zimu grinned at her, and Abeni called out, "Very good, little brother!"

After waiting a moment to let Elicand experience the wonders of the pocket, Abeni lifted his head and called out again. "Shondu! Pikabu pakar!" Tayna picked up the pretendant from where Elicand had draped it over the log, and inspected it curiously while waiting for her friends to reappear. She had an idea for a prank she could play on him when he returned, if she could figure out how it worked. Several moments crept by while she fidgeted with the thing, but when she looked around for help, Zimu just smiled at her confidently. Then a few more moments passed and Abeni's usually infectious grin took on a slight tinge of irritation. After another minute, the Djin shook his head ruefully and called out to Shondu again.

And a few minutes later, yet again.

Time stretched out. Two minutes became five, then ten. In what seemed like a blink, an entire hour had passed and Tayna found herself between the two Djin brothers, searching back and forth through the surrounding forest and marsh, calling. "Elicand! Shondu! Where are you?" Tayna wanted to dart frantically from tree to rock, but she steeled herself to match the slow, methodical survey of every bump and twist of grass that her more experienced Djin companions were using. She twisted her bracelet wrist nervously every few minutes, her own anxiety fueled by Abeni's obvious distress. Even quiet, thoughtful Zimu seemed twitchy and upset. Back and forth they searched, hoping to find their friends hiding behind a shrub, or perhaps injured and lying among the tall reeds following some unfathomable accident.

But they found nothing.

Finally, with literally no stone left unexamined, Tayna dropped her butt to the ground and lay her head on her knapsack, giving in to total exhaustion. But Abeni refused to give up even then, and continued combing the brush, until, finally, Zimu placed a massive hand on the Way Finder's shoulder.

"Searching cannot be done in darkness, my brother, and shouting ill-serves the mute." Abeni's voice had long since been reduced to a hoarse croaking from calling the names of their missing friends over and over. But Zimu was right–there was nowhere left to look and none of them had any strength left to give. The two brothers shared a glance, each mirroring the silent horror of the other's expression. Neither of them wanted to say what was clearly on both their minds.

Nobody lost in the pocket ever comes back. Nobody. Not ever.

chapter 12

"My eyes! Abeni! Your chalat has blinded me!"

The first thing Elicand saw after pulling the bag off his head was nothing. Absolute nothing. The kind of nothing from which the dragon Methilien had fashioned the world. A penetrating, oily black nothing. So naturally, he assume his eyes were the problem, and not the world around him.

"Oh, crop rot!" he shouted. "What good is a blind story uncle?" His anguish echoed wetly from damp stone–at least, it sounded like damp stone–but clearly his hearing was off. He knew for a fact that their camp was surrounded by trees. Sure, there was also the wet, swampy fen, but that was made of plants and bugs and such, not stone. Elicand wound the sack up into a frustrated ball and hurled it as far as he could.

"Abeni? Tayna?"

There was no answer.

"Zimu? Sarqi? Where did everyone go?"

"Fun play?"

Elicand blew a breath of relief and twisted around. "Shondu? Where are you?"

"Pikabu! Pikabu!" Elicand could hear the Brownie scampering excitedly around him, but he had no enthusiasm for such games right now.

"Shondu. Find Abeni. Go get Abeni. Tell him I need help. Hambu is blind and needs him. Okay, Shondu?"

"Pikabu! Pikabu!" the Brownie repeated. Elicand tried several times to get the chalat to understand, but he couldn't make himself understood. The little guy just kept chirping and jumping about. Elicand slumped to the ground, which everybody knew was the best posture from which to hold your head in your hands and moan. But instead of the soft forest floor he'd been expecting, his bones rattled onto hard cold stone.

"Hey!" He reached out gingerly to feel the rough surface, but it didn't make any sense. His fear twisted into anger. "Where did you hide all the dirt you little thief?" It wasn't his proudest moment, but it made him realize how panicky he was feeling. He took a long, deep breath and tried to calm down.

Then he tried again."Shondu? Where did everything go?" There was still plenty of tremor in his voice.

A Brownie's understanding of the world was limited. Most things in it got divided into simple categories: fun and not fun, or tasty and not tasty, for example. Another was sad and not sad, and perhaps Shondu saw that Elicand fit into the former half of this partitioning. Of all the characteristics Brownies are known for, it is perhaps this–their capacity for empathy–that makes them so highly prized as chalats. All of Shondu's instincts for mischief and play now took a back seat to the greater issue of his companion's distress, so he did what Brownies do best. He climbed up into the young man's lap and whirtled his sympathy. Though their speech is limited to about a dozen words, Brownies are capable of other styles of self-expression as well. And what they lacked in vocabulary was more than made up for by the wide range of non-speech sounds they could make, especially for expressing feelings. In the case of sympathy, they produce a sound somewhere between the purr of a cat and the cooing of doves and this so-called "whirtling" is one of the most melancholy and yet comforting sounds in all the animal kingdom.

Elicand felt around blindly until he'd located Shondu's head, and then he stroked at the soft fur between the Brownie's ears. The whirtling got louder. "What are we going to do, little guy? I don't know what's going on, but whatever it is, it looks like we're on our own." With that thought echoing in his mind, Elicand slumped back against the stoney wall behind him, but he barely noticed. His fatigue caught up with him at last, and as his mind raced in tighter and tighter circles of dread, his body abandoned ship, slipping out from under him into the timeless oblivion of total exhaustion.

Elicand woke up some time later, with Shondu still asleep, curled comfortably against his chest. Brownies were notoriously heavy sleepers, so Elicand had no difficulty sliding out from under the little guy without waking him. He then clambered stiffly to his feet. Every bit of skin or muscle that had lain in contact with the stone floor while he slept now ached, and Elicand had to spend several minutes trying to stretch his protesting flesh back into some sort of unclenched usefulness before he was at last ready to turn his attention to the real problem.

The most important issue was the one of his apparent blindness, but, thankfully, that turned out to have been a hasty diagnosis. True, no matter which way he turned his head, the view was identically black–absolutely indistinguishable from having his eyes closed. However, there was one difference. When he rubbed his eyes, he could still see random splotches of color in response to the pressure. Elicand was no Watcher, but he suspected that if he were truly blind, he would not have been able to see anything at all. And that was the key that allowed him to unravel the rest of his puzzle. It was obvious now that he and Shondu had been transported somewhere strange, although he still had no idea how or why or even where. The darkness and the echos of damp stone all around suggested that they were in a cave of some sort, but none of it made any sense. Abeni had said something just before the darkness fell, something about a test. Was this the test? Elicand wasn't sure, but he'd been so distracted by the chalat's antics that he now couldn't dredge up a clear memory of just what it was the Djin had said to him. For all he knew, Abeni was hiding somewhere nearby, laughing to himself and taking notes.

"No matter," he said into the blackness, trying to sound upbeat. "Even if Abeni is here, he isn't helping. And that means," he said, turning to where he thought he could hear Shondu's breathing, "that getting out of here is entirely up to me. The first thing we should do is call up a little light, right?" A moment later, the warm tones of Elicand's spell song blossomed in the darkness and reverberated all around, reflecting back from the cavern walls. This was the song he had learned at his grandmother's knee and it was one of the easiest spell-songs any Wasketchin ever learned. Light was naturally present in all things. It fell upon the things of the world for days and years and was absorbed into them like water into moss. It usually took just the tiniest nudge of song to coax it back out again–even after untold thousands of years lying dormant underground. Elicand sang his song for an entire minute. He sang loudly, he sang lustily, and, toward the end, he even sang a little desperately, but not so much as a glimmer emerged. He tried two or three more times and threw in a couple of other versions of the charm for good measure, still without success.

"Well, that's odd," he said, as he flopped back down onto the cold stone. There was something strange about this darkness. It didn't feel right. It wasn't just that light was absent–it was more like it was being forcibly sucked from the air, and the harder he tried to make it shine, the stronger the sucking got. All he had to show for his efforts now was a slight headache and a feeling of physical exhaustion. He couldn't quite explain it, but his attempted charm had revealed something that hadn't been apparent to him before. There was something fundamentally wrong with this place. It was nothing he could specify, he couldn't point to it and say "That is out of place," but something definitely was, and he decided that caution was going to have to be the main rule until he had things figured out. Elicand turned in what felt like the right direction and called to the chalat. "Come on boy. If we can't see, let's go feel what there is to feel around here."

The echoing of his voice throughout the space brought back to him a vague sense of its dimensions. It felt large, roomy. This was no rabbit hole or even a bear cave. It was bigger than that, for sure, and it sounded larger off to the one side, as though he and Shondu were nestled up closer to one wall than the other. In the total absence of light, he had no way to determine how large the cave really was, so that would be the first job. He stuck his hands out in front of his chest like clumsy antenna and walked slowly forward, waiting to discover the location of the cave wall by bashing into it.

He had only taken three steps when the ground vanished from beneath his feet and he plunged headlong into a yawning abyss.

As it happens, some abysses are bigger than others and, fortunately, the one that Elicand had stumbled into was not very deep at all. His foot found the floor again, only a few inches lower than he had been expecting it. Now, three inches might not sound like much to a normal person, sitting in a comfortable place with plenty of heat and good lighting, but in the cold, damp blackness of an unknown and utterly unlit cave, small distances can seem enormous. For that one brief moment, Elicand had been convinced that he had stepped off the edge of a cliff, and without any useful information coming from his eyes, his brain had filled in the missing details with the most frightful conclusions it could reach that fit the facts. In short, it had decided that, oops, he was now plunging to his death. At first, he had believed his brain completely. But of course, you can't believe everything people tell you, not even if those people are your own brain. During the time it had took for his foot to fall those extra three inches, Elicand found himself with enough time to evaluate the whole of his misspent life, and then to berate himself for the parts he didn't like. And he was especially displeased by that last bit about wandering off a cliff in the dark. But in the end, his plummeting foot struck jarringly onto the slightly lower floor, and his brain quickly sent out an update. Never mind. False alarm. The abyss is shallower than we thought. No death today. Thank you for your attention.

But false or not, the alarms that had gone off in his head had been loud, and the brief panic they triggered had left his skin and bones jangling as though he had just lost a fight with a lightning storm. Now he was terrified of every footstep and every clatter of stone under his feet. It took him almost ten minutes to calm himself down, and three more before he could work up the nerve to take another step, which he wisely took on hands and knees. To his credit, though, that next step, and the ones that followed, were along his original course, toward the near-sounding wall and not, as his instincts were now screaming, back to the sure-footedness of the ground behind him. Perhaps most surprisingly, his progress on all fours was no slower than it would have been if he'd been walking upright. It might even have been faster.

His crawling exploration quickly fell into a rhythm: place a hand on the floor, confirm that it is floor, move forward, repeat with opposite hand. This process gave him confidence, despite his blindness, and with his fear of the uncertain terrain and its yawning pits of eternity diminished, Elicand all but raced across the rocky ground. Soon enough, he found himself beginning to crawl uphill as the floor there sloped roundly up to become the wall. It was hard to believe, but by his estimate, he had only come about twenty feet from where he had started.

Elicand felt around the curves and knobs of rock and loose stone around him, trying to find somewhere to rest. When he found a pair of gnarled outcroppings side by side near the cave wall, he squeezed himself into the gap between them and settled down, facing out. It felt good to be enclosed like this, protected from the unknown on three sides, like a badger in his burrow. For the moment he felt safe.

Now that he had time to think about such things, Elicand realized that he had just come through an honest-to-flowers inspirational experience—one that had given him a new empathy for all creatures hunted, lost, or frightened. It might even make a good premise for a song. Perhaps it seems strange that a young man—trapped, blind and frightened, as he was—would take the time to arrange his experiences into rhyming couplets, but Elicand was a story uncle by training—despite recent setbacks in that plan—and that's just what story uncles did. He was still casting about in his mind, looking for a good rhyme on "plummet," when he was interrupted.

"Food now?"

Shondu's voice murmured from the darkness, and in another moment Elicand felt a pair of furry paws patting at his leg. The Brownie quickly scampered up onto his lap and snuggled in. He, too, seemed to enjoy the protective nook into which they were both huddled. Elicand was a little embarrassed by how quickly he had forgotten his tiny companion, and he was glad nobody could see him blushing.

"Sorry, little guy. I don't have any food for you."

"Not food now?"

Elicand laughed. Even though they couldn't say much, Brownies understood plenty–especially about the important things. Leave it to Shondu to remind him of the most pressing item on their agenda. "I guess we'll have to find our way out of here if we're going to get something to eat, right?"

"Find food! Find food! Fun play! Fun play!" Shondu leapt up suddenly, and the startled Wasketchin could hear his Brownie companion dancing around him in the inky darkness.

"Well, I suppose that means you approve," he said and then he rolled over onto his knees and returned to the long slow process of exploring the cave with his fingers. It was going to be a long day.

Tired as she was, Tayna was unable to find sleep. She just lay on her cot, flipping one way and then the other, with her mind spinning in tight, useless circles. Finally, she sat up and dug her journal out of the knapsack on the ground beside her.

Dear Shammi:

They're gone! And it's all my fault! I mean, I thought I was being so hip, showing how much I knew about peek-a-boo and all that. It was me that put the stupid sack over his head! Abeni showed me that one little bit and I had to go shooting my brain off, proving how smart I was, as if I knew all about it, but if I hadn't done it, poor Elicand would still be here.

I shouldn't even be here. Who am I trying to fool? I mean, peril great? D'uh! What do I know about peril? I'm just a smart-mouth kid. It was all fine enough when peril meant that I was in danger. Or maybe my family, if they really exist. But now it means innocent people who vanish into some pockety nothingness! And I'm still fine? How is that fair?

Maybe it's about time I stopped pretending to be this big, mature adventure seekery chick and admit that I haven't got a clue what I'm doing! There's no secret family waiting for me–that's just a load of cry-baby crap! The only peril around here is the stuff I keep getting other people mixed up in.

And who would send such a stupid message, anyway? A real call for help would have had some details in it, you know? "Dear Tayna. We're all in a heap of trouble and we need you to come home right away to help us out of this jam. Oh. And yes, you really do have a family and we're all just dying to meet you, if we live through the night. Love, you're long lost mother, E'thiel. P.S. In case you need directions, we are currently hiding in a tree stump next to a big waterfall about a ten minute walk north of the place where your friends vanished into the pocket. See you soon." That would have sounded real! None of this mystical as-little-info-as-possible bull-hooey! Whatsamatter? Do message spells cost by the syllable or something?

WHAT AM I DOING HERE? WHY DOES IT HAVE TO BE ME? SHOULDN'T IT BE SOMEONE WHO ACTUALLY KNOWS WHAT'S GOING ON? WHY WON'T ANYBODY TELL ME ANYTHING?

But the letter went unfinished. After having vented the worst of her frustration–and fear–sleep finally caught up to her and pulled its bag of darkness down over her head.

Death was a constant companion on any Wagon Trail, but that usually referred to the Seekers. To lose a member of the Warding party itself was a thing unheard of. The Djin had a saying. "It is a fool of a shepherd who culls his dogs." This was their way of summarizing the pact they held with the Gray Shepherd of Death–or thought they held– that guaranteed the lives of the Warders while the Wagon was on its Trail. Apparently, though, that belief was mistaken. As the sun rose, burning off the mists of night, it did little to burn away the grimness of spirit that had settled over the sons of Kijamon. Zimu had slept fitfully, with his head full of ghosts, while Abeni had found no sleep at all. Of the entire group, only Sarqi had rested well, oblivious to the tragedy that had shaken the others. But when he awoke, the Way Chanter sat up to look around the tent. And the moment his eyes found Abeni's, he knew that things were far from okay.

"Something has happened," he said. Abeni did not respond.

Sarqi threw back the thin blanket and swung his legs off the low traveler's cot to look around. Tayna was still asleep, although she fidgeted in some troublesom dream and would no doubt awaken soon. In the cot beside the girl's, Zimu's sleeping bulk was also plain, accompanied by the distant rock-slide rumble of his breathing. Whatever it was, it had not brought harm to his brothers. But something had happened. A speechless and morose Abeni was so out of character that Sarqi was sure of it. Whatever it was, it was big. He looked around again, inventorying the rest of the tent with rapid, darting eye movements.

"Where is the boy?" he asked suddenly, seeing the empty cot beyond Abeni's. But his younger brother remained mute, staring off into space with haunted eyes and an expression of defeat. When Abeni did not respond, Sarqi stood up and left the tent to investigate further. But even that taught him nothing. When he returned to the tent, he was still as mystified as when he'd left. Clearly, the young Wasketchin was unreliable and had run off, but it did not seem that he had taken anything, or done any harm to the Wagon. And where was Shondu?

All Djin are worriers. They don't like anyone to know it, of course, but they worry. Competence, and its recognition, was the basis of their entire society. But just because they valued competence highly did not mean that it came any more easily to them than it did to any of the other races. It just meant that they worried more about it, and the three sons of Kijamon were as different as any three Djin could possibly be in the way they bore that stress.

For Abeni, competence was simply a matter of doing your best and letting the pebbles fall where they might, so he chose to pretend that he never worried at all. Zimu, on the other hand, walked a much more quiet and thoughtful path. His manner was to analyze all possible outcomes and to prepare himself mentally for each of them in advance. You could always tell when Zimu was worried, because that's when he was at his quietest. Sarqi, however, was the strangest of the three. It is probable that Sarqi worried more than both of his brothers combined. But instead of downplaying his fears, Sarqi's way was to amplify them. Everything he saw, he painted in the most gruesome and horrifying terms possible, lamenting dire ruin loudly and often. He believed that once a fear was voiced, it no longer had the power to become reality. So by speaking his dour predictions of torment and failure to anybody and everybody who would listen, he was actually engaging in his own peculiar version of risk management. Of course, he was also supposed to be one of the powerful sons of Kijamon, so it simply would not do to let anybody else guess the color of his fears. That's why he tried to disguise his heroic, threat-vanquishing thoughts by dressing them up as accusations against those around him, and predictions of utter woe. His brothers knew this about him, of course, which is how they were able to tolerate him so well and work together as a team. Most days. Today, however, Abeni was under considerably more stress than usual, and he had not slept much at all for two consecutive nights.

Sarqi did not yet know this.

"Zimu! Wake up! That fool Abeni has chosen a traitorous brat to spy on us and now he and that stupid chalat have stolen something and run off! I think they're plotting with the Gnomes to–"

With no warning at all, Abeni let out a bellow of rage and launched himself across the tent, clutching Sarqi's throat in a bone-crushing grip.

"You will say no more, little sour puppet, or Abeni will snap your strings and place you in the Wagon himself!"

Tayna, who had been awakened by the shouting, could only watch from her cot in horror. But fortunately for all concerned, Sarqi's complaint had also awakened Zimu, who reached out now, gently, to pry Abeni's fingers from around Sarqi's darkening neck.

"Easy, brother. It is his way. He means no insult." Then he turned to Sarqi. "In time, you will surely be strangled to death by the ropes of your own tongue, little one, but not today. Brother Hambu and the chalat have fallen into the pocket and not returned," he said. "Abeni keens the Kazurwhai for his lost friends, and you bring great shame upon our father's House to speak as you have done: without knowledge. You will amend this when the time is full."

"Yes, brother." Sarqi rasped. He had gone pale at the news, and when he was at last able to get wind enough to speak further, all the customary acid had vanished from his tone. "I did not know. Of course it will be as you say." He turned then to face Abeni and bowed his head deeply to touch the heels of his hands.

"I am shamed by my actions, brother-of-my-grief. You will know how deeply, not by the melody of my words, but by the shape of my actions. I ask only that you grant me time to find a fitting manner in which to bring justice to the injury I have done you."

As Sarqi spoke, Zimu's eyes widened slightly, but he hid his surprise, only nodding briefly to indicate that the apology was acceptable.

Abeni, who had slumped back down to the ground as though it had been he who'd had his strings cut, no longer seemed to realize that his brothers were even there.

In the end, Zimu and Sarqi broke camp without disturbing him. They even managed to strike the tent from around him, without asking him to so much as wiggle out of the way, dismantling the giant red shelter like a stage curtain being withdrawn to reveal a lone, grieving figure at center stage. As they repacked the provisions and gear into the tailbox of the Wagon, each of them stole nervous glances at their younger brother. If the truth were commanded from them, they would each have told how much in awe they had always been of their most boisterous and competent sibling–the one they each judged to be the most in spirit like their legendary father–although they had never spoken of it. To see such a man as that reduced to this current, low state, disturbed them more deeply than they dared to say, and left them both feeling utterly helpless. Tayna, on the other hand, who could do nothing to help with packing, sat cross-legged on the ground in front of Abeni and did something that neither brother could have even conceived doing, and in the act, probably saved him from madness. She held his hand.

It was a foregone conclusion that Zimu and Sarqi would go back to sharing the three Warder's tasks between them, as they had done on their descent from the Anvil, but they had no idea how they were going to manage to get Abeni to come along with them when they set out, and it was sacrilege to even consider placing him in one of the sky tubes. But, to everyone's surprise, when the packing was done and the two older brothers had taken up their stations, Abeni simply stood up and went to his accustomed lead position, waiting silently for the Way Chanter to begin. Once the Wagon was aloft, Abeni struck out along the path through the marsh that he had scouted for them the night before, and Tayna was right behind him.

Sarqi and Zimu exchanged quick glances and then shrugged. Neither of them knew what to say, but as it turned out, words simply weren't of much use to any of them that day. Nobody noticed the angry redness of Tayna's wrist, nor how often she reached out and jerked at it with violent, desperate twists.

It was not a good day.

Over the next twelve hours, the Wagon led them to three different villages, where their party was joined by five more Seekers. If any of the bereaved family members noticed the silent, sullen mood of the Warders, they spoke nothing of it. Perhaps they believed that this was only fitting behavior in the presence of the dead. Regardless, with each new destination, the Wagon grew that much heavier, and the party wended its way, by degrees, further and further out into the surrounding lands. Ever onward. Slowly, their path tended left in a broad arc that, in a week, would bring them fully around the circle of the Throat before crossing over the Lip, curling at last down into Gnomileshi lands—like a granite ship afloat on a rainbow sea, courting the edges of a whirlpool, drawn on by some strange gravity of the dead, down to the harvest tables of the Gnomileshi Horde. That was the way of the Forest.

<hr />

Elicand's hands felt like they had been whipped with a rope of nettles and then bathed in salt-water brine. Every inch of exposed flesh had been scraping, banging or bumping against the rough rock of the cave's floors and walls for more hours than he could count. His poor fingers had been abused, probing into narrow cracks and crevices and his palms had stroked themselves raw against the gritty surfaces of a thousand boulders. The bruises of a hundred stalagmites decorated his shoulders and the top of his head. As a reward for these efforts, though, he was now the Lord High Prince of a domain that stretched sixty-five paces long and fifty-one paces wide at its widest point. It was a kingdom he liked to call Ouchyville, and his aching fingers had discovered three possible ways out of his new domain.

At one end of the chamber was Narrow Gap Passage, where the rock walls narrowed down to within just a few inches of each other. Shondu might be able to squeeze his way through it, but even a starved and sickly Wasketchin youth—which Elicand himself would no doubt become in a few days—could not force himself through such a tiny space. If none of the other exits panned out, though, it was possible that he might have to try to find something to use to chip open a wider gap. This, he called his Plan of Hopeless Optimism. (It was a reflection of Elicand's training that he still clung to crafting stories in his head about his exploits in this strange place, and he believed fiercely that having evocative names for things was an important part of creating memorable stories.)

The second potential exit from Ouchyville was down—an unlikely direction in which to seek escape from an apparently underground cavern—through a large gaping hole in the floor at one end of the cave. This Elicand had named Stupid Uncle Chasm. It was a little less than four paces wide, but a test stone dropped over the edge fell silently for almost eight seconds before crashing against more rocks far below. Even though he had discovered it while crawling on all fours, Elicand had still come perilously close to falling in, because he had allowed the heart-stopping terror from his earlier false-chasm experience to fade from his memory. After several hours of methodical searching without mishap, he'd gotten sloppy with his technique and moved forward before he'd properly tested that the floor under his hand would bear his weight. When it gave way, it was only by dumb luck that his shoulder had hit a hump of rock, which kept the rest of him from sliding in after the hand. If he was going to explore Stupid Uncle Chasm any further, he would have to start by throwing his legs over the edge and then attempting to climb down the unknown chasm wall–if it even had one–by feeling his way to footholds with his bare toes. He called this the Plan of Falling and Dying.

The third exit possibility was about one third of the way around the cavern wall from Narrow Gap Passage, higher up, and marked by a promising lip of stone. So far, he had been unable to get up high enough to feel anything beyond the lip, but it seemed to be a real opening, judging by the breeze. It was subtle, but Elicand was pretty sure he could feel a steady movement of air flowing through the cave, emanating from Narrow Gap Passage and exiting past that high lip of rock. He had labeled this one the Scary Tunnel of Wind Plan and it was by far the least terrifying of the three. But unfortunately "least terrifying" was still horrifying enough to leave him paralyzed with fear as he sat there in the dark, trying to work up the nerve to take the next step. It would be so much easier if he could just see what he was doing. Amazingly, even a thing as simple as walking across a room became a devastating trial of nerves when you had to do it blind and in a strange place, surrounded by a multitude of invisible opportunities for death. At first, he had believed that after a while–maybe an hour, maybe two–his eyes would adjust and he'd be able to see, but it had been something like twelve hours now and he was still just as blind as a granite hammer. He had explored this cave in total darkness and clearly, if he was going to find a way out of it, he would do that in total darkness as well.

In order to give himself some comfort and to organize his search of the cave, Elicand had taken to creating little piles of stones every ten paces, leaving them behind in a growing grid arrangement as he worked his way methodically around the floor. But as he sat there now, trying to summon up the courage to take the next step, it occurred to him that he hadn't heard the tell-tale sound of those stones getting knocked over. He had been hearing Shondu laughing and playing, leaping and dancing around the cave all day, but, somehow, also managing to avoid the little maze of cairns. Elicand realized with a start that Shondu could see in this darkness!

He leapt to his feet immediately and called the chalat to come over. "Lead the way home, boy," he said as Shondu approached. Elicand could hear the Brownie's laughter dancing around him in a circle.

"Pikabu! Pikabu!" Elicand groaned. Not this damned pikabu thing again.

In exasperation, Elicand tried simple Brownie-speak. "No play. Bad trouble. Shondu find Abeni. Take Elicand back now."

"Pikabu! Pikabu!"

Leaf-rot! Brownies just weren't smart enough for rescue work. The brief burst of excitement that had seized him, suddenly leaked out of him then, like water from a punctured wetskin, and Elicand slumped back down to the floor. The truth was becoming clear. Scary Tunnel of Wind Plan was hopeless. He was going to die here, alone, helpless and blind, with no idea where he was or how he had gotten himself into this predicament. Somehow, the magic of Methilien had turned its back on him completely.

───────

The next morning, Abeni was the first to rise. Unfortunately, waking up was a bad thing, a terrible thing, something that he, of all people, should have been incapable of doing on this particular morning. With Gnome territory now so close at hand, and the threat of claim-stringers at its peak, the brothers had decided that a watch would have to be kept. And since it had not been possible for the Way Chanter to participate, given his intense fatigue, the job had been split between Zimu, the Little Fish and himself.

All through Tayna's, and then Zimu's watch, Abeni had been unable to sleep, and he'd been certain that he would be just as unable during his own, so he'd relieved his brother early and sent him off to the tent. But Abeni had misjudged how badly he had needed sleep. And now he had committed the gravest of sins: falling asleep on watch. Hopefully, it had only been a short nap and all would be well.

Abeni shook himself fully awake and stood up. The tree root that had served as his pillow now chastised him with a creak and a groan, as he used it to pull himself to his feet. But the sound was a mere echo of shrieks crying out from within his own body. Every muscle and tendon inside him screamed as he pulled them out of the positions they had stiffened into in the night. Yet he welcomed the discomfort as fitting punishment for his failures. First he had allowed those under his care to be snatched by the Father of Grief, and now he had disgraced his duty to the Wagon itself, by falling asleep when he should have been watching over it. There was no end to his shame, but before he could do anything about his obligations to honor, he would first have to ensure that no harm had come of this latest incompetence. Abeni shuffled away from the tree and made his way over to the Wagon.

Unfortunately, the Wagon was gone.

Abeni stared blankly for a moment, and then once his brain had caught up with the facts reported by his eyes, he spun around, looking in every direction at once. He charged around to the far side of the red tent, sweeping his gaze across the mostly lavender and violet forest beyond, but he knew what he would find even before his eyes had confirmed it. Nothing. The Wagon and everything in it–including the bodies of two kings–had vanished in the night. There was no sign anywhere–not even to his experienced tracker's eyes–of where it had gone or who had taken it.

This was the final humiliation and Abeni's shoulders slumped in defeat as he dropped listlessly against the base of his shame-tree. He spun the iron band around his wrist in a gesture of angry futility, as he had seen the Little Fish do with growing frequency. "Abeni will bring nothing but rust to the house of Kijamon now," he said quietly.

The measure of any Djin's competence was taken by the difficulty of the tasks he had accepted, and the elegance with which they'd been completed. The greatest shame a Djin could imagine would be to botch the assignment, thereby losing any hope that the iron ring binding him to his duty might be transmuted into more lustrous metals. Abeni's arms already boasted a number of such glittering bands–a collection of silver and not just a few golds–that would have been impressive on any Djin twice his age. The thought of now marring that reputation, or those of his father or their House, filled him with remorse. He stared silently at his arm, inspecting the dull iron ring carefully to see if the corrosion had already begun.

"There shall be enough rust and shame for all," said a voice. Abeni nodded his silent agreement as Zimu strode quietly from around the corner of the tent, inspecting his own arm and its identical, dull iron band. The older Djin slumped to the forest floor beside his brother. He, too, had noticed the missing Wagon, and had surmised the rest from the expression on Abeni's face.

"Iron does not perish quickly," Zimu said. "Perhaps we shall sing charms to hasten its death and the bands will be dust within a single year."

"But not before the skin has stained," Abeni replied. They could both think of two or three senior Djin, older even than Kijamon himself, who still bore the orange smears of failure that they had earned long ago, in the dim history of their youth. Both brothers shuddered together at the thought of joining those ranks. They were still sitting there in silent contemplation of their plight when the third brother emerged from around the corner of the tent. Sarqi's eyes were still darting around the scene, searching for the conspicuously absent Wagon.

"What has happened with it you fools? What have you done?" he snarled.

Tayna had been awakened by the strained voices of the Djin brothers, and she lay on her cot rubbing gingerly at her inflamed wrist. Apparently, she'd been twisting her imaginary bracelet all night, and the skin of her wrist was now puffy and raw. She fished around in the folds of her kirfa, looking for the merlhora leaves she had collected the previous day. And this also allowed her to delay getting up. She didn't want to intrude on what she sensed was a private, family moment between the brothers, outside. But she did listen.

By the time Abeni and Zimu had explained what little they knew, and convinced Sarqi that they hadn't simply set fire to the Wagon for sport while he slept, the sun was breaking above the tree-tops. It was Abeni who finally brought them to action.

"Abeni will not return to the Anvil in shame, not while he has strength left to recover what has been taken."

Tayna moved to the door flap of the tent and pulled it back to look out at the brothers.

"The Wagon is gone," Zimu said. "It leaves no tracks to follow. The thief left no footprints to guide our way. Not one among us saw his face nor which way he fled." With her wrist now pleasantly numb, Tayna quietly kicked herself for not having had the foresight to sit watch with Abeni during the night, but she'd been so tired after her own watch, that she'd just fallen thankfully onto her cot and slept like a log.

Abeni climbed wearily to his feet, but there was a light of purpose in his eyes that hadn't been there earlier. "Zimu is correct. The sons of Kijamon do not know what has happened. If they are to preserve the tatters of their names, they must learn what can be learned, no matter the cost." He drew himself tall and puffed out his chest in defiance.

"Abeni will ask the fog." He glared at his brothers, daring them to challenge his decision. Zimu merely raised an eyebrow, but Sarqi spun around to face him as though he had been slapped.

"You're going to involve *them*? Do you think I want any part of their bargain? Who has ever gotten anything but grief from the so-called 'aid' of a sprite?"

"The fog answers only to water sprites," Zimu said. "Trust not in sprites nor the motivations of a Gnome." This was a well-known saying among the Djin.

"Be still, my brothers. No other path is open to House Kijamon. Abeni would sooner face one thousand angry water sprites than the rust-shamed eyes of his father. Perhaps if you are silent," he said, staring directly at Sarqi, "they will not demand the blood-fee." Then without allowing them any further debate, he threw back his arms and gave voice to a deep, bullfrog-throated melody. The air around him began to boil. His singing was like a babbling brook compared to Sarqi's Wagon song. This warmer, burbling sound irritated Sarqi, who hated water in any form—rivers, lakes, puddles. He even hated the *sounds* of water and he secretly believed that Abeni had deliberately chosen his singing style as a child, precisely because of its value for brother-baiting. It was just the kind of subtle tactic a younger brother might employ to annoy an older sibling—one that would go completely unnoticed by their parents. So Sarqi fumed in a silent stew as Abeni sang now, boldly and without restraint, with the voice of a frisky mountain stream. Slowly, the fog bank that had crowded up to greet him, withdrew, leaving the three brothers standing momentarily alone at the center of a growing circular pocket of clear air, until fifteen menacing, black shapes slunk eerily out of the receding fog, surrounding them on all sides.

The sprites had come.

———⟨———

Elicand scrambled his feet against the rough stone wall of the cave and dragged himself up over the lip just as the precarious arrangement of stones beneath him collapsed. It had been a very near thing, but he was now securely up on the ledge. Scary Tunnel of Wind Plan was ready for Phase Two. Whatever that might be.

"Food time?"

The nearness of the Brownie's voice startled him in the darkness. "No, Shondu. Not food time." Elicand heard a quiet sigh of disappointment, but there was nothing he could do about that. His first priority had to be to find a way out of the cave. There was no point in looking for food here, since nothing edible could grow without nutrients and light, and if he wasted time looking for it now, he'd be too weak from hunger to find a way out later. Better to keep moving while he still could.

Scary Wind Tunnel turned out to be a little wider than his outstretched arms and tall enough to stand up in, if he had wanted to. Despite its size and apparent comfort, he proceeded slowly though, feeling carefully all the way around the passage–floor, walls and ceiling–before moving forward, and then repeating the exercise all over again. His progress was achingly slow, but he didn't want to miss any possible side passages or dangerous crevices. Several times he stopped to cock an ear, listening quietly to the dark air around him. It was as if he could almost hear something, a quiet hiss, very low, too low to be sure he had even heard it. Sometimes he would be sure and then he'd tilt his head a different way and it would be gone. The sounds were just too subtle to be certain. He had expected his other senses to become more acute, now that he was forced to rely on them entirely, but instead of hearing every little whisper, he had only begun second-guessing every click and scrape. Even his sense of touch was growing suspect. There were times when he got the strangest sense that the rocks were not just damp, but oily too. Then he would examine them again and find them to be entirely normal. Nothing more than damp stone.

After repeating his search-and-hunch-forward routine several dozen times, the passage turned sharply to his right. Such changes and unexpected features kept the tedious job from becoming too boring, and Elicand greeted the new section of tunnel with some enthusiasm, especially when he realized that he could now definitely hear a hissing noise. Perhaps his ears were indulging in a little wishful hearing, but he thought it sounded like wind rustling in trees. There was still no light to see by, but he reasoned that, since he had no idea of the time, it could easily be night now in the outside world.

Over the next hour–or maybe it was three–the tunnel twisted several more times, and with each twist, the sound of breezes in the forest canopy had grown louder. But there was still no light. Anticipation of an end to this prison of darkness spurred Elicand on faster and faster, and he had to struggle to keep his mind on caution. There was no point rushing, only to fall into an unseen pit right at the very edge of salvation. As a concession to speeding up, though, without sacrificing safety, he decided to skip his examination of the side walls. When he had entered the tunnel, his objective had been to build a mental map of it, including any branches that might provide alternate paths to freedom if this one failed. But now that he could actually hear the wind just a few dozen yards away, other factors became more pressing, such as getting out before he or Shondu starved to death. His excitement began to build.

With his new, faster procedure, the progress of his crawling improved, and he was advancing quickly toward his goal when he reached out and his heart skipped a beat. The ceiling above his head had begun to slope down! Elicand inched forward again and repeated his safety check, with his fingers splayed out, probing the tunnel floor, and then he reached up. Sure enough, the roof was lower again. Panic gripped him. To be this close and have his exit vanish before his very hands was just unfair. Throwing caution into a pit, he crept forward again, keeping one hand on the ceiling and the other on the floor. Step after step he advanced while his hands continued to move slowly toward each other. Finally, with less than a foot between them, the ceiling stopped dropping. It had leveled off again, creating a very shallow tunnel that continued forward. Elicand dropped to the floor and thrust his arm as far into the passage as he could and felt around. Yes, there it was, a lip of stone at the extreme limit of his reach. He could just feel the beginning of a wall rising upward on the other side. An *outside* wall, he was sure of it! With his head down right next to the gap, the hiss of rustling leaves was almost overwhelming. It was impossibly loud, as it echoed and bounced within the close-quartered stone tunnel, but of course it would be loud. His ears were just over-reacting to real sounds now after so many hours–or days even–of grave-like silence.

Without even stopping to wonder where Shondu had gotten to, Elicand pulled himself along the tunnel floor on his back, with both arms stretched out beyond his head, grabbing for purchase against the damp rock walls. Elation filled him as he heaved and struggled, inching slowly forward through the cramped passage. Freedom was only a few feet away! A cool, damp breath of night air tickled his left hand as it emerged beyond the end of the tunnel. Now he was able to grab against that outer wall and pull.

As he dragged himself forcefully through the gap, a bolt of pain shot suddenly through his ribs as they fetched up hard against a protruding lump of stone. He would have cried out if there had been any air left in his lungs, but the knob of rock was wedged tight, pressing down against his chest, forcing his lungs to compress. Elicand's face contorted in pain. He flailed his arm weakly, trying to get a better grip. With great effort, he tried one last desperate pull, trying to heave himself past the obstruction, but he only succeeded in wedging himself tighter. Now the colors played again across his vision, dancing in time to the hammering of his heart. There was no air left in his lungs and with the weight of a mountain pressing down on him, no way to refill them. His strength was failing and his head swam. He realized that he couldn't go any further forward. The colors flashed and flickered and it was getting hard to think. In desperation, he managed to brace a heel into a crevice of rock and pull himself back, feebly. He felt his back budge, just a trifle against the cold, stone floor, but that was all. He had nothing left. He was trapped, half in and half out of his subterranean prison, and in just a moment or two, he was going to die there, unable to breathe, but with the roaring, cascading sound of wind in his ears, ripping through the forest canopy, singing its lament to his passing.

Elicand wanted to scream. He wanted to cry out for help. Most of all, he wanted to inhale. For a flickering moment he was aware of the mighty mountain above him, with its foot planted on his chest and its roar of triumph on the wind. And then the surrounding darkness surged up over his head and he slipped silently from the world.

———————

"Feed me," said one of the inky black shapes.

"And me," said another, and another, and then still another. Soon the forest echoed with the mewling demands of the sprites as they emerged from the fog, twisting and undulating their bodies, which were so dark that they could scarcely be seen, except as patches of blackness against the lighter-colored puffs of mist.

"Sprites are not to be trusted," Zimu said. Tayna nodded her agreement. These guys did not look like Good Samaritan types.

"Why should we feed them?" Sarqi said. They will do nothing for us." Of the four of them, only Abeni had ever actually bargained with sprites before, and he silenced the others with a sharp hand gesture.

"The sons of Kijamon will gladly feed the Kings of Night," he said to the writhing crowd. Then he reached into a pouch at his waist and withdrew a small gobbet of glistening, whitish meat, which he held out so that all the sprites could see it. Immediately, the sinuous shapes converged toward the Djin, and Abeni dropped quickly to one knee. He lowered his gaze and lifted the quivering flesh even higher. "Abeni regrets that he cannot provide such worthy Kings with more than this small token. Yesterday he could have given much, much more of the sacred flapmeat. Plenty for all the Kings to feast upon for a dozen days, but today there is none but this."

As he spoke, the sprites kept one eye on Abeni's hand and one on each other as they jockeyed for position, trying to get close enough to snatch his tribute without getting close enough to any of their kin to risk having it snatched away in turn. The constant shifting and adjusting brought the sprites into a tight circle that began to turn, rotating slowly around the kneeling Djin. Through it all, Abeni kept his eyes down and his hand out, ensuring that the tasty prize was always within sight of the circling fiends. His brothers stared at the spectacle with mounting horror.

"The Djin kneel to none!" Zimu declared.

"You drag our name through the slime!" Sarqi whined. Both brothers moved toward Abeni at the same moment. Perhaps they each thought to bring him to his senses and restore whatever dignity they could to their shared family honor, but they never reached him.

"Be still, my brothers," Abeni said, and then he sang again, briefly. The encircling cloud bank responded at once to Abeni's water voice. Tendrils of fog unfurled and wrapped themselves gently about the torsos of the two elder Djin, who struggled and heaved against these unexpected restraints. "Abeni knows something of the ways of the fog," he said. "Watch your little brother and share in what he has learned." Then he turned his attention back to the revolving circle of sprites. Tayna could only watch, fascinated by the drama playing out around her, and praying that Abeni actually knew what he was doing.

"Will my Kings not take this gift of flapmeat?" The sprites hissed and spat at one another as Abeni held his gift out to them, offering it left and right, enticing each of them, but being careful not to allow any to get close enough to snatch it before he turned and offered it to another.

"It is mine!" said one.

"No, mine!" said another, and soon the forest echoed with alternating claims and denials of ownership. Abeni allowed this to continue for several moments and then, at last, he stood up and placed the scrap of fish back in his pouch.

"Abeni has failed his Kings," he said and he hung his head in shame. "Abeni had more than enough for a feast of feasts, for all the Kings of Dark Water, but Abeni has lost his wagon and the feastflesh with it. The mighty Kings are right to refuse his poor offering. This tiny morsel is not enough. There was much more in the Wagon." As he spoke, the crowd of sprites trembled with frustration.

"The wagon is mine," said one of the sprites, in a flash of problem-solving inspiration. "Bring it to me."

"Bring it to me," said another. "The cargo is mine!" Soon the forest air was filled again, this time with demands for wagons and the tasty treasures they contained.

"Abeni is ashamed that he must disappoint his Kings," he said, "for he does not know where the wagon has gone. It vanished in the night, with all the flapmeat and cream, but Abeni does not know in which direction to search for it."

"Cream?" said one of the sprites. "Bring me the cream!" Again they all fell to shouting their demands, but one voice called out over the others.

"The slave does not know where the cream and tasty meat have gone. I will show him."

"No! I will show him," shouted another.

"No! It will be me!" said a third. In moments the arguing gave way to a piteous wailing that grew in volume as more and more of the sprites joined in. A section of the surrounding bank of fog broke itself off and floated toward the middle of the clearing, where it seemed to condense into a near-solid image—a slightly wispy imitation of the Wagon of Tears. Once it had formed, it drifted over and settled on the exact spot where the brothers had last seen the original Wagon the night before, resting heavily on the crushed grasses where the great silver runners had lain.

"The fog sees all," Zimu whispered. Everyone stared intently at the water-play before them—Tayna from rapt fascination, and the Djin certain that the restoration of their very honor rested on observing every detail. At first nothing seemed to happen, but then another tendril of fog detached itself from the surrounding bank of mist and drifted toward the Wagon. As it moved, it took the form of a smallish man.

"Who is that?" Sarqi demanded. "Who dared interfere with the Sledge of the Dead?"

"To do so is to challenge the Grey Shepherd himself," Zimu announced, but despite their indignation, both brothers continued to watch. The softness of the misty display made the details fuzzy and it was impossible to identify the figure that crept toward the Wagon, but once he had reached it and was standing upright at the Wagon's side, there was one detail that they could all make out easily: more than half the face was made of nose.

"A Gnome!" Zimu said.

"Where did he come from?" Sarqi asked.

They watched as the Gnome raised a long staff and waved it in an intricate pattern above his head. The mist-Wagon rose up off the ground and floated away slowly between the trees, where it vanished into the fog.

Zimu and Sarqi seemed as perplexed as Tayna, but Abeni's eye's flashed with anger. "The Wagon of Tears ignores the villages," he said, "and all of the Seekers who await its passage. Now it seeks directly for the Throat, enslaved to the will of a Gnome." This last he spit out with contempt, then without another word, he turned and strode off into the fog after it.

Tayna looked quickly at Abeni's silhouette vanishing into the mist, and then back to the brothers, still struggling against their bonds. She twisted her wrist fiercely. Once, twice, three times, sending flames of pain up her arm each time. It was an impossible decision! Rescue the brothers and lose Abeni in the fog? Or leave them to the sprites and chase her demented friend on the slim chance she could help?

"Arrgh!"

What she really wanted was to pitch the whole Wagon problem altogether and just get on with the Stinkhole and her *family yours* problem. And maybe, deep down inside, that was the deciding factor. Tayna turned to the brothers, who were still struggling with their foggy bonds, and shrugged. What could she do against Abeni's fog magic or a dozen angry sprites? The sons of Kijamon were probably better equipped to deal with both problems–even tied up–than she ever would be. So she raised her hand in a snappy salute, without a trace of flippancy about it, and then threw her pack over her shoulder and raced off into the swirling mist.

"Abeni! Wait for me!"

Zimu and Sarqi would have to figure things out for themselves.

chapter 13

"I can't part with it for any less than a full grin."

"A grin? Why, it's scarcely worth a wink—a lazy wink, mind you—and still quite dear at that."

"Sorry friend. It's a grin from you or a grin from the next carp. Makes no difference to me who pays, but I'll have the whole value, mark my promise."

Mehklok sighed and set the delicate piece back on the table. He might have gone to a blush, if pressed, but not so much as a chuckle farther. The detailing was excellent, but there were stress faults all through the material where it had been worked with too much heat and too forcefully. The man was putting on airs. Still, he mustn't offend. Not many Gnomes had as keen an eye as he did for these things. There'd be other pieces and other tables. "Die quickly," he said, and then he moved on. Behind him, the merchant nodded politely.

Market day was such a trial for Mehklok. He was cursed with the tastes of a king and the wherewithal of a cat skinner. The pittance he collected from his parishioners was barely enough to keep a working-class dung heap stocked and appointed, let alone enough to rebuild a church of the first rank to its former glory. It had been years since the now-impoverished community of Gash-Garnok had last been home to any nobility—they'd all fled rather than bear the Fury's stare—but you couldn't just pick up a church and run away with it, could you? And that's exactly how long it had been since he'd last received a tithing of any real substance. Since then, he'd been reduced to this miserly existence, seeking out bargains in the late-day heat and appreciating far more than he could afford to buy. He cursed under his breath and pushed his way through the throng of hunched-over shoppers as he made his way up the aisle. Maybe he'd find something at the flesh-worker's stalls.

"Ah, this looks promising," he said as he passed the vulture's wing that marked the entrance to the area reserved for the wet arts. His optimism was rewarded almost immediately. The wares on the third table down still jiggled with the perkiness of recent work. He stooped himself over a bit farther before he approached. It wouldn't do to let the craftsman see him coming, all up and lofty like. Prices would double in a heartbeat.

The stall was like most market stalls–a rickety table standing between two large skins for privacy. Behind it, a smallish woman with long side-teeth and a strong jaw watched him as he moved in to examine her work.

"Is this flapmeat?" he asked, holding one of the displays up to show her which one he meant.

"Don't wave it about like that, you clout!" She lunged forward and took it from his hand, being much more gentle with the delicate carving than she was with his fingers, but Mehklok wasn't in the mood for tipping, so he said nothing and waited for her arm-hairs to lay flat again before pressing her.

"Well, is it?"

She set the piece back on the table and looked up at him with the clearer of her two eyes. "Yes, it is," she said. "*Blind* flapmeat." His eyes widened.

"Really? Where in the depths did you find a blind one? Was it big enough for a set, or is this a solo?"

The piece was quite good. Exceptional, even. If he was lucky and she had three of similar quality, then he knew just where he'd put them. None of the locals would appreciate them, of course, but the district overcaptain had been threatening to drop by for weeks now. Wouldn't that just catch him in the hollow of his throat? Sacramental Raptors made of real flapmeat. Blind flapmeat, at that. Then we'd see who was asking who for favors

"I'll not say where, 'cept that t'weren't an easy climb, let me tell you." The old woman's eyes glinted with the hint of a secret, but Mehklok ignored it.

"So there's only the one then?" She cast an eye over him coolly, estimating how rich his heart might be.

"There's a set," she said. "Four of 'em on ice, and this one out here. I rotates 'em every couple of hours–to keep the stiffening even." Then she turned her face away as she muttered a price.

"What was that?" Mehklok said. "I didn't catch it." Not a good sign. The mumblers were never asking too little.

"I said, the whole set is going for a ludicrous deal. All five for a kiss."

Mehklok actually stumbled, bumping into the table with his hip and setting the display a-quivering. "A kiss? Are you out of your mind? I haven't seen a kiss in... Well, I don't know, but not since your mother was young enough to chase flies."

"I'll go two hugs and a hearty laugh," she said. "But I've got children to feed and the husband is all pink and soft–needs a good liniment, and that'll cost plenty now, won't it?"

Mehklok looked at the raptor again. The outstretched wings had been flayed so delicately. The pin-bones looked like real feathers and they caught the light, gleaming at him in mockery. *We're so beautiful. You can't have us.*

"I only need the three," he said. "I'll give you..." Was he out of his mind? It would leave him flat broke until the next tablefest, but they really were exquisite. "A hug for the three of them, then. That's as high as I'll go."

The little woman looked at the table and then down at the casket of ice beneath it, no doubt doing some quick calculating.

"Sorry, dear. They've only just come out today. If this was tomorrow, I wager I'd be taking your hug then, and be glad to cut my losses. But there's still plenty of light, and all of tomorrow. You're sure you won't take 'em all? For the two hugs? I'll eat the laugh."

Mehklok shook his head sadly. "I just can't," he said. "I've only got the one hug to spend and it has a lot of work to do."

She nodded in understanding. "So maybe tomorrow then?" But he was already shaking his head.

"I've got to be back to the steeple by darkfall," he said. "I will keep an eye open for you though. Next time." He turned and shuffled away.

"You do that, dear. You do that."

He had almost gotten as far as the counting house when she called out to him.

"You say it's for a church, is it? An important one?"

Mehklok shrugged. "It was. Once. Garnok's Rage. It's out in..."

The old woman's eyes doubled in size. "Oh, go on!" she said. "I'm old enough to remember the Garnok. It was a grand steeple in my day. Has it come down as bad as all that?" It had, he told her, sorry to say. Then her expression narrowed, speculatively. "Hmm. Well, I can't break up the set–who would want just a pair? But if I let you take the lot for just the one hug, I'd want your promise they'd be used at the altar."

"Three at the altar," he said. "And one over each portal."

She grunted her satisfaction and then, with a shrug, she lifted the showpiece carefully from the table. "I don't suppose anybody important will see my work at the Garnok these days," she said. "But still, it would–" Mehklok interrupted her.

"Oh, but they will," he said. "At least one overcaptain and possibly his brood-kin as well. I've been waiting for an excuse to bring them in, and your exquisite raptors would be just the thing to make them see how glorious the Garnok could be again. Especially now that the Fury has come down."

She nodded knowingly. "I'd heard tell of that. Qhirmaghen's work, they say. He's a shrewd one, he is. Knows full well what honest folks thought of her Loftiness up there, glaring down like she was staring into filth. Demonstrated great power and awareness of the common folk, didn't he? Can't imagine what any of the other Contenders could do to best him now."

"Perhaps, but still, it all seems a bit backhanded, don't you think? After all, it was only put there because of what the Wasketchin King claims the First Prince did against him. Qhirmaghen could be reminding people that the First Prince is nothing but trouble. Has a bit of an air of self-service to it as well, or so it seems."

"Ar. I take yer point," the woman said. "Must have been good for the old Garnok though, eh? All them stooping young hordesmen o' his, slinking back and forth past your front door all day? I'll warrant you haven't seen so much tribute in an entire moon as ye saw in a single hour of that lot's traffic."

Mehklok shook his head. "Qhirmaghen has few minions," he said. "And those he has, he won't allow to pay respects to the heroes. Says it wouldn't be seemly for the court of a Contender to play favorites, seeking the blessing of Garnok or Ishig and not all the rest. Fact is, when they're about, all they do is scare away my usual visitors–all terrified they'll be pressed into duty. And those that used to come, came as much to see her as to see the Rage. I cannot remember a worse month in all my years, and now, I fear it can only get worse."

The old woman clucked in dismay. "Won't permit proper respect, will he? Well, I never. To think that a Contender for the Crown would deny the very heroes what sprung 'im. What kind of death can we hope for now, if'n we go on, snubbing our dark-fathers like that? And on the eve of Contest, no less." She made a sound of disbelief in the back of her throat, then she seemed to remember the business at hand. "Well, if ye've got it that hard over, you'll be wanting to get back then, and ye've got a long climb to get you there. No use letting these guardians spoil before you gets 'em up where they can be seen proper. You come pay an old woman her due then, and we'll get you packed and on your way."

Mehklok took a deep breath. It had been one thing to offer a hug for the pieces, but it was entirely another to actually pay that much for them. Still, a deal struck is a deal done. He stepped around the table and swept the old girl up in his arms, squeezing her just tight enough to let her know she'd been hugged by a real gentleman. Some folks did a horrible job of it, didn't give full value, but he'd been raised by a proper mother, and educated among the nobles. He knew how to handle these big transactions, even if he didn't get much practice at them. As he set her back on the ground, he couldn't resist himself, and flashed her a full half-row of upper teeth.

"Well, my goodness," she said, blushing and turning away. "Such a thorough hug as I've ever had, and a partial smile into the bargain. You've the mark of a worthy man, you have."

Mehklok relaxed his face to its normal, impassive expression, and bowed low. "Well I'll just take that honest blush of a good woman as my change," he said. Then, since he was still bent over, he scooped up the ice bucket with all five raptor carvings now inside, tucked it under his arm and bid her a good day.

He looked every inch the dandy as he strutted away, although his spine did bend slightly to one side, to balance the bucketful of art that he carried on the opposite hip. A true dandy would have had a bearer for his shopping. Regardless, Mehklok scuttled forward with a lofty, dignified aura that said, "My bearer is ill but I am worldly enough to do my shopping without him." However much outward calm he might have been showing though, he was absolutely screaming on the inside. *What have I done? What have I done? There's nothing left but a blush and some flinches. I'm ruined!*

Elicand's afterlife was a grave disappointment. For one thing, it shouldn't hurt so much, and for another, shouldn't he be able to move? But he couldn't. Not a muscle, not a twitch, except his neck, which he could flex just a trifle, in a sort of nodding motion. That might be helpful. If the ticket to his salvation was in any way dependent on being able to nod "yes," then he was all set. Something was restraining him, but what? Had there been a cave-collapse after he lost consciousness? Was he buried beneath a mile of hard-packed dirt? If so, then why could he breathe?

To say that he was disoriented would be grossly understating the case. It wasn't just the discomfort or the mobility problems–those, he could have lived with. Elicand didn't even know where he was. For that matter, he couldn't even be sure that he *was* at all. How do you prove you're alive when you can't get any useful information from your senses? He was now either completely blind or still in total darkness, and he couldn't hear anything either, save for a deafening roar in his ears, like a... well, like a deafening roar. It wasn't coming from any particular direction–it came from everywhere–and it absorbed all other sounds. He tried to talk, then to yell, and then he screamed for all he was worth. Yet he heard not a peep. And to top it all off, he was freezing. The inky blackness of the hereafter was as cold and penetrating as the teeth of the Anvil biting at the sky. He could feel chill tendrils of eternal nothingness running down his ribs and collecting in a pool against the small of his back. Even his face felt clammy with it and his hair hung damply into his eyes.

Wait a minute. Hair. He wagged his head again, as vigorously as he could manage, and was rewarded by a dozen little pin-pricks of discomfort as his bangs flopped back and forth, jabbing into his eyes. If he had hair, maybe he wasn't dead after all. More than anything else, that thought reassured him. He'd always imagined that hair in the ever-after was a thing of beauty that flowed from one's head like a river of light, not something that was cold and damp and stabbed your eyeballs when you wiggled.

Emboldened by this revelation, he tried again to conjure up a light charm. Come on! Just a little glow. A shimmer even. He sang his charm songs deafly, but he knew them well and was sure that he had made no error, and even though he repeated them a dozen times... Nothing.

He coughed and felt a dull, familiar pain tighten across his chest. Maybe he was dead after all. Maybe the afterlife was an eternity where you relived the last few moments of your life and contemplated what a f'znat you'd been for getting yourself into such a predicament in the first place. That would explain the darkness and the chest pain, and possibly even the whole immobility thing.

(experience self-thou well-being question)

198

Elicand tried to jerk his head around, or tried to, but he couldn't move that far. "Hello? Is somebody there?" But he heard nothing, not even his own question. All the world was a roaring "Shhhhhhhh!" A blanket of static that ate all sound.

(self-mine place-here exist statement)

The voice–no, retract that. The *words* were in his head, but they weren't coming in through his ears. It was like somebody had burrowed into his skull and was sharing the space inside it with him.

(self-mine distinct external exist body-place statement)

Was that an answer? External, as in outside my body? How can you listen to my thoughts if you're not in my head? He wasn't sure he'd understood the overlaid word-ideas he was "hearing." They weren't all strung out in a line, like a sentence. Instead, they seemed to overlap, occurring all at once. It was like a packet of emotional thought maybe, rather than a spoken sentence, but most of all, it was alien and uncomfortable and really, really spooky.
"Where am I?"

(self-thou homeplace exist statement)

Great. I'm at home. Whose home? Mine? Yours?

(homeplace exist all-self ownership statement)

"You can read my mind?"

(thought-think word-pictures radiate self-thou statement)

This wasn't getting him anywhere. He needed to focus on more practical questions. "Why can't I move?"

(protect love heal self-thou statement)

Did that sound like a bit of twisted parent-ish thinking? "We've severed your spinal cord, dear, to keep you from hurting yourself. It's for your own good, you know." Hopefully that's not what the voice meant.

"Am I dead?"

(death one life love flow become both eat statement)

Okay, that one wasn't much better than a random concept stew. He thought he was getting the hang of this way of talking–at least, this way of listening, but it was slow and confusing. What he really needed was to find out something specific and build from that.

"Am I still stuck in the tunnel?" Was this whoever-it-was under-standing him? He seemed to. She? Elicand decided then and there that he would think of her as a she, and that her name would be Calaida. At least until she told him different.

(rock-place self-thou (moving doers selves-us) home-place state-ment) (femaleness self-mine Calaida-label goodness statement)

This time the response was both more complicated and easier to understand. It felt as though there had been two distinct thoughts, but they happened at the same time, even though they appeared to have nothing to do with each other. Some group of people had moved him, to wherever he was now–the "home-place"–and she approved of the name he'd given her. These thought impressions, seemed to make more sense when he focused less hard on trying to understand, and just let them wash over him. Maybe that was the trick–it wasn't so much to *think* the ideas as to *feel* them.

(rightness self-thou empathink relaxation statement)

Despite his progress, and Calaida's apparent satisfaction, Elicand was having trouble keeping up with her. Communicating this way was surprisingly strenuous, with ideas and concepts mashed up against each other and intertwined, instead of being presented in nice, sequen-tial chunks, like real speech. All this feeling-not-thinking was making him more tired than a full day of heavy lifting. Nor did it make him feel any better that Calaida seemed to be going really slow for his bene-fit, trying not to flash-flood him with too much of this... what had she called it? Empathink? The thought of what a full blown conversation with her might be like made him shudder.

"I'm thirsty."

A moment later, he felt something warm and smooth being pressed up against his lips.

(flow life death self-thou within statement)

Here, live it up, drink this bottle of death. Elicand pushed that thought aside—you either trust or you don't, there can be no in-between. And for a deaf, blind and paralyzed maybe-corpse, he didn't really have much choice. He drank deeply. The water was warm and it took the chill out of his bones, leaving behind a sort of oily after-taste. And then five seconds later, the world went out again.

———

The journey home to Gash-Garnok would take him most of the way to twilight, and Mehklok had nothing left with which to buy himself even a skin of traveling gruel. He was so busy berating himself over his hasty purchase, that he scarcely noticed where he was going and in short order, found himself in a blind alley, having gone the wrong way around the counting house. This was the approach to the rear service entrance, and he had intended to trudge past the merchant's entrance out front. He'd been idly hoping to encounter a well-to-do patron coming out in a good mood after a big sale—someone who might have a soft ear for the plight of the Garnok and its keeper.

"Gristle and hair!" he cursed under his breath. The passage was narrow and clogged with wagons and barrows containing expensive wares, the fates of which were no doubt being negotiated inside. He could see bundles of polished thigh-bone, jars of teeth, even an entire bolt of Djin-leather—the kind made from real Djin, not the darkened deer-hide that so many tried to pass off at the less reputable stalls. Mehklok sighed. Such finery was beyond the reach of a simple shrine keeper. Perhaps if he'd been assigned to Ishig's Book or the Spear of Narka's Regret... Those were still at the height of their popularity, and being down low—both of them in the Deep Narrows—they enjoyed much larger congregations, full of wealthy, emotion-spewing merchants.

He was almost all the way back to the mouth of the alley, when something caught his eye from the dim space between two richly adorned wagons. It was a foot. Not a disembodied foot, such as you might find over a hearth or at the center of a rich man's table, but an unharvested foot, protruding from under a coarse blanket of some unusual fleece. The foot had a leg, too, but that was hidden beneath the soiled covering. Mehklok knew he should just keep going. He knew that this was a rich man's wagon, and that the foot and the leg and darkness-only-knows what other parts there might be with them, all belonged to that unknown noble. Still... What harm could a look do? He set his bucket of raptors down gently on a crate and eased his way into the gap to get a better look.

In his youth, Mehklok had apprenticed as a toe-harvester, before he'd heard the siren call of service to the faith, that is. And now, many years later, here he stood, in unabashed envy of the most exquisite brace of toe-bones he had ever encountered. Truth be told, the entire foot was a marvel of perfection. Long and delicately structured, with skin of palest white. Wasketchin. It could be no other. That race was blessed with the most enviable feet of all the races, despite that mad king of theirs. Even the nails were straight and trim–clearly great care had been lavished on them in life, by someone more fortunate than himself. To have been permitted to touch such holy relics...

Mehklok paused. Well, why not? Who would be the wiser? Trembling, he put out his hand and stroked one finger down the side of the great toe. The underlying line of bone was a sheer delight. See how it projected cleanly back to the metatarsal? And how that flowed almost mythically with its brothers toward the cuneiforms and then on to the navicular? It was only through an exertion of self-restraint that he stayed his hand from the harvesting blade that he still wore at his belt. Filch-harvesting from a private collection was a gross indecency. Such a thing could get him flayed, or eviscerated even. Certainly, he'd be beaten. But it was so unfair! Mehklok thumped the end of the wagon with a fist. The cloud-strutting aristocrat who owned this thing didn't have a clue what he'd found. If he had, he'd have kept it under better wrappings than this, and he'd have long since had it properly mounted and preserved. To leave it exposed to the wind and flies was an absolute abomination.

Mehklok flung the cover back down over the exposed foot and wrapped it more securely than he'd found it. Somebody really ought to tuck this prize back up inside the wagon. After all, anyone might come along who knew good material when he saw it, and not have the restraint that Mehklok himself had. He looked at the wagon. Beneath the trappings of wealth, it was a fairly simple affair, with a flat bed and a rail fence running around it to keep its cargo from falling off. The leg was at the side farthest from the counting house–no doubt to keep it hidden. There was a slight space between the wagon and the storage sheds that formed the other wall of the alley. Mehklok thought he just might be able to squeeze himself into that gap and see about shifting the load a bit, to get those toes properly protected. He wasn't actually thinking about stealing it though. Honest.

It took a bit of work, but eventually he did get himself wriggled down the wagon's side, although he scarcely had room to inhale. From here he could see that the fleece-wrapped bundle was longer than he was tall and that there was an empty space ahead of it. The load must have shifted backward during travel. That would explain how it came to be hanging out in the weather, but it still didn't excuse the lout for not having the brains to check his wares upon arrival. Mehklok wormed his way a bit ahead of the fleece and then reached between the side-rails to grab it with both hands. There were some stray provisions strewn about on top of it, but they weren't heavy and he was able to tug the load far enough forward that it no longer stuck out the back. Mehklok grunted in satisfaction and dusted his hands together, pleased with a job well done. The fleece had been bigger and bulkier than he'd have expected for just a leg, though. An image floated casually through his imagination of a whole score of legs, each as slender and delicately boned as the last. It almost made him weep to think of such beauty in the world, such grace. Such power. And to think that he'd actually had the good fortune to see it all.

Well, actually, he'd only seen the one foot. He owed himself that much at least, didn't he? He'd performed a valuable service, after all. Surely that entitled him to simply behold the items he'd so generously protected. Just that, and then he'd turn his back and walk away with his exorbitantly over-priced raptors. That was fair. He reached a gnarled hand in through the rails again and twitched the corner of the cover away to reveal the trove of legs, only it wasn't legs at all.

It was a body.

Mehklok staggered back, so much as the confined space would let him. This was wholly unexpected! The foot was not part of some rich nobleman's private hoard of power bones at all. It was a bootleg corpse! Smuggled treasure! A bundle of legs might have one or two fine pieces in it, perhaps even a second as fine as that dangler, but it was implausible that they'd *all* be its match. Not so with an intact body. In that case, the entire thing was probably as exquisite as the foot. There would be a pair of matching hands, an entire deck of teeth, vertebrae, ribs... And all quite possibly the equal of that one, precious foot. The skin alone would fetch enough that he'd be able to take a wife and, maybe... No, it was too impossible even to dream. Little wonder this had been hidden at the back of the wagon under a dirty blanket and some random oddments of personal housewares–it was worth a king's ransom! Either that, or surround it with a score of guards on round-the-sky duty. It should have been sent to the harvest tables along with all the other mortal remains that had passed into contest. No one man should be permitted to monopolize such a thing–that's what the tables were *for*.

But what should he do now? If he ran off to find a hordseman, the wagon and its contents could be long-gone by the time he returned. Should he go into the counting house and confront the man directly? No, he'd only deny ownership of the entire wagon and get off without so much as a flinch of recompense. Mehklok sighed. There was no other way. He'd have to take the body and go find the hordesmen himself, although he'd leave his precious raptors here in the wagon, as proof of his intentions, and to allow him to prove his claim, if the nobleman denied the charges.

He wormed his way out to the end of the wagon again and hauled on the fleece, pulling the whole thing–body and all–back out through the end rails after he'd only just finished yanking it back inside. That was the kind of life he led–constantly going twice as far as other Gnomes would go, to do the right thing. Once he had his new load balanced over his shoulder, he pushed the bucket of raptors back into the space with one hand, and secured it between a box and a sack to keep it from getting badly jostled or falling out. Then he went off in search of the hordesmen.

Mehklok continued past the front of the counting house, terrified for a few moments that somebody would see him and recognize the fleece or its contents hanging over a simple shrine-keeper's back. But no outcry came. He continued along the main way, dodging and duck-ing as he passed other market-goers coming toward him on their way in, or overtaking them as they too struggled up toward home with their packages. There were no signs of any hordesmen on the march today, and he had gone a good long way beyond the town, into the country-side, before he realized that there were certainly not going to be any out here either. "Oh, well," he said, as if by talking aloud he could convince himself that this was still just an honest citizen's arrest in the making. "I guess I'll just have to keep it."

Then he broke into a run.

(query: conscious-not self-him time-now)

(not-radiate self-him time-now statement) (body self-him repair quiescence necessity supposition)

(statement: unwelcome territory intruder self-him threat-is)

((threat-not self-him statement) intensify) (self-him ambassador stone-told declaration)

(intensify: (statement: disbelief)) (statement: disappointment self-thou judgment)

(respect-mine self-thou statement) (patience-mine self-thou statement) (sympathy-mine self-thou long-life old-mind statement)

(smallness: (statement: acknowledge self-thou rightness possibility))

(body-self-him disposition query) ((fear-mine decision-thou statement) intensify)

(statement: (partial: relent)) (command: body-self-him (movers selves-us-all) above-place)

(gratitude statement) (relief statement) (agreement statement) pause (possibility self-thou (enrager self-mine) realization) (self-him remain home-place time-until heal request)

(statement: exasperation) (statement: tolerance) (statement: possibility future-time regret) (decision: agree)

(gratitude-mine love-mine respect-mine self-thou statement)

Mehklok stood wearily near the crest of a long upward rise. The journey home from Yechnarg was always harder than the trip in, since the more favored Gnomileshi towns were all deep in the Throat, meaning downhill from Gash-Garnok. In the eyes of the sellers and craftsmen, this was good, since they carted or carried their wares downhill to market, but it was unfortunate for their customers, who had to carry them home on their backs, and for most of them, that meant uphill. And if the journey wasn't already strain enough, Mehklok had been given a dose of panic as well. When he'd reached the top of the hill, what had he found but a detail of hordesmen camped at the very prow, apparently watching traffic on the road to either side. They hadn't stopped him, but it had been all he could do not to break into a guilty run as they glared at him all the way up. Still, it was over now, and Mehklok was always pleased to reach this particular spot. Not just because the rest of his journey was downhill from here, but also because it gave him such a good view of his home and its surroundings, and that view now helped to soothe him.

Gash-Garnok was nestled into a shallow fold of ground that hugged the base of the Great Nose–the high ridge that the Wasketchin called "The Outreach." From almost any place in the Throat, the Nose was prominently visible, rising from a point half-way up the slopes of the funnel-shaped region, and then running back out of sight, beyond the Lip. Since the entire region was called the Throat, it made sense that the circular rim around its uppermost extent was known as the Lip. And the fact that such a monumental feature as the ridge was called the Nose, even though it overlapped the Lip and almost projected into the Throat itself, spoke volumes about the unfortunate geometry of Gnomileshi faces.

Even now in the dwindling twilight, the bulk of the Nose dominated the view, blotting out the faint glow of the western sky. It loomed like a protective shadow, standing guard over his once-proud little town and threatening to descend upon any who came closer with ill intent. Though it did look strange now. A trifle bare. After so many years, to no longer have the Fury up on top, screaming her stony contempt down upon all and sundry. Mehklok shuddered. Something told his weary hair that no good would be coming from her collapse. No good at all.

From the center of the town below, he could just make out the slightly paler darkness of the tower steeple known as Garnok's Rage, a slender monument dwarfed within the shadow of the Nose itself. Mehklok loved the view from here, the symmetry, with the white steeple centered below the massive ridge–looking for all the world like a skeletal finger about to pick the Nose. This was the image that people still came to see, and then, like as not, they'd be drawn in further, to place a hand on the tower erected by Garnok himself, a giant spike of defiance aimed at his uphill neighbors. This defiant spirit was now all Mehklok had left to work with—nursing it, and building it, slowly and with great care. It was the only thing drawing the feeble trickle of visitors the shrine still welcomed each season. Hopefully, with the Fury now gone, that trickle might grow once more into a torrent. If he was lucky.

Mehklok grunted at the view in satisfaction, then he repositioned the load on his shoulder and scuttled down the hill, already thinking about a warm fire and something oily to wet his dusty gullet.

The Gnomileshi people were quite different from their uphill cousins—both kinds. While those upright dandies built their homes above the ground, Gnomes were only comfortable below it. And instead of decorating with items of great beauty, Gnomes preferred to surround themselves with items of a different kind of beauty—the beauty of power. And to a Gnome, that meant objects of death and decay. This one aspect of Gnome culture—their fondness for, and preoccupation with, the trappings of death, was perhaps the largest barrier between them and their upland neighbors. Each group simply found the other's tastes disturbing.

Twenty minutes later, Mehklok finally crawled in through the narrow-necked entrance to his hovel, dragging his package along behind him. Once he had it tucked neatly into the putrefaction nook beside the kitchen, he kicked his boots off wearily and flopped down into his favorite chair. Fear had dogged the timid little preacher all the way home, and it continued to clutch at his thoughts now. Who could be so arrogant that he'd deliberately flaunt the harvest rules? And who could have afforded such a glorious specimen in the first place? Who was well enough positioned to keep such a crime quiet? There must have been a dozen or more witnesses to buy off, inspectors to bribe and other squeaky hinges to grease.

And now Mehklok had stolen that powerful man's great treasure. What was he thinking?

While he was preoccupying himself with these fantasies of dread, his left arm groped blindly down and fished around under the chair. It came back holding a flask, full of potent medicine that he kept on hand for emergencies. The cork popped out easily and he took a long, hearty swig, letting the delicious, oily fluid run down his throat. It burned slightly and filled his sinuses with an acrid tang that blurred his eyes and slowly dulled his fears–a twelve-year old middena, left over from the days of Garnok's former glory, and the last of the "good stuff." It had been made by old Arkomek, before he'd been lured away by the richer middens downhill. When this was gone, all that would be left was the thin, watery fozzle that Peshnak still insisted on producing. Sadly, one of the disadvantages of living in such an oxygen-starved little backwater, was that there was no longer enough variety in the local offal-heaps to support a really first-rate effluent. But while it lasted, nothing crammed the stink up his nose like the old Arkomek.

He raised his flask in salute to better days and took another long pull. A minute or two later he raised it again, more loosely this time, with his arm swaying slightly. To salute the fleece-wrapped bundle of trouble parked in the back corner. "Honest or not, you're mine now," he said. "If you're worth a full grin for every step I carried you, you'll bring me only half of what I'm bound to pay out in heartache and regret." And while he sat there, trying to think of something else to salute, his eyes drooped lower, the flask slipped slowly from his hand and his dreams took wing. Soon he was snoring loudly, while the last three swallows of the old Arkomek soaked into his best clothes.

Some time in the night, Mehklok awoke with a start. He wasn't sure what it was that had disturbed his sleep, or maybe rescued him from it, but there had been a noise, so he got up to check. "Probably those young 'uns out picking trophies from the tower again." He got down on his hands and knees and scurried outside to look around.

The moon was in almost full shame, peeking out from behind Mother Night's great, black privy so that only the thinnest sliver of its bald head was showing. Even that feeble light, though, was enough to set Garnok's steeple gleaming. Mehklok peered at it silently, looking for movement, but after a minute or two, he gave up. If there had been any trophy snatchers, they'd run off before he came out. Still, he was already up. He might as well do his rounds, especially since there hadn't been time for more than a hasty circuit that morning, before he'd set off for the market.

Garnok's steeple was six full paces wide at the base, and it rose nearly thirty high, tapering as it climbed, until, from its very peak, Garnok's own thigh bone jabbed itself into the night's eye. The entire tower was constructed of bone, although none but the spike at the top was of people origin–such bones were far too powerful to be used as mere construction materials–the rest of Garnok's steeple consisted mostly of deer and elk.

Mehklok went directly to the offering plate at the altar. Nothing but a small handful of bones and a pair of beaks. Still, it was a better day than most, of late. He scooped the bones up in his hands. Rabbit. Most weren't of any structural use–too thin and fragile–but nothing dead was truly useless, so he dropped the small ones into a pocket. Leaving the pelvis and the two beaks. These were good enough for decorative work. He carried them around to the first portal and stepped through, into the hollow base of the steeple, known as the Chamber of Rage. Here was where he kept the small collection of worthy bones, and he added the recent offerings to the pile. According to tradition, the supply of tower bones was kept on the very spot where Garnok himself was said to have lain after he'd fallen from the Nose during an argument with a group of Wasketchin. The Dragon's Peace ensured that his fall had not been the result of an intentional attack, but it had done nothing to the convince the witnesses to render aid, either. Garnok's leg had shattered in the fall, and despite his cries for help, the Wasketchin had done nothing. Driven into a blind rage, Garnok had wrested the remains of his own femur from out of the useless, bleeding meat that had been his thigh, and used it to curse the sky-dwellers as they looked down at him from their lofty perch.

Since it had been taken from living flesh, that bone had held no death-magic, but it hadn't been wholly without power. Even today, Garnok's fractured leg-bone still had the power to spark Gnomileshi anger over the incident, and over a hundred others incidents like it. So in time, the shrine had grown, as others with grievances had come and left their own offerings of rage and frustration. With those additions, the tower had grown, and always with Garnok's original thigh-bone as its crowning thrust. It stood now as a symbol of Gnomileshi dissatisfaction at the way they were treated by their neighbors, and it had been pointing its bone of accusation up at them for almost three hundred years.

Some said this was why the Wasketchin King had placed his Fury there–to glare his own rage back down upon the Garnok. A tit for a tat, if you like. Others said that such an interpretation was too complimentary to the Wasketchin, for it suggested that their neighbors had at least some slight awareness of Gnomileshi feelings. Whatever the reason, the Fury *had* been erected there, staring down at the town below and its people, with that hideous, stump-nosed face.

The thriving community that Gash-Garnok had been for two hundred and seventy seven years had begun to crumble less than a month later. Some left for fear that the Wasketchin would "accidentally" drop rocks on them from the heights. Others worried that the First Prince truly had been involved in the death of the sky-dweller princess. In their hearts, they worried that the Fury's rage fell deservedly upon the people below, who did nothing to defend her memory. So they too fled–from their own guilt. The rest had fled because fleeing had become the fashionable thing to do. Ultimately, only a single year after the shadow of the Fury had fallen upon it, the town of Gash-Garnok had been reduced from a respectable seven hundred noses to fewer than thirty. And Mehklok's stature as the keeper of the town's most important structure had declined along with it.

The pile of fresh bones kept within the inner chamber were believed to draw from the strength of Garnok's rage, left behind in the soil as his blood had leaked into it. This was a sacred place, and not even the trophy seekers were bold enough to come inside. They satisfied themselves by prying out loose bones from the outside, wherever they could find them, to take home as amulets of power and tokens of their own bravery. Mehklok yelled and chased them whenever he caught them at it–he had to keep up appearances–but the truth of it was that the scavengers were doing his work for him. Only the bones that were weak with decay and drained of power could be pried loose. He stooped over and rooted around in the bone-stack for a moment and selected several mid-sized pieces, which he carried with him outside, exiting through the second portal.

He'd noticed a few missing struts from the steeple's face, directly above the altar, and another that looked perilously close to falling. There weren't enough good bones coming in these days for him to repair everything that needed his attention, but he at least tried to keep things respectable on those parts that were most visible–the lowest section, to a height of ten paces all the way around, and to a height of twenty paces above the altar itself.

Mehklok looked up and fixed his eye on the pieces he'd noticed earlier. A whine formed in the back of his throat. He felt the trickle of power come into him, and he had to fight–as he always did–to resist drawing any from the enormous battery in front of him. Instead, he reached out and drew his death-magic from the decaying leaves and grasses of the landscape around him, and from the body of a small deer that he could sense, lying in the screen of trees that stood beyond his hovel door. This ability, to sense sources of power, and to select between them, was rare among the Gnomes–or any of the races, for that matter. It was this skill that had first lured him to abandon his training as a toe harvester, and to take up the vows that had bound him for forty years now, to the service of Garnok's shrine. When he had collected just enough vim within himself for the task at hand, he released his charm and lowered the weathered old bones from their places in the tower wall. Then he replaced them, floating the new ones up in their stead, where he bound them into place. The whole task had taken less than two minutes, but he still felt drained. It was as though a little more of his life leaked out of him with each repair.

After completing his obligations to the tower, Mehklok scuttled over to the fallen deer corpse and dragged it out of the woods, leaving it to brighten his front entrance while nature did its job. A body on the doorstep was a claim of ownership that none of his neighbors would disrespect. And that reminded him of how long it had been since he'd eaten. With the moon still peeking its bald dome down at his back, Mehklok dropped to his knees and scurried back inside.

This time, the place seemed dark and it was hard to see. He charmed a pair of wall-skulls into a glow and the room brightened with their cheery green light. Not for the first time, he noted that the place needed a good grooming. All around him, he could see evidence of decay and rot that had collected in the corners and crevices. That would all need to be harvested and put to good use, but not today. For now, his stomach was making its demands, so he shuffled himself over to the kitchen area. There was an onion he'd been saving for a while. It was probably getting ripe by now. He reached down and pushed the fleece-wrapped bundle out of the way so that he could get at the mouldering snack below it.

And to his horror, a hand thrust out from within the blankets and grabbed him by the throat.

For some time, Elicand meandered back and forth between consciousness and its various alternatives, although it was extremely difficult to tell the difference. His dreams had begun mimicking his wakeful states, presenting him with blank, sightless visions of disembodied voice-thoughts from strangers who pestered him with abstract feeling-riddles. It reminded him of listening to adult conversations back when he'd been a small boy. Eventually though, he became certain that he was awake. That's when he noticed that something had changed. He could move again. Somewhat.

Everything still hurt, of course, but the pain was now more general, accompanied by a whole-body weakness that hinted at how close to death he had actually been. But after having been immobilized for so long, he welcomed even this simple improvement to his situation, and he tried to sit up.

Some time later, he regained consciousness. Okay. A useful lesson had been learned. This time, he would attempt no extravagant movements. He raised one arm slowly and placed his hand behind his head, then he did the same with the other. A wave of dizziness swept through him, but he rode it out and it soon passed. He was itching to move his legs, too–to stand up and maybe even to dance, but for now, he satisfied himself with the feeling of his hair as it tickled through his fingers. The cuts and abrasions that had covered most of his hands during his time in Ouchyville were now gone. All that was left was the mild itch of healthy new skin.

Speaking of itchiness, his chest and legs were rather tingly too. He pulled one hand out from behind his head–again, slowly–and slid it down to his breastbone. At first, he thought he'd grown a thick, woolly beard on his chest, but then he felt around some more and came to the conclusion that this heavy, fibrous material was not actually growing out of his skin–it was a coating of some kind. It was heaviest over his chest and the ribs down one side, but it was everywhere–on his calves, his thighs and even going around to his lower back as well. In some places, the material was quite stiff, and in others, extremely flexible. In those places, it flaked off easily, and when he felt around the floor, it seemed to be covered with a coarse dust that felt similar to the flaking bits.

Beneath the dust, his fingers found cold, hard stone. Clearly, he was still underground, but for the moment, that didn't bother him. He was alive and it appeared that he was going to recover. In no time at all, he would be back outside. Then he paused. What had happened while he was fumbling around down here in the dark? Was a war now raging? And Shondu! What had happened to the little guy during all of this? Was he okay? "Calaida?"

Distantly, he felt a response.

(acknowledgment statement) (self-mine travel (destination self-thou-body-place) statement) (radiate brilliance health self-thou (happiness self-mine) statement)

Elicand tried to relax. It seemed they could communicate over some distance, but he waited just the same. He got the impression she would not be long.

(happiness clear-think self-thou now-time statement)

"Um. Happiness converse self-thou statement. Self-other companion concern-mine statement. Location well-being self-other companion query?" Elicand still hadn't mastered empathinking more than one idea at a time, and he was forced to think about them in turn, saying each word aloud as he did so. Calaida had told him that this was similar to the way children spoke, and she assured him that, by comparison, he was doing very well. She'd even tried to convince him to continue speaking his own tongue, which she understood fluently, but Elicand was a story uncle, and story uncle's didn't get the great tales by taking the easy way out. He wanted to create an entire saga around this experience, and he was sure that it would be far more riveting if he could convey a sense of how empathink actually felt. So he kept working at it and used it whenever he could.

(sadness statement) (ignorance statement) (aloneness self-thou past-time (discoverer self-mine-one-young) statement)

Elicand sighed. There was a growing certainty at the pit of his stomach that Shondu had fallen into Stupid Uncle Chasm, or one of the other minor cracks and fissures that he had mapped out in Scary Tunnel of Wind. "Self-thou-many search cave-place time-now possibility query?"

(regret statement) (self-other-decider unpermit (goers self-us-any) cave-place statement)

"That's okay," he said, forgetting to translate into empathink. "I think he might be dead, anyway."

(sadness statement)

"Right," he said. "Sadness statement me too."
If it was possible, just saying the words had made his whole world even darker.

Life for Elicand went on, more or less unchanging, for some time. Eventually the tough coating on his body–which he now thought of as bandages–all flaked away, with a little help from his impatient fingers toward the end. With his protective covering gone, he suddenly felt quite exposed. Fortunately, Calaida was there swiftly to return his old clothing. Apparently, with their world shrouded in darkness, her people had never developed a sense of body-shyness and she found the whole idea of clothing a little silly, and for some reason, sad, but he put them on anyway. Not because he was shy, but because the air was *cold*. His kirfa felt good as he adjusted it over his shoulders. The boots, however, seemed a bit floppy and loose. No doubt he'd gotten thinner during his convalescence.

(wholeness now-time self-thou statement) (happiness self-mine statement)

Elicand nodded as he stretched. For the entire time he had been here, he had been unable to stand up or even roll over. He'd been able to sit up, partially, for a few days, but the bandages along his hips and upper legs had clung to the rocky floor with a powerful grip, constraining his movements. It felt good to stretch his legs now and shake off the cobwebs of inactivity. He tried to stand up, but the blood rushed from his head and he got terribly dizzy, sinking back to the floor on his knees before he'd even gotten half way up.

"Whoa. Gotta take it easy," he said into the roaring din. "Maybe tomorrow."

(possibility statement) (regret self-mine statement)

Elicand was puzzled by that. "Regret? Why?" But Calaida wouldn't talk about it. Instead, she seemed preoccupied with repeating the inventory of his various hurts and pains. These they had discussed at length over the course of their growing friendship, and he was pleased to discover that they were all gone. When the checklist was complete, Elicand found himself rather tired from the exertion of rolling and lifting–things he had definitely gotten out of the habit of doing.

(sleep self-thou time-now suggestion) ((walking self-thou time-future-soon desire condition) (energy self-thou require statement))

She reminded him of his mother. *If you want to grow up big and strong, you'll need energy. Eat your salad.* "Yes agreement statement," he said out loud. "I'm looking forward to exploring your... home-place. Imagine the stories I'll be able to bring back to my people wonderment statement." But she was right. He was pretty tired, and he settled down onto his soft dust-covered floor with unusual delight. Tonight, he was going to be able to sleep on his side!

(sleep-destination time-now self-thou statement) (journey self-thou pleasantness statement)

"Good night, Calaida. See you in the morning prediction." The thought of actually *seeing* her made him smile though, and in a matter of seconds, Elicand was snoring.

The hand that held Mehklok's throat was not particularly strong, but his fear made it seem like the unyielding vice-grip of a demon. Clearly, this once-dead body had rejected the peace of Grimorl and decided to return to this world to pick up its life where it had left off. Such a thing was an abomination—a reversal of the natural order—but something that was well known to be within the power of the greatest Wasketchin wizards.

Mehklok dropped to his knees and whimpered for mercy.

Within the blanket, the body made no sound—a clear sign of its evil intent. For several moments, Mehklok knelt there, weeping his terror into the soil of his kitchen floor. Then, a second hand emerged, folding back the corner of the blanket to reveal the face of a woman. She had been hard used of late, and a wild look burned in her eyes, but she was every inch the skeletal goddess that had been promised by the bones of her feet. Mehklok trembled all the harder in the fire of her glare and waited for her to end his pathetic existence with a word.

Bu no word came.

The witch-goddess took her hand from his throat and gestured toward her mouth. Mehklok began to quake. She wasn't just going to kill him—she was going to to eat him! *Oh, why oh why oh why did I have to go stumbling down that stupid alley? If I'd been paying attention* as I ought, I'd be sitting happily with raptors at all stations and the overcaptain on his way. But no! I had to take a misturn, and then I went and stuck my snob in where it didn't belong. And what do I get for all that? Eaten, that's what! He raised his head, ready to accept the inevitable.

The witch was still making movements toward her mouth. And chewing. She was already eating something—but what? His soul? All his future joys? Then he cocked his head. Her dinner?

Mehklok got his legs back under himself and prayed to the Worm that he was right. "You w-want food, is that it?" His gaze darted nervously around the kitchen. "N-not sure what I've got f-for a sky-dweller's stomach," he said. Then he remembered the deer on his front stoop. It wasn't aged nearly enough yet for his tastes. The blood was probably still liquid, but he'd heard that life-magic folk preferred it that way. He raised his hands in a calming motion. "Stay here. I'll be right back." Then he dropped to his knees and scuttled out the door.

"Get away from that, you!" Mehklok kicked at a crow as it hopped from one foot to the other, edging its way cagily toward the witch woman's dinner. "What's wrong with you above-grounders, anyway? Do you not know enough to let your food age properly?" Mehklok's idea of fresh meat was when it could be scooped from the bone with a spoon. Speaking of which, how did one go about preparing it when it was in this state, anyway? Is one part any better than another? After looking at the thing from a couple of different angles, he still couldn't make up his mind, so he shrugged, pulled his harvester's blade from its ceremonial sheath on his belt, and went at it.

While he struggled with the butchery, Mehklok also struggled with a growing urge. To flee. He paused for a moment, wiping his nose with the back of a bloodied hand, and looked up at the near-dead moon hanging above the Lip, and at the wide-open road below it, just yards away, beckoning. It would be so easy. Just chuck it all—the hovel, his trophies, the skin swatches of his ancestors... Everything! He'd done his best here, and what did he have to show for it? Nothing, that's what. He'd spent his entire budget in a last ditch effort to build it all back up, but then he'd gone and left the centerpiece of that grand plan to rot on the back of some rich carp's wagon! There was nothing left, and nothing here for him anymore. There hadn't been in years.

But a glimmer called to him from the corner of his eye. The Garnok.

And Mehklok let out a long sigh. Who was he kidding? He couldn't leave–not the Garnok–not after everything he'd already endured in its name. And especially not if that meant leaving it in the clutches of some foreign witch demon. No. Maybe she hadn't killed him yet, but she was going to have to if she wanted all this. She'd probably wait a bit, until she'd been fed, anyway. Or maybe she'd want her nits harvested and her toe-nails sharpened first, too. After all, why waste a good trembling minion? But sooner or later, she'd make her move to take it, and if he still had air in his chest, he'd be there to stop her. She'd have to kill him first. And if that's the way it had to be, well, at least then he would be able to hold his head high in Grimorl–a chaplain of a church of the first rank, right to the bitter end.

Mehklok stood up and lifted the ragged hunk of deer meat into the light. He'd driven his knife through it so he could hold it without getting any more blood on him than he already had. His stomach writhed. Solid meat! The thought of it was unnatural, but at least he didn't have to eat the stuff. She did. With a sigh, Mehklok dropped back down and scuttled inside, holding her dinner above his head, lest it touch the ground on the way and be judged unfit by Her Holiness.

Back at the carcass, the crow had only flown a short distance away, and he swooped back in a flash, settling onto the now-ready-for-business all-night buffet. Time for a little snack.

He was still tearing at his first beakful when a talon-curling shriek erupted from the hole in the hillside next to him, interrupting his meal. This was followed immediately by the deep, percussive sound of something heavy hitting something hollow. And then a heartbeat later, a second figure shot out of the hole on all fours. The crow paused to look at her, a red tuft of meat stretched taut in mid-tear between his feet and his beak. The woman rose into a crouch with the wicked looking knife held low in one hand, her eyes fixed on the hole.

The crow blinked.

Dagger woman's eyes darted toward the movement, and then toward the buffet table beneath him. Her eyes widened.

Several minutes later, the crow returned again to the buffet. This time for good. He croaked a challenge out into the night air, daring anyone to shoo him away again.

There were no takers. Only the sound of running feet and the *Tash! Fush!* of somebody moving quickly away through the underbrush.

chapter 14

"Abeni! Hey, Big Whale! Wait up!"

Tayna plunged blindly through the fog. She still hadn't sighted Abeni since dashing after him into this crazy mist. Of course, for all she knew, she could be walking past him right now. She couldn't see a thing. What she was hoping for was a grunt or a snarl of some kind to steer by. But so far, nada.

According to Sarqi, the Wagon always went straight, and Abeni was good at tracking it, so *he* probably wasn't wandering around aimlessly. But Tayna? Well, she thought she'd been holding a steady course, but every tree that loomed at her suddenly from out of the fog was another threat to her certainty. Sooner or later, she was going to take a detour and lose her bearings. And when that happened– Oh. Never mind.

Just like that, the fog was gone. It hadn't just petered out, nor had she simply stepped into a clear space. One minute she was worrying about getting lost in its pea-soup thickness, and the next minute, it had turned itself inside out and vanished. Off to her left, Tayna could hear the sounds of heavy crashing through the trees. She ran to catch up.

"There you are! Where did all the fog go?"

Abeni was in the middle of stooping under a half-fallen tree, and now he paused and turned his head toward her. He did not look happy to see her. "The Little Fish should not have come," he said grimly. "Abeni walks the path of rust, and a friend would not behold such shame." Then he turned away, as though that was all that needed to be said on the subject.

"Hold it, Beluga Boy. You're going to have to try harder than that if you want to shake me."

Abeni's massive shoulders sagged, his face full of defeat. "The Little Fish does not know the ways of the Djin," he said. "The Bearers of Rust are not to be trusted. They cannot protect even their own reputations. How can they be trusted to protect their companions? You must go back. Sarqi and Zimu will help you to reach the bone house. Abeni cannot." Tayna's mouth hung open in shock.

"What is with you?" she said at last. "Sure, the situation is entirely suckesque, no question, but which part is it again that makes you the village idiot of the story? The fact that your plans didn't work out perfectly? Or the fact that you didn't have every glitch fixed in five minutes? I mean, it's been a whole day since Elicand and Shondu went missing, and almost four hours since your precious "garbage truck of the dead" was stolen, and here you are with nothing solved yet. Not even a clue to work with. No wonder you're out here doing your big, green, Incredible Sulk–you're clearly incompetent. I'm surprised your brothers haven't killed you by now, or whatever it is you Djin do with traitors to the family honor." Tayna had been hoping that the verbal abuse would make him angry, make him defend himself, but instead, Abeni only nodded in silent agreement and hung his head even lower.

And that made her furious.

"Gaaah!" She grabbed him by the arm and pulled, but he didn't move so much as a twitch. He just looked down at her hands, which were clamped to his iron bond-ring. "Look! See?" she said, tapping it with a finger, pointedly. "No rust yet! That'll take days! What do you say we put the 'poor stupid me' party on hold, huh? At least until you get some real rust flakes to complain about. You wouldn't want to celebrate your change of status until it's official, would you?"

But Abeni wasn't listening. Now that the fog had cleared, he had no time for her well-meaning distractions. He gently pried her fingers from his arm, and turned away to resume tracking the Wagon. Tayna watched him go, totally frustrated at his sudden, pig-headed stubbornness–not that it interfered at all with his tracking abilities. Even on auto-pilot, Abeni seemed able to see signs that were completely invisible to her. Fortunately, she didn't have to follow vague signs hidden in a field of waving grass. She had the Glum Avenger to follow.

That, however, quickly became easier to say than to do. Despite having to read the tracks, Abeni continued to pull further and further ahead of her. The Way Finder seemed to be possessed and completely oblivious to her attempts to match pace with his great, ground-eating strides. In a matter of only minutes, she'd lost sight of him again. But Tayna didn't give up. For the moment, her happiness-challenged friend was not making any effort to stay quiet, and she was able to track him by the sounds of crashing underbrush and the occasional scampering of little animals that fled from his stomping wake. She wasn't sure how long she'd be able to stay close, but she was determined to find out.

What she wasn't expecting was to actually catch him.

After half an hour of chasing the ever more distant sounds of rustling and crashing, at last they stopped, and Tayna was pretty sure she'd lost his trail for good. The fact that she continued moving forward was more out of a sense of momentum than anything else, and she was trying to figure out what to do next when she stepped out through a cluster of trees and almost ran into him.

Abeni was standing in the middle of a small clearing that looked as though it had recently been used to hold ballroom dancing lessons for cave trolls. Against their will. The grass was torn up in great heaves and mounds, and the soil beneath it had been gouged into confused furrows, forming a more or less circular pattern.

"What happened here?" she said, as she came up to stand beside him.

Abeni's eyes never ceased their darting pattern of concentration, drinking in the details of the scene. "A struggle," he said over his shoulder, apparently resigned to the fact that she was still following him.

"Somebody tried to attack the Wagon?"

"No," the Djin said. "The thief tried to turn it."

Tayna stared around at all the soil carnage. "Turn it? Why bother? Why not just make it choose a new target? We already know he can do that."

Abeni shook his head slowly. "It makes no sense," he said. "But that is what he tried to do. And he failed." His large head swung up, gazing at a point between the trees, on the far side of the clearing. He took a step forward. "And after failing, he continued in this direction."

Tayna hurried to catch up, but something caught her attention in the grass and she turned back to investigate. It was a piece of whitish wood. A carving of some kind. She knelt down. Oh crap. The carved turtle. "Abeni?" Her voice was hushed with sadness, remembering where she'd last seen the little toy, and a heavy weight settled over her heart as she reached down to pick it up.

Then there was fire.

———⌐———

She felt the heat on her cheeks first, and across her brow. Scorching, acrid heat. It was hard to separate the sensations from the smells, as waves of both rushed up her body, filling her skull from the inside out.

She could remember dreaming stuff like this before, only this was no dream. Tendrils of glowing sulfur befouled her hair and insinuated themselves everywhere, in her sinuses and beneath her kirfa. Steam rose from the heavy fabric and it began to darken and then smoke at the corners. The only place in the universe that could still remember coolness was the smooth dry wood of the turtle, gripped tightly in her fist, but no matter how hard she tried, she couldn't open her hand to drop it. Her eyes had snapped shut when the first blast washed over her and now she was terrified to open them, for fear of what the flames might do, but she felt an overwhelming need to look.

So she did.

To her surprise, the soft, liquid orbs were not flash-boiled in her skull, but what they saw quickly dowsed any relief she might have felt. In the distance, Abeni had turned to look back at her, seemingly oblivious to the flames that crawled up his arms, his legs, and danced in sultry yellow rhythms across his broad Djin shoulders. The forest beyond was in full rage, dark and orange, streaming with ribbons and gusts of blackest soot, all racing for the sky. And beyond that–though she couldn't actually see it–she knew that the rest of the Forest was a conflagration of Hell's own fury. Each and every person–Djin or Wasketchin–everyone she had met since crossing over was consumed by it. Nor was the searing destruction limited only to this world–it crossed even into Grimorl. Rachel and Eliza, Becky–all of them were just as surely caught in this inferno as well–a suffocating furnace of rage had swept out of a child's carving, and now it threatened to consume every person and every world she'd ever known. She had not been told so. There were no signs, no billboards proclaiming it.

She just knew.

Tayna looked down at her own arms, her chest, her legs. She was surprised to see that there were no flames on her own body. Not yet. Then her skin began to smolder. She watched, horrified, as everything she knew as part of herself erupted. Not into open flame, but bursting instantly into thick, oily black smoke. Her smoke-self simply hovered there, stupidly, billowing in turbulent clouds of black and gray. She was a column of undulating soot, vaguely cylindrical. Insubstantial. Hellsmoke incarnate.

Waves of heat scalded her. Cascades of sweat ran down her face of smoke and then boiled away, leaving scars and blisters in their wake. She couldn't think. Somewhere, a little girl was screaming in terror. In agony.

A shape broke from the wall of incandescence in front of her, rolling and bouncing toward her, flinging careless beads of fire to either side. It came straight for her. Tayna tried to cry out. She wanted to scream, but she couldn't force any sounds out through the soot-choked caverns of her lungs and mouth. All she managed was to taste the silent char of her tongue. She wanted to run, to hide, but the flames just rose higher around her as the bounding shape closed in.

Then suddenly, it was over. She found herself lying on her back in the dirt, surrounded by a charred circle of grass only ten feet wide. Beyond that circle, the flames had been nothing but illusion, and they were gone. The smoke was gone, too. There was only her, in regular skin, lying on her back between the scorched furrows of mud. Tayna took a deep breath, calming the panic that had threatened to drown her. Then she sat up.

Beside her, lying on the grass-char, where he too had fallen after body-slamming her out of the flames, Abeni pulled himself slowly to his knees. His shoulder and arm were burned black. Ugly rivulets of muddy blood and crisped tatters of flesh slid freely down his skin. Most of his back, neck and scalp were equally charred, as were all the ribs down his left side. Even his proud Djin ponytail had vanished in the flames.

"Abeni?" Tayna was up in a shot and she raced to his side, reaching out her hands, then withdrawing them, afraid of doing more harm than good. The Djin was silent.

"Ohmygod! Abeni? Say something!" Tears welled up in Tayna's eyes as she stared helplessly at her friend, who was clearly in agony–an agony that he had suffered while rescuing her from her own stupidity. She let out a sob, angry at her stupid self and at her own stupid talent for getting other people hurt.

The Djin, still on hands and knees, shook his head stiffly, obviously fighting down waves of pain. "Little Fish. Cries. For Abeni." he said, between clenched teeth. "She. Is unhurt?" His concern for her just made her sob all the harder.

"Oh shut up you giant potato! Tell me what to do!"

———⌣————

Elicand was dreaming about birds. All his life, he had loved the sound of birdsong–the sweet, trilling music of the trees. As a child, he had spent days upon days sitting in the boughs of one tree or another, just drinking in the excited chatter of his flighty neighbors. From them, he had learned the rhythms of the forest, the seasons of mating and hatching, fledging and migration. He'd learned their politics, listening raptly to their reports of food and danger, scarcity and abundance, and to tales from the eternal war between the crows and the sparrows. It had been a happy time, and his first training in the great skill that would mark him later in life: that of listening.

Dreaming of them now though, should have been a happy experience–a reminder of the joys of his home, sent to warm his heart in this time when he was so far removed from them. But they were not happy. There was trouble in the forest of his dreams, trouble tinging every chirp and warble. Cries of distress and of danger echoed in his head, cries of fear and of fleeing. Cries of rage and pain. Even the nightingale was alarmed.

((DANGER (SELF-THOU SELF-MINE SELF-OUR) TIME-PRESENT-NOW) INTENSIFY!)

The young story uncle tossed fitfully, unaccustomed to such darkness in his usually contented sleep. The panicked chattering of the birds ruffled and coursed around him as flocks and flocks–flocks of flocks–thrilled around him, each racing in a different direction, each fleeing for their very lives. And behind it all, the steady, relentless pounding of drums. Strange that birds would use drums, but dreams are funny that way.

(DANGER DANGER FLEE SELF-THOU TIME-PRESENT-NOW) (ENEMIES BORDERS-CRUSHING LOCATION-HERE KILL-ALL SAFETY-SEEK) (INTENSIFY! INTENSIFY! INTENSI-)

Elicand rolled over and sat up, blinking sleepily in the darkness. Something felt wrong.

"Calaida? Are you there query?"

The air around him still throbbed with that deafening, static roar that ate all sound. Tonight it reached even into his head. There was no answer.

"Calaida?"

All around him, there was nothing but the roaring silence.

———

Abeni reached out with his good arm. "Help Abeni. To sit," he said.

Tayna took the offered arm and hauled against it, helping him roll over onto his butt. He sat there, cross-legged on the grass, but hunched forward awkwardly, leaning to his right, with his left arm held high in the air and his head low, trying to keep the burned flesh away from the ground.

"Now what?" she asked, her voice poised on the edge of panic. Moving him had caused the wounds to stretch and tear, and they now seeped and bled freely.

"Abeni must... Healsong." He gasped as a fresh wave of pain washed through him. Tayna could only whimper and hold his good hand, not knowing what else she could do to help. Beside her, the big Djin began to hyperventilate. Fear gripped her tighter. Was he going into convulsions or something? A moment later, he moaned as well, but it became a sort of rhythmic moaning. And then she understood. Abeni was in too much pain to sing, so he was making music the only way he could manage. Without even thinking about it, Tayna stroked his hand and breathed along in time with him, humming in a nervous counterpoint to his moans–doing what little she could to let him know that he was not alone–that she was right there at his side.

Their song was hypnotic, weaving a spell of timelessness over the two friends as they sat huddled together–pained together–beneath the strengthening rays of the morning sun. Tayna had no idea how long they sat there, breathing together, him moaning, her humming, but she was pretty sure that the next time she took note of it, the sun had moved appreciably across the sky. She was trying to judge how far, when she realized that the ragged moan of Abeni's breathing had stopped.

"Abeni!" Tayna leapt to her feet in stark terror. "Come on, Big Whale! Breathe!" She spun around in front of him and grabbed him by his massive shoulders, trying to shake some life into him. How do you give CPR to someone the size of a hippo? But nothing worked, and when she put her ear to his chest, all she could hear was death. No breathing. No heartbeat. Nothing.

Tayna pounded against the bleeding flesh of his shoulder and screamed. It was a wordless, shapeless sound. It said nothing. It conveyed everything. She clawed frantically at her wrist, trying to strip her own invisible bond ring from where it had never been and fling it back at the gods, or the Dragon, or whoever it was who had saddled her with it in the first place.

"Take it back!" she screamed. Her voice was hoarse and came out as little more than a croak. "I don't want it! I don't care about *peril great*! I don't care if there's a *family yours*! I don't want it! Not any of it! Not if this is how it has to happen! TAKE IT BACK!"

And then she slumped over and wept herself into unconsciousness.

———————

"All aboard for Medicine Falls, Wilmerton and Lake of Angels. Now departing from Platform Three."

It was some time late in the afternoon and Tayna stirred groggily. Her face felt sticky and she pushed back, wiping at the mess with the sleeve of her kirfa. It was Abeni's blood, caked on her cheek. She recoiled in horror and rolled away, coming up into a crouch, her eyes darting around the clearing suspiciously. She had heard something. The more immediate horror lying in the grass beside her was something she was no longer willing to see.

"Departing at nineteen twenty hours. Passengers for Medicine Falls, Wilmerton and Lake of Angels please proceed to Platform Three."

Tayna got unsteadily to her feet and looked around. The sound seemed to be coming from beyond the trees to her left. Numb from the ears inward, and with no particular plan in mind but to move, she wandered off in that direction. As she reached the trees, she realized she could hear other sounds too. The general clanks and thumps of urban life, the clatter of glass doors opening and closing, footsteps, and the low, throaty rumble of large vehicles. As she passed between the first pair of trees, a low, concrete building came into view, right in front of her. A sign above the entrance said, "Methilien Bus Depot."

She opened the door and went inside.

The lobby was just as she imagined any small-town bus depot lobby might look. There was a ticket window on the back wall, but a hand-printed sign was stuck to it. "Closed for Psychotic Episode." A few vending machines dominated the rest of that wall, but they had all seen better days and Tayna doubted she would have risked a quarter in any one of them, even if she had one.

On her left was the door leading out to the bus platforms, and next to it, a large plate glass window allowed travelers to see the buses waiting for them, through the grime. The center of the room was devoted to several rows of long wooden benches. The waiting room. Half a dozen people sat or stood, scattered around the place. None of them looked to be in any kind of hurry.

A gargantuan fat lady sat on a chair against the back wall, slowly feeding jelly beans one at a time into the constantly chewing maw of her face. A policeman sat to Tayna's right, sipping coffee, with his chair tipped back to lean against the wall opposite the window. There was a buff-looking soldier woman doing push-ups on the floor, and on the bench, a middle aged couple were gathering their suitcases and arguing about who had the tickets. Behind them, an old man sat by himself, throwing pebbles at a small flock of pigeons who were bobbing and pecking at the ground around his feet.

The loudspeaker crackled to life over Tayna's shoulder.

"Last call for Medicine Falls, Wilmerton and Lake of Angels. Departing now from Platform Three."

The young couple looked up in alarm and quickly ran toward the door, dragging their belongings behind them in a confusion of thumps and bangs. A frantic moment later, they were out the door and onto the platform. Tayna walked over to the window and looked out. She could see them talking urgently to the driver while he stowed their gear in the big luggage cavern of the bus's belly.

"Mama? Papa?" Tayna turned around at the sound of the voice. It was a little girl, maybe four years old. She had just come out of the washroom, but she was filthy. She looked like she'd been playing in a campfire all day and had done nothing to wash off the clumps of ash and soot and roasted meat that clung to her face and hung from her hair.

"Mama? Papa? Where are you?" Tayna caught her eye and pointed out the window, but the little girl just stared at her, refusing to break eye contact. Tayna turned her head to gesture toward the window, where the girl's parents were now waving their tickets and gesturing confusion at the driver. The little girl's head turned in time with Tayna's own, and that's when she realized she was looking at a mirror that ran along part of the back wall. With sudden horror, she also realized that it was *her* parents that were about to leave.

"Wait!" she yelled, and then turned to bolt for the door.

"Keep the noise down, dammit!" The old man didn't even look up from his pigeon-pelting.

But Tayna couldn't make her feet move. Her eyes went frantically back to the grimy window, but instead of seeing her parents, her eye settled on her own reflection. And it winked at her.

What?

"It's okay," her reflection said. "They always leave." Then Tayna and her reflection both turned at the same time and waved their little hands at her parents, who were settling down into the bus's empty front seat. Reflection-Tayna's wrist wore a beautiful bracelet–a solid ring of silver, with square panels of turquoise set into it–that glittered and sparkled, even in the weak bus-station sunlight. Tayna reached up instinctively and stroked at the raw, bleeding skin of her own wrist. In the reflection, her fingers bobbled at the bracelet. Beyond the grime, Tayna saw her mother suddenly smile. Then she waved, revealing an identical bracelet on her own arm.

"Cool, huh?" Her reflection grinned at her. "Granna made 'em for us. As long as we got 'em, I can't get lost. When I'm lonely or scared, all I gotta do is touch it and she'll hear me. Like you just done. Or if sump'n bad happens, I just gotta turn it, an' she'll come running. She promised."

Tayna fingered her own puffy wrist again, tenderly. "I think I lost mine," she said. The eyes of her reflection widened. "But you can't lose it," she said. "See?" Then she gripped the ring in her little fingers and tugged. It was obvious that it was too small to slide over her hand. "It grows when I get bigger," her reflection said. "But it's always too small to come off. Mommy's had hers since she was a little girl."

"But how..." Tayna was suddenly sure that she had once had a bracelet of her own, just like the one in the window. Her reflected face grew grim and determined.

"Somebody stole it!" her reflection hissed. And Tayna knew it to be true. "That's not fair! How will your mommy know how to find you? You gotta get it back!" The little girl in the window was horrified, and her shrill voice echoed throughout the lobby.

"Baw! Boo-hoo! Somebody stole my sparkly!"

Tayna's head jerked around instinctively at the interruption. The old man with the birds was making crying motions with his fists under his eyes. When he saw Tayna staring at him, he broke into spasms of wet, cackling laughter. Tayna turned back to the window, but it was too late. Her little-girl reflection was gone, and there was only her plain, ordinary self staring back at her from the glass.

Tayna spun around, her eyes blazing fiercely. The old man was still glaring at her. "Quit yer bawlin' and get on with it," he said. "Ye got people waitin' on ye. Maybe even dyin' on ye." Then his eyes flashed with mockery. "Oh, I fergot. Ye don't care about them others."

"Shut up!" she spat. "What do you know about caring, sitting there chucking stones at helpless little birds? And I should be taking advice from you?"

The old man cackled and sputtered as though he was about to spew a lung. When he finally got it under control, he looked at her with watery eyes. "Now who's yakking without a clue?" he said, pointing to the floor at his feet where the pigeons were gobbling up his pebbles almost as fast as he was throwing them. "Little buggers ain't got any teeth," he said. "They *need* the stones. Swallows 'em into their gizzards so it'll grind up their food for 'em. Otherwise, they'll starve–even with a belly full of worms."

Tayna blushed. "I knew that."

"Course ye did. Ye just forgot is all." The old man winked at her and then jerked a thumb at the seat beside him. Tayna was too confused to argue, so she just went over and sat where he'd indicated.

"The problem is, yer trying to do things part ways," he said. "Part of ye in one world, part in the other. Part of ye believing, the other part denying. Kind of bucking the system–both systems. Like a bus station in a magical forest." He winked broadly.

"But–" The old man waved her interruption away.

"Figure out what world you're in, girl, and *be* in it," he said. "All the way. With all the rights and privileges, so on and so forth."

"What's that supposed to mean?" she asked. The old man cackled again.

"Jiggity, girl, look at yerself! Ye come storming through this here forest, demanding that it produce ye some parents, but yer ignoring what's going on around you. The place is in crisis, girlie, but are you pitching in to help with any of *their* problems? Course you ain't. Yer just a typical teenager, head down, running full tilt for what you want, and paying diddly squat attention to the rest. Consequences be damned. Gonna get yer family and get out again, quick. Well, what if this world ain't willing to part with 'em on those terms? Didja ever think of that? What if it *won't* part with 'em, or anything else ye want, until ye show that yer willing to give something back in return?"

"Like what?"

"Ain't fer me to decide," he said. "But I'd start by taking a more active interest in what's painin' the folks around ye. Hell, the Watcher even told ye that much. 'No taking without giving. Balance is the way of all things.' Remember?"

Tayna slumped back down into her chair. She did remember. But she'd been so consumed by the news that her parents might really be alive that she'd pushed it aside at the time. And then promptly forgotten it.

"Oh crap. I've really screwed this up, haven't I." Beside her, the old man made a tsk'ing noise in his throat and he shook his head.

"Look kid. Yer running flat out. Ye got the pedal to the metal through a world you didn't even know existed last week, let alone one you understand, and you're trying to do everything by yer lonesome. Captain, pilot, navigator, the whole shebang. And where's that gettin' ye? No rest, no guide, an' nobody to talk to. Hell, yer psychic pressure's been in the red for so long, it's a wonder you didn't go kablewie three days ago. Look at this dump! It was right pretty last week. Ye've had friends traipsing through here on just 'bout every bus I've seen. Eliza, Rachel, the Watcher, Winry, Arin, Lan'ia, the story uncle, yer big Djin fella, his family... Comrades in a crisis, girl! All of 'em, if you'll let 'em. All of 'em waiting fer ye to trust 'em, tell 'em what's goin' on. Ask fer their help. Hell, you collect 'em like flies on a corpse. They seems almost drawn to ye, though I ain't got the slightest why. Ye seem kinda whiny to me. But now where are they? Huh?" He gestured around at the room full of strangers.

Tayna looked around at the tattered walls, the splintered edges of the wooden seats. It did look kind of run down.

"Well I'll tell ye where they went," he said. "They're gone! That's where. Moved on. Hung around just so long, and then left. No point their wastin' time if yer not gonna give 'em a ticket fer the rest of the trip." The old man hooked a thumb toward the schedule on the chalk-board by the ticket booth. It was mostly smudged off, but she could still read the top two lines. Destinations "Friendship" and "Trust." Both were crossed out, with the words "Service halted indefinitely" scrawled over top.

Tears spilled down her cheeks. Had she really pushed all those people away? "What am I supposed to do now?" she asked, quietly.

The old man waved an arm at her. "Hell, I don't know, girl. This is your hallucination. Not mine. That's yer look out. Always has been. I'm just telling ye what I see."

Tayna's eyes narrowed in sudden suspicion. "Are you the Dragon Methilien?"

The responding laughter from deep in the old man's chest almost had kidneys attached to it. "Don't ye get it girl? I ain't the Dragon! I'm you! Or a part of ye, anyway." The old man swept his arm around the lobby, taking in the rest of the weary travelers "We all are!"

"All of you?" Around the room, each of the others met her eye and nodded. Tayna could tell in the twinkle of their expression that it was true. They *were* her–all of them. Each a different aspect that made up part of the whole. Some were easy to pick out. The cop, that was a no-brainer. The soldier woman–that one made a little sense too, especially recently. But the fat lady in the chair bothered her. That didn't feel familiar–not the way the others did. Tayna got slowly to her feet and went over to meet this seeming stranger in the cast of personalities that apparently lived inside her head.

"Excuse me. Do I know you?" she said as she approached. The fat lady looked up at her and then suddenly stopped the mechanical motion of jelly-bean to mouth, as she noticed Tayna approaching.

"Oh, hello Tayna, dear. I was just clearing up the board in here and I think I've made a frightful mess." The schedule chalkboard was next to her, and Tayna suddenly recognized the tell-tale smudging.

"Sister Diaphana?" Tayna could barely recognize the woman. She was easily a hundred pounds heavier than she was supposed to be. And without all the usual nun-garb, she was almost a different person. But the woman was shaking her head.

"No dear. I'm you, just like the others."

"But somehow, a sort of Diaphana-me?" Diaphatayna nodded her head.

"That's right, dear. You don't recognize me because I'm all soft and mushy." The woman prodded her ample flesh with a finger to emphasize her point. "But I'm a mighty big part of you, you know, even if you don't want to realize it yet. Maybe the biggest."

Behind her, the soldier barked a warning. "Time to move out, Generalissimo. We've got work to do."

"But I don't want to go! I won't be able–"

Diaphatayna smiled sweetly up at her. "Of course you're able dear. You've always been very able. I have faith in you, we all do." All around the room, heads were nodding in agreement. "We're counting on you, you know. And so is your big friend." Then she went back to fishing in her bag of candy.

"Wait!" Tayna cried, but she could already feel invisible hands pulling at her, tugging like a hundred little chains, dragging her back toward the entrance. She looked back at the fat lady. "You never told me. What part of me are you?"

This time it was the cop who interrupted. "Hey, Rookie! Have a look at this!" Tayna turned to meet his gaze and had to dart a hand up quickly to catch whatever it was he had thrown. It was the carved wooden turtle. "Arson," he said. "A deliberate trap, left by the guy who stole the Wagon to delay any pursuers. Watch your back around that one."

Tayna nodded her thanks to him as the doors opened and she glided back out through them. Again she turned and found the fat lady looking at her, smiling sweetly.

"What part of me!" Tayna yelled.

The enormous woman smiled and waved, with big, exaggerated Diaphana arm motions.

"I'm the part that falls in love, silly! Bye bye!"

Then the doors closed.

It was some time late in the afternoon and Tayna stirred groggily. Her face felt sticky and she pushed back, wiping at the mess with the sleeve of her kirfa. It was Abeni's blood, caked on her cheek. She recoiled in horror and rolled away, coming up into a crouch, with her eyes darting around the clearing suspiciously. She had heard something. Then she looked more closely at the horror lying in the grass beside her.

"You're breathing!" she exclaimed.

"Yes. Abeni does breathe," he said. He still hadn't moved from where he'd slumped over, however long ago it had been now. "Although he does not know how such a thing can be."

Tayna pulled his injured shoulder toward her. The skin was still black with soot, and clumps of charred Abeni-meat still clung to his back and ribs, but underneath all that, he was completely healed, except for the missing hair.

"Whoa!" she said, filled with more than just a little awe, as she let go of his shoulder. "You Djin guys really know your healing magic!"

Abeni reached up with his unscorched arm to check out the repairs for himself. "No, not Djin magic," he said slowly. "No Djin can heal such wounds." Then he turned to look her in the face, his eyes wide with wonder.

"It is Little Fish magic."

They talked about it for quite a while. Tayna was sure that it had not been her doing. She'd have felt something. But Abeni would not listen.

"Abeni does not know how. He does not understand Wasketchin lore. But he is certain that the Little Fish has performed a great magic. She has saved Abeni from Death. And Abeni must now share half his life with her." The stupid Djin even leaned forward onto one knee and bowed his head low over joined wrists.

"How may Abeni be of service?"

Tayna snorted through her nose. "Oh shut up, you big goof! You can't be my slave unless I say so, and I don't. I didn't do anything. Trust me. For now, let's just call it a miracle and move on. Okay?"

Abeni looked up at her suspiciously. "The Little Fish tries to trick Abeni. She has great fire magic. She survives unharmed in the heart of the flame for many minutes, while Abeni roasts like a feast in just one second. Surely she has great power."

Tayna's eyes popped. "All that happened just while you were knocking me down?" The Djin nodded. "Holy crap! And I was in there for, what, at least a minute. And I got away with nothing?" Again he nodded. "And so now you figure I must be some kind of fire-magic priestess or something?" Nodding was getting to be a habit for him.

Tayna rolled her eyes in disbelief. "Fire magic? Me? Look, I'll show you fire magic." She marched over to the trees and grabbed a fallen branch, then she marched back, holding it out in front of her. "Come on, baby, light my fire," she sang, raising the branch before her like a holy relic. "Try to set my stick on fi-er! Come on, baby, light my fi-errr!"

Nothing happened.

She thrust the end of the branch toward Abeni's face. "Go on. Touch it. Is it even hot?"

He reached up and touched the stick gingerly, fully expecting his fingers to be burned. But they were not. Abeni sat back and looked at her.

"The Little Fish truly does not have fire magic?"

Tayna shook her head. "Not even a little bit."

"Then how did she–"

"I don't know what happened, Abeni. But it wasn't me, okay? Maybe I'm fireproof–I don't know–but if so, that's all it is. I promise you, nothing would make me happier than finding out that I could do magic." Then she grinned, and brushed her fingers unconsciously over her earlobes. "Well, nothing except maybe finding out that the whole magic husband-ears thing was a mistake. But I'm serious. If I could do magic, I would do magic. All the time. It's only, like, the biggest dream most kids I know ever have. So if I could do it, you know I would. But I can't, so I don't, okay?"

Abeni got to his feet. "Abeni believes the Little Fish," he said.

"And we'll stop all this nonsense about you owing me half your life?"

"Abeni will stop," he said, grinning slyly. "Unless he finds out later that the Little Fish does have magic. Then *she* will have to protect *him*–for many, many years. The Djin live a very long time."

Tayna grinned. "Deal. So now what?"

Abeni's gaze narrowed and swiveled back to the trees where he knew the Wagon had gone several hours earlier. "Now we return to hunting for thieves," he said. "This was a powerful trap. The one who set it is a danger to all the forest. He will be found. He will be stopped." Then Abeni's eyes blazed as he took the wooden turtle from Tayna's hand and hefted it.

"And he will never disturb the chamber of a Seeking child again."

It was Abeni who'd first suggested it. "The Wagon must go like an arrow," he said. "Always it takes the straightest path. Especially if the thief cannot make it turn."

"Right," Tayna said. "The shortest distance between two points is a straight line."

"Shortest, perhaps," Abeni had replied, with a gleam in his eye. "But fastest?"

So here they were now, with darkness beginning to fall, plunging down a river as it cascaded down the slopes of the Throat, clinging rigidly to a ten-foot log while Abeni muttered his version of the Way Chanter's song to keep it from flipping over and crushing or drowning them both. The wild-water route. It was their third hour of this torture, but he also assured her it was their last. After the fire trap, Abeni had used the last known direction of the Wagon to project its path, and to his surprise, there had only been one destination lying on that course that had made any sense: the great bone-field of the Gnomileshi Horde, site of the Harvest of the Dead, which, coincidentally, was also the final destination of every Wagon.

"The thief did not change the Wagon's path at all," Abeni'd said when he had realized where it was going. "It has only been made to forget its duty. This explains much." By skipping all the waiting Seekers, Abeni was sure that the Wagon would now simply make a bee-line for its ultimate stop–the Gnomileshi harvest tables. "And there is another ceremony in that place, which Abeni thinks now is very, very important."

When Tayna looked at him, he scowled. "It is where Contenders

for the Gnomileshi crown must gather to announce their feats of bravery," he said. "Those who wish to become King must prove to both the
people and to the dead that they have great power, that they are strong,
and that they understand the needs of all Gnomileshi. They must per-
form a deed to show these things, and then announce it from the top of
the Braggart's Arch before the Dead Moon." By this, he meant the new
moon, which would set the following night. If the Wagon had been
stolen by a Contender, he would have to announce himself before then.

Tayna nodded. "I can't think of anything that would make a better
feat in the eyes of the Gnomes than stealing the sacred Wagon of Death,
and reclaiming the body of their dead king. Can you?"

"Indeed not," Abeni said. "The thief is very wise. It is a good plan.
He will make a most formidable king."

"Isn't that a good thing, though?" Tayna said. "If he's that smart
and he gets voted king, won't he be likely to stop all this war garbage,
too?"

Abeni shook his head ruefully. "Such a one as he knows that the
Djin will not forgive such treachery. It can only be that he is one who
already hungers for war, for by his actions, he assures that Abeni's
people will now bring one to him."

"Excuse me? What idiot would actually want a..." Tayna's eyes
suddenly snapped to attention. "Oh gimme a freaking break! Him?
Again?" Abeni nodded. "What, is he, like, the only Gnome on this
entire freaking planet? He's everywhere evil needs to be!" She turned
to look at her friend. "So what do we do now?"

"Abeni's duty has not changed," he said, tapping the cold iron of
his bond ring. "Abeni must regain the Wagon and stop the First Prince
from becoming King of the Gnomes."

Tayna dropped her head. "Why do I get the feeling this is not going
to be as easy as all that? Do you have a plan?"

"Abeni must be first to reach the Braggart's Arch. There, he will
track back to the Wagon and take it from the First Prince, before he can
reach the boasting place." Then he had explained about the wild-water
route.

But all her fears had proven unwarranted—as most fears usually do—
and she pulled herself now up onto the heavily overgrown banks of the
river as Abeni pushed the log back out into the current and came to
join her.

Moss hung in dripping ropes from the trees and covered the rocks,
the colors here tending toward shades of browns and grays. It was ev-

erywhere and it gave the jungle around them an odd, two-tone palette of drab and decay.

This low down into the bowl of the Throat–in the Deep Narrows–the sun was no longer visible. The sky above was dark blue-gray–still lit, but the Lip of the Throat held the sun at bay, and smog of some kind hung in the air above them, darkening it to its present color Tayna swatted at the swarm of flies that had discovered her as soon as she'd climbed ashore. And humid! The air was thicker and heavier than any she had ever experienced. It was like being in a sauna with your wet-suit on–or at least, what she thought that would be like.

"Whew! Crazy-hot day, huh?"

Abeni shook his head. "This air has no meat," he said. "The Little Fish should come here in the Months of Fire. On such days, it is as muscular as Zimu, and twice as dark." He pointed up at the smog bank. Tayna had seen smog that was thick enough to paint with before, but she had never seen anything like this. "What is it?"

"It is the Great Gnome Crop."

When Tayna cocked her head and shrugged, Abeni smiled and added a single word that made her flesh crawl.

"Flies."

Suddenly, the swarm of insects that were flying their tightly woven pattern of annoyance became more disgusting. The Gnomes actually eat these things? After wrestling her intestines back down where they belonged, Tayna forced her attention back to their mission.

"So this is what we're looking for? The Great Bragging village, or whatever?"

Abeni nodded. "It is," he said. "But Gnomes do not live in 'villages.' They prefer to make homes in the dirt."

Tayna nodded. "So caves, huh? Like bats?"

The Djin smiled awkwardly. "It is a little like bats yes, but not caves. When Abeni said 'dirt,' he was being polite." Then he shrugged. "It is said they live in their *own* dirt."

"Oh, gross!" Tayna's face cringed into a prune of disapproval and the tip of her tongue darted several times from her mouth, as though it was pushing out something foul. She managed to regain her composure, but for the rest of that day, she would continue to catch herself wiping her hands on her clothes as though trying to remove a stain that just wouldn't go away.

"Okay," she said, once the worst of it had passed. "I suppose there are other things I'd better know. Somehow, I don't think being down here is going to be quite as much fun as visiting the Wayitam."

Abeni nodded. "Indeed, they are a strange people. As long as the Little Fish is with Abeni, she will be safe. Abeni will do all the talking, if talking is needed. There is only one thing that she must remember. The Little Fish must remember never to show emotion upon her face."

"That's it?" she said. It seemed too simple. "Just remember not to smile, and everything else will be fine? No need to worry about having a hand lopped off for asking the time, or being fed to weasels if I do something outrageous like turning my head to the left?"

Abeni shook his head. "That is all. The Little Fish must not show happiness or sadness, anger or fear. She must find a neutral gaze and drape it upon her face like the skin of a dead otter."

"Poker face. Got it. But why?"

Abeni sighed. "It is a difficult thing to tell," he said. "For the Gnomileshi, feelings do not occur in the heart by themselves, they must be manufactured. When Abeni is happy, his face knows it before he does."

Tayna grinned. "Squirrels nine trees over know it before he does," she said. "You might be a big strong Djin hero, but you couldn't hide a smile with a leather hood and an iron helmet. Even your elbows give you away."

Abeni smiled. "Just so!" he said. "And the Little Fish could not disguise her scorn, not even if she were as invisible as the mist. All in the forest would hear the snorting of her contempt." Tayna frowned. It wasn't that bad, was it? But Abeni continued. "Yet this is Abeni's meaning. For the Djin or Wasketchin, the feelings of their hearts show themselves upon the face—it is a thing as automatic as filling their lungs, but this is not so for the Gnomes. For them, a feeling is something to be made, as you would make a mug or a dagger—a thing that can come only from deliberate effort. Once made, they must then choose whether to hoard the feeling to themselves, or give it to another by displaying it. They must think very carefully, decide what might be earned by the showing. Between the Gnomes, a smile or a frown can be traded as the Djin trade gold."

"They use emotions as money?"

Abeni nodded. "This is why the Little Fish must keep such treasures to herself. Those who received nothing from her generous fountain of wealth would become vengeful. It would not be safe for her."

"Great. You mean I could end up with even more people trying to kill me? No thanks. I'm trying to cut down." And then, to emphasize the fact that she was joking, she stuck out her tongue.

Abeni glared at her, drawing attention to the fact that, even after having been warned, she was still drenching the countryside in an unrestrained hailstorm of emotional content. He sighed and shook his head sadly. "Misfortune truly walks the trail with Abeni this day," he said. "To think that an armor against such troubles began the journey with him and has been lost... It is yet another burden of regret he bears."

"Armour?" Tayna's curiosity was roused. What kind of armor could protect you against greed?

Abeni shrugged. "It matters not," he said. "Abeni should not have spoken of a thing that cannot be had. Perhaps it continues to bring happiness to Hambu in Grimorl. That is enough."

Tayna frowned. What on earth was he...? Then she reached inside her kirfa. "Um, Abeni? Are you talking about this?" From a pocket she withdrew the pretendant and held it out hopefully.

The Djin's eyes widened in surprise. "Indeed! Abeni was speaking of just this thing." He reached out and took it from her extended hand. "How did the Little Fish come to possess it?"

"Well, Elicand took it off when we stopped to make camp. He said it was giving him a headache—making him bump into things all the time. After he... well, afterward, I found it on the log where he'd left it. I picked it up and haven't really even thought about it since then. We've been kind of busy."

Abeni seemed to be of mixed feelings. On the one hand, the topic that they had both been avoiding was now well and truly opened, exposing to the air all the raw feelings that he had been trying to smother. But on the other hand, this was good news. The golden chain was coiled around his massive fingers like lace, and the pendant itself seemed to hang tiny against the vast plain of his palm. A grown Djin of Abeni's stature would never have admitted it, assuming he was even consciously aware of the fact, but he was inordinately fond of the little talisman, and it was no small boost to him now to find that it had not in fact been lost.

He turned and gave Tayna a more Abeni-like smile than she had seen in days, raising the pendant between them. "Perhaps the Little Fish will not die after all," he said.

"Oh, good," she said. "Then I guess I like this plan."

According to Abeni, they were less than a mile upstream of the Braggart's Arch, and would now have to climb down the rest of the way. The walls of the Throat were quite steep in the Deep Narrows, and it was a matter for linguists to decide, whether traversing it would best be called walking or down-climbing. But no matter what you called it, their progress was slow. With the waning of the Dead Moon, the banks on either side were crowded with anxious Gnomes, all waiting to see which of the many pedestrians using the Arch to cross the river would be the next to stop half-way and make a speech. Definitely not a good place for a young Gnome girl and her Djin friend to climb off a log if they were trying to blend in. Abeni had been right to leave the river when they did.

The disguise of the pretendant did nothing to trap any heat around her–illusions make poor insulators–but she couldn't help feeling twice as hot and stifled as soon as she'd hung it around her neck. It was the nose. She was constantly having to turn her head to see around the enormous, baguette-shaped thing that protruded like a tumor from the center of her illusory face. It stood to reason that if there was something covering her face like that, then surely it was also trapping her humid breath in close, and adding it to the sweltering heat that clung to her skin. At least, that's what her brain kept telling her.

The journey into town had passed with little incident, save for the wonders of entering into a new realm. If anyone had noticed that it seemed to be the Djin who was leading, and his young Gnome "guide" who followed, nobody had mentioned it–not that they got to speak to the locals much. Wherever they went, heads popped out of hovel-holes to look, and then, just as quickly, popped back out of sight. But none actually ventured out of the security of their homes to talk. More than once, Tayna came near laughter at this bizarre sight, but each time, a massive, muscular hand had found its way to her shoulder, or her arm, and squeezed just enough to remind her of his rule, and the giggle had died upon her lips before it could bloom and be stolen. The pretendant did a good job of masking the little emotional flickers, but not even a magic bauble could disguise outright laughter. And the locals really had looked funny. Roadside Whack-a-Gnome.

With each step downward, it seemed that the heat and humidity increased a little more, and the clouds of flies thickened. Tayna had never seen so many insects packed together in so tight a space, except for once, in a TV commercial about bug repellent. Fortunately, Gnome flies–as Abeni called them–did not bite, but that was about the only obnoxious thing they didn't do. They got stuck in her hair, they crawled in her ears, they squirmed in her kirfa... Those that didn't touch her, buzzed around her head like an airborne motorcycle gang harassing a tourist. After almost an hour of walking through this nightmare jungle of people, flies and heat, Tayna was close to a burst of rage, but again, the giant, meaty hand seemed to sense her impending outburst and lighted upon her shoulder with a gentle reminder.

Show no emotions.

At last they came to a widening of the road, with an unusual number of hovel-holes arrayed on the hillside around it. The ground here was much more uneven than it had been higher up. There were blind hills and knobs of land, and clumps of trees that all gave the landscape a surreal quality. And then, as Abeni led her around a last outcropping of rock, she saw it.

The road they had been following paralleled the river, but here, it swerved away before banking sharply back to hit the river at right angles. Where they met, a vast stone arch curved up out of the hillside and leapt over to the river's farther bank. It was easily twenty paces wide, perhaps ten high, and the river boiled and tumbled through the empty space beneath it. At its peak, a large multi-panelled gong hung from a pole.

"The Braggart's Arch," Abeni said. "All who contest for the crown must stand upon it and bang the gong before the setting of the Dead Moon. There they must recount the tale of their deeds."

Beyond the Arch, Tayna could see a vast empty field, which Abeni told her was the bone-field itself–home of the death wardens and the site of the Gnomileshi harvesting tables.

"So what happens?" Tayna asked. "Contenders make their spiel and then what? Go home to wait for a fax?"

Abeni wrinkled his face at the unfamiliar word. "They may leave if they wish, but such a thing would not be wise. Who would remind the gathered horde of their great deeds once the next Contender had spoken his competing claims?"

Tayna looked around. The trees that slumped over everything looked sickly and twisted. Their roots clung tenaciously to every fissure and crack that could be found in the steeply sloped rock. Curtains of moss draped from branch to boulder, and from root to crown, in sickly mustard yellows, dull browns tinged with bile-green, and every combination of dank, damp gray imaginable. Everywhere in between was shadows, flies and drabness. But the locals seemed to love it. Crowds of adults gathered along the banks, fanning outward for several hundred yards in each direction, centered on the Arch. Beyond them, children ran free, occasionally leaping into the air, snatching handfuls of the local "crop" and stuffing it into their mouths like candy. Older children, teens mostly, lounged decadently nearby, ignoring the festivities, but not far from them either, criticizing everything while laying belly-down on the slime-covered rocks, drawing out the warmth like furry salamanders. And everywhere, the air was charged with expectation. Tomorrow was the end of the White Contender's Moon, and when it set, that's when the real fun would begin. Only then would the full ballot be known and the gathered horde at last able to get on with the business of proclaiming their new King.

"So, how far to Igli's Book?" Tayna asked.

Abeni turned to face her. "The great Gnomish Library of the Dead is rightly called by the name of its first shrine-keeper," he said. "And *Ishig's* Book is near to us, beyond the harvest field. But time closes like a trap, and Abeni must leave soon if he is to meet the approaching Wagon. The Little Fish must now decide, would she sleep here, lingering to witness the excitement of the Gnomes for a time, or would she have Abeni take her at once to the doorstep of the Great Library, and be done?"

Tayna wiped a hand up the side of her head, behind her ear. It came away smeared with insect gush. Getting out of the flies might soon become her biggest priority. "I don't suppose there's a hotel half-way between the two?"

A grim look slid across Abeni's face and he sighed. "Gnomes little understand the ways of their 'above-grounder' cousins. There is indeed a place for travelers. It lies a little way beyond the Braggart's Arch, but the Little Fish would not find it pleasing. She should do as Abeni will do, and sleep upon the ground."

"The ground?" Tayna said, incredulously, as she smacked at a fly that was inspecting her right nostril. "Anything has got to be better than lying in the open underneath this bug storm. Even if all they've got is a leaky tree-house, I'm in. Take me to it." Abeni shrugged his shoulders and gestured for Tayna to follow, as he turned and strode toward the river.

The Braggart's Arch was a natural formation, carved by raging water from the same stone as the rest of the landscape. Moss clung to its dark underside and nestled into the corners where it merged with the riverbank. Just as eons of coursing water had carved its shape, centuries of foot-traffic had left their mark too, wearing a shallow depression into its upper surface, forming very shallow, rounded curbs along either edge, which was all that stood between pedestrians and a very wet and violent end. Abeni led her into the steady progression of people crossing over.

When they reached the half-way point, he paused to let Tayna inspect the large, multi-panelled gong. It was square, about five feet wide, and it hung from two leather straps below a heavy wooden post that had been driven into the stone at a lopsided angle.

An older-looking Gnome was stooped over at the base of the post, rooting around in the rocks that lay there in a loose pile. When he saw Tayna watching him, he sized her up and then grabbed a stone out of the heap and held it out to her.

Tayna accepted it with a nod–remembering not to smile her thanks–and turned it over in her hands. It was solid and fit her grip snugly. "So," she said, waving the rock toward Abeni. "to be a Contender, all someone has to do is bash the gong with one of these and then give a speech? That's it?"

Abeni nodded. "Theirs is a simple way," he said.

On either bank of the river, the murmur of the crowd had dropped below the rush of the the river, and the Gnomes crowded toward the bridge. Tayna realized with a start that they thought *she* might be a Contender, preparing to throw her hat into the ring. She handed the rock hastily back to the old Gnome and walked away quickly, fully expecting a laugh from the crowd, but it never came. Tayna darted quickly forward through the crowd, almost dragging Abeni along behind her. With every step she waited for the mocking laughter to finally erupt, and her flinch-meter continued to ratchet upward. But it never came. Their whole emotionlessness thing was just plain creepy, and somehow, it seemed even worse coming from a crowd than it did from just one or two Gnomes.

They were just about to step off onto the far bank, when a low, booming crash shook the air. With her nerves already stretched tight, Tayna almost screamed. She could actually feel the reverberations of the gong vibrating the fabric of her kirfa against her back. Wait a minute–the gong! She whipped around to see what was going on.

The old Gnome was still standing next to it, and when he saw Tayna looking at him, he raised the rock in salute. Her rock, she realized. Did the crazy old buzzard think he was hitting the gong for her? She shook her head and made rapid, downward patting motions with her hands. No! Put it down! I'm not one of your stupid Contenders! The Gnome ignored her pantomimed pleas and turned back to face the throng of Hordesmen who were now pressing toward the bridge. He drew himself up to his full height, and suddenly, he looked years younger. Almost dignified. Then he spoke.

"Marchers of the Horde, attend me! I am Qhirmaghen, and I would contend for your Crown!" Even the river below him seemed to fall silent. Seeing that he had their full attention, Qhirmaghen continued.

"I look out upon you, and I see things that should not be." His voice was loud, commanding, but not harsh. "I see backs bent from labor, and I see backs bent from humbleness. These are good, these are as things should be." His eye scanned the crowd, resting briefly on any who would make eye contact, and giving them a nod, before moving on. "But I also see backs stooped to the ground, lower even than the feet that carry them. These backs cry out to me. They say, 'We are ashamed! A blight has been placed above us, weighing us down with fear. Fear that evil has been done in our name! Fear that we have done nothing to cleanse our name of this act.'" Some heads in the crowd were beginning to nod. "And yet, there is fear also that no evil was ever done–that we stand falsely accused–and that still we have done nothing to cleanse our name!" The nodding was beginning to pick up strength.

"So here we stand, all of us, crushed, not by what has been done to us, nor by what has not been done to us. But by what we ourselves have failed to do *for* ourselves! Where among us has been the leader who would take up the mop and pail of vengeance, and lead us out to cleanse our name? Where has been the leader who would reclaim this once-great nation? Where has been the leader who would dare all for honor, for pride, and for the everlasting glory that is the Gnomileshi Horde?"

A clatter of sound rose up. Tayna watched the crowd, but none of them was shouting or even appeared to be speaking. Then she saw. Hands. Not clapping, but pounding together, a stone clasped in each palm, smacking and smacking, again and again, louder and louder. There wasn't a whisper of emotion on even one in the sea of faces, but they approved of this Qhirmaghen and the message he was bringing them. After a few moments, he raised his hands and the noise died down so that he could continue.

"My name is Qhirmaghen. For all my years, I have been nothing–a simple charm-trimmer–and like you, I have born shame heavily upon my back. But tonight, I tell you, 'No more! ' No more will I bow and scrape below skies filled with my 'betters.' No more will I beg for scraps of dignity from those who would be my masters! No more will I allow my children to go to bed feeling shame for who they are!

"I asked you before, where have been the leaders who would pull us from this cycle of madness, and I tell you now, that *I am that leader*! As proof, I offer you this trophy!" He turned and pointed to the brow of a low hill beyond the crowd, where another Gnome, an underling of some kind, pulled a screen of dull blue tree branches away, revealing a tall, slender boulder that was silhouetted beautifully against the fading glow of the twilight sky. "Behold the pointing finger of the Fury herself!" Qhirmaghen cried. "She fell by my hand, and by my hand alone! Her reign of tyranny over our heads is at an end! And by this pledge, I! Would! Be! Your! King!"

The roaring of the applause stones was long and loud. All around her, Gnomes were quickly turning to one another.

"He's got it. He's the one."

"Knows how we all think, he does."

"Pulled it down by himself, he says."

"Big job, and him nothing but a charm-trimmer."

Seeing that the excitement was over, Abeni beckoned Tayna to follow, and pushed his way through the throng of people who had pressed forward onto the road from the hills beyond.

"Wow," Tayna said, when they had gotten far enough away that they could hear each other again. Abeni was silent. "You didn't think it was an impressive speech?" she asked.

Abeni nodded. "Abeni worries that perhaps it was too impressive. Like the First Prince, this Qhirmaghen also does not seem to wish for peace."

Tayna shook her head. "I don't know," she said. "Maybe there's a difference between wanting a war and just wanting to be treated better." If there was one thing Tayna could empathize with, it was how crappy it felt to think that somebody was always out to crush you.

Abeni eyed her curiously. "Does the Little Fish say that he will not fight?"

Tayna shrugged. "How should I know? He might. Especially if there's no other way to get what he wants." She thought back to her own skirmishes against evil overlords. "Respect is a really powerful magic too, you know."

Abeni nodded thoughtfully at that, and they said nothing more about it as they walked on, paralleling the river and dropping steadily downhill in silence. They still hadn't passed anything that looked even remotely like a house or a hotel, and Tayna was beginning to wonder if Abeni had forgotten where it was he was supposed to be taking her. Then all at once, he stopped, with his back against a filthy, slime covered rock, and sketched a low bow.

"A wish from the Little Fish is like a ring of iron to Abeni," he said. "Allow him to present the place of honor for travelers in the land of the Gnomes."

Tayna looked around. "Excuse me? All I see is you, the river, a mossy rock and some mud."

Abeni looked around to ensure that they were alone, and then risked a smile. "Not one rock," he said. "That would be insulting, even for Gnomes. The Little Fish sees *two* rocks. And what is more, they lean together. Is this not a shelter fit for a visiting king?"

"That?" Tayna said, pointing at the rock behind him. It appeared to have fish guts and sea slime dripping from its upper edge, and a putrid, yellowing muck clung to its lower flanks, that may very well have washed up during a recent puke flood. With some difficulty she was able to keep her stomach in place as she approached. One hand was clamped firmly over her mouth and nose, but it did nothing to hide the stench. Sure enough, there was actually a second rock behind the first, and the two were leaning together, as advertised. Or possibly, clinging to each other in horror.

"They expect us to sleep here?"

"As Abeni has said, they mean well, but have no understanding of houses above the ground. Such a thing is an abomination to them: to sleep, separated from one's earth. They attempt to make even this simple rock hut more home-like. Alas, 'home-like' to a Gnome means, 'appointed with stinking dead things.' Abeni prefers to sleep upon the ground."

"You think?" Tayna shuddered. She wouldn't even let a Goody sleep in a place like this. But then, as if the mere thought of the Sisters of Good Salvation had summoned them, a crack squadron of stunt flies chose that moment to do a fly-by in tight formation. Right into her eye. She could almost hear the nunnish laughter now.

Tayna sighed. It felt like it was going to be a long night.

After abandoning Hotel Gnomileshi, Abeni had helped the Little Fish to find a more suitable place to sleep. It was a safe location, near to the bone house of the Gnomes, far back from the road, behind many large boulders, with the shelter of a tree above, and a thick mat of moss for a bed. The bone house was very important to all Gnomes, and Abeni had assured the Little Fish that she would be very safe in such a place. No hordseman would dare to risk earning the displeasure of the dead. They had talked for a while, and before she knew it, Tayna had told Abeni everything–even about where she had really come from, but if it bothered him, her large friend had kept those concerns to himself. With the burden of her secrets lifted, at least a little, Tayna had settled in, and then Abeni took his leave. Tonight, he, too, would sleep upon the ground, as he had told her. But not before he had performed the duty for which he had come here.

The Djin are not procrastinators. A job worth doing was a job that should probably have been done long ago. Through all the long hours of Gnomish twilight, while the Little Fish slept safely down below, Abeni had climbed steadily back up the Throat, toward his duty. And his revenge. It had been a long, uphill journey–one that, for the Little Fish, would have been exhausting, but Abeni was not only a Djin–he was also a Way Finder, no stranger to the climbing of mountains. By the time the sun was truly setting in the west, Abeni had climbed all the way to the western Lip, using his Finder's skills to close the gap between himself and the coming Wagon. He could feel it calling out to him as it approached on its unerring path, straight toward the harvest tables down below.

There was no charm that could be sung to give one this ability. Such a thing only arose from many long years of faithful service to the silent calling of the Wagon, and from a deep understanding of its nature. What few in all the forest knew was that the secret of its magic was grief. For while it was true that the Wagon had been constructed by the Djin, none save the family of the Wagonsmith himself had ever learned that it was the tears of the Dragon's own sorrow that were used to quench the silver runners from the heat of the forge. Tears which bubbled forth from the stone of the Bloodcap itself, and could only be collected when a new Wagon was to be made ready. Only with this secret quench-water could the wagon that was built, truly become a Wagon of Tears. But Abeni did know these things, and so it was that he could sense it now, and he knew that it was close.

"Come to Abeni," the big Djin said quietly, as he scanned the grassy brow of the Lip. "Abeni has a gift to give the one who would stain

Kijamon's House with rust." He hefted a massive oaken tree-limb in one hand. "A very heavy gift."

Judging the line upon which he was sure the Wagon would float, Abeni found a large boulder that lay just a little to one side, and stepped into its shadow to wait.

It was perhaps twenty minutes later that he heard the rustling of leaves and branches that signified something large moving through the screen of trees. Mere minutes later, he could discern the padding of feet in the grass, and the low, nasal hum of what must surely be a Gnomileshi Way Chanter's song. The thought of such abominations sent a cold shiver down his spine and to comfort himself, he tested his grip on the handle of his "gift." Only a few moments more...

Anger and excitement welled up in the powerful Djin as the silver runners and granite body of the Wagon coasted into view past the edge of his boulder. This would be sweet and glorious revenge. Not only for the Way Finder, and for House Kijamon, but most importantly, for a nameless little boy whose only token of this world had been snatched from his slumbering hands and desecrated in a repugnant act of cowardice.

The last sky-tube came into view, and with a roar of righteous anger, Abeni raised his gift above his head and leapt out from his shadowed place of hiding, to bring justice to those responsible.

chapter 15

Dear Shammi:

OMG! I can't believe how much has happened! And I feel so good! The old pigeon man was right! I told Abeni everything, and it's like this huge load is just gone! I can't believe I let Veest get me so worried. I mean, the big galoot wasn't even freaked out about the whole Grimorl thing. I guess he's seen so much weirdness lately that my story was just another blip on his Djin radar screen. I hope he's okay. He went to go hunt down the Wagon thief, but he's like, a mountain, right? How could he not be okay?

And hey, can you believe it? Here I am, sitting like maybe a hundred yards from actual answers! Of course, you already know what I'm going to find out, don't you? But you've never bothered to share your secrets. Oh never mind. I've decided I'm going to forgive you. I mean, you must have your reasons for whatever it is you do or don't do around here.

So who was the woman on the bus? Huh? That's what I want to know. Was it E'thiel, the forest auntie? I couldn't see much, but she seemed very homey and down to Earth. That part fits at least. Could you even imagine me as Tayna, daughter of Constance Parkindale-Chesney and Mr. Reginald Townsendbury, Vice President of Overseas Investment for the firm of Copperton, Pitchbottom and Barleycorn? Oh god! What a prison sentence that would have been, huh? Prep schools, and tea societies, debating club and eventually pledging to mamma's old sorority, so that I could meet my own Mr. Doofigus McSillywaddle? No way! That's a game for the Lovables. Me, I'm definitely more of a working-class orphan.

Whoa. It just hit me. I might actually have to stop saying that word. "Orphan." Funny, isn't it? How you can think about something as being part of you for so long that, even though it makes other people *all weepy, it's just like, the most normal thing in the world to you? I wonder if kids with cancer feel that way, or kids whose parents have been divorced. Sure, it makes you sad sometimes, but you still gotta live your life, right? Even normal kids get sad–it's what people do, I think. So everybody stop feeling sorry for me just because my sad thing is different from your sad thing, okay? Can't we all agree to focus on the happy things instead?*

Oops. There I go, sounding like little Sally Happypants. It must be the excitement. I never thought I could feel so tingly like this. Do people with families feel this tingly all the time? I guess not. It probably wears off, like all the other tingly things in life. I wonder if this is how Lies feels when she makes up her stories. If it is, then I guess I can see why she does it. It's kind of a cool feeling. But what if, right? And then, what if that? And then the next thing? My mind's going at a million spins a second and I can't shut it off! What if there are uncles or aunts or grampas even, still around, who'll be happy to find out I'm still alive? Where would we live and what would we do together? Are there cousins? Maybe they have a sailboat. I've always wanted to try sailing.

See? I keep doing it. Running off at the imagination. I'm glad I'm here, writing this to you, and not sitting someplace where other people could hear me going on and on about this stuff, like some stupid, puppy-love victim, dreaming about her first kiss or something. "And will he be dreamy?" That touchy-feely motor-mouth-of-happiness thing is so not me. Or, I mean, usually it's not. Do I really have a Diaphatayna hiding inside me? I'm not sure where she'd fit, though. Sigh. I miss Lies. She'd be so into this whole thing. If she were here, then I'd be able to sit back and be all Tayna about it, and she could be all Lies about it for me. Oh well, I guess I'll just have to be both of us this time. Or is that the fat lady talking?

Anyway, I've got to try to get some sleep. The heat here isn't so bad, now that I'm not moving around in it, and the flies are surprisingly un-thick too–maybe because there are so many more people to bother back by the bridge. Whatever. This is as quiet a place as I'm going to get, so I better get at it.

Oh, and do me a favor, would you? Check in on Abeni. I know he's an adult and all, but I think he's really just a kid at heart, driving around in the body of a he-tank, so have a look for me, okay? Don't let the

big guy get into too much trouble, because there's nobody there to get
him out this time if he does. I'll check in with you tomorrow to let you
know how everything goes here. I plan to be there first thing in the
morning. Sounds a little gee-whizz-eager for me, huh? Just call me
Little Tayna Happypants. I'm in such a good mood, I wouldn't even
care if you did.

G'Night,
LTHP

When Tayna awoke the next morning, Abeni was still gone, which was
a good sign. It meant everything had gone according to plan, and
Abeni should now be on his way back to the Verge with the Wagon, to
resume the Trail of Tears. And hopefully he'd find his brothers along
the way too. But contemplating Abeni's success gave her little comfort
now as she neared the completion of her own journey. Today, in the
dank, overgrown depths of the Gnomileshi heartland, alone and every
inch the clueless tourist, things seemed a lot less certain than they had
last night. In the Verge, many things had struck her as odd, but at
least the people there had made a strange sort of sense. But here, the
operative word wasn't so much "odd" as "creepy." Sleeping in dung-
holes? Buying food for a grimace and three giggles? There was just
no way a girl fresh out of the repressed existence of the Old Shoe was
going to be able get on top of a place like this without help.

The very look of the Gnomes was disturbing too, with that bloody
great hotdog bun nose of theirs, flopping about in the middle of their
faces. Hell, even her illusory one was a constant irritation. How the
Gnomes managed to eat without half-swallowing that huge flap of dangling meat with every second bite, she couldn't begin to imagine. Aside
from the noses though, the rest of the Gnomileshi features were normal enough. Their close cropped, flat-topped hair style gave them all
a vaguely military look, and their deep-set eyes were spaced a little
widely—just enough to call attention to the fact, but not so much as to
seem inhuman. After all, Angiron had managed to pass for human,
once he'd done something about his nose.

Tayna stretched in the cool morning air. It was almost refreshing
and she allowed a full-bodied yawn to possess her for several long
moments before she remembered the flies. She snapped her mouth
closed with a clopping sound, but fortunately, no flies were trapped in

the process. The breeze coming up from the river had none of the heat and humidity (or mass) that it had held the night before. Abeni had said that the mornings would be more pleasant, before the heat got up. And that, more than any other factor, convinced her that she'd better get going. There was no telling how long her luck with the flies would hold.

Before he'd left, Abeni had shown her the place where a narrow trail branched off the main path below, turning up a side gully. She scrambled down there now from her sleeping nook and followed the meandering passage a short ways to its end, where the two side walls narrowed until they merged together in a dead-end corner, choked and overhanging with green and purple weeds and moss and a few tiny pale white proto-tree seedlings clinging desperately to their soilless, rocky perch.

But there was no cave.

Tayna wondered if she might have missed a turn, or if maybe she'd taken the wrong trail from the get-go. But then she inhaled. The stink that assaulted her was almost enough to drop an ox. A nose raised in a world of disinfectants, of scented candles and perfumed dryer sheets, is a nose entirely untrained for dealing with the gruesome reality of a world-class stench, and this one greeted her with all the force of an unexpected punch in the face. Some trick of the wind had hidden the smell from her as she'd approached up the narrow defile, but now that she'd reached the end, there was no hiding it any longer, and there was no doubt. She had definitely found the Stinkhole. To find the entrance, all she had to do was follow her nose.

Which is how she found the narrow crack between the two rocky walls, down low, below her knees. Tendrils of long, stringy moss had hung over it like a curtain, hiding it from her eyes, but not even charms of invisibility could have kept it's location a secret with that smell to guide her. The closer she got, the more physical it became, and now, as she crouched down, brushing the mossy curtain aside to take a peek, that physicality oozed and flowed around her like the current of a molasses river. Tayna's eyes watered, and the muscles around her nose twitched, flexing spasmodically, as though they were trying to muster the strength to clamp her nostrils shut out of sheer desperation.

Tayna nodded to herself. The Stinkhole. Ishig's Book. Answerville. This was the place. And everything she knew about herself was about to change. Throwing caution to the stink, Tayna dropped down on her hands and knees and crawled forward into the gloom.

Tayna knew she had reached a cavern when the scuffling of her knees on the well-worn rocky floor changed tone. Not a ray of daylight had followed her and she was suddenly very nervous. Was it safe? What if she plunged into a shaft, or got buried under a collapse of stone? But it was much too late for such thoughts now. Safe or not, she was here. The place felt exactly like what she imagined death would feel like. Inky darkness, bad smell. At least there weren't any nuns.

She had thought she was alone, but then the silence was broken by a voice that gruffed at her from somewhere near at hand.

"You seek the past."

Tayna shook her head, as much to fight down her nervousness as to contradict the voice. She had come too far and too much rode on her questions to be cowed now by some faceless Walmart greeter at the edge of the abyss.

"No, I seek my future."

The voice grunted. "Perhaps, but you have come here, to the shrine of Ishig's Book. Written in bone, its pages know nothing of the future, nor the present, yet here you are. You seek the past."

Tayna shrugged. "Fine," she said. "I seek the past. Po-tay-to, po-tah-to. So how does this work?"

There was a sound of movement at her elbow and then, suddenly, a gnarled hand clutched at the pretendant hanging around her neck. "You dare seek to deceive the bones? Think you that the ancients are so easily misled? Those who dwell in darkness?"

Tayna reached up and wrapped her fist protectively around the cool metal talisman. Bones? What did bones have to do with anything? But she didn't want to advertise her ignorance. "I have no idea how gullible they are," she said. "But what's the point of lying? Wouldn't that just spoil the answer I'd get?"

This time the voice sparkled in agreement. "So it would," he said. "Nonetheless, it is a gambit chosen by many. Persist in your illusion if you wish. No matter. The bones know all. What do you offer?"

"Offer?" She hadn't expected there to be a charge.

"Yes, offer. What will you surrender in exchange for your answer?"

"Um." Tayna fidgeted nervously. This was not like any library she'd ever heard of. She cast her mind back, frantically, trying to re-member everything she'd been told about this place in the last few days. And then she realized. There was no book–no ledger with names and dates in it, as she had expected. This was a book in the sense that it was a collection of information, but it had something to do with bones and dead people, not sheets of tree pulp. "Uh, don't the bones belong to everyone? And why should the ancestors charge for their answers? They're dead. They can't spend it."

A tired sigh reached her ears. It was a sound that can only be made by frustrated civil servants dealing with people who haven't bothered to learn the rules before getting in line. "Fine," he said. "Ask away. I'll just sit here. I'm curious to see how much you are able to learn without my help."

"Oh. Sorry. I didn't think about that." The voice muttered something about how they never do, but Tayna didn't hear him. She was trying to remember what it was that Abeni had said about Gnomes using facial expressions as currency. "Uh, would a laugh be enough?" Tayna could almost hear the Gnome's eyes narrowing as he appraised her.

"Girlish or full-bellied?"

"I'm sorry?"

The voice repeated himself, drawing each word out to ridiculous length and raising his voice, as though she were hard of hearing. "Gir-rrllishhh. Orrrr. Fffulllll. Beh-lllllied?"

"Oh. Definitely full-bellied. I'm quite a laugher."

"I'm sure you are. What else?"

"What else? Like, what other payment? Er, how about a shriek of fear?"

Tayna could almost hear his toes tapping the cave floor in strained patience. "No, not more emotions. I'll have the laugh, but do you take me for a fly-chasing child? You're a sky dweller. Such payment is as little to you as blood-stains to a harvester. What will you offer that you value?"

"You mean, money? I didn't think anybody used it around here, I mean, everyone seems to just be willing to do good and all that. I don't have–"

"No! No Djin trinkets! I asked not of the things your fellows might take in fair exchange. I asked for something you value." Tayna wasn't sure what to say to that. After a long moment filled with awkward, the voice sighed wearily. "Look, you seem earnest enough. But perhaps you should learn the way this is done and try again at another time..."

Tayna panicked. "No! Please! I'm sorry! You're right. I do understand, but this has all been happening so fast and there's just not much that I actually own that I can give you. Except this." She dug blindly into her knapsack, fumbling in the darkness, but once she got it open, what she was looking for wasn't hard to find. She drew it out and held it into the dark air in front of her. Her voice was trembling when she spoke. "It really is the only thing I have that I value. Will this be enough?" There was no answer and her breath caught in her throat. "I'm sorry! Really, it isn't much. I know that. But if you only knew how important it is to me, you'd understand how valuable it is. You see, it's the only thing I've ever really owned. Just a collection of letters, really–to a... a friend, only she never reads them, but it's the most important thing I have and I really need this question answered. If this is the only way to get it, then you can have it." To have come all this way, and then to have the chance snatched away from her? Tayna's arms trembled as she waited for him to speak.

"Come forward, girl. Ask your question."

She shook herself in surprise. "Really?" She stepped forward and held it out toward the voice. Her journal. But the gnarled hand pushed it gently back toward her.

"Keep your writings," he said. "Ask your question."

"I don't understand. You said–"

"The thing with sky dwellers," the voice said, cutting her off, "is that you all assume that, because you can produce a laugh, you must be rich once you enter the Throat." Then, as suddenly as a hail storm, the cavern was filled with a deep, rasping wheezy sound. "You see?" he said proudly. "We too can produce hollow laughter. Such braying is valueless. What we crave, the tokens of this realm, are real emotions. Those we cannot mimic. We can receive them from others and repeat them. But only once. We are unable to do so again until we've experienced it anew. The second uttering is as empty and without shape as any we create of our own."

"So asking for something I really valued..."

"Was a way to lead you to a true feeling," he said, completing her sentence for her. "And you honor me. Rarely in my years as Reader of the Book has any supplicant offered so much for the privilege of my counsel. Your quest is true, and I shall do all in my power to aid you. My name is Urlech, and I am yours to command. Now, what is your question?"

For the longest moment, Tayna just stood there. How do you sum up a lifetime of anxieties and fears, and spit them out in a single question? She fought down the urge to twist her bracelet. "I need to know about my parents," she said. Immediately she felt as though it was the stupidest thing in the world to say. It wasn't even a question. But the Gnome–Urlech, he'd said–didn't laugh.

"That is all?" he said. If anything, there was almost a hint of disbelief in his voice. "You don't come to ask the name of your one true lover? Or the path to some fabled stash of Dragon's Scales that cannot be charmed?"

Tayna grinned. She suddenly realized how boring his job must be, and the usual kinds of problems he had to deal with. Like Einstein forced to work in a donut shop or something. "Nope," she said. "Sorry. Just want to know if mom and dad are doing alright." Not to mention, who the freak they are.

She could almost hear Urlech shaking his head in wonder. "As you will," he said. "Tell me their names and I shall ask."

Tayna blushed. "Well, that's kind of like the problem, okay? I don't actually know their names."

The Reader drew a surprised breath. "No matter. Tell me of their deeds then, and of their kin." But Tayna just shook her head in the darkness. Somehow, the old Gnome saw the gesture. "Really?" he said. "Nothing?" Tayna shook her head again. "No cute pet names, or distinguishing marks? No best childhood friend? No mother's mother or father's uncle? Actually nothing?"

"Nothing."

Urlech fell silent, lost in thought. It was a puzzle like none that he could remember.

"And I suppose you have no trinket given you by them? Or can tell the name of even a distant relative or casual acquaintance? No favorite nose pick or discarded scrap of clothing?" Tayna shrugged her shoulders high and did her best to look apologetic.

"Well then, we've no other option," Urlech said. Tayna heard him move toward her, and then what sounded like metal sliding on leather. Like a blade being draw from a scabbard. It was enough to send a chill down her spine, but she held her ground.

Urlech gripped her by the wrist and then spun around, locking her arm against his side as he turned to shout back into the cave. "Fathers and mothers, hear me!" he cried. "Sing your joy in recognition of the daughter of your blood!" While he spoke, she could feel him move, raising an arm up into the air. And where his hand should be, she thought she could see the barest glimmer of light winking from a keen-edged blade. But still she fought to remain calm, trusting in this odd little Gnome, even though she had no real reason to do so.

With a flash, the gleam descended, whipping past her outstretched fingers, but she felt nothing. Then Urlech squeezed and she felt a sudden flare of pain along the length of her index finger. She could feel the blood welling up from the razor-sharp gash and run down her finger to drool onto the floor. In her mind's eye, it was a fire-hose, a fountain. But she stood her ground and refused to let her stomach complete any of the back-flips it was struggling to make. She started to ask a question, but Urlech hissed under his breath. "Silence!" And for several long seconds, all she could hear was the sound of her own life draining out onto the cavern floor.

Then Urlech stopped squeezing, but he continued to hold her still as a few more seconds passed. During this time, she heard nothing but the clattering of one rock settling against another, and the occasional drip of water from somewhere high up. It was very disappointing. When a full minute had passed, Urlech shifted his claw-like grip to Tayna's wounded finger and muttered a charm. In an instant, the flesh had mended itself and the sting had begun to recede. The Reader released her hand and clucked wisely to himself. "Interesting," he said.

Tayna gaped at him. "Interesting? A slashing blade, a bucket of blood and an echoing cave screaming out in total silence is interesting?"

Urlech clucked again. "A bucket? You lost more the last time you bumped your nose," he said. "And as for the screaming silence, don't you think I'm a better judge of that than you are? After all, this is my shrine. You're just a visitor."

"You mean you actually got something out of all that not-making-any-sound-whatsoever?"

Urlech seemed surprised. "How exactly did you think the bones would communicate with us? Did you expect them to talk? Chant poems, perhaps? Or did you think they would somehow take control of my body and make me talk for them? They're bones! They're lying in a wet cave! They can do precisely two things: click and drip. That's all. And girl, I haven't heard a greater clamoring from the ancestors in years. You've got a horde of your own in here."

Tayna's heart leapt into her throat. "You mean, they're here?"

"Of course they're here," Urlech insisted. "They all come here, eventually. You're maternal grandmother was quite definite about it. Crazy old bat pretty much screamed at me. Imagine! Three entire drips from a single bone. I'd say she wanted to declare a holy feast in your name, but she wasn't the only one—just the loudest. The others are all here as well. Paternal great-grandfather and his wife, maternal great-great-grandfather. Even an uncle, on your father's side. Yes, my dear. Quite a showing of support, I'd say."

Tayna's voice was scarcely more than a whisper. "And my parents? What about them?"

"Eh? What?" the Gnome asked, absently. He was still riding the thrill of such a heart-felt reaction. By his standards, this had been a bonus day. It wasn't often you got emotion from the bones. "Parents? No. No parents in the chorus. That much I can say for sure."

In her sudden excitement, Tayna grabbed the Gnome by the collar of his robe and jerked him in close. "No way! Really? You mean they're not dead? E'thiel and Alon are alive?" She wanted to say more, but Urlech reached out and put a hand over hers, shushing her with a hiss. A moment later he released her.

"I thought you didn't have any names." he said.

Tayna blushed. "Well, I don't, actually. Those are just the names that somebody told me *might* be my parents. I didn't want to jinx anything by assuming it was true." Urlech grunted in approval.

"And you were right," he said. "But did you hear? The two you just mentioned called out after you said their names. They're here, and two sprats with them."

A lump rose from nowhere and settled in Tayna's throat. "They're here?"

"Sorry if that is not what you wanted to hear. Near as I can tell, she died birthing the second child. Him not long after. Broken heart probably. Happens all the time with sky-folk."

The feeling of sadness drifted down Tayna's throat and settled into her chest. Then she brightened a little. "You said two sprats–that's kids, right?" Urlech grunted in the affirmative. "That means they found their older girl, here? The Lost One? And she's dead too?" Again he grunted.

"Well, it's nice that they found each other," Tayna said. "But it means they couldn't possibly be my parents." And then she realized two more things, almost at the same time. If her grandparents were here, like he'd said, then she really *had* been born in Methilien. Veest was right!

Tayna clutched at the shrine-keeper's arm in excitement as she gave voice to the second part. "So somewhere out there, my parents are still alive!"

Urlech extricated himself from her grip and smoothed his robes.

"Well, I didn't say that, now, did I? Can't ever be sure whether a body's dead or not–only whether they're here or not. Could be that they died in a fire, or drowned in a river. Could have fallen from a cliff. Even then, if any bones survive, one of them will usually find its way here, but that could take decades. Can you imagine how long it takes for a finger bone to wash down a mountain stream, get eaten by a fish, that gets eaten by a bird, and then just happens to get dropped outside this cave? Why just last week I found one at the door that was over three hundred years dead. Can you imagine? Three hundred! And it only found its way to me now. But like I say, some part of them almost always winds up here in the end."

Tayna grinned from ear to ear, not caring a flip about how much she might be overpaying the little Gnome. She didn't even have room in her heart to be sad at losing her connection to E'thiel. That had never been more than a slim hope, anyway, not matter how much she'd tried to Lies it up. But now? "I can live with those odds," she said. "If you had to bet your life on it, you'd say they were more likely still alive?"

"Oh, yes. Certainly. Not many escape Ishig's Book, not even for a short time. That's why the harvest tables are so close. Keeps things nice and orderly. And it's a far shout less likely that both mother and father could avoid me. Too bad, though. If the grand-sires were so enthusiastic, imagine how loud the parents would have been."

Tayna stood up straight and took a big breath of air, completely oblivious to the fetid stench of decay. "I am so glad I came," she said, grasping at his hand in delight. "You have no idea how much this means to me. If you'll just give me their names, I've got a whole bunch of reuniting to take care of!"

Urlech jerked back in shock. "Names? How would I know that?"

"But? You said you'd heard from my grandmother's grandfather, and my father's uncle, or whatever. How could you know that...?"

"And not know their names?" Urlech said, finishing her question for her. Tayna nodded. "Listen," he said. "If your whole family was gathered at a feast and I walked in and shouted out, 'Who here is related to this girl?' How would they have answered me?"

"I don't know. Maybe raise their hands, or shout out 'Yo!'"

Urlech nodded. "Well that's pretty much what just happened here. Notice how you didn't suggest that any of them would have shouted out their own names, or a list of villages that they'd once lived in?

"When you've been at this game a while, you get so you can tell a few things. Accents and the like. The shape of a drip's echo, the flatness of a bone's click. So I can tell some, but nothing so specific as a name."

Tayna sighed. "Then we have to ask another question." She held out her other hand, ready to pay the blood price, but Urlech gently closed her fingers and pushed her hand away.

"There is no question you could ask. About the only way you could do it would be to read out a list of every man and woman in the history of Methilien and ask each time whether that person was your kin, but you'd be long out of blood before you got through the list of a single mid-sized village, and the bones would probably be bored with the questions by then anyway. They can refuse to answer, you know."

"So that's it, then."

Tayna refused to let her shoulders sag. Maybe it had been silly to hope for actual names. If there was one thing she was learning quickly, it was that magic wasn't always as useful as you might want it to be. It never seemed to actually do anything. Not when you compared it with the spectacular kind she'd been raised on in books and movies. But on the other hand, compared to the entirely magicless world of Grimorl? Even this was huge. She knew more now than when she'd first come in. And even though Urlech wasn't sure, she was. She knew it. Somewhere, right now, in this very forest, two people were walking around, breathing. Living.

Her parents.

Her freaking, honest-to-God, parents!

chapter 16

As Tayna walked back up the slope toward the bridge, her mood kept bouncing between giddiness and regret. Giddy at the thought that her parents might actually be alive, and regret over the loss of E'thiel. Something about that name had really resonated for Tayna. Or maybe it had been nothing more than the humble honesty of their professions: a forest auntie and a waterbringer. It was exactly the kind of people Tayna would have been proud to come from. Whatever the reason, though, she'd been setting mental roots down into those maybe-parents without even realizing it. So, although Urlech's bones had offered good news, there had been sadness as well. And losing that kind of stung.

The Gnome ahead of her stopped walking, but Tayna didn't notice and ended up walking straight into his back. He turned and, seeing Tayna's height and upright posture—neither of which could be hidden by mere illusion—he stooped over lower, almost cringing at the tall, proud she-Gnome.

" 'Scuse the blunder, Missus."

Tayna gawked at him. "But I walked into you," she said, cocking her head in confusion.

The smaller fellow cocked his own head, and looked up at her with one eye. "An' I 'scused ye for it, din't I? Must be taxin' on ye, I imagine—getting four squares a day with yer head shoved so far up into the crop that ye can't even see yer own feet. Grimey! It's yer lot what Qhirmaghen's gonna fix, it is. Yer days of loft and priv'lege are done for, girlie." And then he was gone, scurrying off into the crowd that seemed to have congealed out of the very air while she was walking. And come to think of it, the air was getting thick enough—and meaty enough—for that to have been actually true.

Tayna waved a hand at the flies in front of her face. The crowd around the bridge had nearly doubled since last night, and as she looked at it now, she wasn't exactly enthusiastic about plunging back into its midst. Off to her right, the bonefield stretched back away from the river and its crowds. Apparently, the reverence the Gnomes had for the place acted like a force-field of respect, and the throngs of the king-curious flowed out around it, above and below, but gave the harvest field itself a wide berth.

Tayna wasn't nearly so shy.

The first "table" she came to–a rock, really, with a flattish top and rounded sides–was low to the ground where even the most stooped-over Gnome would be able to reach whatever was laid out across it. The top itself was slightly cupped and it sloped gently to one side. At the lowest point, there was a small notch in the edge, and below that, a rough knob of stone stuck out of the side. Tayna looked up at the vast field. At a guess, there must have been four or five hundred of these tables–all more or less the same, but in slightly different sizes and heights. They weren't arranged into any sort of grid, though, which is why they were so hard to count. Tayna wondered if maybe it had once been just a field of boulders from which the tables had all been carved, right where they stood.

Obviously, the one in front of her was not in use, and apparently hadn't been for some time. A little further up, though, she could see that a few of those closest to the bridge were not so lucky, and that the three or four Gnomes were moving slowly back and forth between them. With a grim swallow, Tayna marshaled her stomach into obedience and edged herself slowly in that direction to check it out.

The first body she actually came to was that of a Gnome. A dozen or so tufts of colored string were visible, tied in various places. Claim-strings, no doubt. Man or woman, Tayna couldn't be sure. He (or she) was lying face down. All the bodies were. There seemed to be about ten occupied tables around her, the bodies all in varying states of... completeness. Apparently, harvesting was not a quick–or tidy–process. The poor Gnome in front of her seemed to be entirely intact though, which was why she'd come to this table. But the presence of a large pail hanging from that little knob of rock below the notch, spoke volumes about the messiness that was to come.

Tayna risked a look over to the next table, which was not quite so pristine as the one in front of her now. From the looks of things, the harvesting on that one was about half-way done. And suddenly, she knew that she'd seen all she needed to see of the death harvest. It was fascinating, in theory–a sort of full-service recycling program for all things vim related, where even the wonder of decomposition and death could be harvested and returned to the great Circle of Magic, or whatever it was called. But theory was about as far as she wanted to go, now that she'd seen something of its practice. She turned her back on the tables and walked away as quickly as she could.

As she moved back out onto the roadway, the tide of Gnomileshi movement quickly caught her up, and rather than fight it, Tayna allowed it to sweep her on toward the middle of the crowd, although she had to be quick on her feet to avoid being trampled by the buggies and carts full of who-knows-what. Apparently, Contender time was a popular time for moving house, judging by the size of some of the loads being maneuvered down the busy roadway. But all that bustle was good for catching snatches of conversation and doing so gave her a quick read on the latest news.

"Only a few hours yet, and still he hasn't shown."

"Knows he can't outdo Qhirmaghen, I'll wager."

"Nah, he's a proud one, the First Prince is. He'll not back down."

"Yer daft! It's his pride what'll keep him away, ye ninny!"

On and on it went, with only two real themes. "Isn't Qhirmaghen great?" and "When will the First Prince show up?" Tayna smiled to herself. She wanted to shout, "Never! My friend Abeni ruined his plans! He's probably licking his wounds in Grimorl even as we speak!" but something told her that this would not be a wise bit of news to share with this particular crowd. They were pretty disappointed that they weren't going to get the big prince-fight showdown that they'd all come here to see. Above the heavy traffic on the Arch, the Dead Moon was already descending toward the Lip.

As the morning wore on, pangs of hunger slowly returned–after having abandoned her suddenly at the bonefield. Not surprising that they should return, though, since she hadn't eaten anything other than the small pouch of trail-mix that Abeni had left her with last night.

Now that she was looking for them, Tayna realized that there were food vendors everywhere, moving through the crowd, collecting smirks and scowls and handing out all manner of Gnomish dainties in return. The most popular dish by far was some kind of slimy strips of foul smelling stuff that looked to her like snake organs drenched in motor oil. One sniff was all she needed to decide that she certainly would not be trying that one any time soon.

Another guy was selling something that at least wasn't disgusting to look at, but turned out to be a sort of eggshell paste smeared into roasted chicken-beak crackers. Her grimace of revulsion caught the eye of the vendor, who brightened at such generosity, and tossed her three of the things before she could wave him off. Later, she realized that his brightened expression had probably been her change.

Tayna stuck her tongue out tentatively and let it touch the "cracker." To her surprise, there were no noxious oils or slimes on it. Just chicken beak. The shards of eggshell distributed all through the goo-ball on top would make for some nasty chewing, but it didn't seem completely vile. Tayna tucked the morsels into her kirfa, which she was still wearing underneath the rags of the illusion. If all else failed, she'd try to eat them later. They had a sort of earthy smell—not bad, really, just not exactly food-like either—so they didn't trigger her hunger reflexes, and she was able to ignore them while she continued searching for something more appetizing.

Her height advantage over most of the Gnomes around her made the job a little easier. She could actually see the food hawkers, in addition to hearing their cries of "Gopher rings!" "Kidney thrash!" and a dozen other names that were both hopelessly alien and disturbingly familiar. Her size helped in another way too, because it allowed her to push more easily through the crowd.

One of the vendors seemed to be really popular with the kids, who would run up and gabble about at his feet, snatching his stick-treats as fast as he could hand them out, and then run away. But she never saw them put the sticks in their mouths. Curious, Tayna made her way over, excusing herself politely, and elbowing her way through where politeness failed.

Upon closer inspection, she still couldn't tell what they were. The sticks were about as long as her forearm and as thick as her pinkie. Some tar-like goo covered the top third, which flared out into a paddle maybe three fingers wide. Listening to the children dicker with the candy man made it sound like the goo came in different flavors, but they were indistinguishable in color, so that was only a guess. Tayna decided to follow one of his happy little customers and see what she could learn.

Some things never change, though, and being smaller and more boisterous than everyone else had exactly the same advantages in the Gnomileshi world as it did in her own. The kid was fast! And it was all Tayna could do to keep up with him as he darted in and out between the legs of his elders and dodged under a heavily-burdened cargo cart, moving steadily toward the fringes of the crowd. Tayna dashed after him, keeping back though, so that he wouldn't know she was following.

Behind her, a steady wake of shouts and curses flowed out from her path, as one bumped or jostled hordesmen stumbled into another. The occasional yell of "Sorry!" thrown over her shoulder did little to stem the cursing. Eventually though, her quarry broke free of the sea of legs and made it onto open ground. What he did then was enough to jerk her to a halt and turn her around, without so much as a glance over her shoulder. The disgusting little twerp had leapt up into the air as high as he could, waving his stick at the end of an outstretched arm, collecting a solid coating of flies on the sticky flavored goo. She didn't want to witness what came next, even though her imagination insisted on showing it to her, over and over again, in high-def slow-mo.

Her search for food was now, officially over. She'd seen just about as much of Gnomileshi cuisine as she was going to be able to handle, and if the beak-paste was the least noxious thing she'd encountered, then that was just going to have to be breakfast, like it or not. She pulled one of the eggshell snacks from out of her kirfa and nibbled at it daintily.

It turned out to be not so bad—the paste part, anyway. Not good, mind you, but not so bad, either. She found that the best way to eat them was to pry the putty out of the cracker and pop the whole ball into her mouth, sucking it slowly and letting the paste part—which tasted a bit like Cream of Wheat—dissolve from between the bits of shell, which she was mostly able to spit out. A few of the really smallest shards got swallowed, but even that was a somewhat familiar experience. Lies was a bit of a horror show when it came to making omelets, and Tayna was accustomed to dealing with eggshell fragments in her food. With her hunger abated for a while, what she really needed now was something to wash it down with.

But Tayna was far from the only one with that notion, it seemed. In fact, the entire crowd appeared to be organized around that idea. From the center, a steady stream of people flowed in a more or less straight line toward the river. Once there, they peeled away to left and right, curling back on the left, toward the base of the Arch, where they could look to see if anything was about to happen, and to the right, wandering off downhill to what Tayna assumed were the local equivalent of port-a-potties. Of course, she knew that in Gnome-town, such a concept was probably far more disgustingly managed than that wonder of modern plastic efficiency that she was familiar with, but it was one delusion she insisted on clinging to fervently. When she reached the river, she intended to go left.

The banks here were sloped, probably by centuries of crowds just like this one, which made it easy to reach the water. Tayna cupped her hands into the violent current, mimicking the people to her left and right, and felt the river's rage tug relentlessly at her hands. This was no babbling brook! She lifted a palmful of water to her lips and sighed. It was icy cold and better than anything she could ever remember drinking–even boh-choh. Once, twice, three more times, she dipped her hands into the torrent and drank. There was a constant pressure at her back, as more Gnomes pressed forward, waiting for their chance at the river's edge, and Tayna wondered how any of the smaller ones managed to keep from getting pushed out into the current and swept away in a blink, but it never happened.

She was just about to move on when a flicker of movement caught the corner of her eye and she turned. What had she seen? A dozen or so yards to her left, someone was using a mug instead of their hands.

And it looked all the world like a Djin mug!

"Abeni! Over here!" Tayna pushed her way through the crowd, toward the place where she'd seen the mug flash into the water, but already she could see that there was no mountain of dark Djin kneeling on the banks. Only Gnomes. Why would a Gnome be drinking from a foreigner's mug?

By the time she reached the end of the line of drinkers, she still hadn't been able to spot the mug-holder. She was just about to give up when, to her left, she heard a curse.

"Hey you! Watch where yer sloshing that stuff!" Tayna turned quickly toward the shout and saw a hand withdraw, still clutching the gray vessel.

"Pardon this humble servant," said the mug-holder. Was he looking nervously back at Tayna? And then he was off, pushing his way toward the bridge.

Try as she might, Tayna wasn't able to catch him. He seemed particularly skilled at bobbing and weaving his way through the crowd of elbows and knees without slowing, and even though Tayna was pushing and shoving like a freight train with a schedule to keep, it seemed that every shove had its cost. She kept slowing down, and the mug man kept speeding up. Eventually, she lost him as two Gnomes carrying a long, heavy roll of turf blundered in between them, and she found herself forced to a halt at the base of the Arch, fuming. She hadn't seen so much as a fork or spoon in her entire time in the Throat. And now suddenly, when three of her Djin friends were missing or unaccounted for, along with a wagon-load of their camping gear, that's when some no-account Gnome decides to get all continental, experimenting with the ways of other folk? She did not like the odds on that being a coincidence.

Tayna was still turning slow circles, trying to catch sight of the guy, when a loud crash pierced the thrum of conversation. The gong! She turned to see who'd struck it, but she was pressed up against the very flanks of the Arch itself, and its own bulk kept her from seeing the top. She pushed away, trying to move away from the Arch so she could turn and get a look, but the crowd had other ideas and was pressing back toward her. Above her, she heard a voice call out, and its familiar tones made her heart sink.

"Hordesmen of the Gnomileshi Nation, hear me! I am your First Prince, eldest sprat of the fallen Grinyak! My name is Angiron, and I would contend for your Crown!"

———————

Inside her chest, Tayna's heart pounded. How had he managed to give Abeni the slip? And where was her Djin friend now? Her eyes scanned what little of the pressing crowd she could see, but that wasn't much at all, and it contained no Djin. Finally, she realized that she'd never be able to see anything from here–she needed to get up higher–so she edged her way along the base of the Arch until she reached the lowest slope of the up-bound ramp, and then pushed her way onto it, through the crowd of people, wagons and baggage.

"You know my life!" Angiron cried. "You know of my long history of service to the Horde!"

To her surprise, the crowd wasn't quite as densely packed on the bridge as it was on shore. They were probably afraid of falling off. Perhaps the thin curbs at the sides of the ramp didn't seem like such good security between you and the pounding death of the river below. Unencumbered by any buggy-loads of her own, Tayna was able to thread her way cautiously up the slope, faster than the sluggish flow of traffic.

"You know of my father, and of his long years of service! Grinyak! Proud king of a proud people!" Those people still hadn't reacted much to the sudden appearance of their First Prince. He'd surprised them all, and with less than an hour to go til moon-set, they'd all pretty much written him off. They were probably still too busy adjusting to this change in circumstances to figure out how to respond.

"Some," Angiron shouted, "would have you believe that we are not a proud people!" Tayna could see Qhirmaghen, standing on the far shore, bristling visibly at this thinly veiled jab.

"Some would have you believe that we are trodden beneath the boots of our sky-loving betters! He believes that the Gnomileshi Horde are cowed by the likes of some pouting hump of Wasketchin stone!" He spat a huge wad of phlegm in the general direction of the Fury's severed finger. "Pah!"

"This Pretender paints you a picture! He tells you we are nothing! And that without him as your king, we will always be nothing!" That seemed to draw people finally out of their stupor, and the crowd began to murmur. Tayna took the moment of their distraction to scuttle under one of the larger carts and managed to gain a few paces more toward the crest of the Arch.

"He believes that a lump of worthless stone is enough to fill each and every Gnomileshi heart with self-loathing!" The murmuring grew louder. "And to prove his worth as your king, what did he do?"

Somebody in Qhirmaghen's entourage called out. "He tore down the Fury, that's what he did!" There was a rally of response from Qhirmaghen's followers, but it wasn't much and Tayna could hear Angiron's snort of contempt from where she stood.

"He sucked the piddling remains of life-magic from her like a leach!" Angiron shouted in reply. "Pah! It's not even death-magic! That is not leadership! That is not power! Destroying their toys teaches the sky-dwellers nothing! It only makes them hate us more. When I am your king, we will turn that hate into fear! And their fear–their emotions–will wash over us like a glorious tide! Make me your king, and the Gnomileshi Horde will rule all of Methilien!"

By this point, Tayna had worked her way to the very apex of the Arch, with only one, last hulking crate in her path. Like all the other cargo on the bridge, it was now at a dead halt, waiting for the speech to end. There was no chance that it was going to move for her. The dusty red cloth draped over it went all the way down to the stone of the Arch, so ducking under was out, and along its left side, the bridge was clogged tight with traffic, which just left the narrow curb to the right. Of course, that route was free and clear. Not to mention just a little bit crazy. But if she was going to get a look at what was going on, that was her only option, so she skirted around the end and worked her way up along the crazy side.

"But what have you done to earn the Crown?" somebody else

shouted. Tayna was pretty sure that Angiron had been waiting for exactly that question.

"What have I done? What a good king should do, that's what! A good king does not bemoan yesteryear! A good king looks to the future! A good king secures tomorrow! And a great king secures all the tomorrows! Behold!"

As Tayna inched her way along the side of the crate, the tarp that was draped over it suddenly leapt into the air, startling her badly. She felt its roughness tugging at her arms and head as it whipped up past her face, and for a teetering moment, she was afraid that she was going to topple off the ledge into the raging water below. Meanwhile, the gathered Horde had gone deathly silent. A horrible, sinking feeling opened up in the pit of Tayna's stomach. Were they looking at her?

"I give you what should rightfully have been yours for all these long centuries! I give you the heartstone of all death-magic! This, my token of magic, is the first of three that I offer, as proof of my abilities!"

From somewhere near the back of the crowd, the buzz of approval stones clacking together started up, but it was not quiet for long. For Tayna, the world had dropped into slow motion. As she turned to see what they were all looking at, hollers of approval rose up to surf on top of the growing storm of clacking, and still she turned. The energetic surge got faster and faster, and then, finally, there it was. At last she could see the cargo that she had been creeping past for these last several minutes.

The Wagon of Tears.

It hovered there, four or five inches above the stone of the Arch, its nose still pointing straight toward the bonefield, just beyond the end of the bridge. Beside her, only a few feet away, the tarp that had covered it now fluttered on the wind as it drifted slowly down toward the river below. And now she recognized that too–the enormous Warder's tent. Somehow, Angiron had managed to get it, even though it had not been on the Wagon when he'd taken it. A cold chill went down her spine. What had happened to Zimu and Sarqi? But the strutting Prince, still hidden from view beyond the front of the Wagon, was not yet finished.

"My second token! Of all who protect the Sledge of Power, there is one who is known by all, famed for his strength and agility!" Tayna's heart rose into her throat. Oh please, no. Not that. She turned and shuffled back the way she had come, searching frantically. Where was he? He had to be around here somewhere. If only she could reach him in time.

But she was too late.

"Behold, the Eyes of the Sledge, sprat of Kijamon, the Thief of the Dead himself! A sprat I defeated easily in single combat this very morning!"

Tears filled Tayna's eyes, and she could only watch in horror as, from the sky-tube directly above her head, the now laughterless form of Abeni rose silently into the air. No! No no no no no no no... The noise from the crowd redoubled and the buzz of approval now blurred into a solid, low-pitched hum that rattled her very bones. Abeni! Tayna sobbed. What could she do? How could she help him? Alone? Against Angiron and the entire Gnomileshi Horde? As if carried by her tears, all the fight flowed out of her, and Tayna slunk slowly back to the end of the Wagon, no longer interested in trying to get a look at that fetid little skunk as he strutted and crowed.

But she could still hear him. "And best for last! To affirm my understanding of the hearts and the wills of you, my Hordesmen, I give you my final and most treasured token! I return to you the one who was denied the solace of your tables, the one whose loss has grieved you most, the one whose death at the hands of the sky-dwellers enrages you most deeply. I give you, Grinyak!"

From another tube on the far side of the Wagon, the smaller, grayer form of a dead Gnome rose up, just as Abeni slipped back down into his. All around the Arch, the buzz of approval rose still higher, compressing itself into an almost physical force that forced Tayna hard up against the cold granite of the Wagon's frame. Sensing a grand finale, the entire crowd surged forward, leaving a space down the side of the Wagon, and despite herself, Tayna couldn't help but follow along, staring into the air above her, mesmerized by the floating king. She followed, helpless, as Grinyak passed beyond the last tube and settled down, slowly, toward two outstretched arms, visible beyond the Wagon's bulk. No doubt, the loving arms of his favorite son.

Before the body settled, the arms reached aside to an aide and handed him the long, bone-and-jewel rod that he had been using to channel his magic. It was a newer-looking staff than the one she'd last seen driven through the body of a rabbit. He'd been using it now to hold the Wagon aloft, and to float Grinyak's body toward him—a task the aide now stepped in and assumed smoothly. Tayna wasn't at all surprised to recognize him as the little mug-thief that she'd been following earlier.

With his hands now free, Angiron's arms reached out to accept the body of his father, disappearing behind the Wagon as he held the corpse tightly to his chest for a moment, and then reappearing as he raised Grinyak back up triumphantly over his head.

"At last my father is home! Back where he belongs! Ready for his release! Ready to surrender his flesh to the magic! To the people! And to the hungry blades of the Gnomileshi Horde!"

As Tayna walked out past the end of the Wagon, Angiron turned toward her, with his father's body still raised high above him. Their eyes met. "You!" he cursed, in a voice only loud enough for her to hear. His eyes were filled with surprise. But not as much as hers.

"NOOOooooo!"

Tayna's shriek managed to pierce even the loudest noised of the crowd and every Gnome head now turned to gape at the screaming girl on the Arch. Not a Gnome girl, but a Wasketchin. Where had she come from? When the tarp had erupted up off of the Wagon, it had caught on the clasp of the pretendant and jerked it from Tayna's neck. So there she stood, undisguised, in front of the man who had been making her life a living hell since the first moment she'd met him. That's what had caused his eyes to widen. He'd recognized her, standing there, in just about the last place in two worlds where he'd expected to see her, and one of the few places he had not yet searched.

But that was not why she screamed. What she saw was far, far worse. Something snapped inside her then, and without even thinking about it, she knew that this was it. She had to do something. Anything! In the same tiny sliver of time that it takes a hummingbird's heart to beat just once, Tayna whirled around and heaved against the Wagon with all her might. Slowly, like a car accident remembered in excruciating detail, its giant bulk began to slide. There could be no doubt that hers were the hands of grief, and the Wagon responded willingly to her slightest touch, floating with dream-like ease toward the curb. Behind her, Angiron dumped his father hastily to the ground and turned to snatch at his staff, but the aide had stepped forward to better see what he was doing, and that was all the time she needed. While confusion and panic bubbled all around it, the Wagon calmly passed beyond the edge of the curb, tipped, and then dropped like a shot toward the river. Finally, Angiron managed to lay his hands upon the instrument of his power and he shoved the aide violently to one side, just as Tayna turned to look back at him over her shoulder. She still refused to believe what her eyes were telling her, but that did not stop her from throwing one last finger of defiance at him, before she turned and dove head-first over the curb, following the Wagon into the turmoil below.

But the last thing she saw was not the water rushing up to meet her. Her mind was filled with another vision. It was Angiron, screaming in rage, and whirling his staff above his now shocking and impossible head.

Then the river took her.

All the world is a circle. A large circle. Grayish and blustery looking. It is surrounded by blackness.

Several long moments passed before Abeni could open his eyes all the way, but even then, he could see nothing but that circle, and its enveloping blackness. This was bad, he was sure of that much, though for the moment he could not remember why. Making matters worse, he was cold and uncomfortable. The smoke was clearing from his mind, but too slowly.

It wasn't until he tried to reach up to rub his face with his great, Djin hands, and banged them into the cold, hard resistance of the blackness in front of him, that he finally understood what had happened.

He was in the Wagon of Tears.

With a roar of outrage, the Way Finder shot his legs out against the floor of the tube, propelling himself to the top of the sky-chamber, but not out. Only his shoulders had cleared the smooth, circular ring of its mouth–a ring not unlike the ones around his own arm–and he had to suppress a wave of shame when it became apparent that he would actually have to touch the cool, shiny metal with his bare hands if he was going to undo the greater disgrace. He did so, and moments later, dropped himself to the ground at the Wagon's side, breathing heavily as he struggled to remember how such dishonor could have been forced upon him.

The First Prince. Vividly now, he recalled leaping out from his hiding place to confront the Wagon thief, only to be ensnared in a heavy fog of death magic. The Gnomileshi Prince had been waiting for the attack and had defeated Abeni easily. Shamefully. It never occurred to the proud Djin that his failure might have been the result of several days of sleepless exhaustion, or his harrowing and recent recovery from near-fatal burns. Excuses were not a tradition of House Kijamon. He had simply engaged in combat, and been defeated. All else was weeping and rust.

Shuddering with the weight of his shame, Abeni did his best to stand tall as he took stock of his current situation. The sky was a perplexing gray, streaked with whiteness, and a bitter wind whipped the whiteness around him, slashing at the bare flesh of his arms and legs. It was a sky of madness. All around him, the world was strange–white and gray and black. The only colors at all were in his clothing, and reflected in the gleaming smoothness of the sky-chambers above him.

The Wagon itself was settled deeply into the cushion of whiteness that lay draped over the ground and every part of the landscape. The only sound, other than the screaming of the wind, was the low throb of his own mind seething against his shame and railing at the strangeness of this place.

"Can't be happening. Can't be true. Not happening. Just a mistake."

Over and over, those words came to him, in snatches, between the shriekings of the wind. Then he realized that, if they really were coming from his own mind, shouldn't he be able to hear them even when the wind was blowing?

Abeni made a slow, methodical circuit of the Wagon, searching for another explanation for what he was hearing, and it didn't take long to find it. Under the rear of the Wagon, the Little Fish lay curled on her side in a ball. Blood flowed freely from great tears in the skin of her forearm, which she continued to twist viciously with her other hand as she chanted. Her eyes were glazed over in the manner common to the deeply grieving.

"Not happening. Not true. Can't be real..."

His young friend gave no sign of acknowledgment as he knelt beside her. Gently, Abeni placed his hands over hers and pried her fingers from the blood-slick and tattered skin of her wrist. But even then, she did not look up, did not relent in her chant of denial.

"Easy, little one. Abeni will help you now, as you have helped him."

But Tayna did not respond, not even to his voice. It was as though she could not hear him through whatever torment had gripped her mind, so Abeni lowered himself down to the cold, white ground beside her and wrapped his enormous arms around her, cuddling her tightly to his chest. It was instinct, but it seemed the right thing to do. Of course, he could not know how many, many long years it had been since anyone had ever held her like that, compassionately, trying to draw the pain out of her with nothing but the simple warmth of his skin and the comforting presence of his arms around her.

But deep inside her, Tayna knew how long it had been–exactly how long–and now, after ten long years without it, she melted into that nurturing embrace, and the icy glaze of her eyes thawed into tears.

"Oh Daddy, it was horrible," she mumbled into the Djin's massive chest. "I dreamed about a bad man. He was hurting people, my friends, and I just couldn't make him stop!"

Abeni didn't know whether to speak or hold his tongue, but she gave him no time to decide. Before he could draw his next breath, the Little Fish spun in his arms and beat at his face and shoulders with her bloody hands.

"And it's all your fault! How could you let it happen?! How?! I saw them, up there on the bridge, his ears, like mine, all big and blue and dangly! You did it! You let him be my... my... *husband!*"

Then Tayna lapsed into wordless sobbing, leaving Abeni too startled to think of anything to do or say, except to hold her close and continue rocking gently back and forth, mystified, as the wind whipped whiteness and confusion out of the sky and hurled it into his upturned face.

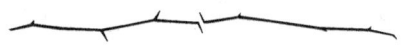

We should talk

Really, I'd love to hear from you. Feel free to make contact at any of these coordinates. Tell me what you loved, what you hated. Send me a picture you drew of Tayna, or a poem you wrote about evil nuns. That stuff really energizes me.

Google+ (+JeffersonSmithAuthor)

CreativityHacker.ca (my blog)

Twitter (@Jefficus)

Facebook (Jefferson.Smith.585)

Can I ask a favor?

Would you consider rating this book at one of the online sites? Just go to GoodReads or Amazon and then click on the star ratings to tell people what you thought. Even that little bit would be very helpful.

And if you happen to go further and write an actual review, don't keep it to yourself–let me know about it. Contact me through one of the above coordinates and shoot me a link to what you posted. Reviews really do help, so as my way of saying thanks when you post one, I'll send you a free ebook. And then we can do the dance all over again.

So that's it from me. Thanks for spending your time in Methilien, and I hope you'll come back for the next exciting instalment in *Oath Keeper*.

Books by Jefferson Smith

Finding Tayna series
Strange Places

Oath Keeper

Inverted Worlds Short Stories
The Old Soft Sell

Bodies of Evidence

Famine, With Fries

(Shorts available free at creativityhacker.ca)